RESOUNDING PRAISE FOR
JAMES GRIPPANDO
AND
WHEN DARKNESS FALLS

"James Grippando is a very inventive
and ingenious storyteller."
Nelson DeMille

"Thorough research, intelligent plots, and
white-knuckle tension are the hallmarks of
James Grippando's previous novels, and *When
Darkness Falls* is no exception. It contains
all these attributes skillfully employed."
Miami Herald

"From the get-go, it's beaucoups suspense—and
then Grippando puts pedal to metal. . . . It's the
relentless pacing that makes this one sizzle."
Kirkus Reviews

"Grippando excels."
St. Paul Pioneer Press

"Grippando shows storytelling brilliance."
San Diego Union-Tribune

"Pardon the pun, but Grippando
grips from the first page in a thriller
that will keep you up all night."
Harlan Coben

"Grippando writes in nail-biting style."
USA Today

By James Grippando

Need You Now+
Afraid of the Dark*+
Money to Burn+
Intent to Kill
Born to Run*+
Last Call*+
Lying with Strangers
When Darkness Falls*+
Got the Look*+
Hear No Evil*
Last to Die*
Beyond Suspicion*
A King's Ransom
Under Cover of Darkness+
Found Money
The Abduction
The Informant
The Pardon*

And for Young Adults

Leapholes

* A Jack Swyteck Novel
+ Also featuring FBI agent Andie Henning

JAMES GRIPPANDO

when darkness falls

HARPER

An Imprint of HarperCollinsPublishers

This is a work of fiction. Names, characters, places, and incidents are products of the author's imagination or are used fictitiously and are not to be construed as real. Any resemblance to actual events, locales, organizations, or persons, living or dead, is entirely coincidental.

HARPER

An Imprint of HarperCollins*Publishers*
195 Broadway
New York, NY 10007

Copyright © 2007 by James Grippando
Author photo © Monica Hopkins Photography
ISBN 978-0-06-208794-2

First Harper premium printing: May 2012
First Harper mass market printing: December 2007
First Harper hardcover printing: January 2007

Printed in the United States of America

Visit Harper paperbacks on the World Wide Web at
www.harpercollins.com

10   9   8   7   6   5   4

For my father,
James Vincent Grippando.
Seeing is not believing. Believing is believing.

when
darkness
falls

Sergeant Vincent Paulo couldn't see the man who had climbed to the very top of the William Powell Bridge. Paulo couldn't even see the damn bridge. He heard the desperation in the man's voice, however, and he knew this one was a jumper. After seven years as a crisis negotiator with the City of Miami Police Department, there were some things you just knew, even if you were blind.

Especially if you were blind.

"Falcon," he called out for the umpteenth time, his voice amplified by a police megaphone. "This is Vincent Paulo you're talking to. We can work this out, all right?"

The man was atop a lamppost—as high in the sky as he could possibly get—looking down from his roost. The views of Miami had to be spectacular from up there. Paulo, however, could only imagine the blue-green waters of the bay, the high-rise condominiums along the waterfront like so many dominoes ready to topple in a colossal chain reaction. Cruise ships, perhaps, were headed slowly out to sea, trails of white smoke puffing against a sky so blue that no cloud dared to disturb it. Traffic, they told him, was backed up for miles in each direction, west toward the mainland and east toward the island of Key Biscayne. There were squad cars, a SWAT van, teams of police officers, police boats in the bay, and a legion of media vans and reporters swarming the bridge. Paulo could hear the helicopters whirring all around, as local news broadcasted the entire episode live into South Florida living rooms.

All this, for one of Miami's homeless. He called himself Falcon, and the name was a perfect fit. He was straddling the lamppost, his legs intertwined with the metalwork so that he could stand erect without holding on to anything. He was a life-size imitation of an old-fashioned hood ornament, without the chrome finish—chin up, chest out, his body extended out over the water, arms outstretched like the wings of a bird. Like a falcon. Paulo had a uniformed officer at his side to describe the situation to him, but she was hardly needed. It wasn't the first time Paulo had been called upon to stop one of Miami's homeless from hurting himself. It wasn't even his first encounter with Falcon. Twice in the past eighteen months, Falcon had climbed atop a bridge and assumed the same falcon-like pose. Each time, Paulo had talked him down. But this time was different.

It was Vince's first assignment since losing his eyesight.

And for the first time, he was absolutely convinced that this one was going to jump.

"Falcon, just come down and talk. It's the best way for everyone."

"No more bullshit!" he shouted. "I want to talk to the mayor's daughter. Get her here in fifteen minutes, or I'm doing a face plant onto the old bridge."

The Powell Bridge is like a big arc over Biscayne Bay. Cyclists call it "Miami Mountain," though as suicides go, it is no match for the Golden Gate in San Francisco or the George Washington in New York. The crest is only seventy-eight feet above mean tide. Even with the added thirty vertical feet of the lamppost, it was debatable whether Falcon's plunge into the bay would be fatal. The old causeway runs parallel to the new bridge, however, and it is still used as a fishing pier. A hundred-foot swan dive onto solid concrete wouldn't be pretty—especially on live television.

"You ready to punt yet, Paulo?" The voice came from over Vince's left shoulder, and he recognized the speaker as Juan Chavez, SWAT team coordinator.

Vince cut off his megaphone. "Let's talk to the chief."

The walk back to the police van was clear of obstacles, and Vince had memorized the way. His long white walking stick was almost unnecessary. He and Chavez entered the van through the side door and sat across from one another in the rear captain's chairs. An officer outside the van slid the door closed as Chavez dialed headquarters on an encrypted telephone. The call went directly to Miami's chief of police, who was watching the standoff on television. Her first words weren't exactly the vote of confidence Vince needed.

"It's been over two hours now, Paulo. I'm not seeing much progress."

"It took me almost twice that long to talk him down from the Golden Glades flyover last winter."

"I understand that," said the chief. "I guess what I'm asking is, are you comfortable doing this?"

"Now that I'm blind, you mean?"

"Don't get me wrong. I'm glad you decided to stay with the force and teach at the academy. I called you back into the field because you have a history with this guy, but the last thing I want to do is to put you in a situation that you don't think you can handle."

"I can handle it fine, Chief."

"Great, but time is a factor. I shouldn't have to remind you that no one in Miami keeps gloves in the glove compartment. If this sucker doesn't climb down soon, one of those stranded motorists is going to reach for his revolver and take him out for us."

"I say we move in now," said Chavez.

Vince said, "Don't you think a three-oh-eight-caliber, custom-built thunderstick is a bit of overkill against a homeless guy perched on a lamppost?"

"No one's talking about a sniper shot. I just want to move our team closer into position, make them more visible. We need to send a message that our patience is wearing thin."

"If he thinks SWAT is coming up there after him, he'll jump."

"The same tactic worked just fine the last time."

"This time is different."

"How do you know?"

"I can tell."

"What, going blind made you psychic?"

That made Vince blink, but dark sunglasses hid plenty of pain. "Shove it, Chavez."

"All right, fellas, knock it off," said the chief.

"I'm serious," said Chavez. "This isn't the first time we've had to deal with a homeless guy threatening to hurt himself. Nine times out of ten, they just want a little attention. I'd like to know what makes Paulo think this is the real deal."

"That seems like a fair question," said the chief.

"All right," said Vince. "For one, it may be his third time up on a bridge, but it's the first time that Falcon has made a specific demand. And it's a fairly rational one at that. It's not as if he wants us to make the bubble people stop stealing his thoughts. Just as important, he's set a time limit. A short one—fifteen minutes. You factor in the stress in his voice, and you've got a man on the edge."

"Wait a minute," said Chavez. "Because he shows some signs of clear-headed thinking, that makes him more of a danger to himself?"

"In some ways, yes. The only way Falcon climbs down from that lamppost is if he gives up on his demand to talk to the mayor's daughter. Because he still shows some signs of rational thought, he will very likely feel overwhelming humiliation when the television world sees him fail. If we send the SWAT team up that pole before he's ready to accept his public failure, you might as well push him off the bridge yourself."

"How about soaking him with a fire hose?" said the chief. "Or maybe a stun gun."

"There again, we're on live television," said Vince. "You knock him off that lamppost and we'll have two dozen personal-injury lawyers handing him business cards before he hits the ground."

There was silence, each officer thinking it through. Finally, the chief said, "I suppose we could promise to give him what he wants."

"You mean let him talk to the mayor's daughter?" said Vince.

"No, I said *promise* it. That's his only demand, right?"

"Bad move," said Vince. "A negotiator never promises anything he can't deliver. Or that he has no intention of delivering."

"For once I agree with Paulo," said Chavez. "But I think—"

Vince waited for him to finish, but Chavez seemed to have lost his train of thought. "You think what?" said Vince.

"I think it doesn't matter what we think. The mayor's daughter is here."

"What?"

"I can see her through the windshield right now."

Vince picked up the sound of approaching footsteps outside the van. The side door slid open, and he could feel her presence. "Hello, Vince," she said.

Alicia Mendoza was not merely the mayor's beautiful twenty-seven-year-old daughter. She was a cop, too, so it was no surprise that she had gotten through the police barricade. Still, the sound of her voice hit Vince like a five iron. Instinctively, he began searching for the memory of her visage—the dark, almond-shaped eyes, the full lips, the flawless olive skin—but he didn't want to go there. "What are you doing here, Alicia?"

"I hear Falcon wants to talk to me," she said. "So I came."

Vince's sense of hearing was just fine, but his brain was suddenly incapable of decoding her words. That familiar, soft voice triggered only raw emotion. Many months had passed since he'd last heard her speak. It was sometime after he became a hero, after the doctors removed the bandages—following the horrific realization that he would never again see her smile, never look into those eyes as her heart pounded against his chest, never see the expression on her face when she was happy or sad or just plain bored. The last thing he'd heard her say was, "You're wrong, Vince, you're so wrong." That was the same day he'd told her it would be best to stop seeing each other, and the unintended pun had made them both cry.

"I want to help," she said as she gently touched Vince on the wrist.

Then go away, he thought. *I'm so much better now. If you really want to help, Alicia, then please—just go away.*

2

Miami criminal defense lawyer Jack Swyteck wasn't looking for a new client, at least not one who was homeless. Granted, many of his past clients hailed from an address that even the pushiest real estate agent would have to admit was undesirable—death row, to be specific. Jack's first job out of law school was with the Freedom Institute, a ragtag group of idealists who defended "the worst of the worst," which was a nice euphemism for some very scary and guilty-as-hell sons of bitches. Only one had actually been innocent, but one was enough to keep Jack going. He spent four years at the institute. Nearly a decade had passed since his last capital case, however, and it had been just as long since he'd defended the likes of a Falcon.

"So, your real name is what?" said Jack. His client was seated on the opposite side of the table, dressed in the familiar orange prison garb. The fluorescent light overhead cast a sickly yellow pall over his weathered skin. His hair was a thinning, tangled mess of salt and pepper, and his scraggly beard was mostly gray. An open sore festered on the back of his left hand, and two larger ones were on his forehead, just above the bushy right eyebrow. His eyes were black, hollow pools. Jack was reminded of those photographs of Saddam Hussein after he crawled out of his hole in the ground.

"My name's Falcon," he said, mumbling.

"Falcon what?"

The man rubbed his nose with the palm of his hand. It was a big, fleshy nose. "Just Falcon."

"What, like Cher or Madonna?"

"No. Like Falcon, fuckhead."

Jack wrote "Falcon Fuckhead" in his notes. He knew the man's real name, of course. It was in the case file: Pablo Garcia. He was just trying to start a dialogue with his new client.

Jack was a trial lawyer who specialized in criminal defense work, though he was open to just about anything if it interested him. By the same token, he turned away cases that he didn't find interesting, the upshot being that he liked what he did but didn't make a ton of money doing it. Profit had never been his goal, which was precisely the reason that Neil Goderich, his old boss at the Freedom Institute, referred Falcon's case to him. Neil was now the Miami-Dade public defender. Falcon flatly refused to be represented by a PD—anyone on the government's payroll was part of "the conspiracy"—but he desperately needed a lawyer. The dramatic live news coverage on the bridge, coupled with Falcon's apparent fascination with the mayor's daughter, gave the case a high profile. Falcon took a swing at the first PD assigned to the case, so Neil pitched it to Jack. Falcon was happy, if only because it could be fun to mess with the son of Florida's former governor. Jack had been happy, too. He made it a practice to do two or three freebies a year for people who couldn't pay, and he was reasonably confident that his old buddy Neil wouldn't toss him a lemon.

Jack, however, was beginning to have second thoughts.

"How old are you, Falcon?"

"It's in the file."

"I'm sure it is. But talk to me, okay?"

"How old do I look?"

Jack studied his face. "A hundred and fifty-seven. Give or take a decade."

"I'm fifty-two."

"That makes you a little old for the mayor's daughter, don't you think?"

"I need a lawyer, not a smartass."

"You get what you pay for." Sometimes a little wisecracking loosened these guys up, or at least allowed you to keep your own sanity. Falcon was stone-faced. *It must be decades since this one cracked a smile.* "You're Latin, right?"

"What of it?"

"Where you from originally?"

"None of your damn business."

Jack checked the file. "Says here you became a U.S. citizen in nineteen eighty-two. Born in Cuba. My mother was from Cuba."

"Yeah. She was great, but I ain't your daddy."

Jack let it go. "How did you get here?"

"A leaky raft and a boatload of luck. How'd you get here?"

"Just luck, I was born here. Where do you live now?"

"Miami."

"Where in Miami?"

"It's a little place along the Miami River. Right before the Twelfth Avenue Bridge."

"Is it a house or an apartment?"

"It's actually a car."

"You live in a car?"

"Yeah. I mean, it used to be a car. It's been stripped a hundred times over. Doesn't run or anything. No tires, no engine. But it's a roof over my head."

"Who owns the property?"

"Hell if I know. There's this old Puerto Rican guy named Manny who comes around every so often. I guess he owns the place. I don't bother him, he don't bother me. Know what I mean?"

"Sure. My dad and I had the same arrangement when I was in high school. So, let me ask you this: How long have you been homeless?"

"I ain't homeless. I told you, I live in the car."

"Okay. How long have you lived in this car?"

"Few years, I guess. I moved in sometime while Clinton was still president."

"What did you do before then?"

"I was the ambassador to France. What the hell does that have to do with anything?"

Jack laid his notepad on the table. "Tell me something, Falcon. How is it that you've lived on the street all these years, and the only time you seem to get into trouble is when you climb up on a bridge and threaten to kill yourself?"

"I'm a smart guy. Keep my nose clean."

"You ever had any contact with the outreach people from Citrus Health Network, or any of the folks over at the mental health clinic at Jackson?"

"There's this woman named Shirley who used to come visit me. Kept trying to get me to come with her back to the hospital and get some meds."

"Did you go?"

"No."

"Did Shirley ever tell you what kind of a condition you might have?"

"In her opinion I showed signs of paranoia, but she thought I was well compensated."

"What did you say to that?"

"I said thank you very much, it sure sucks to be crazy, but it's nice to have a big dick."

Jack ignored it. "Have the police ever come to take you by force to a crisis center for a few hours, or maybe even a day or two? Has anything like that ever happened to you?"

"You mean have I ever been Baker-Acted?"

It didn't surprise Jack that he knew the terminology. He was definitely well compensated, psychologically speaking. "Yeah, that's what I'm asking."

"If I was crazy, they'd have me over in the A Wing."

The A Wing at Miami-Dade county jail was for psychiatric patients. "No one's saying you're crazy," said Jack.

"You people are the crazies. You're the ones who walk around pretending that guys like me are invisible."

Jack didn't disagree. Still, he jotted "possible anasognosia" in his notes, a medical term he'd picked up while working death cases. It meant the inability to recognize your own illness.

"We'll talk more about that later," said Jack. "Right now, let me explain what's going to happen today. You're charged with a variety of things. Obstructing a bridge, obstructing a highway, creating a public nuisance, indecent exposure—"

"I had to piss."

"You probably should have come down from the lamppost to do it. But hey, hindsight's twenty-twenty." Jack continued with the list: "Resisting arrest, assaulting a police officer—"

"That's a total joke. Paulo told me that if I came down, I could talk to the mayor's daughter. The minute my feet hit the ground, three SWAT guys were all over me. Of course I resisted."

"I'm just reciting the charges, I'm not the one bringing them."

"What kind of a country is this anyway? A guy wants to jump off a bridge, why should it be illegal?"

"Well, if they made it legal, then you'd have everybody wanting to do it. Kind of like gay marriage."

"The only reason they're going after me like this

is because I asked to talk to the mayor's daughter."

"Now that you bring it up, exactly what did you want to say to her?"

"That's between me and her."

"I have to correct you there, pal. If I'm going to be your lawyer, let's get something straight from the get-go: There's *nothing* between you and Alicia Mendoza."

A worm of a smile crept across Falcon's lips, a kind of satisfied smirk that Jack had seen before—but only on death row. "You're wrong," said Falcon. "Dead wrong. I know she wants to talk to me. She wants to talk to me real bad."

"How do you know that?"

"I saw her standing by that police van. I'm sure it was Alicia. I asked her to come, and she came. They just wouldn't let her talk to me."

"That's probably because they didn't want to do anything to encourage the obsession."

"I'm not stalking her," he said sharply. "I just want to talk to her."

"Mayor Mendoza probably doesn't appreciate the distinction. Most people wouldn't."

"Then why didn't they bring any stalker charges against me?"

"You only contacted her once, so trying to prove stalking would needlessly complicate the case. You gave the government a much easier way to put you away for a good long time. It's called possession of narcotics. That's also on the list, and it's a felony, my friend."

"I didn't have no crack."

"It was in your coat pocket."

"I didn't put it there."

"Uh, yeah," said Jack. "Save it for another day. All we have to do this morning is enter a plea of not guilty, no explanation needed. The judge will hear briefly from me on the issue of bail. I'll argue this, that, and the other thing. The prosecutor will say it's this way, that way, and the other way. After everyone's had their say, the judge will stop counting the number of tiles in the ceiling and set bail at ten thousand dollars, which is pretty standard in a possession case like this one."

"How soon do they need it?"

"Need what?"

"The ten thousand dollars?"

Jack was amused by the question. "As soon as you can get it, you're out of jail. Or we can post a bond. You'd have to come up with ten percent—a thousand dollars—which is nonrefundable. And you'd have to pledge sufficient collateral for the balance. All this is academic, I'm sure, since you obviously don't have ten cents, let alone—"

"Not a problem. I got the ten grand."

"What?"

"I don't need to post no bond. I can pay the ten thousand dollars."

"You can't even pay me," said Jack, scoffing.

"I can pay you, and I can make bail."

"You live in an abandoned automobile. Where are you going to get your hands on that kind of cash?"

Falcon reached across the table and laid his hand, palm down, flat atop Jack's notepad. The fingernails were deformed and discolored from a fungus of some kind, and that open sore on the back of his hand was oozing white pus. For the first time, however, Jack detected a sparkle—some sign of life—in those cold, dark eyes. "Take notes," he said in a low, serious tone. "I'll tell you exactly where to find it."

3
·

Jack's flight landed in Nassau just after nine a.m. He hated small aircraft, but a forty-five-minute hop over the Gulf Stream on Zack's Seaplanes came at an irresistible price. It was absolutely free, thanks to Theo Knight.

Theo was Jack's all-purpose assistant, for lack of a better term. Whatever Jack needed, Theo went and got it, though Jack knew better than to ask how he got it done. Theirs was not a textbook friendship, the Ivy League son of a governor meets the black high-school dropout from Liberty City. But they got on just fine for two guys who'd met on death row, Jack the lawyer and Theo the inmate. Jack's persistence had delayed Theo's date with the electric chair long enough for DNA evidence to come into vogue and prove him innocent. It wasn't the original plan, but Jack ended up a part of Theo's new life, sometimes going along for the ride, other times just watching with envy and amazement as Theo made up for precious time lost.

This time, it was Theo's turn to go along for the ride—to Falcon's bank.

"Greater Bahamian Bank and Trust Company," said Theo, reading the sign on the building. "I hope they got casinos in here."

Jack had called the bank beforehand and confirmed that it did in fact have a safe deposit box for Pablo Garcia. He then faxed over the executed power of attorney, which would authorize him to access the box. Sure enough, the signature of his client matched the specimen on file at the bank. Jack still didn't believe there was money inside, but the flight was free, and even a break-even day at the casinos beat a good day in the office, especially if Theo was the one rolling the dice. He didn't always win, but the guy never seemed to lose money at the crap table. Jack didn't dare ask him how he did that, either.

Bay Street was essentially Main Street for high-powered finance in the Bahamas, and the Greater Bahamian Bank & Trust Company represented one of hundreds of foreign institutions that thrived on the legal protections and secrecy that countries like the Bahamas afforded to offshore branches. While there were many recognizable names—Royal Bank of Canada, Barclay's, Bank of Nova Scotia, and others—some of these so-called banks looked more like a doctor's office, basically just an office in a strip mall that might as well bear the name JOE'S BANK OF THE CARRIBEAN. Greater Bahamian was somewhere between the two extremes, occupying the ground floor of a three-story building. The main entrance to the bank was tidy and simple, a mix of chrome, glass, and indoor-outdoor carpet. Two security guards patrolled the lobby, each packing a nine-millimeter pistol in a black leather holster. Another armed guard stood watch at the door. Theo greeted him with a folksy "How goes it, bro?" The same greeting from Jack would have come across like Garth Brooks doing rap. Theo, however, was an imposing man with the brawn of a linebacker and the height of an NBA star, sort of a cross between The Rock and a young Samuel L. Jackson on steroids. Just to look at him, you would guess (correctly) that he'd spent time in prison. That bad-boy image served him well. Very few people ever got in his way. The rest of the world—even armed security guards—just stepped aside and smiled, hoping that "How goes it, bro" was Theo's way of saying "Relax, dude, I don't have time to rearrange your face." On occasion, Jack needed a friend with that kind of firepower. Mostly, he found Theo entertaining, like cable TV and satellite radio rolled into one big, amusing, friend-for-life subscription.

"Hey, I almost forgot to tell you," said Theo as they crossed the lobby. "Katrina has a friend she wants to fix you up with."

Katrina was Theo's on-again, off-again girlfriend, a tough and sexy Latina with a Russian accent who had once laid Jack out on the sidewalk with an awesome left hook—no exaggeration. "I'm really not interested in any blind dates."

"Katrina says she's hot."

"A woman will always say her friend is hot."

"No. A woman will always say her friend is pretty, which probably means she's not. But if she says her friend is hot, trust me, dude, she's hot."

"That was almost poetic," said Jack.

"It did kind of rhyme, didn't it?"

"Like Eminem, without the profanity."

It was midmorning, and perhaps a half-dozen customers were in the bank, not counting Jack and Theo. In the personal banking center to the left, a dozen or more bank officers were at their desks, busy on the telephone. With customers all over the world, the Greater Bahamian Bank & Trust Company transcended time zones.

"Interesting place for a homeless guy to do business," said Theo.

"Depends on the business," said Jack.

The court hearing had played out exactly as Jack had predicted. Falcon entered a plea of not guilty, and the judge set bail at ten thousand dollars. Before leaving the jail, Jack retrieved a bit of Falcon's personal property from lockup. It was a necklace made of metal beads, which Falcon had worn around his neck for years. Attached to the necklace was a small key. Jack had Falcon's key in his pocket as he headed toward the sign marked SAFE DEPOSIT BOXES.

The boxes were located in a windowless wing of the private banking section. Jack left his name with the receptionist and took a seat on the couch. The well-dressed man seated beside him was reading the stock quotes. An elderly woman on her cell phone was speaking Portuguese. Lasers of light flashed from a three-carat diamond ring with each wave of her hand. Jack tried to imagine someone like Falcon walking in and stinking up the place. It didn't compute.

"Mr. Swyteck?" a woman said, standing in the doorway. Jack answered, and she introduced herself as Ms. Friedman, vice president. It seemed like everyone in a bank was a vice president. Jack and Theo followed her to a small office behind the reception desk.

Jack presented her with the original power of attorney and his passport. Ms. Friedman inspected both. She then excused herself, explaining that she needed to verify the signature once again, and left the room. Jack sat in silence, waiting. Theo grabbed a magazine from the rack and started flipping through the pages. He never really read anything, save for a menu, and he seemed bitterly disappointed to discover that this month's issue of *Bahamian Banker* was short on photographs. Jack needed to find something to talk about before his friend tore the place apart in search of *Sports Illustrated*.

"So, why does she want to meet me?" said Jack.

"Why does who wanna meet you?"

"Katrina's friend—the blind date you were talking about."

Theo smiled. "Ah, so you *are* interested."

"No. I'm just curious. Why does Katrina think we'd be a good match?"

"I'm told that she likes a man with a sense of humor."

"Right. All women just love a man with a sense of humor. But as it turns out, they're usually referring to the humor of Jude Law, Will Smith, or George Clooney. Apparently, those guys are a stitch."

The bank officer returned. "Gentlemen, come with me, please."

They followed her to the end of the hall and stopped at the security checkpoint. Another armed guard was posted at the door.

"How goes it, bro'?" said Theo.

This time the guard said nothing, no pleasant smile. This was the bank's inner sanctum, the place where things got serious, where security was equal to Theo Knight.

The guard unlocked the glass door to allow Jack and Theo to enter. Ms. Friedman was right behind them. The door closed, and the guard relocked it. The safe deposit boxes were arranged from floor to ceiling, as in a locker room. Everywhere Jack looked was another box with a brushed-metal face. The larger ones were on the bottom. Smaller ones were on top. Ms. Friedman led Jack to box 266, one of the larger ones. It had two locks on the face. She inserted her key into one lock and turned it.

"Your key is for the other lock," she said. "I'll leave you in privacy now. If you need me, check with the guard. There is a convenience room in back with a table and chairs. You can take the whole box with you and open it there, if you wish. No one else will be allowed in this area until you've finished."

Jack thanked her, and she gave him a little smile as she left the room. He kept an eye on the keyhole as he reached inside his pocket for the key. "What's your guess, Theo? You think there's really ten thousand dollars inside that box?"

"Five minutes ago I would have said no way. But who knows? Everything has checked out so far."

Jack inserted the key. The tumblers clicked as he turned it clockwise. With a steady pull, he removed the box from its sleeve. It was longer than he had expected—about two feet from front to back. It was heavy, too. He laid it on the bench behind him.

"And the answer is . . ." he said like a game show host as he flipped the latch and removed the lid.

Jack was suddenly speechless.

Andrew Jackson was staring back at them, many times over. Crisp twenty-dollar bills were stacked neatly side by side. Jack removed the top bundle. There were more beneath it. The box was stuffed with cash, top to bottom, front to back.

"There must be a couple hundred thousand dollars in here," said Jack.

"At least," said Theo. "Which certainly makes you wonder."

"Why would a guy live in an abandoned car if he's got all this money in the bank?"

"Maybe for the same reason he wants to jump off a bridge," said Theo. "Or maybe he just wants to be homeless."

Jack laid a hand atop the money, thinking. "Or both."

4

When Vincent Paulo was a little boy, he was afraid of the dark. He and his older brother shared a bedroom. The lower bunk was for Danny, who never had trouble falling asleep. Vince had the top bunk, which was part of his mother's strategy. She knew that no matter how frightened he became, little Vince wouldn't dare crawl down from the top bunk in the middle of the night. He couldn't risk waking his big brother, unless he wanted a certain bloody nose. Vince would lay awake for the longest time—for hours, it seemed, the covers pulled over his head, afraid to make a move. "Just close your eyes and go to sleep," his mother would say. But Vince couldn't do it. The room, at least, had a night-light. Closing his eyes would mean total darkness, and it was in that black, empty world that monsters prowled.

Ironic, he thought, that he now lived in that world—and that it was indeed a monster who had put him there.

Vince tried not to think about the day he'd lost his sight, or at least not to dwell on it. Hindsight could eat you up, even on the small stuff. *If only I'd remembered that Elm Street was a speed trap. If only I'd sold that stock last month.* But how many people could say, "If only I hadn't opened that door, I would never have lost my eyesight"? Of those, how many could actually live with the result—truly *live* with it, as in live a happy life. Vince tried to be one of those people. He refused to be doted on or smothered by those of good intentions. He refused to change careers. He refused to stop living. There would be major changes and adjustments, to be sure. Teaching at the police academy wasn't exactly active duty, but it was important work. It was certainly better than taking disability and fading into oblivion. Hopefully there would be more cases like Falcon on the bridge, where Vince could play a role in a real-life hostage situation. But even if that didn't happen, he would go on with his life, and he would be happy. That was a good place to be, emotionally, and it had taken him many months to get there.

It had taken only the sound of Alicia's voice to send him tumbling back to square one.

"I'm taking off now," his uncle said. "Are you going to be all right?"

Each evening, Uncle Ricky picked Vince up from work, drove him home, and helped him cook dinner—usually grilled steaks and ice cream. Richard Boies was the uncle everyone wanted, sort of a second father and best friend rolled into one. The things he did for family were from the heart, not out of obligation, and his mischievous streak and quick sense of humor always lifted Vince's spirits. Just the thought of this tall, slender man with bright red hair, blazing blue eyes, and glowing red skin from the Miami sun was enough to make Vince smile. They could no longer share Uncle Ricky's love of photography, but they would listen to music, tell stories, and play cards or dominoes until it was time for bed. Uncle Ricky was a dominoes master. Vince got even at poker. He had a long way to go before he mastered Braille, but Vince knew a full house when he felt one.

"I'm good," said Vince.

"You sure?" said Uncle Ricky. "Nothing I can get you? Glass of water? Remote control? Winning Lotto ticket?"

"Get outta here," said Vince, smiling.

"I have to be going too," his brother said. Danny had a wife and three kids, but he did manage to visit Vince on poker night. Uncle Ricky made sure he didn't cheat.

"There's a nasty cold front coming through tonight," his uncle said. "You want me to drag an extra blanket down from the closet?"

"I can get it," said Vince. "Thanks anyway."

The goal was for Vince to do more and more for himself every day. A caregiver came at six every morning to help him work toward his goal of complete independence in various personal matters, everything from grooming and hygiene to little tricks in the closet that would prevent him from walking out of the house wearing black pants with brown loafers. Uncle Ricky would be back at seven a.m. to take him to work.

His uncle slapped him on the shoulder and started toward the door. Danny followed and said, "Texas Hold 'Em next week?"

"I'll be ready," said Vince.

The front door opened, then closed. Vince remained in the armchair as he listened to the fading sound of footfalls on the sidewalk. Uncle Ricky was the first to leave. His brother waited behind on the porch. It was the same drill every week. Danny would stand there alone, searching for the right thing to say to Vince, and wishing that he had Uncle Ricky's easy way about himself even in the face of adversity. Vince knew in his heart that Danny wanted to open the door, step back inside, and have that conversation they'd been avoiding—to be the big brother. But it never happened. He would give up and go home, saying nothing.

The engine fired, and Vince could hear the car pulling away. His brother was gone, and it was like old times. Back then, they would lie awake at night in those bunk beds, talking. Oh, the things brothers could talk about while staring into the darkness. Then Danny would fall asleep, and Vince would be alone. And afraid.

Get over it, Vince told himself.

His childhood fears notwithstanding, Vince had grown up to be brave, good-looking, and full of confidence. He came to the police force straight out of the marines, after a tour of duty in the first Gulf War. Before enlisting, he'd earned a degree in psychology from the University of Florida, where he was also a standout on the swim team. At six-foot-two and 190 pounds of solid muscle, he was a walking Speedo advertisement. He hated those banana hammocks, however, and he wore them only to compete. What he loved was police work, and he loved being a cop. The psychology degree and his coolness under pressure made him a natural for crisis management. In his five years as a negotiator, he was known as a risk taker who didn't always follow the conventional wisdom of other trained negotiators. His critics said that his unorthodox style would eventually catch up with him, and they were right. A few of them predicted that he'd end up dead someday.

Even they didn't see blindness coming.

The telephone rang. He rose and, with the aid of his walking stick, went to the kitchen and answered it. The voice on the other end of the line halted, though it was a familiar one. "Vince, hi. It's me. Alicia."

The call didn't shock him. "Professional" was perhaps the best way to describe his behavior toward his ex-girlfriend during that crisis on the bridge. He felt no animosity toward her, and he had conveyed none. He simply felt better equipped to move forward without Alicia in his life, without a constant reminder of the bright future he'd lost. Vince didn't want anyone sticking by his side just because she felt sorry for him. No matter what she said, a woman as active, adventurous, and gorgeous as Alicia was bound to leave her blind boyfriend behind eventually. Her dumping him would only make it worse. He had explained all of that to her many times before. Perhaps he should have told her again. "What's up?" he said.

"Nothing. I just wanted to tell you that I thought you did an amazing job yesterday with that jumper."

"Thanks. But it really wasn't anything to be proud of."

"You're being too tough on yourself. I think you should consider branching out beyond just teaching at the academy. I really do."

"It's nice of you to say that. But honestly, the way things went down on that bridge, we're lucky no one was hurt."

"Luck is always part of the job."

"Sometimes it's with you, sometimes it's not."

"This time it was," she said.

Last time, it hadn't been. No one needed to say it.

An awkward silence gripped the phone line, and Vince could sense that she had something more to say. He kept them focused on business. "We should never have promised to let him speak to you," he said. "It's always dangerous to feed a stalker's obsession, and getting caught in a lie can spell disaster."

"I was actually willing to talk to him, if you thought it was a good strategy. Lying to him wasn't my idea."

"I know," said Vince. "But that was how the chief wanted to play it, so who am I to argue with results? As long as you're comfortable."

"I'm fine with it."

"You should be. I don't think Falcon will be getting out of jail any time soon. Like his lawyer said, if the judge wants to set bail at ten thousand dollars, he might as well set it at ten million."

"Well, apparently Swyteck changed his tune. The station called right after dinner. Falcon made bail."

"You're kidding? How?"

"I don't know," she said. "But that's enough about Falcon. I'm just glad I was able to help. That's the reason I went to the bridge."

The implicit message was that she hadn't gone there just to see him. "I understand what you're saying," he said.

"No, maybe that didn't come out right. What I'm trying to say is that if I wanted to talk to you, I wouldn't show up on a bridge in the middle of some homeless guy's suicide. I would just call you up on the phone and say, hey Vince, I want to talk to you."

"I know you would."

She paused, and Vince could feel the change in tone coming. "Hey Vince, I want to talk to you."

Again, there was silence. He could feel the tightness in his throat, the emotional vice grip. He drew a deep breath and let it out. "It's not that simple, Alicia."

"It's a heck of a lot easier than trying to act like total strangers."

"Let's not go over this again, okay?"

"You're right. Let's not do that. There's a jazz festival on South Beach this weekend. Some of the clubs are kicking things off Friday night. You like jazz even more than I do. Want to go?"

"I don't think—"

"Don't think. Just do it."

He paused just long enough to give her an opening. "Great," she said. "I'll pick you up around nine."

Part of him wanted to say no, but that would have been his fears talking—the fear of destroying what they'd once had, the fear of discovering that they had no future, the even greater fear of confirming that he could never build a life with a sighted woman. "Okay," he said. "I'll see you tomorrow night."

She said a quick good-bye and hung up. Clearly, she wanted to disconnect before he could change his mind. There was no chance of that, however. Vince was a man of his word. If he said he would go, he'd go. It wasn't in his nature to second-guess his decisions.

Except for that door. That pockmarked door at the end of the dark hallway—the door he should never have opened.

Vince found the clock on the kitchen counter and pressed the speaker button. "Ten fifty-two," the mechanical voice announced. Time for bed.

He took three steps to the right and opened a drawer that was directly beneath the microwave oven. His medication was in a foil package, third bin from the left. The doctor had prescribed Mirtazapine, thirty milligrams, in a dissolvable-tablet form, to be taken each night at bedtime. It was an antidepressant. It didn't seem to make him any happier, but it did knock him right out.

He opened the package and placed the tablet on his tongue. The bitter lemon taste brought a sense of calm, even security. Eight hours of sleep, guaranteed. Eight glorious hours of sight.

In his dreams—even in his worst nightmares—Vincent Paulo was never blind.

5
.

Alicia didn't feel the cold night air until she switched off her cell phone.

The bar was packed and noisy, so she'd been forced to step outside and call Vince from the sidewalk. Miracle Mile was an upscale shopping boulevard, the heart of downtown Coral Gables. This time of year, it had that eclectic mix of palm trees and Christmas decorations—colored lights everywhere, storefront windows frosted with artificial snow, reindeer and candy canes suspended from lampposts. The bar at Houston's Restaurant drew a twentysomething crowd on Thursday nights, and the waiting line wrapped all the way around the corner to the valet stand. The singles on queue seemed to eye one another with added interest. This was definitely snuggle weather. Alicia was the only person on the block without a coat. She felt like one of those Jersey girls who ended up on the evening news each year, determined to show off her new bikini and steal a suntan despite forty-degree temperatures without the wind chill.

Alicia wasn't out on the prowl. Thursdays were her nights out with old girlfriends, a chance to break away from a shrinking social life that seemed to revolve more and more around being a cop. All the guys stepped aside and checked her out as she went back inside. She drew dirty looks from several women who assumed she was using that hot body to cut in line. It was amazing how so much of society and basic social interaction was built on eye contact. That little observation just seemed to pop into her head for no reason at all. But things rarely happened without a reason. She was thinking about Vince, and her painful awareness that he could never again cut a glance across a room was exactly what had triggered her thoughts. She was suddenly angry with herself. He would push her away for good if he knew she was feeling sorry for him.

The bar seemed even louder and more crowded as Alicia forced her way back to her friends' table. The effects of two-for-one margaritas were beginning to wear off, and she was already regretting the impulsive telephone call to Vince. She knew better than to let alcohol do the talking for her, but somehow it had worked out fine.

Finally, she reached her table, only to find a waiter clearing away empty glasses as five women settled up the bill.

"You owe sixteen twenty-five," said Rebecca, never looking up from her miniature calculator. Rebecca had been Alicia's friend since college, and she was still the same. Bills were divided to the exact penny.

Alicia checked the back of her chair for her purse, but it wasn't there. She checked the floor around them and even under the table. "Did one of you girls grab my purse by accident?"

The others shrugged and looked at one another. No, uh-uh, not me.

"Well, shit," said Alicia. "Somebody stole my purse."

"Are you sure?"

"Yeah. I took my phone out to call Vince, and I left my purse right here on the back of my chair." Presently, the back of her chair was up against some guy's butt. Their table was surrounded—practically smothered—by a standing-room-only crowd. Someone could have easily brushed by the chair and lifted her purse without Alicia's friends taking notice.

"I'll cover your share of the bill," said Rebecca. "Why don't you check with the hostess? Maybe someone turned it in."

"All right," said Alicia, though she knew in her heart that it was more likely in the Dumpster and that some slob who now called himself Alicia Mendoza had already purchased a sixty-inch plasma TV with her credit card. It was a sea of humanity between her and the hostess. She had to turn herself sideways and rub against two dozen strangers before reaching the stand.

"Did anyone turn in a purse?" Alicia asked.

"What's it look like?" asked the hostess.

"Black shoulder bag. Kate Spade."

The hostess pulled the bag from beneath the counter just as Alicia's friend emerged from the crowd. "You found it," said Rebecca. "Where was it?"

The hostess said, "One of our waitresses found it in the ladies' room."

"I didn't leave it in the ladies' room," said Alicia.

"Maybe it was one of your margaritas that left it there," said Rebecca. "Check to see if anything's missing."

Alicia opened the bag, but the restaurant was almost too dark to see inside her purse. She and Rebecca went outside, and the cold night air hit them immediately. The temperature was dropping by the minute, but Alicia was flushed with adrenaline as she sifted through the contents of her purse. To her relief, her wallet was still there. The credit cards were still in place, and so was all her cash.

Rebecca snatched a twenty-dollar bill and said, "For the drinks. Now I owe you three seventy-five."

Alicia stepped away before her friend could claim ownership to anything else. She checked the side pocket and the zipper pouch inside. "My lipstick is gone."

"Yuck," said Rebecca. "No offense, girl, but who would steal your lipstick?"

An uneasy feeling came over her. She imagined some pervert writing her initials on his balls with Dusty Rose No. 3. Probably an overreaction on her part, but the mind went in those directions when you were a cop. "Only one person I can think of."

"You mean that guy on the bridge who wanted to talk to you? I thought he was in jail."

"The station called right after I left work to tell

me he was back on the street. Somehow he made bail."

"If a homeless guy came wandering into Houston's, wouldn't somebody notice?"

"Maybe they cleaned him up before he left jail."

"Enough to get into the ladies' room? That's where they found your purse, remember?"

"That's true."

"But it has to be him, doesn't it? If it's not, then who's the lipstick bandit?"

Alicia's gaze shifted back toward the restaurant. With the reflections off the huge plate-glass windows, the packed crowd seemed to double in size. "I have no idea," she said.

6

The night Falcon returned to the street was the coldest of the year.

It was well after dark before his lawyer finally posted the ten-thousand-dollar bail. Swyteck wanted to have a full and frank discussion with his client before springing him loose. Falcon wanted out of there immediately. Predictably, Swyteck turned on the social-worker speech, the deep concern for his downtrodden fellow man. Get yourself an apartment, Falcon. Get some warm clothes, get a life—for Pete's sake, do something with all that money you have squirreled away in a safe deposit box. As if any lawyer really cared about his poor, homeless client. Falcon was no fool. He didn't need to sit around and wait for Swyteck to work his way up to the obvious burning question. The guy was a lawyer, and he wouldn't be much of a lawyer if he didn't worry about where the money had come from. Not that those bastards didn't take dirty money. Lawyers just knew well enough to take precautions before taking their take. Take, take, take.

"Back off, Swyteck!" he said aloud, speaking to no one. "You can't have it."

The Miami River was an inky black belt in the moonlight. It was quiet along the riverfront tonight, except for the cars whirring across the drawbridge. Rubber tires on metal always seemed louder in the cold, dry air. Falcon wasn't sure why, and he didn't care. He had to take a piss. He stopped beneath the bridge, unzipped, and waited. Nothing. The traffic noise from above was bothering him. Vehicles passing at the speed of light, one after another, quick little bursts that sounded like laser guns. It was breaking his concentration. His stream of water wasn't what it used to be. It took a clear head and determination just to empty his bladder. He gritted his teeth and pushed. One squirt, dribble. Another squirt, more dribble. To think, this used to be fun. What the hell ever happened to the mighty swordsman who could hose down a park bench from ten feet away? Falcon hadn't completely finished his business, but it was way too cold to keep your pecker hanging out all night. Especially when you were well compensated, right, Swyteck?

He buttoned up and prepared himself for the final leg of the journey. He was almost home. The bend in the river told him so. He loved living on the river. In fact, seventy-degree river water would feel mighty good on a night like tonight. A regular poor man's hot tub—except that Falcon wasn't poor. Ha! The rich are different. "Yeah, I'm good and different, all right," he said to no one.

His breath nearly steamed in the crisp night air. It just kept getting colder. How was that possible? This was Miami, not Rochester. Swyteck had offered to drive him to a shelter, but Falcon was going home. Yeah, it was an abandoned car, but it still had all the comforts. Had himself a TV, a stereo, a toaster. He was sure they would still work, too, if only he had electricity. He could even have laid claim to a dishwasher, had he been able to lift the damn thing. The stuff people threw out was just amazing. Most trash wasn't really trash at all, just things people got tired of having around the house. It wasn't broken, wasn't worn out, and sometimes it wasn't even dirty. Out with the old, in with the new. Lawn mowers, radios, blenders, the Bushman. Especially the Bushman. That's right, you heard me. You're trash, Bushman! YOU ARE NOTHING BUT STINKING, SMELLING TRASH!

"Who you calling trash, mon?"

Falcon turned around. He was still standing under the bridge. His friend the Bushman was lying on the ground and glaring up at him. That crazy Jamaican was sucking the thoughts out of Falcon's head again. Or maybe Falcon had been talking out loud without realizing it.

"Sorry," said Falcon. "Didn't mean nothing by it, buddy."

The Bushman grumbled as he pulled himself up to the seated position. A tattered old blanket was wrapped around his shoulders. He had the thickest, longest dreadlocks of anyone outside of the Australian Bush, which was the reason Falcon called him the Bushman. Normally, those dreadlocks would hang down loose, all dirty and gnarly, like the tufted fleece of a yak. Tonight, however, they were wrapped around his head like a turban, held in place by an old metal colander that made a pretty nice helmet. His jeans were filthy, as usual, but the sweatshirt looked to be clean and in good shape.

"New sweatshirt?" said Falcon.

"Folks from the shelter came by an hour or so ago. Passed out some goodies." He held up his hands to show off a pair of socks that he was wearing like gloves. "You missed out, mon."

"They take anybody back with them?"

"Nope. Not a one of us."

Just ahead, barely visible in the moonlight, a heap of cardboard started to stir. It was Uhm-Kate. Whenever anyone asked her name, the response was always, "Uhm, Kate." She looked twice her normal size. It was a trick Falcon had taught her: stuff your clothes with old newspapers on cold nights. There were other ways to keep off the chill, but they usually came in a bottle.

"Hey, Falcon's back," she said.

More moving cardboard. The underbelly of the old drawbridge was like one big homeless slumber party. There was the Bushman, Uhm-Kate, half a dozen more. Eager as he was to get home, Falcon thought he might just stay here tonight, until he saw Johnny the Thief. He didn't actually see him—just the glinting eyes in the darkness. It was the cough that revealed his identity. Johnny had one of those deep, lung-shredding coughs that hurt your ears just to hear it. He denied having AIDS, but everybody knew. When he first came to the street, he was Johnny the Pretty Boy. He wasn't so pretty anymore. Now he was Johnny the Thief, always stealing everybody's dope.

"Got any shit, Falcon?"

"Nothing for you, Johnny."

"Come on, man. You're a celebrity now. One of the beautiful people. Beautiful people always got the shit."

"I'm not a celebrity."

"Yes, you is," he said, and then he started coughing. "You was on TV. I saw you. I watched in the emergency room over at Jackson. I told everyone in the joint: Hey, that's my friend, Falcon!"

Falcon could no longer feel the cold air. Hot blood was coursing through his veins. "I'm not your friend, Johnny."

The Bushman rose and came to him. "Take it easy, mon. Don't pay Johnny no never mind."

"What you mean you ain't my friend?" said Johnny.

"I don't have any friends," said Falcon.

The Bushman seemed genuinely hurt. "Aw, now dat can't be true, mon."

"Bushman's right," said Johnny. "That's not true at all. I know it, you know it, everybody who was watching you on the TV knows it. You gots a friend, all right. You gots a *girl*friend."

"You shut your ugly face, Johnny."

"It's true. That's why you ended up in jail. You wanted to talk to your *girlfriend*."

"She's not—"

"Falcon gots a girlfriend, Falcon gots a—"

Before the taunting could even build up a rhythm, Falcon lunged straight at Johnny's throat and took him to the ground. Johnny landed on his back. Falcon was kneeling on his chest. He had both hands around Johnny's neck and was squeezing with blind fury.

"Stop!" the Bushman shouted.

Falcon kept squeezing. Johnny's face was turning blue. He clawed and scratched at his attacker, but Falcon did not let up. Johnny's eyes looked ready to pop from his head.

"Let him go!" shouted Bushman. But Falcon didn't need anyone telling him what to do. He knew what Johnny deserved. He knew how much suffering a human being could take. He gave one last squeeze, pushing it to the limit, then released.

Johnny rolled onto his side and gasped for air. Falcon watched him for a minute, saying nothing, displaying no emotion of any kind. Johnny kept coughing, trying to catch his breath. The Bushman started toward him slowly, concerned. "Johnny, you want some water?"

"No!" shouted Falcon. "He can't drink yet. If he drinks, he'll die. No water!"

The Bushman made a face, confused. "What are you talkin' about, mon?"

Falcon couldn't find a response. His thoughts were scattered, and he was too tired to chase them. He looked at the Bushman, then at Johnny. No one said anything, but Falcon no longer felt welcome.

"I'm going home." He stepped right over Johnny and continued on his way, following the footpath along the river.

Slowly, the rush of anger subsided, and he was beginning to feel the cold again. His thoughts turned toward home. He would definitely sleep in the trunk tonight. That was by far the best place on cold nights, offering complete shelter from the elements. Just thinking about it brought a warm feeling all the way down to his toes. Forget those losers and their scraps of cardboard under the bridge. Who needed their insults and aggravation?

He was just a few yards from home when he stopped in his tracks. A fire was burning beside his house. Not a big, raging, out-of-control fire. It was a little campfire. A stranger was seated on a plastic milk crate and warming his hands over the flames. No, not *his* hands. *Her* hands. Falcon's visitor was a woman. She spotted Falcon and rose slowly, but not to greet him. She just stared, and Falcon stared right back. In this neighborhood, her appearance was far more curious than his. Hers were not the clothes of a homeless woman. The overcoat fit her well, and it still had all the pretty brass buttons in place. There were no holes in her leather gloves, no fingers protruding. The shoes were new and polished. Her head was covered with a clean white scarf. It almost looked like a nappy. A well-dressed older woman with a diaper on her head.

Falcon took a half-step closer, then stopped.

"Who are you?"

She didn't answer.

"Who *are* you?"

Silence. Falcon tried another angle.

"What do you want?"

Still no answer. Instead, she simply started walking around the campfire, walking in circles, walking in silence. Falcon's hands started to shake. He clenched them into fists. He bit down hard on his lower lip, but a fireball was burning inside him, and there was no containing it. "Get away, get away from me, GET AWAY FROM ME, WOMAN!"

He shouted at her over and over again. He shouted at the top of his voice. He shouted until he couldn't shout anymore. He gasped for air, and it felt so cold going down that he thought it might sear his lungs. He wanted to run, but there was no escape.

Because he did indeed know who she was, this Mother of the Disappeared.

And he knew exactly what she wanted.

7.

It was after midnight, and Alicia was still standing outside Houston's Restaurant waiting for the valet attendant to bring her car around. That was one way to crack down on drunk drivers, make everyone wait till dawn at the valet stand. Next time she would be sure to drive her yellow Lotus or red Ferrari and get "preferred parking" right at curbside.

Her cell phone rang inside her purse, which, in turn, was inside a doggy bag. She planned to bring the whole thing into the lab in the morning to have them check for fingerprints, which could confirm that Falcon was the lipstick bandit. She let the phone ring to voice mail, but it started ringing again. Someone was psycho calling her. She wrapped her hand in a tissue, carefully removed the phone, and answered it. It was her father. He wanted to know where she was, and she told him.

"Sweetheart, your mother and I think you should come home tonight."

"I am going home."

"No, I mean here, with us."

She was twenty-seven years old, and her parents still thought of their house as her home. It was a price she gladly paid for being the only daughter of a Latin father. "*Papi*, it's late, and I have to work in the morning. I'll come by this weekend."

"We're just concerned for you, that's all."

There were times in her life when she could have sworn that her parents knew everything about her—including whom she was dating and whether he called her or nudged her in the morning. But could they possibly know that her purse had been stolen? "Why are you concerned?"

"You know why. That Falcon wacko is out on bail."

"That seems to be the top news for the night."

"This is serious, Alicia. The state attorney assured me that setting bail at ten thousand dollars was as good as throwing away the key on this guy. That obviously didn't turn out to be the case. He may be a drifter, but we have to be very careful with him."

She couldn't have agreed more, but she didn't want to worry her parents further by telling them about the stolen purse. "Look, I can't come over tonight. But I promise, first thing tomorrow I'll meet with the chief and the state attorney about tacking on a restraining order to the terms of release."

"All right. That's a good plan. But be careful going home tonight."

"I'm a cop, remember?"

"You're my daughter first. We love you, that's why we worry."

"Love you, too. I'll talk to you tomorrow."

The valet brought her car around as the call ended. The drive home took fifteen minutes, which she spent in total silence, no radio. The stolen purse had given her plenty to think about, enough to make her stop worrying if the call to Vince had been a mistake—for now, anyway. Phone calls to old lovers, particularly those made from a bar, usually didn't start replaying in your mind until about three a.m.

Alicia lived alone in a Coconut Grove townhouse. The Grove was part of the City of Miami, an area unto itself that was well south of downtown. Alicia was one of eight of "Miami's bravest" assigned to patrol it. Long before the developers took over, the Grove was known as a Bohemian, wooded enclave, a haven for tree lovers and flower children of the 1960s. Some of that charm had managed to survive the bulldozers and wrecking balls. The sidewalk cafés on Main Street were as popular as ever, and finding your way through the twisted, narrow residential streets beneath the green tropical canopy was a perennial right of passage in Miami. But to Alicia—to any cop—the Grove was essentially a world of extremes. It was a place where some of south Florida's most expensive real estate butted up against the ghetto, where the mayor's multimillion-dollar mansion was just a short walk from his daughter's "questionable" townhouse. The Grove could service just about anyone's bad habit, from gangs who smashed and grabbed, to doctors and lawyers who ventured out into the night in search of crystal meth, to the distinguished city councilman in need of a twenty-dollar blow job. But yes, it did have some of that old charm, whatever that meant, and Alicia couldn't imagine living anywhere else in Miami.

"I hate this place," she muttered. Searching for a parking space always made her feel that way. Naturally, some jerk had taken her assigned space outside her townhouse, so she was forced to cruise the lot for a visitor's spot. She found one next to the Dumpster, which of course meant that her car would be covered with raccoon tracks in the morning. She turned off the ignition, but her Honda continued to run. It sputtered twice, the chassis shook, and then it died. Never before had she owned a car that made such a production out of killing the engine. This one was such a drama queen, which was why she'd named it Elton.

She got out and closed the car door. An S-curved sidewalk led her through a maze of bottlebrush trees and hibiscus hedges. A rush of wind stirred the leaves overhead—another blast of Arctic air from one doozy of a cold front. She walked briskly, with arms folded to stay warm, then stopped. She thought she had heard footsteps behind her, but no one was in sight. Up ahead, the sidewalk stretched through a stand of larger ficus trees. The old, twisted roots had caused the cement sections to buckle and crack over the years. It was suddenly darker, as the lights along this final stretch of walkway were blocked by sprawling limbs and thick, waxy leaves.

Again, she heard footsteps. She walked faster, and

the clicking of heels behind her seemed to quicken, matching her own pace. She stepped off the sidewalk and continued through the grass. The sound of footsteps vanished, as if someone were tracing her silent path. She returned to the sidewalk at the top of the S-curve. Her heels clicked on concrete, and a few seconds later the clicking resumed behind her. She turned and said, "Who's there?"

She saw no one, and there was no response. In the darkness beneath the trees, however, she sensed someone's presence. *I wish I had my gun*, she thought. She never carried it when out drinking.

She turned toward her townhouse, and her heart leapt to her throat. A man was standing on her front step. She was a split second away from delivering a martial-arts kick, then stopped.

"It's me, Felipe," he said.

A wave of relief came over her, though she still felt like killing him. "Don't ever sneak up on me like that. What are you doing here?"

"What do you think?" he said.

Felipe was one of her father's bodyguards. He was about six-foot-six and built for the fireman's calendar, with handsome skin that was just a shade too dark to be called olive. His crew cut was nicely groomed, except for the crescent-moon bald spot on the crown of his head. The scar was exactly the size of the bottom of a beer bottle, and it smacked of a bar fight gone bad. His five-o'clock shadow was perpetual—at least in the sense that it was there without fail every time Alicia saw him. The first time they'd met was at a victory party the night her father was elected to his first term as mayor. Felipe was a hottie, she had to admit, and she figured that he must have been drunk and off duty when he introduced himself by saying that he'd like to guard her body. It soon became apparent that he was just another sober jerk, with one redeeming quality: He loved the mayor like his own father and, if he had to, would probably take a bullet for him. That kind of loyalty more than made up for the occasional and mostly harmless lousy come-on.

"Did my father send you?" she said.

"Of course. He just wanted to make sure you got into the townhouse safely."

"I know. But I think you can see that's not really necessary. I'm sorry you had to come all the way over here so late." She started up the stairs. He followed. She stopped at the front door and said, "You can go home now, Felipe."

He had a smug expression, as if he knew how much this was going to bug her. "Your dad specifically told me to go inside ahead of you and check things out. Make sure no one is hiding in the closet, that sort of thing."

"Oh, for Pete's sake. I'm a cop."

"Hey, I'm just doing as I'm told."

This was turning into a night that she'd sworn would never happen—the two of them standing at her front door as Felipe the Conqueror flashed the macho man's grin, the kind that came only with the right to enter. But it was too darn late to phone her father and argue about it. She unlocked the door and stepped aside. "Make it fast, please."

Felipe gave her an obnoxious little wink as he crossed the threshold and switched on the light. "Nice place," he said in a breezy tone, as if he were expecting her to turn on some music and offer him a drink.

Alicia's townhouse was cozy—a nice way of saying "small." The kitchen and living room were downstairs. There was no dining room per se, just a dining area that was really part of the living room, separated from the kitchen by a little pass-through opening over the sink. Alicia followed him to the sliding glass doors. He unlocked them and stepped outside to check the patio. It was late, she was tired, and she was losing her patience for this. Then something caught her eye. Her computer was in a little work area directly off the kitchen. She had DSL service, so her computer was always online, and she noticed several new e-mails in her in-box.

"All clear. Where's the bedroom?" Felipe asked as he came in from the patio.

"Upstairs." She wasn't about to go up there with him, and her expression had apparently conveyed as much.

"Be right back," he said.

Alicia's attention returned to her e-mails. There was the usual smattering of spam, but it was another message from an unknown sender that caught her eye. The subject line read, ABOUT YOUR PURSE. She opened it with a click of her mouse, and her heart skipped a beat. The sender was identified only by a jumble of numbers and characters, not a real name. She read the message once, then read it again. It was short, to the point, and downright creepy:

"I'm sorry. Please don't be frightened. Soon you will see, it is only out of love that I seek you."

Felipe was back. "Everything's fine upstairs. Are you—" He stopped himself in midsentence. "Are you okay?"

"I'm fine." She managed an awkward smile, trying to keep it cool as she showed him to the door and opened it.

"I'll let your dad know that everything checked out okay."

She was about to say good night, but he interrupted. "You sure you're okay?"

"Yes, I'm sure."

"You look like you seen a ghost."

"Nope. No ghosts here," she said. *None that I care to tell you about*, anyway. "Good night, Felipe."

"Good night."

She closed the door and locked it, her thoughts awhirl. This was no longer a drifter's one-time demand to speak to the mayor's daughter. The stolen lipstick, the e-mail—this was outright stalking.

Alicia checked the lock again, making double sure that the deadbolt was secure. Then she went upstairs to her closet—to get her gun.

8
.

The next morning, the Miami-Dade crime lab found a fingerprint on Alicia's compact that didn't belong to her. A scientific confirmation that Falcon had stolen her purse would have made things pretty simple. Nothing, however, was ever simple.

The print didn't match Falcon's.

"That's weird," she said. "If it's not mine and it's not Falcon's, then whose is it?"

"No one in any of our databases," was the answer she got.

She wanted to ask if they were sure, but she knew these guys were thorough. Fingerprint analysis wasn't just a matter of pushing a button and seeing what came up on the computer, the way it was portrayed on television. The Miami-Dade crime lab checked and double-checked. When they said "no match," there was no match.

Around ten o'clock, Alicia headed over to the tech geniuses in the audiovisual department. Her laptop was in the hands of Guy Schwartz, one very smart geek, who had done the trace on the "Sorry about your purse" e-mail.

"The message was sent from the Red Bird Copy Center," Schwartz said. "That's in the big shopping plaza on the corner of Red Road and Bird Road. Easy to find, but now comes the hard part."

"How do you mean?"

"The Red Bird Copy Center is the kind of place that rents computer time by the hour, like an Internet café without the lattes. People can come in off the street and send e-mails to whoever they want. I can't just look at your computer and determine the sender's identity. Your only hope is that the clerk at the copy center can tell you who rented the particular computer in question. Or maybe you can pull a fingerprint from the keyboard or mouse."

"I'm on it," she said.

Twenty minutes later, Alicia and Detective Alan Barber were in the Red Bird Copy Center. Alicia had "a personal stake in the case"—a rather lame way to say "the victim," but such was police lingo—so she had to beg for permission to accompany Detective Barber and his team of crime-scene investigators. The last thing the prosecutor needed was for Alicia to testify at trial as both the victim and the investigating officer. She was allowed on the scene strictly as an observer. Period. End of discussion. Alicia was okay with that.

Detective Barber had twenty years on the force, and he was probably about six months away from perfecting his Joe Friday monotone. Miami was rarely cold enough for a trench coat, so the chilly weather was like costume day for Barber. He was standing at the counter near the cash register, his hands buried deep in his coat pockets, his fleshy brow furrowed into the anatomical equivalent of the Spanish Steps. A glossy color photograph, Falcon's mug shot, lay flat atop the glass. Last night's desk attendant was leaning on one elbow, staring down at it, studying the image. It was Barber's standard interrogation tactic. Never ask the witness to describe someone out of the blue. Put the photo in front of him, let it jog his memory. "Ever seen this guy before?" said Barber.

The young man scratched at the tattooed dragon on the left side of his shaved head, just above the ear, directly below the scalp ring. "Nope."

It wasn't the response that Alicia or the detective had expected. "You sure?" said Barber.

"Dude, I think I'd remember this loser if I saw him."

Barber kept his composure. Alicia resisted the urge to jump in with her own line of questioning. Standing on the sidelines with a virtual gag on her mouth was proving much more difficult than anticipated.

The computer in question was in pod number three. The crime-scene investigators were proceeding in their usual methodical fashion, dusting for prints and searching for other physical evidence that might identify the person who had sent Alicia the e-mail.

"Do you remember who was using that computer last night?" asked Barber.

"What time?"

Barber fumbled for a copy of the e-mail. Alicia filled in the blank for him: "The e-mail was sent from your computer number three at ten twenty-two p.m."

Barber shot her a look, as if to say "No talking, that was our agreement."

"Ten twenty-two p.m.," he repeated.

"Don't remember exactly. But I think it was a woman."

"A woman?"

"Yeah. An older woman."

Barber shoved the photograph toward the clerk again. "You sure it wasn't this guy?"

"I don't think so."

Barber seemed annoyed. "Can you describe for me the last three customers you dealt with last night?"

"Sure. One was a woman, and—Uh. No, two were women, and the last one was a man. I think. I don't know. It was either a man or a woman."

"That certainly narrows it down," said Barber.

Alicia waited for him to follow up, but the detective was suddenly more concerned with the text message on his vibrating cell. Alicia asked the clerk, "Do your customers sign a log book or anything like that?"

"No, they just pay by the hour and go."

"The woman who rented pod number three, did she pay with a credit card? Anything to create a written record?"

"Uh-uh. We don't take credit cards for anything

under twenty dollars. I'm pretty sure I had only one credit card transaction all night."

Barber was still reading from his text message, so Alicia forged ahead. "Do you have a security camera on the premises? Could we get a look at her that way?"

"No. We respect our customers' privacy." Translation: How would *you* like it if someone watched you surf the porn sites?

Barber was suddenly drumming his fingers across the glass countertop. "Anything else you'd like to ask, officer?"

Alicia backed away. She wasn't trying to upstage him, but she could tell that his heart wasn't in her case. Barber was a top-notch homicide detective, with plenty of homicide cases that needed his full attention. He was assigned to a stalking case only because Alicia was the mayor's daughter. Alicia didn't like it any more than he did, but if he wasn't going to pursue the obvious questions, she would. Perhaps she'd pushed it a little too far. "You go right ahead, detective. Sorry."

Barber said, "Can you describe this older woman for us, kid? The one who rented pod number three?"

The clerk made a face, as if it hurt to search his memory for something that happened all of fourteen hours ago. "Not really. Hispanic, maybe. Kind of short. Just another customer, you know. We get lots of customers."

Barber asked a few more follow-up questions, none of any consequence. He ended by passing the clerk his card and asking him to call if anything came to mind.

"I hope I was helpful," said the clerk.

"You were, thank you," said Alicia.

Barber checked with the CSI team, which had about another hour of work on computer pod number three. They could handle it on their own. Barber gave the signal, and Alicia followed him outside to the sidewalk.

"You think the boy's covering for somebody?" she asked.

"No," said Barber. "I don't think he pays much attention to who comes and who goes from the place. It's just not important to him."

"You don't actually think it was an old woman who stole my purse and sent me that e-mail, do you?"

"Could have been a woman who sent you the message. I have no idea who stole your purse."

"Are you saying two people might be involved in this?"

"Look, Alicia. You ask a lot of questions, and that's a good thing in this business. But see, the trick is to ask people who might possibly know the answers. How the hell do I know if there's two people involved or not?"

He started walking toward his car. Alicia followed. She was thinking about what the clerk had told them. "It just doesn't add up. Someone steals my lipstick, and then a little old lady sends me an e-mail saying that it's only out of love that she seeks me?"

"The kid could have been confused."

"What if he's not? What if it was a woman who sent me the message?"

"Hey, stranger things have happened, honey."

She climbed into the passenger seat and closed the door. Barber started the car and backed out of the parking space. Alicia looked out the window toward the Red Bird Copy Center.

"Not to me," she said as they drove away. *Honey.*

9
·

Mayor Raul Mendoza didn't like what Jack Swyteck was telling him.

"This is my daughter we're talking about," the mayor said into the telephone.

"I'm definitely sympathetic to that," said Swyteck. "But I would see it no differently if we were talking about a member of my own family."

The mayor sank back into his big leather chair at his office in Miami City Hall. Felipe, his trusted assistant and bodyguard, was seated in the armchair on the opposite side of the old teak desk. All of the mayor's furniture was made of teak, a nautical decorating theme that, together with his corner-office view of the marina, only served to remind him that he never had time to sail anymore. He barely had time for anything that wasn't official business. Except when it came to his daughter.

Mendoza had always made time for Alicia, from her soccer games as a little girl—he never missed one—to her graduation from the police academy.

He loved his wife, and they were still together and happy after twenty-nine years. Even after he was married, however, the concept of dying for someone else seemed a bit unreal, more like a melodramatic metaphor for the depth of one's feelings than an actual commitment. That all changed with Alicia. When she was sick as an infant, he begged God to make him sick instead. When she cried, he couldn't bear to hear it. When some homeless pervert was stalking her—well, all bets were off. It didn't matter that the mayor was nearing the end of his term and facing an uphill battle for reelection. It didn't matter that the fund-raising had to be done long before voters went to the polls, or that he had places to go, hands to shake, checks to cash. He was trying hard to be diplomatic with Falcon's lawyer, but this was about his daughter's safety, and he had little patience for anyone who refused to open his eyes and see things as any father would see them.

The mayor said, "I know it's unorthodox for the victim's father to call the defense lawyer, but hear me out, please."

"It's happened in other cases," said Jack. "Worse cases."

"Then you understand how disappointed I must have been when the prosecutor called to tell me that you wouldn't agree to revise the terms of release."

"This is nothing personal," said Jack. "The law requires the prosecution to show some new facts to the judge, something that makes my client a greater flight risk or a greater danger to the community than originally thought."

"Your client continues to stalk my daughter. Isn't that enough?"

"If the prosecutor had evidence to support that claim, we'd be in court this afternoon."

Swyteck had hit the nail on the head. A defense lawyer had no way of knowing all the weaknesses in the state's case, particularly at this early juncture, but the prosecutor had laid them out in painstaking detail for the mayor. Without anyone noticing, a homeless bum had to get inside an upscale Coral Gables bar, take a woman's purse, and ditch it in the ladies' room. The desk clerk at the copy center said it was a woman, not a man, who rented the computer that was used to send Alicia the e-mail. Falcon's fingerprints were found nowhere, and the lone extraneous fingerprint on Alicia's compact didn't even match his.

"You're a very insightful attorney, Mr. Swyteck."

"In cases like this, it's really just a matter of doing my job."

"And I imagine there is much discretion in that job description."

"I suppose."

"Then why not agree to a restraining order that prevents your client from coming within five hundred yards of my daughter?"

There was silence. He could sense that Swyteck wanted to agree. Was it possible—a criminal defense lawyer with a conscience? No way. Any inroads into the lawyer's moral sensitivities were due entirely to the mayor's persuasive powers. *Damn, I'm good.*

"I'm sorry, I can't do it."

That took the air right out of the mayor's inflated ego. "Why not?"

"Because it's not in my client's interest."

"You want something in return? A little quid pro quo? Is that it?"

"Mr. Mayor, I'm really not at all comfortable having this conversation with you."

"Seriously. If there is something you want, tell me."

Again, he could sense that Swyteck was struggling. The lawyer said, "Please don't take this the wrong way. I can't even imagine what must go through a parent's mind when it comes to a child's safety, even after she's a grown adult. But we need to avoid these conversations. They will only feed the public perception that the case against my client is driven not by reasoned legal judgment but by raw emotion from the mayor's office."

The mayor gnawed his lower lip. It was a good thing Swyteck wasn't in the office with him. He might have clobbered him. "Thank you for that," said the mayor. "I should have expected nothing less from a money launderer."

"Excuse me?" said Jack.

"The ten-thousand-dollar bond your client posted. It's no secret that you smuggled the cash out of the Bahamas."

"I didn't smuggle anything," said Jack. "And the

reason there are no secrets surrounding the bond is precisely because I did everything aboveboard. My client has access to cash in the Bahamas. I set up a ten-thousand-dollar savings account in his name at his Bahamian bank. The money was sent by wire transfer, the necessary currency transaction reports were completed, and the feds were completely in the loop. End of story."

"No, it's not the end of the story. Thanks to you, this won't be over until that crazy son of a bitch comes after my daughter again. Then let's see if you're so smug." He hung up the phone without saying goodbye, doing nothing to mask his disgust in the presence of his bodyguard. He rose and walked to the window. Not even the sailboats and the flat, blue-green waters of the bay could soothe him.

Felipe said, "You want me to speak to this Swyteck?"

"Don't be an idiot," he said, still looking out the window.

"You want me to pay Falcon a little visit?"

The mayor turned to face him as he considered it, forcing a little smile. Felipe smiled back. Before long, the two men were grinning so broadly that the mayor could hardly contain his laughter. Felipe, too, was on the verge of laughter, though he clearly didn't know why. "What's so funny, boss?"

"It just amazes me, how stupid you can be."

Felipe's smile vanished. "What do you mean?"

The mayor's expression was deadly serious. "In the great American tradition of executive-office conversations that never happened, let me ask you two questions. One, isn't it obvious what needs to be done?

"Two, why on earth would you ask *the mayor* before doing it?"

10

Jack Swyteck liked to think of himself as a full-service attorney, but he did not make house calls. That was the rule, which, like most rules, was swallowed by its exceptions. He did visit clients who were in jail, who didn't have a car, or, apparently, who *lived* in a car.

"You sure about these directions?" said Theo.

Jack was leading the way down a footpath along the Miami River. A commuter train rambled along the track two hundred feet above them. A lazy tugboat churned downriver toward the bay, its wake breaking against a rusted, half-submerged barge. "Am I sure?" said Jack. "These directions rolled right off the lips of a clinically paranoid homeless stalker who threatened to throw himself off a bridge if the mayor's daughter didn't talk to him. Why would I question their accuracy?"

Theo considered it, then said, "Do you speak Globalish?"

"Do I speak what?"

"Globalish. It's the universal language of the homeless. Like Esperanto."

"What the hell is that?"

"You never heard of Esperanto? It was invented by some Polish dude, but it's more like Spanish or Italian. A second language for everyone. That's sort of what Globalish means. It's English, combined with global, meaning worldwide, though it can also mean 'great tits,' depending on the context. Globalish. It's probably what Falcon was speaking when he gave you the directions."

Jack wasn't sure how to respond. Theo had this uncanny ability to make no sense and make perfect sense at the same time.

They kept walking. Earlier that morning, an unexpected phone call from the state attorney had lasted only a few minutes. Jack knew almost immediately that the prosecutor was bluffing. If the state could prove that Falcon was continuing to harass the mayor's daughter, the prosecutor would have been in court faster than a bailiff could say "All rise." Jack would not agree to a restraining order. The personal call from the mayor had made it considerably more difficult to maintain that position, but it was his job to put emotions aside and to act in his client's interest. He still had a conscience, however. If his client was determined to continue breaking the law—if Falcon refused to give up his pursuit of Alicia Mendoza—then it was time for him to get a new lawyer. Jack had defended plenty of clients who had committed horrible crimes. Anyone who had a problem with that had no business being a criminal defense lawyer. It was something altogether different, however, to provide legal protection for someone who was steadily working his way up to the big kill.

And *that* was his problem with Falcon.

"We there yet?" said Theo.

Jack ignored him. The Miami River stretched five and a half miles in a southeasterly direction, from the airport to downtown Miami, where it emptied into Biscayne Bay. Over the centuries, everything from raw sugar to raw sewage had floated down its tea-colored waters. At any time of day, you might find a ninety-foot yacht bound for the West Indies sharing the right of way with a rusted old container ship weighted down with cocaine. It was truly a working river, handling over four billion dollars a year in legal cargo, and a walk along its banks was like a slide show of Florida history. There were two-thousand-year-old relics from the Tequesta Indians, warehouses and dockyards built by the Florida East Coast Railroad, an old fort from the Civil War, marinas, public parks, historic homes, mangroves, run-down apartment buildings, and even some pretty good restaurants.

Theo grumbled to get Jack's attention. "Hey, Swyteck. I said, ain't we *there* yet?"

"Almost." The Big Fish restaurant was one of the landmarks Falcon had mentioned, so Jack knew they were getting close. Right on the river, it was actually one of Jack's favorite lunch spots. It was nothing fancy, just a relaxing place to eat fresh dolphin, tuna, or shrimp ceviche while soaking up a historic stretch of river, a piece of old Miami where mariners from houseboats at the west end of the river sidled up alongside bankers and lawyers from the office towers to the east. Jack led Theo around the restaurant, past the trash bins and a nearby marina, where the combined odor of diesel fumes and discarded fish guts nearly gagged him. He imagined that Falcon had scored many a meal right here, rooting through the Dumpsters for leftover french fries or hush puppies.

They passed beneath a bridge, and when they emerged on the other side, the river started its jog to the northwest. A brisk wind was blowing straight into their faces. Though the sun was shining, south Florida remained in the grip of an abnormal and persistent cold front. Every fifteen steps, Jack heard Theo huffing in an unsuccessful attempt to see his breath steam. Cold was a relative concept in Miami.

"That must be it," said Jack, pointing. There was an abandoned car about twenty feet off the riverbank, near an old warehouse—just as Falcon had described it.

Instinctively, they slowed as they closed the last twenty yards, caution in their steps. The car was little more than a burned-out metal shell. All of the windows were gone, including the windshield. The steering wheel and front seat were missing as well. The backseat was still in place, but it had been slashed many times over, and the stuffing was coming out.

There was no sign of Falcon.

"Reminds me of the last time we saw your Mustang," said Theo.

He was talking about Jack's pride and joy, a vintage 1966 Mustang convertible with rally pack gauges, wood steering wheel, and pony interior. His first major purchase out of law school, it was nothing short of a work of art until some angry drug dealers put a match to it.

"That was harsh, Theo."

"Sorry, dude."

They stepped closer. Theo walked all the way around the vehicle and stopped directly in front of it, facing the grillwork. "All Mustang jokes aside, it actually is a Ford."

"You think?"

"Definitely. Late seventies, I'd say. Ford Falcon."

"A Falcon?" said Jack.

"Yeah. Funny, huh?"

"I figured he called himself Falcon because he was ready to fly off a bridge. Turns out, it's just an extension of where he lives." Jack took a slow walk around the car, inspecting it. Rat droppings were scattered across the sun-baked hood. Cockroaches hid in the darkness of the wheel wells. Scattered about the interior were some dirty Tupperware bowls, empty coffee cans, an old raincoat, and a tattered sheet of plastic. "Imagine living here," said Jack.

"Beats the hell out of death row," said Theo.

As usual, Jack couldn't argue with the big guy's perspective.

Theo said, "So what do we do now? Sit around and wait?"

"It's not as if I can call my client on his cell phone and set up a meeting."

"You want to leave a note and a quarter, tell him to call you?"

Jack thought about it. "Let's give it a few minutes. He said if I ever needed to find him, afternoons were the second best time to catch him at home."

"When's the best time?"

"After midnight, but I'm not about to come out here then. Not even with you watching my back."

Theo scratched his head as he searched for someplace to sit. He went to the rear of the car and hopped up on the trunk lid. It made a funny noise as he landed, as if the lid and latch no longer fit just right. Just then, Jack noticed some brown droplets on the bumper. He squatted down for a closer look.

"What'd I do now?" said Theo.

Jack wasn't sure what it was, but he had a pretty good idea. "Theo, don't touch anything. Just climb down slowly."

The tone of Jack's voice made it clear that he wasn't kidding around. Theo slid down until his feet touched the ground. As his body weight lifted from the trunk, the old spring hinges creaked, and the lid opened on its own power.

Then they saw the body—or what was left of it. It was a mangled heap at the bottom of the trunk. A rat the size of a small dog scurried away from its lunch, giving them both a start.

"Holy shit," said Theo.

Blood, everywhere, so much blood. "My thought exactly," Jack said quietly.

11

Jack watched from behind yellow police tape as the crime scene investigators tended to the body in the trunk. It was like watching a well-oiled machine—swabs taken, photographs snapped, evidence gathered. He probably would have stayed even if Detective Barber hadn't asked him to stick around, but it was near sunset, and Theo was clearly ready to leave.

"Don't you got any actual living clients you should be back in the office overchargin'?" said Theo.

"Oh, be quiet," said Jack. "Have you no respect for the dead?"

"That's odd."

"What's odd?"

"Beginning a sentence with the word 'have.' It's like starting with 'to whom,' which, studies have shown, can't possibly happen—no way, no how—without a stick up your ass."

That was Theo, on a perpetual mission to save the world from itself.

Jack signaled to the detective. He was standing

across the yard, near the abandoned vehicle, and talking with one of the investigators. In due time, he finished the conversation and walked over to the police barricade at the outer edge of the crime scene.

"Sorry to keep you waiting," said Barber.

"Sorry?" said Theo, his hands buried in his pants pockets. "We been standin' around for over an hour, pal. It's cold as hell out here."

Jack wondered about the origin of that expression—"cold as hell"—but that was a debate better had over beers. "Theo, why don't you see if you can steal us some hot coffees from that restaurant we passed on the way over here?"

"Like that's gonna help." Theo did another one of his little huffs, trying to make his breath steam. This time, it worked—barely—which set Theo off like a boy in his first snowfall. "Did you see that? We're in Miami, it technically ain't even winter yet, and my breath steamed!"

Jack was tempted to say something about the expulsion of hot air, but he let it go. "Theo, how about that coffee?"

He finally took the hint. When his friend was out of earshot, Jack said, "Look, detective, I'm willing to help you out here. But why don't you just call me later on tonight, unless there's something you really need to ask me right now."

Detective Barber glanced toward the abandoned car. The examiners were getting ready to lift the body onto a gurney. "Just one thing I'd like to know," he said, his gaze turning back toward Jack. "Where's your client?"

It sounded like a stupid question, but the detective's expression said otherwise. Jack said, "Are you telling me that's not Falcon in the trunk of that car?"

Detective Barber shook his head.

Jack said, "I didn't want to touch anything, so we didn't move the body. He was all wrapped up in blankets from the cold. I guess we didn't get that good a look. I just assumed—"

"Don't beat yourself up," said the detective. "With the victim's face bashed in that bad, about all you could do was assume. At least until we got here."

"You're sure it's not him?"

"Not unless he had a sex change in the last couple days."

Jack felt a rush of panic. "It's not—"

"Alicia Mendoza? No, no. If that were the mayor's daughter, we'd have every media van in the tri-county area upon us by now. This is a much older woman, fiftysomething, maybe sixties. I suspect she's another one of Miami's homeless. Falcon probably found her all snug and warm in his favorite spot, freaked out, and let her have it."

"You have a murder weapon?"

"We suspect it was the lead pipe found next to the car. Traces of blood and human hair on it. It would take something substantial like that to account for the blunt trauma. Your boy literally bashed her face in."

"He's not my boy," said Jack.

"No, that's true," Barber said, smiling. Then he chuckled. "He's just your client."

"What's so funny?" said Jack.

"No offense, counselor. But something deep inside my jaded cop existence takes perverse pleasure in the fact that a criminal defense lawyer called the cops to report a murder committed by his own client." He was chuckling again. "Sorry. I just can't help myself."

Jack could already hear the Swyteck jokes coursing through the hallways of the Miami-Dade Criminal Justice Building. In these situations, there was only one comeback. "How do you know my client did it?"

The detective's smile faded. "I think we can safely assume—"

Jack held up his hand, stopping him. "One erroneous assumption per crime scene, please."

"Oh, come off it, Swyteck. In another two hours, we'll have enough physical evidence against your client to fill an entire crime lab."

"But you still may not have my client."

"We'll find him."

Jack leaned closer, as if to make it clear that he wasn't kidding around on this point. "When you do, be sure you remind him to call me."

Suddenly, someone near the river was shouting at the top of his voice. Both Jack and the detective turned to check out the commotion. It was a combination of words and wailing, loud but utterly incomprehensible. The detective said, "Looks like we got a friend of the victim. Excuse me, Swyteck."

Jack stayed put as the detective headed toward the river. He watched only long enough to make sure that the screamer wasn't his client. It wasn't. Jack turned away from the police tape and started back toward the footpath in search of Theo.

"Hey, mon. You Falcon's lawyer?"

Jack turned at the sound of the Jamaican's voice. He was dressed in blue jeans and an old hunting jacket, with thick smears of black grease amid the blotches of camouflage. The boots were in even worse condition, and they were both for the left foot. His tangled dreadlocks were tucked up into a bulging knit cap atop his head. It probably wouldn't have looked quite so strange if he hadn't wrapped it in aluminum foil.

"Who are you?"

"They call me the Bushman."

"Do you know Falcon?"

The man's eyes darted back and forth. He gestured frantically with both hands, telling Jack without words to keep his voice down. Whoever this guy was, he appeared to be even more paranoid than Falcon. "Falcon and me is friends," he said, then stopped himself. He seemed eager to tell Jack more, but it was equally clear that he wanted to get away from the crowd. He jerked his head, a movement so quick that it bordered on spastic, but he was merely signaling Jack to follow him back toward the bridge. They walked until the Jamaican seemed comfortable with their distance from the crime scene.

"Do you know where Falcon is?" said Jack.

"He's running."

"Running from what?"

The Jamaican glanced back toward the cops, but he said nothing.

"Did Falcon kill that woman?" asked Jack.

The Bushman grimaced and stomped his foot, as if he'd just bitten into a sourball the size of a melon. "Shhhhhhhh," he said, putting his finger to his lips.

Jack lowered his voice to a raspy whisper. "I'm his lawyer. You can tell me why he's running."

"He runs cuz he scared, mon."

"Scared of the police?"

The Bushman scoffed so bitterly that he made a spitting sound. "He's not scared of no police. He's scared of her."

"Who is she?"

He didn't respond. Jack sensed that he knew the answer, but he just wasn't ready to share it. Then Jack noticed the necklace around the Jamaican's neck. It was identical to the one Falcon had worn—the one with the key to the safe deposit box on it. "Hey, that's an interesting necklace you're wearing. Where'd you get it?"

"Falcon gave it to me."

"He gave it or—" Jack checked his words, not wanting to shut down the conversation by coming across as too accusatory. "Or did you borrow it?"

"I don't borrow nothin', mon. He gave it to me. For protection."

"Protection from what?"

The Jamaican's gaze drifted back toward the crime scene. "Dat's what I'm trying to tell you. Falcon says we all need protection. From *her*, mon."

"The dead woman? Who is she?"

The Bushman leaned closer, cupping his hand to his mouth as he whispered, "She the Mother."

"Mother? You mean like a *bad motha'*?"

"No. She's *their* mother."

"Whose mother?"

His voice became so soft that Jack could barely hear him. "Of the Disappeared, mon."

"She's the mother of the disappeared?" said Jack, confused.

A look of horror came over the Jamaican's face, as if he could scarcely believe that Jack had uttered the words aloud. Jack said, "What does that mean— she's the mother of the disappeared?"

The Jamaican stepped away in obvious fright, balling his necklace tightly into his fist and clutching it against his chest. "No, you can't have it! Get your own protection! Dis one is mine!"

Jack searched for something to say, something to calm him, but the words didn't come fast enough. The Jamaican turned and sprinted toward the bridge, one arm pumping, the other held close to his body. He kept on running until he vanished somewhere in the twilight beyond the marina.

He was a troubled man, the conversation had been very odd, and Jack stood there in the waning moments of daylight as he pondered what seemed to be the strangest but most certain thing of all.

The Jamaican surely would have killed him before giving up his gift from Falcon, his protection—that necklace of metal beads.

12

Around nine p.m., Alicia met Detective Barber at the Joseph H. Davis Center for Forensic Pathology, a three-building complex on the perimeter of the University of Miami Medical Center campus and Jackson Memorial Hospital. The nearby cancer center, eye institute, and spinal project were top-notch, but when it came to medical science, Miami's living had nothing on its dead. The Davis Center was a first-rate, modern facility, with some of the best forensic specialists in the world.

The body in Falcon's car had put the City of Miami police on high alert. A down-on-his-luck homeless guy with his eye on the mayor's daughter was one thing. A vicious killer was quite another. Investigators were covering every angle, so it seemed wise for Alicia to take a look at the victim before an autopsy made her unrecognizable. Fingerprint analysis having turned up nothing, the woman's identity was still unknown. The face was battered beyond recognition, but perhaps Alicia would recognize something else about her. If there was some connection between the victim and Alicia, police wanted to know about it from the get-go.

An assistant medical examiner escorted Alicia and Detective Barber to examination room three. Barber was a familiar face around the Davis Center; he had worked homicides for several years. Alicia, however, was a newcomer. "Have you seen an autopsy before?" the assistant ME asked her.

"Once," said Alicia, "during training."

"Good. But if you feel light-headed, just let me know."

The pneumatic doors opened, and they were immediately slammed with the indoor equivalent of an Arctic blast from the air vents in the ceiling. Alicia felt as though she'd just discovered the epicenter of Miami's latest cold front. Bright lights glistened off the white sterile walls and buff tile floors. The unclothed, ashen cadaver lay face-up on the stainless-steel table in the center of the room.

The examiner knew the detective, and he introduced himself to Alicia as Dr. Petrak. Then he said something in such a heavy Eastern European accent that Alicia couldn't understand him.

Detective Barber translated. "He says we're just in time."

From the looks of things, Alicia would have guessed they were too late. The autopsy was well under way. Two deep incisions ran laterally from shoulder to shoulder, across the breasts at a downward angle meeting at the sternum. A long, deeper cut ran from the breastbone to the groin, forming the stem in the coroner's classic "Y" incision. The liver, spleen, kidneys, and intestines were laid out neatly beside a slab of ribs on the large dissection table. The cadaver was literally a shell of a human being, and just the sight of it was making her a little queasy. Or was it the sweet, sterile odor that was getting to her?

"Are you okay?" asked Dr. Petrak.

"I'm fine," said Alicia.

The doctor was examining the victim's battered right cheekbone, working beneath an intense white spotlight. His powers of concentration were such that his bushy gray eyebrows had pinched together and formed one continuous caterpillar that stretched across his brow. He laid his tweezers aside and snapped a digital photograph.

Alicia's gaze drifted across the lifeless body. Lifeless—that was a very fitting word. Whoever she was, she had been without a life for a long time. The fingernails were jagged, several of them bitten back to the quick. The toes were deformed, presumably from shoes that didn't fit. The calluses on her knees were thick and discolored. They told of a woman who'd spent day after day on Miami's sidewalks, looking up to passing strangers, begging for spare change. They might never ascertain her true identity. Alicia felt sorry for her, then she felt embarrassed for herself. It seemed that people always felt compassion after it was too late to help.

"Interesting," said Dr. Petrak. "Verrrry interesting."

Alicia was suddenly reminded of an old episode

of *Laugh-In* that she'd seen on cable. Dr. Petrak sounded like that comedian with the cigarette and wire-frame glasses who used to dress up like a German soldier from the Second World War. *Vaht vahs his name?*

"What's very interesting?" said Detective Barber.

Arte Johnson. That was the guy. Alicia wasn't trying to check out, but little mental journeys helped take her mind off the odor and bring the blood back to her head.

The doctor said, "Officer Mendoza, what do you think when you see a woman with an Adam's apple?"

Alicia suddenly felt as though she'd been caught daydreaming in ninth-grade science. "A woman with an Adam's apple?"

She had stated her question as if it were an answer. It worked.

"*Exactly*," said Dr. Petrak. "It can't be, right?"

"Unless she used to be a man," said Detective Barber.

Dr. Petrak looked up, his expression deadpan. "Don't get crazy on me, okay, detective?" He refocused on his work and carefully opened the victim's mouth with a long, probing instrument. "What this bump tells us is that there is something lodged in her throat."

Alicia took a half-step closer. Dr. Petrak was right: This *was* getting interesting.

"Of course, the X-ray didn't hurt my diagnosis much, either." The doctor shined a laser of light deep into the victim's gaping mouth. The front teeth were missing, though it was difficult to tell if that was a result of the beating or of simple neglect over the years. The shattered molars, though, were clearly the work of the same lead pipe that had demolished her cheekbone. Dr. Petrak probed with his forceps, his hand as steady as a heart surgeon's. The bulge in her throat was due mostly to the missing molars, but Dr. Petrak seemed to be searching for something else. Finally, with a turn of the wrist, he had it. He carefully removed the object and placed it on the dissection tray.

"What is it?" Alicia asked.

He held the tray before them for a closer look. "What does it look like?" he asked.

Alicia studied it for a moment. "A metal bead," she said. "Like those add-a-bead necklaces that preppy girls used to wear."

"Except that this one is lead, not gold," said Dr. Petrak. "I found six others just like it inside the victim's stomach."

"You mean she swallowed them?" said Detective Barber.

"Apparently so," said the doctor.

"Why would she do that?" said Alicia.

"You can answer that as well as I," said the doctor. "Think in very simple terms. To do this work, you must constantly remind yourself not to skip over the obvious. So, she swallowed them because . . ."

Alicia wished otherwise, but she had no idea where the doctor was headed.

"Think in the most basic sense," he said. "Why do we do anything in life?"

"Because we want to?" she said.

"Very good," said Dr. Petrak. "Or?"

Alicia considered the possibilities. "Because someone forces us?"

"Excellent," said the doctor.

"But why would anyone force her to swallow metal beads?" said Alicia.

"Ah," said Dr. Petrak as he switched off the spotlight. "That's where my job ends. And yours begins."

13

Falcon was on the run. Or, perhaps, "in flight" was a better way to put it.

One foot in front of the other. That was his mantra. Had to keep moving. The night air was cold, but he didn't feel it. In fact, he was sweating heavily beneath his layers of clothing. He was wearing everything he owned—two T-shirts, a sweatshirt, a windbreaker, and his winter coat. The layers did more than fight the cold. He was a veritable walking suitcase, packed up and moving on to a more hospitable corner of the uncivilized world. He knew he would never see his car again. Going back to the river was not an option. Standing still was a luxury that he could ill afford. He had to keep moving farther and farther away, until his legs gave out and he could travel no more. What was that saying—just because you're paranoid, doesn't mean they're not out to get you? Maybe it was time to leave Miami. Maybe even the country. But how?

The money. His Bahamian safe deposit box held

more than enough to take him anywhere he wanted to go. True, he had vowed never to touch it. Many times over the past several months, he had even tried to give it to the rightful owner. The fact that Swyteck had been able to withdraw ten thousand dollars for his bail, however, told Falcon that his offer had been rejected and that the money was still sitting there. Unless Swyteck stole it. He wouldn't do that, would he? Ha! Who could resist that temptation? There was absolutely no risk of ever being caught.

Where's my money, Swyteck?

What money?

The cash in the safe deposit box.

There was no cash in that box.

I had two hundred grand in there!

Yeah, right. Tell it to the police, pal.

"Damn you, Swyteck! You stole my money!"

Falcon was cutting through a parking lot behind an all-night restaurant, and he noticed a woman headed toward her car. The expression on her face told him that his little tirade directed toward his lawyer had indeed been audible. The woman quickly found her keys—probably some pepper spray, too—and jumped inside her car.

Gotta get off the streets, he told himself. *Go someplace they can't find me.*

The alley led him behind another restaurant, past a noisy tavern. The Dumpster looked like a good place to relieve his bulging bladder, but someone had beat him to it minutes earlier.

"Son of a bitch," he said, stepping out of it.

He continued down the dark alley, though he was

suddenly thinking about *her* again. He didn't dare say her name, not even to himself. Even with all his extra clothing, he felt naked without his necklace of metal beads. He was without any protection whatever. Part of him realized that he didn't need it; she was gone. The other part—the loudest part, the part that was speaking to him now—told him that she would never leave, that he could never have enough protection.

The alley grew darker with each additional step. On either side were the unadorned backs of buildings—a bar, a drugstore, a Laundromat. A half-block ahead, the lights from Eighth Street were a glowing dot in the darkness, like an oncoming locomotive. The walls were cinder blocks painted beige and white. Every door and window was covered with black security bars. If he narrowed his eyes, Falcon could almost see one set of hands after another gripping those iron bars, hands without faces—nameless faces that were linked inextricably to the secret prison cells of his past. Those were memories that he battled every day. But with the barred doors and windows all around him, his mind carried him back to a place where demons roamed, a time so long ago. A quarter-century was an eternity; a quarter-century was yesterday. It all depended on how closely he was being followed by the Mother of the Disappeared.

"Prisoner number three-zero-nine," the guard said in Spanish.

The prisoners did not move. There were nearly

seventy-five of them, men and women, crowded into a room that could have comfortably accommodated no more than two dozen. Whether asleep or awake, most of them sat on the floor with their heads down and their knees drawn in toward their chests. Others lay on one side, curled into a fetal ball, trying to deal with various pains that made it impossible to rise even to a seated position. Many were from the nearby university—students, teachers, or staff in their twenties or thirties. The oldest was a union leader in his sixties. The most recognizable was a journalist from a major newspaper. A few were teenagers who had gone missing from local high schools. Some had been imprisoned for months; others, just days. None had bathed since their detention began. No prison garb was issued. They wore whatever they'd happened to have been wearing when they were plucked from their home or place of work and hauled off to prison. For many, a short-sleeve shirt or cotton blouse was not nearly warm enough for an unheated cell. The inmates were not told the exact location of the prison. They had no visitation rights; no phone calls or correspondence with loved ones; no television, radio, or contact of any kind with the outside world. They ate stale bread or a disgusting gruel that smelled like rotten cabbage. Some days, they ate nothing at all. Complaints, however, were never uttered. No talking of any kind was allowed—not to guards, not to other prisoners, not to oneself, not to anyone, ever. Violators were punished severely.

"Prisoner number three-zero-nine," the guard

repeated, his voice taking on an edge. He was a bulky man, broad-shouldered but bulging around the middle, like a heavyweight boxer who had gone soft. The thick, black hair on the back of his neck and forearms had earned him the nickname El Oso—the bear. It was not a term of endearment. Nicknames among the guards were a necessity. No one went by his real name.

A middle-aged man rose slowly and started toward the door. He took short, reluctant steps, walking on the balls of his feet, as if unable to place any weight on his arches or heels. He stopped at the bars, never looking the guard in the eye. "She is not feeling well," he said softly.

The guard grabbed him by the hair, jerked him forward, and slammed his head against the bars. "Are you prisoner three-oh-nine?"

The man grimaced. A rivulet of fresh blood trickled down his forehead. "No."

"Did anyone give you permission to speak?"

"No."

"Then sit down!" El Oso said as he shoved him to the floor. His angry gaze swept the cell, then settled on a woman huddled in the corner. "Three-zero-nine. Here. *Now!*"

No one moved. Then, just as El Oso was on the verge of another outburst, the woman stirred. The cell had no lighting on the inside, only the fluorescent fixture on the guard's side of the bars. Even in the dim glow, he could see the outline of her body. She came toward him, submissive, obedient. His eyes narrowed, and an evil smile creased his lips.

"Three-zero-nine?" he said.

"Yes," she replied.

El Oso could barely contain his excitement. He didn't normally get the pretty faces. It made him hard just to think about it.

He'd done plenty of women before, but never one who was pregnant.

"*Bienvenidos, chica. Bienvenidos a la Cacha—la casa de la bruja.*"

Welcome, young woman. Welcome to La Cacha—the witch's house.

"Hey, cat-food monster. Move it."

Falcon turned to see a busboy standing in the open doorway to the back of a restaurant. His stinging glare stirred Falcon from his memories, but he was still not completely focused. He was barely aware of the fact that he had urinated all over his own left foot.

"I said beat it!" the busboy shouted as he hurled an onion at him.

It hit Falcon in the chest and fell to the ground. Falcon picked it up, inspected it. It was rotten on one side, but he took a bite out of the good side, signaled a silent thank-you to the busboy, and shoved the rest of it in his pocket. He didn't bother zipping up his pants before continuing down the alley. He counted off twenty steps, then turned to see if he was still being watched. The busboy was gone.

Falcon caught sight of the old metal fire escape. It was black and rusty, and the base of the retractable staircase was fastened to the wall with a heavy metal bracket. The wall was made of cinder blocks. Falcon counted off the blocks until he found the third one from the bottom, and the tenth from the corner. He leaned closer and shoved it to test his recollection. The block moved. He shimmied the loose block from the wall and dropped it to the pavement. The two oval-shaped openings inside the block were stuffed with plastic bags. Falcon removed the bags, opened them, and smiled. It was all there—the money he had put away for a rainy day.

And he had the distinct feeling that the clouds were about to burst.

He stuffed the cash into his pockets and started making plans. New clothes, a hot shower, and maybe even some hair dye were in order. A pistol or two with plenty of ammo wouldn't hurt, either. You could get just about any firepower you needed on the streets of Miami, and no one knew them better than Falcon.

Then, it would be time to deal with Jack Swyteck.

That thief.

14

Jack and Theo caught a Miami Heat game downtown at the American Airlines Arena, the Triple A, as it was known. If ever a corporate sponsorship had gone sour, the Triple A was it. Imagine an airline spending millions of dollars to attach its name to a state-of-the-art, bay-front basketball arena, only to have everyone in town give the credit to a motor club.

"Feel like getting something to eat?" asked Theo.

Jack kept walking through the Purple Zone of the crowded garage, trying to remember where he'd parked his car. "You had three hot dogs, fries, nachos, a pretzel, and the better half of an ice cream bar from the kid sitting next to you. How can you be hungry?"

Theo shrugged. "That was an hour ago."

They found his car in the Orange Zone, and as a compromise, hit a fast-food drive-thru on the way back to Jack's house. After much pestering, Jack had finally agreed to meet Katrina's "hot" girlfriend on

South Beach. Jack was still wearing his courtroom attire, so a quick stop for a change of clothes was essential. The ride to Key Biscayne took only twenty minutes, though it seemed much longer. Jack lost the coin toss for control over his satellite radio. Theo stuck him with a station for which he had absolutely no use, the unending string of rhyming expletives punctuated by the sound of Theo smacking on a candy bar for dessert.

"We need to talk about your fat intake," said Jack.

"It's a diet chocolate bar."

"Says who?"

"Says so right here on the label. Forty-five percent less fat."

"Less fat than *what*? A humpback whale?"

Jack was suddenly praying for car trouble—*anything* seemed better than a night of Theo and his girlfriend simulating sex on the dance floor while Jack and the mystery woman shouted themselves hoarse just trying to make small talk over the music. Jack wasn't much of a clubber, and he hated setups, especially the late-night variety. Midnight, however, was the South Beach equivalent of happy hour on the mainland.

"Don't even think about it," said Theo as they pulled into Jack's driveway.

Jack shifted into PARK and killed the engine. "Think about what?"

"Bailing on me."

Jack shot him an incredulous look. The guy was a mind-reader. "Don't worry. I'm going. And I'm sure I'll thank you. Someday. In your dreams."

They went inside the house. Jack took a quick shower and put on a change of clothes—black, of course. Theo ordered a movie and a middleweight boxing match on pay-per-view, then nearly blew a gasket as he tried in vain to figure out the picture-in-picture function on Jack's TV set. By eleven-thirty, they were out the door and ready to go.

"So what's her friend's name?" said Jack as he locked up.

"Sabrina."

Jack halted. "We're going out with Sabrina and Katrina?"

"Yeah. Cool, huh?"

"It sounds ridiculous."

"Okay, her name's not Sabrina."

"Good." Jack started toward the car again. "Then what is it?"

"Is a name really that important?"

"I have to call her something."

"All right. Her name is Cindy."

Jack hated to trash the past, but his response was almost a reflex. "You're fixing me up with a woman who has the same name as my ex-wife?"

"To be honest, they share more than just a name."

"Don't tell me they look alike, too."

Theo paused, then said, "Even more than that."

"Act alike?"

A big, exaggerated shrug rolled through Theo's entire body, as if to say "Sorry, dude."

"Theo, why in the hell would you—"

Theo lost it. "Gotcha," he said, snorting.

Jack could breathe again. "Not funny."

"No. But it do put things in perspective, don't it, bro'?"

Jack glared over the car roof, then opened the door and got behind the wheel. Theo was still chuckling as he slid into the passenger seat. Jack turned the key in the ignition and said, "So does this mean Katrina's friend is really named Sa—" He stopped cold.

"Don't move," came the voice from behind the headrest. "You neither, black boy."

Jack felt a ring of cold metal pressing behind his left ear. Theo did a quick check over his shoulder. "Eyes front, hands on the dashboard. Or this lawyer's brains are all over the windshield."

Jack summoned a calm voice and said, "Do as he says, Theo."

Reluctantly, Theo obliged, his gaze locking onto the glove box. Jack stole a quick glance in the rearview mirror. There was barely enough external light shining through the tinted windows for Jack to make out the gun and the hand that was holding it. The backseat and gunman, however, were in total darkness. Jack and Theo had been too caught up in the joke about his date to notice that the dome light hadn't blinked on when the car door opened. The dashboard lights were off, too, leaving it too dark to have noticed anyone hiding on the floor. *He must have tinkered with the settings.*

"Everybody just take it nice and easy."

Jack recognized the voice. "Falcon, you don't want to be doing this."

"Shut up!"

The engine continued to idle. For what seemed

like an eternity, it was the only sound in the vehicle. Finally, Theo said, "Ironic, ain't it?"

"Quiet!" said Falcon.

Theo didn't have to explain. Jack knew exactly what his friend was thinking. The way this was going down, it was very much like Theo's very first car ride with Katrina.

Falcon said, "Now, nice and slow motion like. Put the car in gear."

"This is not smart at all," said Jack. "The cops are looking for you."

"No, not for me. For a homeless guy, the old me."

"I'm sure you clean up nice. But they're all over town. They'll find you."

"Those idiots don't have a clue. All they care about is guarding the mayor's daughter. I could have walked over here naked, saved the cab fare."

Jack debated whether to say more, or at least how to say it. "Did you kill that woman?"

Falcon didn't answer.

"Who was she, Falcon?"

"Nobody. All of them were nobody."

"All of who?"

He groaned, as if Jack were grabbing his various strands of thought and tying them into painful, knotted memories. "Stop asking so many questions, damn it."

"Listen to me. It doesn't matter what you did. I'm your lawyer. I can help you, but not if you add kidnapping and carjacking to your troubles."

"Shut up and drive."

"Just put the gun down."

He shoved the weapon even harder against Jack's skull. "No more talking!"

"All right," said Jack. "Where are we going?"

The question hung in the darkness. With the utmost discretion, Jack caught a glimpse of Falcon's face in the rearview mirror. His lips were moving, but the words wouldn't come. Or was he talking things over with himself?

Falcon said, "You and your buddy are going to show me where you put all my money."

"What money?"

"Don't pull that shit on me again, Swyteck. The money in the safe deposit box!"

"All I took was ten thousand dollars to post your bail. Not a penny more."

"You took all of it, I know you did!"

"Dude, we didn't take your money," said Theo.

"You gotta have it! The bank's crawling with cops, I know it is. They're just waiting for me to come get my money, see? If it's there, I can't possibly get at it. So you better have it. You just fucking better have it!"

Jack felt the gun shaking, as if Falcon were fighting the urge to pull the trigger. Whether the money was actually missing or not was irrelevant. In Falcon's paranoid mind, it was gone, and Jack had taken it. Charged, tried, convicted. Any further denial would only have unleashed the execution. "All right," said Jack. "I'll take you to it."

15

.

"Y ou seem distracted," said Vince.

"No. I'm okay," said Alicia. She flagged the cocktail waitress and signaled for another round of drinks.

It was almost eleven o'clock by the time Alicia had finished up at the medical examiner's office, driven home to get ready, and picked up Vince at his place. Vince's blindness had thrown a curveball into her routine. Selecting what to wear, putting on her makeup, blow-drying her hair—did any of those things that she would normally do really matter to him anymore? She wasn't sure why, but even raising those questions in her mind made her feel guilty. She debated whether to talk it out with Vince but decided it was better to keep the conversation light. The band was quite good, and they listened to music at the bar for a half-hour. When a table became available, they went out to the sidewalk café, where they could hear each other talk. The cold front was still a factor, but the bar had outdoor space heaters to warm things up. It was a crisp, clear night, and the moon over the ocean was so large that you could actually see the shadows on the lunar surface. She wondered if she should tell Vince about it.

"You keep looking around when we're talking," he said.

She did a double take, wondering how he knew.

"I can hear it," he said. "When you're not speaking directly toward me, the voice projects differently."

"Really? That's amazing."

"It's a skill I've been working on. I get a little better at it every day. But we weren't talking about me. Why are you looking around?"

"I'm sorry. I didn't mean to be doing that."

"Am I making you uncomfortable?"

"No."

"Are people looking at us?"

"Looking at us? No. Of course not."

He paused, then smiled smugly. "This is awesome."

"What is?"

"I've done most of my practicing on people I know only on a casual basis, but it works even better with people I know well."

"What are you talking about?"

"My hearing. And my ability to tell when people aren't telling the truth."

She returned the smile, even though he couldn't see it. "Okay, okay. We are being watched."

"Happens every time I go out. People staring and saying, 'Hey, who's the lucky girl with that incredibly hot blind guy?'"

That drew a little laughter. The waitress brought

them fresh drinks—white wine for Alicia, another Heineken for Vince. When the waitress was gone, Alicia said, "Actually, it's my father who's watching over us."

"Is that so? Maybe my hearing isn't as good as I thought it was. I completely missed the band's spontaneous rendition of 'Hail to the Chief.'"

"He's not here, turkey. What I mean is that about half the City of Miami police force is within a three-block radius of me at all times. I can count three off-duty cops right now."

"Your father's concerned for you," he said, taking on a more serious tone.

"That's an understatement."

"It's only natural. Things have changed, now that we know your stalker is a killer."

She thought back to the autopsy room. "It was absolutely brutal, what he did to that poor woman."

"You could have called me to cancel tonight. I would have understood."

"It's good for me to get out. Even if we are being watched."

"Pretty cushy job for those guys. I would imagine you're still easy on the eyes."

She didn't know how to respond.

Vince said, "Have you changed much? Your appearance, I mean."

"Well . . . no. Not really. It's only been six months. I was upset when we split, but I didn't get crazy and cut off all my hair or tattoo a ticking biological clock on my forehead."

He drank from his beer glass and carefully placed

it back on the coaster. "I'm starting to forget what people looked like."

She looked at him—not with sympathy but intrigued. Vince had never been one to speak freely about his feelings, and it was a little disorienting to hear so much from his heart. He was different now, in so many ways. Not all of the changes were bad. Not bad at all. "I suppose that's another skill you'll develop with time. You'll learn to reconstruct those images in your mind."

"I don't think so."

"Why not?"

"It's strange, really. My grandmother, who has been dead for over two decades, I can picture perfectly in my mind. But with my brother, who I see every week, it's now almost impossible for me to attach a face to his voice."

"What about your uncle Ricky?"

"Of course I remember the red hair and those blue eyes. But with the distinguishing lines of the face, it's like everyone else. The best way to describe it is to imagine that there is a big photo album in my mind. If people are part of my past, they stay there forever, just as they were. But if I make them a part of my new life, their image fades. The more contact I have with them, the more they are defined by things that don't depend on sight. For those folks, there will eventually be nothing left in the photo album but the shaded outline of where the picture used to be and a little label that tells me who it was."

Again, she found herself struggling for a response. "There's more to a person than just a face."

"Thank God for that. Because the way things are now, a face is nothing."

"I don't think I agree with that."

"It's true. There are no expressions that I can pick up, no little nuances of an arched eyebrow or parted lips. No more talking without words. I try to direct my face toward yours when we're having a conversation, but it's simply a matter of projection. That's all any face is now. Just a place where the voice comes from."

Alicia gazed at him, wondering if he could sense it. She wanted to say the right thing, but words seemed inadequate. She hesitated, then followed her impulse. She reached across the table, took his hand, and held it in hers. Slowly, she drew it toward her and pressed it against her cheek. Even after she let go of his hand, he left it there, cradling the side of her face, taking in her warmth and softness.

A lump came to his throat, followed by a sad but appreciative little smile on his lips. "Well," he said softly, "I can't always be right."

16

Jack had no idea where he was headed. The trick was not to let Falcon know that he was completely ad-libbing.

Theo shot him a nervous glance from the passenger seat. Jack kept driving. A gun to his head didn't make it any easier to bluff his way through this treasure hunt. They were headed north on Biscayne Boulevard, away from the downtown area. On the left was the Freedom Tower, a distinctive Mediterranean revival–style high-rise where thousands of Cubans, including Jack's mother, had been processed through immigration in the 1960s. Across the street was the basketball arena, with a five-story likeness of Shaquille O'Neil that almost qualified as life-sized.

"Watch your speed," said Falcon. He obviously didn't want to be pulled over by a patrol car. Jack slowed the car to thirty-five miles per hour.

For years, city planners had made much of the "Manhattanization" of Miami's skyline, but its downtown area was still a far cry from the city that never sleeps. Beyond a handful of clubs and restaurants around the design district and Little Haiti, the stretch of Biscayne Boulevard north of the old Omni Hotel basically shut down by midnight, even on the weekend. Many of the storefronts were secured with roll-down metal shutters, and the homeless slept in doorways on cardboard mattresses. Cross-traffic was minimal, but that didn't stop the traffic-planning geniuses from scheduling red lights for no apparent reason. Jack was thankful for any reason to stop; he still hadn't figured out where he was taking Falcon. They were at the Twenty-first Street intersection, virtually on the doorstep of the famous "blue-tile building," Miami's first example of Cuban-inspired architecture that didn't sport the classic Mediterranean look. Jack knew it only because it was Theo's favorite building in Miami, though his taste had nothing to do with the fact that the building was blue and Cuban, or red and Russian, or green and Martian. It mattered only that it was the U.S. headquarters for Bacardi spirits.

"Probably a few hundred grand sitting around in there somewhere," said Theo.

"No talking!" said Falcon.

The traffic light changed, and the journey continued. "How much farther?" said Falcon.

"Not too much," said Jack.

"Where are we going?"

"The marina. It's where I keep my boat."

"That's a lie. There's a boat behind your house."

Jack was caught, but a trial lawyer was nothing

if not quick on his feet. "That's my little boat. We need my really *big* boat to get to the Bahamas."

"Is my money still in Nassau?"

"If I tell you, you'll just shoot me and go by yourself."

"Maybe I'll just shoot you now."

"And then you'll never see your money."

Falcon's voice tightened. "Don't tell me what I'll see or won't see."

Theo said, "Dude, get a grip."

"Shut up, both of you! I'm in control here."

"Do you even know what control is?" said Theo.

Jack shot him a sidelong glance, as if to say, "Who asked you?"

The gun pulled away suddenly, but it returned with a vengeance. The metal butt landed in front of Jack's ear, just below the temple. The blow stunned him. The car swerved, but Jack fought it off and quickly recovered. Falcon jabbed his gun at the side of Jack's skull.

"Don't tell me I'm not in control," he said.

Jack felt blood oozing down the side of his face. He could hear the paranoia in Falcon's voice, feel the desperation in the air. The situation was only getting worse, and he had to do something fast. Just ahead, the traffic light changed from green to amber. Jack noticed a squad car at the cross street, waiting for a green light. On impulse, Jack hit the gas, knowing that he couldn't possibly make the light. The squad car was already in the intersection as Jack sailed past at nearly double the speed limit. Jack's light could not have been redder.

Blue flashing lights swirled behind them as the squad car screeched onto the boulevard and gave chase.

"You did that on purpose!" said Falcon.

Jack heard a click behind his ear—*the hammer cocking*?

"Outrun him," said Falcon. Jack didn't react fast enough. Falcon pushed the gun even harder against his head. "Floor it, or I'll kill you!"

Jack hit the accelerator, and the car lurched forward. The squad car was a half-block behind them and in hot pursuit, siren blaring. The engine growled, and the speedometer dipped beyond seventy miles per hour.

"Jack, spin it!" said Theo.

"Faster!" said Falcon.

"Spin it!"

Jack hit the brake and jerked the steering wheel hard left, then hard right, trying to pull one of those smooth sliding maneuvers that professional drivers do on television commercials. It wasn't so easy. The car was skidding out of control as Theo lunged across the console. Jack felt the tip of the barrel slide across his head as Theo and Falcon struggled for the weapon. There was a deafening noise—it was like shooting off a cannon inside a cave—and the sunroof exploded. Pellets of shattered glass rained down all over them. The pain reached deep into Jack's ears. Theo was shouting, and the tires were screeching like banshees, but it suddenly felt as if he were two hundred feet underwater—tons of pressure in the ears and no sound whatever. Then the ringing started, and with Theo and Falcon still going at each other, it was impossible for Jack to stop the car from careening across the boulevard. He wasn't even sure who had the gun anymore.

"Theo!" Jack shouted, though he could barely hear his own voice.

Rubber burned against the pavement as the car cut across three lanes of oncoming traffic. Horns blasted, vehicles swerved out of the way, and the bright white beams from several pairs of headlamps shot in every direction. Jack's car slammed into the curb, but the vehicle was going plenty fast to jump right over it. It was like a big speed bump on a NASCAR track. The car was airborne for an instant and came down hard on an asphalt parking lot. Jack managed to catch a glimpse of a neon sign that read VACANCY, as the car barreled into the Biscayne Motor Lodge. It scored a direct hit on room 102. All of the rooms had outdoor entrances that faced the parking lot, and the external walls were the flimsy, prefabricated aluminum-and-fiberglass packages typical of motor lodges—a door, a picture window, and a climate-control unit all in one piece. It was like driving into a one-car garage without bothering to open the garage door. Both the driver's and passenger's airbag exploded. The car leveled everything in its path, like a high-speed bulldozer, shoving lamps and dressers and two double beds against the back wall of the hotel room. The mountain of debris had acted like a giant cushion, not exactly a soft landing but better than crashing into a concrete pillar. The airbags had saved their lives.

It took a moment for Jack to regain his bearings and realize that they had indeed come to a complete stop. The room looked as if a bomb had detonated. It was almost completely dark, brightened only by the streetlights that shined through a gaping hole that was once the front of the hotel room. The ceiling had partially collapsed into a cloud of dust. Electrical wiring, twisted water pipes, broken furniture, chunks of drywall, and other debris were strewn everywhere. Jack refocused just in time to hear the squad car squealing into the parking lot. The blaring siren drowned out all sounds—except for the gunshots. Falcon was shooting at the cops as he crawled out of the car through the shattered rear window. Jack wasn't sure if it was a different gun or the same one that Theo had tried to wrest away from him. The officers scrambled for cover and returned the fire. Jack ducked down in the front seat and told Theo to do the same.

There was another exchange of gunfire, and the nine-millimeter slugs fired by the police made a popping sound as they hit the interior walls of the demolished hotel room. The wrecked automobile was suddenly bathed in white light. The police had switched on the spotlight that was fastened to the squad car. Another shot rang out, and the light was history. Falcon had nailed it with one shot from a distance of at least a hundred feet. The police returned fire.

Theo quickly glanced at Jack, making just enough eye contact to convey the understandable fears of a man who had spent four years on death row for a crime he didn't commit. They were sitting ducks in the car, and Theo's expression said it all: No way was he going to hang around and hope that a pair of white cops would peg the big black guy for an innocent victim. Before Jack could even try to stop him, Theo was sliding through the shattered windshield, determined to find a better hiding spot while the spotlight was dead.

Another crack of gunshot drew Jack's attention back to the parking lot. He saw an officer fall to the pavement. The other went to his aid. Another shot echoed from somewhere within the mountain of debris, and the second cop went down equally hard. Jack couldn't see Falcon, but wherever he was—*whoever* he was—he was one crackerjack marksman.

The downed officers didn't flinch, didn't make a sound. Sirens blared in the distance, signaling that law-enforcement backup was on the way. Jack spotted a fast-moving shadow on the wall, on the opposite side of his car. It was Falcon. He was trying to escape, but he was on the wrong side of the car. There was too much clutter to get out that way, no way to reach the parking lot, unless he climbed over to the driver's side.

"Run for it!" shouted Theo.

Jack sprang from his hiding spot behind the front seat and moved quickly over the mound of clutter. On the other side of the car was Falcon, but he had no apparent interest in Jack. His focus was on the only way out—a side door that, presumably, led to an adjoining room. With a single shot, he destroyed the lock. Jack heard him force the door open, and a woman screamed. Someone was in the adjacent room—the one Falcon had just entered.

"Theo!" Jack shouted, but he was too late.

Theo had heard it, too, and he was already up and over the car, chasing after Falcon, answering the woman's scream.

Before tearing after him, Jack spotted a weapon on the ground, beside one of the fallen officers. He went for it.

"Freeze!" the other officer shouted. His left shoulder and neck were covered with blood. He was wobbling, unable to stand but trying to stay centered with his weight on one knee.

"I need your help," said Jack. "My friend is—"

"I said freeze!"

"But listen to me, please."

"Facedown, on the ground, now!"

The gun was aimed straight at Jack's heart, giving him no choice but to comply. As he did, another scream emerged from somewhere behind the closed door of the motel room. A single gunshot followed—then silence. Jack lowered his forehead to the pavement and closed his eyes. The shattered searchlight and two wounded cops quickly flashed in his mind. Falcon had yet to miss a target all night.

And Theo Knight was one big target.

17

Things were moving way too fast for Jack to be scared. He was still facedown in the parking lot behind the squad car. The driver-side door was open. The wounded officer was down on one knee, struggling to reach for the radio control and at the same time keep his gun trained on Jack. Jack's ears were still ringing from the discharge of Falcon's pistol inside a closed vehicle, but he thought he could hear voices from somewhere across the parking lot. The sound of a car crashing into a building was nothing short of the blast of a bazooka, and it had sent neighbors scurrying out of their apartments and into the street like a swift kick to an anthill.

"You people get back inside!" the cop shouted, but his voice was weak. He tried to stand but couldn't. He propped himself up, elbow on the running board, groaning in pain as he managed to key the public address system on his vehicle. "Everyone, back inside your homes. You are in extreme danger!"

He dropped the microphone and grasped the radio control. Jack could hear sirens approaching from the north and south—or was it that damn ringing in his ears? No, it was definitely sirens. They were getting louder, closer, with each passing moment.

"Six-one, this is McKenzie," the officer said into his microphone. "Who's out there?"

"Fernandez," the reply came back. "Where are you?"

"Biscayne Motor Lodge," the cop said, his voice fading. "Officer down. I'm hit, too."

"Hang on, buddy. I'm one minute away."

"It's bad. Real bad. Lopez took one in the head. Send a full-crisis team. Got a possible hostage situation."

"Roger."

Jack was under orders not to speak, but his silence was helping no one. "Tell him that it's Pablo Garcia, aka Falcon. The homeless guy who was stalking the mayor's daughter."

McKenzie's breathing grew heavier, as if he were summoning the strength to tell Jack to stay quiet. Or perhaps he was just processing the information. Finally, he keyed his microphone and said, "Tell the chief to send Vince Paulo."

The bullet had flown right past Theo's left ear.

"On the floor!" Falcon shouted. He was holding a young woman as a human shield, her eyes wide with fright. The gun was jammed against her right temple.

It wasn't the first time Theo had been locked in a stare-down with a gunman, but calculating his next move against a deranged man with an innocent hostage was unlike anything he'd ever faced.

"Down on your belly, now!"

Theo's mind was awhirl. The guy had a gun. It was obviously loaded. He'd hit two cops already. The chances that he'd miss Theo a second time seemed pretty slim.

Falcon jabbed his finger into the girl's eye, and she screamed again.

"Okay, okay!" Theo said as he went down on the floor.

Falcon pushed the girl onto the bed, grabbed a ropelike sash from the draperies, and tied her hands behind her back. His movements were quick and efficient, as if he'd done this before. With the gun aimed at Theo's head, he patted him down for weapons. Theo had none.

"Get up!" said Falcon as he grabbed the girl and pulled her up from the bed. Again, she was his shield. "Everything goes up against the wall," he told Theo. "The mattresses, the dressers—everything. Right now!"

Theo climbed to his feet and started moving furniture.

"Faster!"

Theo was practically throwing things into place, creating a mountain of debris behind the wall, window, and door that separated them from the police in the parking lot. There wasn't enough to cover the entire window, and some light from the parking lot seeped into the room through the top of the draperies. When the task was finished, Falcon said, "On your belly!"

This time, Theo didn't wait for him to savage the girl's eye. He went down quickly. Falcon came to him and pressed the muzzle of the gun against the back of his skull. Theo could smell gunpowder from the previous rounds. He wondered if this was the end, if Falcon was of the mind that two hostages were more than he could handle.

"Let the girl go," said Theo. "You don't need her."

"Don't tell me what I need."

"Seriously. Swyteck can help you."

"Swyteck can't do shit."

"That's not true. He helped me, and I was on death row."

"Death row, huh?"

"That's right."

"I got news for you, big guy," Falcon said as the gun barrel burrowed into the nape of Theo's neck. "We're all on death row."

The next few minutes unfolded like a war zone around Jack. At least a dozen squad cars roared up Biscayne Boulevard and positioned themselves around the motel in circled-wagons fashion. An ambulance was right behind them. Two City of Miami cops jumped out of their cars and ran toward Officer Lopez, who lay motionless in the parking lot. A quick round of gunfire from room 103 turned them back and sent them scurrying for cover behind their vehicles. Another squad car squealed across the

parking lot and stopped between the downed officer and the motel to create a shield. On hands and
knees, a paramedic crawled toward Officer Lopez.
Thirty feet away, closer to the street, another
paramedic hurried toward Officer McKenzie. Jack
watched it all unfold from a worm's-eye view, his
cheek flat on the asphalt.

Another officer rushed to McKenzie's side.
The name tag on his breast pocket said D. SWANN.
"Where you hit, Brad?"

"The shoulder," he said. "There's innocents
inside that building. You guys have to hold your fire.
How's Lopez?"

"Don't know. Paramedic is with him now."

With a jerk of his head, he pointed toward Jack.
"This guy was driving the car that crashed into the
building. Could be dangerous."

"I'm not dangerous, I was carjacked," said Jack.

"I'll take care of it from here," said Swann.

The paramedics placed McKenzie on a gurney,
and the ambulance whisked him away. Swann patted
Jack down, but before he reached Jack's wallet, he
said, "You're Jack Swyteck, aren't you? Governor
Swyteck's son."

"Yes. That's what I've been trying to tell you
guys. That's my client in there with—" He stopped,
his chain of thought broken by another round of
gunfire.

Swann keyed his microphone. "Hold your fire!"
He looked at Jack and said, "What's your client
armed with?"

"Handgun."

"Pistol or revolver?"

"Pistol, I think."

"How many ammunition clips?"

"I don't know."

"What's his name?"

"Pablo Garcia. He goes by Falcon."

Swann keyed his public address system. "Falcon. This is the City of Miami Police Department. You are surrounded. Please, just calm down, and hold your—"

The crack of gunfire sent him diving to the pavement. For a split second, Jack thought Swann had been hit, but he was just taking cover. "That's one pissed-off client you've got there, counselor."

"No kidding. What you need is a trained negotiator."

"Got one on the way."

"Good," said Jack. "Tell him to hurry."

18

At twelve-forty a.m. Alicia dug her ringing cell phone out of her purse and checked the display. It was Renfro, the chief of police. She and Vince were still seated at their outdoor table, talking and listening to music. Alicia plugged one ear with her finger to silence the sounds of the nightclub and took the call. The chief gave her a quick update on Falcon and the possible hostage crisis.

"Where are they?" asked Alicia.

"Biscayne Motor Lodge. You know it?"

"Of course." Any cop who knew anything about twenty-dollar prostitutes and petty drug deals knew the Biscayne Motor Lodge. "Anyone hurt?"

"Two officers down. Juan Lopez and Brad McKenzie."

"How bad?"

"McKenzie called for backup. Lopez—It was a headshot."

"Is he . . ."

"Yeah, he's dead."

"God, no. His wife just had a baby."

Vince said, "What's wrong?"

The emotion in Alicia's voice was more than enough to signal that it was something serious. She reached across the table and touched his hand, as if to say "Just a sec."

"You're shaking," he said.

She wasn't sure that she was, but Vince had definitely picked up some sign of her distress. Nothing cut through cops like the loss of their own.

The chief continued, "I know that Paulo has pretty much settled on the idea that teaching at the academy is the right place for him, long-term. But he and this Falcon have a history. He at least has that much going for him to start up a dialogue. Do you think—"

"I'd bet my badge on it," said Alicia.

"Talk to him first. You'll know what to say to him. Then have him call me."

"Will do." After a quick good-bye, Alicia hung up and laid a twenty-dollar bill on the table to cover the last round of drinks. "We have to go, Vince."

Vince handed the money back to her and opened his own wallet. The bills were folded differently, according to denomination—singles lengthwise, fives widthwise, and so on. He unfolded two tens and laid them on the table. "You bought the first round," he said.

"Thanks, but we really have to go."

"What is it?"

"Not good," she said. "I'll tell you on the way."

Ten minutes later, they were speeding across the

Julia Tuttle Causeway on their way to the mainland and the Biscayne Motor Lodge. Cruise ships in the Port of Miami lit up the bay like floating hotels. To the west was the Miami skyline, a jagged assortment of modern skyscrapers bathed in a rainbow of colored spotlights. Alicia gave Vince all the details, and the chief's proposition was hanging in the silence between them.

"I don't think it's a good idea," said Vince.

Alicia changed lanes to get around a truck. "All you have to do is talk to the guy. He knows you."

"Talking a homeless guy down from a bridge is one thing. But we're dealing with a clinically paranoid gunman holed up in a hotel room with at least one hostage, possibly more. That leaves zero margin for error."

"It's a phone call, Vince."

"No, it's a hostage negotiation. Slight difference."

"Do you really think that's beyond your capabilities?"

"I don't know."

"Do you think someone else can do it better?"

"How *can* I know, damn it?"

"Don't get testy about it. Just take this for what it is—a vote of confidence from the chief of police."

He drew a deep breath and let it out slowly. "You just don't understand."

"No, I probably don't. Tell me."

"I'm so tired of the extremes."

"How do you mean?"

"People either pity me to death and think that I can't possibly manage a minute of my life without a sighted person holding my hand, or they think I've been magically transformed into some kind of blind mystic with extrasensory powers. Well, that's not the way it is. I've been using my white stick for six months, and I still on occasion walk straight into a lamppost; my sense of smell does not rival a blood-hound's; and even if Bruce Willis and M. Night Shyamalan were sitting right next to me, I could not see dead people. It's just plain old me, get it? I'm not helpless, but I'm not a blind Superman, either. I'm just a regular guy who's doing a pretty decent job of making my life a little better from one day to the next."

Alicia kept her focus on the string of orange tail-lights ahead of her. With the old Vince, she would have pressed harder. The new Vince was more complex, and maybe he had a point. She was probably as guilty as the next person, assuming that any man who lost his sight could suddenly sniff out an apple from across the room or pick up body rhythms over the telephone. Granting Vince those little pluses, at least in her own mind, helped her deal with the enormity of his loss. "You're right. This isn't my decision. It's yours."

"Thank you," he said.

She glanced to her right. His head was turned away from her, as if he were looking out the passenger window. He wasn't, of course. It was all about body language, a signal that the discussion was over. It was the kind of behavior that she would never have let the old Vince get away with, and Alicia wasn't going to start now, simply because he was blind. "Just get the negotiations started, all right? If you don't feel comfortable, then pass it off to someone else."

He didn't answer.

"Vince, please. If you say no to the chief this time, there's not going to be a next time."

There was still no reply.

"Damn it, Vince. What do you want to teach at the academy? How to be a quitter?" She worried that she might be hitting below the belt, but after a minute or so, her words seemed to have the desired impact.

"All right," he said. "I'll get it started."

She wished that he could see how proud she was of him. Instead, she reached across the console and squeezed his hand, and they rode the rest of the way in silence to the Biscayne Boulevard exit.

19
.

Biscayne Boulevard was completely shut down, both north and south, for as far as Jack could see. Eerie was the mood on a normally busy street that was suddenly deserted, particularly at night, with the swirl of police lights coloring the neighborhood. Jack hadn't seen Miami's main boulevard so empty since Hurricane Andrew ripped through South Florida. It made the arrival of the SWAT transport vehicles even more dramatic. There were two of them, one from the City of Miami, and the other from the Miami-Dade Police Department. Rather ominously, another ambulance trailed right behind them, just in case.

Jack prayed that Theo wouldn't be the one to need it.

Jack was standing in the parking lot of a fast-food restaurant, across the street and down a few hundred yards from the Biscayne Motor Lodge. Law enforcement was setting up a makeshift command post right outside the restaurant. Its location was strategic—close, but not too close, to the motel—and a ready source of burgers, fries, and coffee certainly didn't hurt.

The wound on the side of Jack's head was no longer oozing blood. One of the paramedics had cleaned and bandaged it, and Jack declined a trip to the hospital. After some forty-five minutes, the ringing in his ears had finally subsided. Discharging a firearm inside a closed vehicle was definitely not something he would recommend to friends.

The SWAT vehicles and the ambulance rolled up through the drive-thru lane and parked alongside the restaurant. Moments later, a large motor van bearing the blue, green, and black logo of Miami-Dade Police Department arrived. The antennae protruding from the roof signified that it was equipped with all the necessary technical gadgets to survey the situation and make contact with the hostage-taker. The rear doors to the SWAT vans flew open, and the tactical teams filed out. They were armed with M-16 rifles and dressed in black SWAT regalia, including helmets, night-vision goggles, and flak jackets. They appeared ready—eager, in fact—to go on a moment's notice.

A uniformed officer led Jack to the City of Miami police van and introduced him to Sergeant Chavez, the crisis-team leader. "Wait right here," said Chavez. "I definitely need to talk to you." He turned and went directly to the crisis-team leader from MDPD. Almost immediately, Chavez and the MDPD officer were embroiled in a heated discussion, as if the face-to-face confrontation were a mere continuation of an argument they'd been conducting by telephone or radio. Jack couldn't hear their conversation, but he knew a turf war when he smelled one.

Fortunately, the men and women in the field weren't quite so paralyzed. Jack watched as they moved from building to building, door to door, making sure that no one in the neighborhood ventured out onto the street. A helicopter whirred overhead—low enough for Jack to read the Action News logo on the side.

"Too close!" shouted Chavez, this time speaking in a voice that Jack and everyone else could hear. "Get them to back off—now!"

Another officer picked up a loudspeaker and told the intruding chopper to mind the restricted air space. It seemed to have no effect.

For several minutes, Chavez and the MDPD officer continued to haggle for control of the situation. Two fully armed and outfitted tactical teams awaited instructions, doing exactly what many believed to be the true meaning of the SWAT acronym: sit, wait, and talk. Jack was losing his patience. The motel had been silent for almost fifteen minutes, since the last exchange of gunfire. Jack could only speculate as to Theo's condition, but he knew one thing for certain: Falcon was still alive and in control. The gunfire had told him as much. The best Jack could hope for was that Theo was now a hostage. He didn't want to consider the worst.

Jack approached Chavez and the MDPD officer. It was time to settle their differences. "Who's in charge here?" said Jack.

"I am," they said in unison.

"Who are you guys?" said Jack.

Chavez reintroduced himself. The other man said, "Sergeant Peter Malloy, crisis-team leader, Miami-Dade Police Department. Who are you?"

Chavez said, "This is Jack Swyteck. He's a criminal defense lawyer."

Malloy's expression soured, as if Chavez had just said, "He's a pedophile who teaches kindergarten."

Jack said, "That's my client in there, Pablo Garcia. Homeless guy who calls himself Falcon. He was out on bail after climbing up the Powell Bridge."

Chavez said, "He's got a thing for the mayor's daughter, who also happens to be a City of Miami police officer. That means I got one cop dead, one wounded, and one stalked. That's three good reasons for me to be in control here. How many do you got, Malloy?"

"Dozens. I got a tactical team, a negotiating team, a traffic-control team, a communications team, and supervisors to control their actions. And unlike you folks at the city, we're trained to do this full-time."

Jack was about to slap them. "Hey, I got the best reason of all to be here. His name's Theo Knight. He's the hostage. And he's my best friend."

That silenced them for a moment, but the sound of his own words seemed to hit Jack hardest of all. As long as he'd known Theo, and as much as it felt true, Jack wasn't sure he'd ever used those words before—"He's my best friend."

"Might be a woman in there, too," Jack added.

"I heard a scream when Falcon went into the next room. Theo went in after her. That's when the standoff started."

Malloy glanced toward the motel. Spotlights had been rigged up on the rooftop of the office building directly across the street. Two powerful beams of light cut through the night, one trained on the door to room 103; the other, on the demolished room 102 and Jack's car. Malloy said, "That your vehicle?"

"Yeah."

"How the hell—"

The ring of Jack's cell phone brought the conversation to an abrupt halt. Jack quickly checked the display. The number made his heart thump. He'd dialed Theo's cell phone several times in the past half-hour, only to get no answer. Now, a call was coming back. "It's Theo's cell phone."

"Answer it," said Chavez.

"Wait," said Malloy as he handed Jack a Dictaphone.

Jack held it to his phone, pressed record, and then hit the talk button. "Theo?"

"Oh, that's funny, Swyteck."

It was Falcon. Jack said, "Where's Theo?"

"He's, uh . . . Let's just say he can't come to the phone right now."

"You son of a bitch. If you—"

"Don't bore me with threats, Swyteck."

Jack struggled to quell his anger. Self-control was the key to dealing with the clinically paranoid. Particularly when they were well armed. "All right, let's both of us just take a deep breath here. If anybody's hurt—you, Theo, anybody—let's take care of him okay? Do you need a doctor?"

"Are you kidding me?"

"I just want to make sure everyone's okay, that's all."

"Kiss my ass. I want to deal."

"Good. There's a negotiator right here with me."

"I don't want a negotiator. Tell the cops they can go to hell. Even Vince Paulo screwed me over on that bridge, and we go way back, long before he was blind."

"Could be different this time. You're holding the cards now."

"Damn right I am. That's why I'm giving you this chance. You got one shot to show me you're the man."

"What do you want?"

"You can start by returning the money you stole from me."

"I didn't steal—"

"Stop right there!" he shouted.

Jack was silent. It was impossible to tell over the telephone, but Jack could almost see Falcon biting back his rage, fighting to keep control. Falcon's voice lowered, but it was still tight with anger. "I don't want no excuses. No denials. Bring me my money. That's the demand. Got it?"

"I'll see what I can do."

"No. I said, 'Do you got it?'"

Jack hesitated. "I want to talk to Theo."

"No way."

"Tell me who else is in there with you."

There was a click on the line. It wasn't a hang-up. It sounded more like the hammer cocking on Falcon's pistol. "One more time, Swyteck: Do you got it?"

Jack took the warning to heart. "Yeah. I got it."

"Good. As soon as the money's here, we can talk about my other demands."

"What other demands?"

"You'll see. This is going to get very interesting."

"This is not a game, Falcon."

"Couldn't agree more. This is very serious business."

"Then cut the crap. Tell me what you want."

"I got a better idea. Just ask Vince Paulo. He knows what I want. Problem is, I don't trust him to give it to me no more. Which means it's all on your shoulders. So bring me that money, and we can talk. But don't take too long. The battery on your friend's phone won't last forever. And when it dies . . ." His voice trailed off, and the ensuing silence seemed interminable.

"You still there?" said Jack.

"Yeah. Come on, man. I'm waiting. Fill in the blank. When the battery dies . . ."

Jack didn't want to say it, but this wasn't a fight worth picking. "Theo dies."

Falcon gave him a mirthless chuckle. "Wrong again, genius. *Everybody* dies."

The line disconnected. Jack stood frozen for a moment, thinking the kind of thoughts that were anything but helpful in a crisis of this magnitude.

An hour earlier, he and Theo were on their way to South Beach. Now, one cop was dead, another was in the hospital, Theo was a hostage, and Falcon was calling the shots. Add to that the unidentified woman's body in Falcon's trunk, and it was almost too much to comprehend. Jack closed his flip phone and dabbed away a drop of blood from the bandaged wound at his temple.

The crisis-team leaders were watching him, their expressions filled with anticipation. Sergeant Chavez said, "Well, what's the word?"

He looked at Chavez, then at the crisis-team leader from MDPD. "I think you've just been fired."

"Who's fired?" said Chavez.

"All of you," he said, gesturing toward the SWAT vans. "Except for me and Vince Paulo."

20

Tires screeched as a dark green sedan flew around the corner and entered the parking lot via the fast-food restaurant's drive-thru exit. The brakes grabbed, and the front bumper nearly kissed the pavement as the car came to an abrupt halt just a few feet away from Jack.

Sergeant Chavez was standing nearby, speaking to the traffic-control leader by radio. Jack couldn't hear every word, but he gathered that media vans with satellite dishes were starting to back up at both the north and south barricades on Biscayne Boulevard. The fleet of television helicopters whirring overhead had grown from one to three, their bright white search lamps cutting through the clear night sky. Meanwhile, the tactical teams stood idle outside the SWAT van, drinking only decaffeinated coffee, careful not to get too stimulated.

The moment the car door flew open, Jack recognized the mayor's daughter from the recent photographs in the newspaper. The passenger door opened, and the man with the sunglasses and long white cane could only have been Vincent Paulo. As they approached, Jack noted the way Officer Mendoza guided her blind partner through unfamiliar territory, his hand resting in the crook of her elbow. She wasn't steering him, nor had they locked arms like sweethearts, but Jack detected a level of comfort and familiarity between them, a certain naturalness to the physical contact.

"Any word on McKenzie?" she asked the sergeant.

Chavez cut his mike and said, "Took one in the belly. He's in surgery now. We're hoping for the best. I guess you heard about Lopez."

Her nod was slow and deliberate, conveying only sadness. Jack suddenly wished he were invisible, as if his status as Falcon's lawyer placed him somewhere between the outsider at a family funeral and an accomplice to murder.

"Any contact with the subject yet?" asked Paulo.

Chavez cast a glance in Jack's direction. "His lawyer just took a phone call."

"Where's his lawyer?" asked Paulo.

"I'm right here," said Jack.

Paulo turned at the sound of his voice, and they shook hands. Sergeant Malloy then introduced himself as the crisis-team leader from the Miami-Dade Police Department. The round of introductions ended with Jack facing Alicia.

There was always a level of discomfort when meeting your client's victim, even if she was, relatively speaking, one of the lucky ones. Her demeanor toward Jack was professional, however, no daggers in those big brown eyes. She was wearing a stylish cropped leather jacket, black slacks and sweater, and heels that left her shorter than Jack and Sergeant Paulo but a good two inches taller than Chavez. If any doubt remained, the perfume and makeup confirmed that she had been summoned from an off-duty location. The photographs in the newspaper had presented the mayor's daughter as quite an attractive woman, and Jack could now attest to the fact that the camera hadn't lied.

Paulo asked, "How certain are we that Falcon has taken a hostage?"

"Very," said Jack. "His name's Theo Knight. He was riding with me when Falcon hijacked our car. The phone call came on Theo's cell phone. Could be a woman in there, too."

"I need more details," said Paulo. "Who can bring me up to speed?"

Chavez gave him the rundown on police response thus far. Jack filled in everything from the carjacking to the call on Theo's phone. Finally, they replayed the tape recording of Jack's conversation with Falcon. For Jack, it was only a little less stressful the second time around. He was already starting to second-guess the things he'd said, and the way he'd said them, with Theo's life in the balance.

Just as the tape finished, a helicopter cruised by so low that it stirred the cold night air around them. "Is that one of ours?" asked Paulo.

"Media," said Chavez.

"We need them to back off."

"No shit," said Chavez.

Paulo looked up to the sky, which struck Jack as curious. He seemed to be responding to the sound and the wind. Paulo said, "Are you sure the telephone call came by cell?"

"Positive. Theo's number came up on my display."

"The crash may have taken out the phone lines. Chavez, you'll need to check with the phone company. If there's still phone service to the motel, block out all calls except those coming from our communications vehicle. We don't need him talking to some overactive journalist. By the way, has anyone contacted Building and Zoning yet?"

"Not yet," said Chavez.

"We'll want blueprints of the building. The more detailed, the better. Bearing walls versus nonbearing walls, crawl space, duct work, attic clearance. Have you located the water main?"

"We're working on it," said Chavez.

"Good. We may want to turn that off at some point. The same goes for electrical."

"Any moron can see—" Chavez stopped himself, but he didn't apologize for the slip. "The electricity is already out, at least in the room they're in. The crash seems to have taken care of that."

"Let's not assume anything," said Paulo. "I don't want Falcon watching us on television, especially with these media choppers revealing our positions. So let's get on it and cut the power as soon as possible. Is anyone else still inside the motel?"

Chavez said, "We went door-to-door as much as we could and evacuated the guests. Seems to be plenty of vacancy. We've accounted for sixteen guests. Some were already out on the street. They ran like hell when the car crashed into the building. I'm sure it must have sounded like a bomb going off."

Paulo asked, "Was there anyone inside the motel room that Mr. Swyteck's car crashed into?"

Jack felt a sudden chill. With all the commotion, he hadn't yet stopped to consider the possibility of another victim crushed beneath his vehicle.

"We don't know yet," said Chavez.

"Is there a hotel manager or front-desk clerk we can ask?"

"Haven't found him yet. It was pandemonium out here until traffic control cleaned things up."

"Is there a guest registry in the front office?"

"Yeah, but about half of the guests we've talked to so far aren't even listed on it. Some of these rooms seem to rent by the hour, if you know what I mean."

Malloy interrupted, flashing an annoyed expression. "Excuse me, Sergeant Paulo. But exactly what is your role here?"

Alicia answered, "He has a history of negotiations with Falcon, going back almost two years. He's here at the request of Chief Renfro."

"You mean he's going to be the lead negotiator?" said Malloy.

Paulo said, "I'm not trying to sound like a jerk, but would everyone please stop talking about me as if I weren't here? I'm blind, not invisible."

"Sorry," said Alicia.

"To answer your question: No, I'm not going to be lead negotiator. I've agreed to get a dialogue started. But once that's done, I'm out. You guys can take it from there."

Jack said, "Sorry, but that won't work. You heard the tape of the phone call. The only person Falcon wants to talk to is me, and he told me to talk to Vince Paulo if I needed help figuring out what he wants."

Malloy said, "Let's get something straight right now. A lawyer is not going to be our lead negotiator."

"Then it has to be me and Paulo."

An uneasy silence came over the group. It was impossible for Jack to read Paulo's expression, the eyes hidden as they were behind dark glasses. Finally, Paulo said, "Let's take it one step at a time. First thing we have to deal with is the demand. Tell me more about the money he wants."

"He has cash in a safe deposit box in Nassau. He thinks I took it, but I didn't. I left all but enough to cover his bail right where I found it, back in the Bahamas."

"How much money are we talking about?"

Jack hesitated. His criminal defense lawyer instincts were kicking in, but the bottom line was that if this lawyer-client relationship hadn't died with the carjacking, then it definitely took a backseat to the gun Falcon was holding to Theo's head. "I counted exactly two hundred thousand originally. His bail was ten thousand."

The cops exchanged glances. Chavez said what they all were thinking: "How on earth does a homeless guy have that kind of money in an offshore bank?"

"Probably not from washing windshields," said Jack.

Paulo asked, "Any idea why he wants his money now?"

"No. He just wants it."

"It doesn't matter why," said Malloy. "The director has made MDPD's position on this crystal-clear. We don't give money to hostage-takers. Period. You learn that in hostage negotiations one oh one."

"All rules have exceptions," said Paulo.

Jack said, "Are you saying that you want me to fly to the Bahamas and get the money?"

"How long would it take you?" asked Paulo.

"Are you serious?" said Jack.

"This isn't going to end quickly, my friend. Last time out, Falcon tied up traffic on the Powell Bridge for almost four hours. It took close to six and a half hours the time before that. And those negotiations were *without* hostages. So how long would it take you?"

"Theo has a friend who operates a fleet of seaplanes out of Watson Island. If I told him that it was a matter of life and death, I'm sure he would have me there in an hour, if you can arrange clearance. But factor in the ground time, and that's still four or five hours, round-trip. That's assuming that I can find someone to let me into the bank in the middle of the night."

"I have a contact at Interpol who can work with you on that. And the air clearance is no problem."

Malloy chimed in again. "You can't give this Falcon a suitcase full of cash."

"What's the downside?" said Paulo.

"It's against the rules."

"I'm still not hearing a downside," said Paulo.

Jack was starting to like this guy.

Paulo said, "We have to build some goodwill. My last exchange with Falcon was when I talked him down from the lamppost on the Powell Bridge, only to have SWAT pounce all over him. I have to make up for that. If we can meet his first demand, we reestablish trust. Giving him cash—his own cash, mind you, not ours—isn't like giving him ammunition."

Malloy said, "If you give him money, then he'll want ammo."

Paulo said, "Last night, Falcon killed a woman and stuffed her in the trunk of an abandoned car that he calls home. So far tonight, he's shot two police officers, one of them fatally. He has absolutely nothing to lose by killing again. If we can buy back a hostage with his own money, I say that's a good deal."

Jack said, "So you want me to go?"

"You mean you're still here?" said Paulo.

Jack was definitely starting to like this guy.

21

"Wall 'em up, wall 'em up, wall 'em up." Falcon had been repeating the same words, over and over again, for at least fifteen minutes. It was driving Theo crazy, but he held his tongue.

With Theo's help, Falcon had turned the room into a makeshift fortress. Anyone coming through the front door would have to pass through a mountain of furniture to reach the hostages. The entire room had been cleaned out, except for the television. There was a crack of light at the edge of the wall and along the top of the window. The drapes were so old and worn that, in spots, the lining had lost its blackout quality. The room brightened every few seconds as the intermittent swirl of police lights seeped in from the parking lot. Falcon had tried the light switch, but they were obviously without electricity. That didn't stop him from pushing the on-off button on the TV every few minutes, determined to get a picture.

"Can't you see that the power's out," said Theo.

"Shut up!"

Judging from the number of sirens blaring in the past twenty minutes, Theo figured that an army of police had taken up positions outside the motel. He was pretty sure that he'd heard helicopters as well, though he had no way of knowing if they were part of a tactical team or the media. As best he could tell, the police were regrouping. The gunfight was over. It was time to negotiate. Theo hoped that Falcon was lucid enough to realize that police didn't deal for dead hostages.

Falcon walked to the corner near the window. Minutes earlier, he'd broken through the glass and fired off two quick shots from that same position. He seemed to have a view of the parking lot from that vantage point.

"I can't breathe," the woman hostage said. She was seated on the floor with her back to the wall, her hands tied behind her waist, and a pillowcase over her head. It was cold outside, and the room was comfortably cool. Even in the dim lighting, however, Theo's eyes had adjusted well enough for him to see the tiny beads of sweat glistening on her arms, physical manifestation of her fear and panic.

Falcon started mumbling to himself again. "Wall 'em up, wall 'em up, wall 'em up."

Theo's hands were tied, but his head was uncovered. Falcon appeared to be on a mission to find another pillowcase somewhere in the pile of furniture. "Wall 'em up" seemed to be his way of saying that the hostages should be hooded and blindfolded.

"I really . . . can't breathe," the woman said, groaning.

Falcon was pacing furiously, not even listening to her.

Theo said, "You need to loosen the knot around her neck." Falcon didn't respond. Theo said, "Hey, did you hear me? She's going to suffocate."

"Quiet! I can't think!" Falcon had a crazed look in his eyes. The room glowed with each flash of police lights in the parking lot, and it gave his face an angry red sheen.

"This won't get you nowhere, man," said Theo.

Falcon glared, then turned away and resumed pacing. "Wall 'em up, wall 'em up."

"I need some air!" the woman shouted.

"Take the pillowcase off her head, jerk-off!"

Falcon wheeled and swung his arm around violently. The butt of his gun made a dull thud as it crashed against Theo's skull. Theo fell hard to the floor. It was like a one-two knockout punch—the blow from the gun and his head hitting the carpet. "Shut your trap," he heard Falcon shouting, but sounds and sights were all just a blur. He fought to remain conscious, refusing to close his eyes. He tried to focus on something, anything, to keep his brain functioning. A trickle of blood ran into his left eye, and Theo tried without success to blink it away. His other eye, the one closest to the carpet, was staring at the bathroom door. It was closed. Like the rest of the room, the dark slat at the threshold of the bathroom door brightened with each pulse of colored light from police vehicles in the parking lot. Theo struggled to concentrate. In the intermittent light available, he could see something on the bathroom floor, on the other side of the slat. It was directly in front of the base of the toilet. The lights pulsed again, and he saw something that looked like a shoe. Two shoes, in fact—men's shoes.

One of them moved.

Theo showed no reaction, and he wasn't sure if this was a good or a bad thing. But with each flash of light, he became more certain.

Someone was in there.

22

Within the hour, Jack was on a seaplane headed back to Nassau. The ocean below was as black as the night, making it nearly impossible to distinguish the low-hanging stars from the scattering of lights across the island landscape. Jack was glad that it wasn't his job to discern up from down. He rode in the copilot's seat beside Theo's friend and the owner of the aircraft, Zack Hamilton. A City of Miami police officer was in the row behind them.

The Bahamas are made up of some 700 islands and 2,400 cays, though only about thirty are inhabited, and two-thirds of a total population of 300,000 lives in Nassau. Jack couldn't count the number of times that he and Theo had, on a whim, hopped on his motorboat and made the sixty-mile trip from Key Biscayne to the nearest Caribbean refueling station—gasoline for the boat, Mount Gay rum for the boaters—on the island of Bimini. Nassau is farther northwest, but it still seemed as though their seaplane had just leveled off when it was time to begin their descent. Slowly, the seemingly random arrangement of glowing dots ahead organized themselves into long, parallel lines of blue guiding lights.

"Prepare for landing," said Zack. He was speaking into the microphone on his headset, his voice tinny but audible over the drone of the twin prop engines.

"Are you going to put us down on a landing strip?" said Jack.

"Beats the hell out of the forest."

It was the kind of wiseass response that Jack should have expected from one of Theo's oldest buddies. "I meant as opposed to the water. This *is* a seaplane."

"Runway's a lot safer at night. But we can do the water, if you really want to."

"No, thanks," was what he said, but he was thinking, *Not in this flying death-trap.*

Zack checked his flight instruments as he finished off his last swallow of orange Nehi and sucked the greasy remnants of a party-sized bag of Cheetos from his fingertips. He seemed to possess an insatiable appetite for anything orange and edible, so long as it was artificially colored and of absolutely no nutritional value. It was just one more trait that served to underscore the fact that Jack was unlike Zack in every conceivable way but two: Their first names rhymed, and they were both friends with Theo Knight. A side-by-side comparison of the two men would have yielded unassailable scientific proof that the tiny fraction of DNA that differentiated one human being from the next was unquestionably the most significant fraction of anything in the entire universe. Zack was nearly seven feet tall, and he wore his hair in cornrows that hung down longer than Jack's arms. His build made Theo look slight. A knee injury in his rookie season had deep-sixed his NBA career, but fortunately, the signing bonus was big enough to set him up in his own business. Flying became his new passion, and Jack had to admire a guy who had managed to turn a fallback career into something he loved. Still, it was hard to imagine that anything less than the power of Theo could have brought Jack and Zack together at two o'clock on a Saturday morning.

They landed and quickly deplaned onto the runway. With the assistance of local law enforcement, they cleared customs and immigration in expedited fashion. A Bahamian police officer met them in the terminal and took them straight to a squad car parked in a no-parking zone in front of the airport. Jack and Zack rode in the backseat, and the Miami cop took the passenger seat. The car didn't pull away fast enough to suit Jack.

"We're kind of in a hurry," he said.

The Bahamian cop glanced in his rearview mirror. He had a round, pudgy face and the eyes of a hound dog, at once dull and expressive, if that was possible. "'Course you is, mon."

Traffic was light at this hour, and until they reached the outskirts of Nassau, Jack counted more stray goats and chickens than oncoming automobiles. Twenty minutes later, they arrived at the Greater Bahamian Bank & Trust Company. Jack climbed out of the car, and the others followed him up the concrete stairway. The front doors were solid glass, and the inside of the bank was dark, save for the typical security lights that burned after hours. A security guard emerged from the shadows and came to the door. He spoke through an intercom that crackled like a grease fire. "We're closed."

Jack held his tongue, but Zack blurted out exactly what he was thinking. "Don't you think we know that, Einstein?"

Jack hoped it had gone unheard. He leaned closer to the speaker box and said, "The manager was supposed to meet us here and let us in."

The guard shrugged and said, "Mr. Riley's not here."

Jack gave up on the guard and turned to the local cop. "Where is Riley?"

The Bahamian flashed those hound-dog eyes again. "He be late."

"He can't be late. When's he getting here?"

"Soon."

"How soon?"

"Soon as I call him."

"Well then, would you call him, *please*," said Jack, his tone more impatient than polite. "Like I told you before, we're really in a hurry."

The Bahamian started slowly back to his car, presumably toward his radio. "'Course you in a hurry, mon. The whole world be hurryin'."

Jack felt a throbbing headache coming on. Theo

would have known exactly how to deal with these chumps. For a split second, Jack found himself wishing his friend were there, until he quickly realized that if Theo were there, that would have eliminated any need to come in the first place. Jack massaged away the pain between his eyes.

I'm losing my mind.

Sergeant Paulo was reacquainting himself with the inside of the police communications vehicle. It was familiar territory to him. He had everything he needed: his favorite chair, his old coffee mug, a bone mike to communicate with his team leaders in the field, and a telephone within easy reach, to speak with Falcon.

The coordination of efforts between city and county law enforcement was a work in progress, but the key roles had been defined. Like most crisis units, this one included several teams: negotiations, tactical, traffic control, and communications. The lead negotiator was Paulo, whose primary responsibility was to speak directly to the subject. Sergeant Malloy of MDPD was the secondary negotiator. His job was to assist Paulo and take notes. Intelligence officers from both MDPD and the city would conduct interviews and gather information for the negotiators. A staff psychologist was on hand to evaluate the subject's responses and recommend negotiating strategies.

The two departments would share responsibility for traffic control, and the tactical teams also overlapped. Snipers from each department assumed strategic positions on rooftops across the street from the motel. The assault teams stood ready to go. It was agreed, however, that if they were forced to use breachers—specially trained tactical-team members who could blow open doors or windows— MDPD would go in first.

It was also agreed that Alicia would be Paulo's eyes.

"You nervous?" she asked as she poured fresh coffee from a Styrofoam go-cup into his mug. It was just the two of them in the communications van, as Paulo had requested some time alone to organize his thoughts for the initial contact.

"I have a sinking suspicion that I'm in this for the long haul."

"Would you rather it was in the hands of someone like Chavez or Malloy?"

"Part of me would, yeah."

"How can you even think that way?"

He drank from his cup. "If this goes badly, you know how the headlines will read, don't you?"

"'Blind Guy Blows It'?"

It was kind of funny, the way his literal mind immediately conjured up the image of "BLIND GUY BLOWS IT" beneath the *Miami Tribune* masthead. "You always did beat around the bush, didn't you?"

"Sorry. But I wouldn't be so direct if I actually thought you were going to blow it."

The side door opened. "Who's there?" said Paulo.

She introduced herself as Lovejoy, one of the intelligence officers. "I found the property manager," she said. "The good news is that there was no one in room one-oh-two when Swyteck's car crashed into it. But he has some info on the occupants of one-oh-three. I thought you might want to talk to him."

"Definitely," said Paulo. "Is he with you?"

"Yeah, he's right here. His name's Simon Eastwick."

"Mr. Eastwick, how are you?"

The man paused, and Paulo presumed that it was because he had misjudged where he was standing. It sometimes disoriented people when he wasn't looking straight at them. "I'm fine, thanks," he said finally.

"Can you tell me who was in that room before the crash?"

"Uh, it's two Latina girls," said Eastwick.

"By 'girls,' do you mean young women, or, literally, 'girls'?"

"I mean they were teenagers. Maybe eighteen or nineteen."

"Do they speak English?" said Paulo.

"One of them speaks very well. The other is so-so."

"Do you have their names?"

"No. They paid day-by-day, cash."

"Do you know if they were both inside the room at the time of the crash?"

"Sorry. Couldn't tell you that."

Paulo said, "How long have they been staying at the motel?"

"One of them just got here yesterday. The other one, I don't know. A few days, maybe longer."

"Did they have many visitors?"

"I wouldn't know."

Alicia said, "How about customers?"

Eastwick was suddenly indignant. "Like I said: I wouldn't know."

"Ah," said Alicia, "the don't-ask-don't-tell motel. Is that it?"

Eastwick said, "What people do in their private time is their business."

"Not if they're underage," said Alicia.

"Like I told you, they looked to be eighteen or nineteen to me. I was just giving them a place to stay."

In exchange for a cut of their business? That was what Paulo *wanted* to say, but it wouldn't do any good to get the property manager's back against the wall and shut down his cooperation. "Is there anything else you can tell us about these girls, Mr. Eastwick?"

"Not that I can think of."

"I'd like you to sit down with the tactical team, explain every conceivable point of access to that room. Could you do that?"

"Sure."

Eastwick started toward the door, but Paulo stopped him. "One other thing. These girls, as you call them. Is there any possibility that they would keep a gun in their room?"

The man considered it for a moment. "I'd say that's a very definite possibility."

"Thank you, Mr. Eastwick. That's some very helpful information."

Everything looks different at three a.m., and the inside of the Greater Bahamian Bank & Trust Company was no exception. The lobby was completely still, and the palpable silence made Jack aware of the sound of his own footsteps, the gum in Zack's mouth, and the loose coins in the security guard's pocket.

After three radio calls, Otis Riley, the bank manager, had finally shown up. He was a short man with a dark island complexion that radiated good health, but Jack could still see the sleep in his eyes. Riley offered very few words as he took them down a hallway and then to a set of locked doors that opened to the safe deposit box room. "I believe that Mr. Swyteck and I can take it from here," he told the group.

Zack, the security guard, and the Bahamian police officer did not object. The Miami cop said, "I need to stay with Swyteck."

"Why?" said Jack.

"Because I was told not to let you out of my sight."

"What do you think I'm going to do, shove a stack of twenties in my pocket?"

The cop was stone-faced.

"Oh, for crying out loud," said Jack.

The cop said, "It's my job to make sure that the exact amount of money that comes out of that box goes directly into police hands back in Miami. That's the only way the feds will allow that much cash to cross an international border."

"All right," said Riley. "Come with us, then." Riley used his access card to unlock the door, and the three men entered the safe deposit box room. The manager went into the office and returned with the key to box 266 in hand. "Do you have your key, Mr. Swyteck?"

Jack nodded. Riley went to the box and inserted the bank's key. The lock clicked when he turned it. Jack inserted his key, and there was another click. Jack pulled the handle, and the box opened like a drawer. It was halfway open when his heart sank. He opened it all the way and found himself speechless.

"It's empty," said Riley.

"What happened to all the money?" said Jack.

"We have never had a mishap in our eleven-year existence," said Riley, as if a decade plus one were more than enough to establish a tradition of excellence in the world of offshore banking. "I'm certain that every last bill can be accounted for."

"Has someone accessed the box since I was here last?" said Jack.

"I'll check the records straight away," said Riley.

"That may not be necessary," said Jack. "There's a note."

The cop said, "Don't touch it."

Jack wasn't about to smudge it with his own fingerprints. The scrap of paper was the size of a business card, and a handwritten message was scrawled across the front. With the tip of his pen, Jack slid the note from the back of the drawer to the front, close enough for him to read it aloud. "*Donde están los Desaparecidos?*"

"Is that Spanish?" said Riley.

"Yes," said Jack.

The men were silent, as if trying to decipher it. "What does it mean?" said Riley.

The cop said, "It translates to 'Where are the Disappeared?'"

"That's the easy part," said Jack. "But if you want to know what it means . . ."

"Yes?" said Riley.

Jack stole another glance at the note. "I don't have a clue."

23

Alicia was asleep in the backseat of her car when her cell phone rang. Vince had warned her that the Falcon and Theo show might well have the legs of a PBS telethon, so she grabbed the opportunity for a quick catnap. Her car was parked right beside the command center, in case she was needed. The missed call went to her voice mail, but she recognized the number on her call-history display. She hit speed dial, and her father answered on the first ring.

"Alicia, where are you?"

"I'm at a mobile command center. There's a hostage situation on Biscayne."

"I know. Chief Renfro called me, and I just turned on the news. Why are you there?"

"Because I might be able to help."

"Please don't talk to that psycho. He's killed one cop already, shot another."

Alicia checked her face in the rearview mirror. Once upon a time, she could have curled up in the backseat, slept off a night of two-for-one cosmopolitans, and made it to her eight a.m. accounting class with no makeup and a smile on her face. Those days were gone. "I'm not in any danger. I'm way outside the line of fire."

"Good. Just don't go anywhere near that building. Please, promise me you won't go there."

"I'm not going anywhere."

"Don't even talk to him on the phone."

"He hasn't asked to talk to me."

"He will. He asked to talk to you when he was on that bridge, and he'll ask again."

"If he does, I'll do what the negotiators think I should do."

"No. Listen to your father. Do not talk to him. Do you hear me?"

"*Papi*, calm down, all right?"

"I am calm. Just promise me you won't talk to him."

"Okay, I won't talk to him. I promise. Unless the negotiator thinks it would help."

"By 'negotiator,' do you mean Paulo?"

"Yes."

"For heaven's sake, Alicia. The last time that man was in a true hostage crisis, a five-year-old girl was nearly killed, and he ended up blind."

"That wasn't his fault."

"That's your opinion."

"Yes, it is my opinion, which is to say that I trust his judgment. Now, I've done the best I can to honor your wishes. I promise that Falcon won't even know I'm in the neighborhood, unless Vince thinks it's absolutely necessary."

"No, not *unless* anything. You can't talk to that lunatic."

The desperate tone surprised her. It was almost irrational, certainly unreasonable. "I'm sorry. I can't promise you that." There was only silence on the other end of the line. "*Papi*, are you okay?"

"Yeah, I'm fine."

"Are we good then?"

He made a noise that was somewhere between a sigh and a groan. "I hate to be the one to point this out. But sweetheart, when you and Vince first started dating a year ago, you used to tell me how worried you were about him. You said yourself that he doesn't exactly play by the book."

"That's not what got him hurt."

"Maybe it didn't. But maybe it did. I just don't want to see the same thing happen to you. Can you understand that?"

"Yes, I can. But you have to understand my side of it, too."

"I know. You do what you have to do."

"Thank you. I will."

"We both will."

"We both will what?" she said, not quite sure what he was trying to say.

"Nothing. I love you." He said good-bye and hung up.

Four o'clock in the morning. Had the night gone according to their original plan, Jack would have been in bed, only dreaming of the Bahamas or some other slice of paradise, and Theo would have been rolling in from the clubs on South Beach right about this time. Instead, Jack was going on his twenty-second hour without sleep, and he was reporting back to a hostage negotiator by telephone from the Nassau police station.

"What happened to the cash?" said Paulo.

Officer Danen, the City of Miami cop, had told Paulo about the missing money. Danen and Jack were now on speakerphone, as time was of the essence and Paulo wanted nothing lost in translation. Jack leaned closer to the squawk box atop the desk and said, "Someone beat us to it two days ago. The bank won't give us a name because of the bank secrecy laws. Whoever it was, they cleaned it out."

"But you still have a power of attorney from your client. Why won't they tell you who opened the box?"

"Until their lawyers get out of bed and advise otherwise, the bank's position is that the power of attorney is limited to a right of access. It doesn't give me a blanket right to information protected by bank secrecy."

"You're not playing games with me, are you?"

"No way. You can ask your own man, if you don't believe me. He was right at my side the whole time. We opened the box, and it was empty. Except for a note."

"A note?" said Paulo. "What did it say?"

Jack told him. Paulo said, "What's that supposed to mean?"

"NFI," said Jack.

"NFI?"

"Sorry. That's a Theo-ism: no idea," he said, leaving out the colorful adjective.

"Did the bank let you keep the note?" said Paulo.

"I didn't ask for permission. I just kept it." *Another Theo-ism*, thought Jack.

"Good. Danen, make sure he doesn't contaminate it. We'll want to check it for prints."

The Miami cop said, "I'm one step ahead of you. Bahamian police pulled a thumbprint from the front and an index finger from the back. We did an electronic scan and sent it off to the FBI and Interpol from the station here in Nassau. Everything's in the works."

"Good, but it could turn up goose eggs. Let's keep the pressure on the bank to cough up a name. Do we need to involve the FBI?"

"Only if we want everything all screwed up," said Danen.

Jack held his tongue, but he often found the turf wars in law enforcement to be nothing short of the Hatfields versus the McCoys. And people say lawyers have egos.

Paulo said, "Where does it stand now, exactly?"

"The only thing the bank will confirm is that someone definitely accessed the box between three and three-thirty p.m. last Thursday. I might be able to get beyond that in the morning, but in the middle of the night, we can't get the machinery in motion to pierce the Bahamian bank secrecy laws."

"Do they realize that we have a hostage situation here?"

"Of course. But no offshore bank wants to get a

reputation for opening its secret records every time a U.S. law enforcement agency shows up in the dead of night and claims to have an emergency on its hands."

"Especially if they screwed up," said Jack.

"What do you mean?" said Paulo.

"I had a case once against a Cayman Island Bank that let my client's ex-husband into her safe deposit box. The deadbeat took about a half-million dollars in jewelry that didn't belong to him. Turned out to be an inside job. A bank employee let him in, even though the husband's name had been removed from the approved access list long before the divorce. Then it was up to my client to prove there was actually that much jewelry inside the box. We couldn't, of course. The jury gave us twenty-five thousand dollars just because they knew something was fishy. I suspect that the bank threw one hell of a Christmas party that year."

"Are you saying that's what happened here?"

"I don't know," said Jack. "But from my experience in the Cayman Islands, the bank isn't going to tell us squat until they've lined up their own legal defense."

There was silence on the line. Then Paulo said, "How soon till you hear back on the fingerprint check?"

"Could be within the hour," said Danen.

"Good. Stay in Nassau and do the follow-through with the bank in the morning."

Jack said, "You want me to stay here, too?"

"No," said Paulo. "I have to start a dialogue with

Falcon. It's too damn quiet inside that motel room, so I'm going to make the call as soon as we hang up."

"Be careful with that," said Jack. "The more you talk to him, the sooner the battery on that cell phone wears out. And he warned us what happens then."

"I know. But I've waited as long as I can. We've got to start talking, make sure he's not freaking out on us. At the very least, I need to be able to reassure him and tell him that you're on your way back from the bank."

"All right," said Jack. "I'll see you before sunrise."

24

Theo remained on the floor, his cheek pressed to the carpet. His head was throbbing from Falcon's blow.

It had been a good half hour since Falcon had removed the pillowcase from the girl's head, but her breathing was still shallow and rapid. It seemed that she just couldn't get enough air. Fear could do that to a person. At least Theo hoped it was fear. This was neither the time nor the place for a real medical emergency.

Theo was still staring at those shoes on the bathroom floor. They had twitched once or twice, but the person behind the closed door was doing an impressive job of remaining absolutely still and quiet. Theo wondered if he should try to make contact with him—he assumed it was a *him*, based on the shoes.

Falcon continued to pace furiously, practically wearing a path in the carpet. Had he sat for just a moment, or taken a position at the window, that would have been Theo's chance to slip a whisper through the slat beneath the door: "Tap your foot once if you're alone. Tap twice if you have a gun." Theo wasn't the type to sit around and wait for someone else to solve his problems. But if he was going to make a move against Falcon, he needed to know who was on his side, whether they could be of any help, or whether they'd just be in the way. As it was, Theo could only wait for the right opportunity.

"Relax, why don't you?" Theo told his captor.

Falcon ignored him. His lips were moving furiously. The guy was deep in conversation, perhaps rehearsing his lines, perhaps fighting off the demons in his head.

"Dude, give it a rest," said Theo.

Falcon stopped, looked down at Theo, and pointed the gun at his knee. "You interrupt me one more time, and you'll be setting off metal detectors for the rest of your life. You understand me?"

Had Theo been just a foot closer, he could have hooked Falcon behind the knee and brought him to the floor with a roundhouse kick. But then what? Theo's hands were bound behind his waist, the girl beside him was tied up, and Theo had no way of knowing whether the guy who was hiding in the bathroom would come out to help or sit tight and let Falcon shoot them. Theo said, "Yeah, I understand you."

"Good. Now get up off the floor."

Theo didn't move. It gave him a sinking feeling, the thought of breaking off any chance to communicate with the man in the bathroom.

"Now! Up against the wall, next to the girl."

Slowly, Theo complied. It was just as well. He'd seen enough cop shows on television to know that the two most dangerous points in time for hostages were right off the bat, at the taking, and later, when someone tried to escape. It was like flying: takeoffs and landings accounted for ninety-nine percent of the fatalities. They'd made it through the takeoff, so to speak. Halfway home. He needed a plan of attack, not a knee-jerk reaction, if they were going to bring this baby home for a safe landing. Until he had a game plan, it was a virtual certainty that all hell would break loose when that bathroom door opened.

"I have to pee," the girl said.

"Hold it," said Falcon.

Damn straight, cross your legs, thought Theo.

"I can't. I've been holding it for two hours. Please, just let me go to the bathroom."

Falcon made a face. "All right. I'll let you use the bathroom. But if you try anything," he said, aiming the gun to Theo's head, "the black guy gets it. *Comprende?*"

She nodded.

Beautiful, thought Theo. *Just beautiful*.

The phone rang. Theo recognized the ring as his own, but his cell phone was in Falcon's pocket. Falcon froze. The pulsing ring continued. Three times. A fourth.

"You gonna answer that?" said Theo.

It rang a fifth time, then a sixth. A chime followed— way too cheery-sounding for the circumstances—

indicating that the unanswered call was going to voice mail. Falcon stood frozen, as if paralyzed with indecision.

At the front of the room, the opening above the drapes suddenly brightened. The cops had switched on a spotlight in the parking lot. Theo heard the click of a public address system outside, then an amplified voice that sounded almost mechanical.

"Falcon, it's me. Vince Paulo. I'm dialing again. Answer the phone, please."

There was utter silence for thirty seconds. No one moved.

Then the phone started to ring again.

"If he doesn't answer this time," said Chavez, "it's time to start thinking about a breach."

A breach meant a forced entry. Vince wasn't ready to go there yet. "He'll answer."

He waited in the silence of the cool night air, precious seconds ticking away with each hollow, unanswered ring of the telephone. The call went to the sixth ring, and then Theo's voice-mail message came again. Vince ended the call.

"How much longer do you intend to keep this up?" said Chavez.

"It's early. I know this guy. It takes a while to get him talking."

"How long can you stay sharp without sleep?"

It was a fair question, but it suddenly had Vince wondering about his medication. It was back at his house. Even if he'd brought it with him, he couldn't take it, since it made him sleepy. Antidepressants, however, weren't something to stop cold-turkey. He hadn't missed a dose since starting the prescription six months ago. One night would probably be okay. But what if this standoff stretched into two? Or three? Or longer? "I'll let you know when it's time to make a change."

"They could all be dead in there already," said Chavez. "I think you should get on the PA again and tell him to answer the phone or we're coming in."

"Let's hold off on the threats, okay?" Vince redialed the number. This time, the phone rang three times and stopped, but there was only silence on the line. Vince gripped the receiver a little tighter. "Falcon, are you there?" No one answered, but the line was definitely open. "Falcon, this is Vince Paulo."

"What do you want?"

Vince tried not to sound too happy to have a voice on the line. "Just checking in. Wanted to make sure everything is okay."

"Passable. I would have liked a view of the swimming pool, but what can you expect without a reservation?"

A sense of humor was a good sign. Guys on the edge rarely cracked a joke. "Are you hungry?" said Vince.

"I live in a car, remember, asshole? I been hungry for eleven years."

"We could get you some food. How about some burgers?"

"Sounds good."

"How many?"

"Two. Some french fries, too."

"How about for the rest of the gang?"

"Sure. Bring some for them, too."

"How many burgers we talking about then?"

"I don't know. Bring two more."

"One for each of them?"

"Yeah. One apiece. That's enough."

Vince raised two fingers, signaling to the others. He'd confirmed it: two hostages inside, no more. "Okay, that's four burgers and some french fries. I'll throw in some drinks, too. But you know how this works, Falcon. We've done this before. My boss won't let me give you something for nothing."

"I can pay for it. Just as soon as Swyteck brings me my money."

Vince had to handle this one carefully. Sooner or later they needed to address the missing money, but this negotiation was doomed if he didn't let Falcon know straight up that he couldn't just send his lawyer out for cash and then buy whatever he needed. "It's not a matter of money, Falcon. Why don't you let the hostages go?"

"Why don't you stop talking shit?"

"This is not doing any of us any good, Falcon. I can't help you with innocent people at gunpoint."

"I'm not letting them go."

"I can understand how you might think that way, but let me be straight with you. This is not a threat. All I'm trying to do is give you an accurate picture of what's going on out here. The police have surrounded the entire building. There are City of Miami cops here. Miami-Dade Police

Department is here, too. They have shut down the entire neighborhood. Escape is not an option. So let's make a deal here and now, all right? You don't try an escape, I don't send in the SWAT. We cool with that?"

Falcon didn't answer. Vince saw that as a good sign. Immediate rejection punctuated with profanity would have been a bad sign. "I understand you have a woman in there with you. Is that right?"

Still no answer.

"Can you tell us her name?" Vince waited, but he got no reply. "Maybe you don't know her name. Why don't you ask her and tell us?"

"Sure thing," said Falcon. The ensuing silence was long enough for Vince to build up hope that Falcon had covered the mouthpiece and was actually speaking to his hostage.

"She says her name is Amelia Earhart, and she wants to talk to Geraldo."

Geraldo? thought Vince. Obviously, he hadn't watched television lately. "That's a good one, Falcon. But it's important for us to know her name."

"I told you enough already."

"Yeah, you're probably right. You just take your time and think about what I said before. And think hard about letting those hostages go. It would count for a lot if you did, Falcon. Judges like it when you show some goodwill."

"Who the hell are you to be talking about goodwill? You told me to come down from the bridge and I could talk to Alicia Mendoza. That didn't happen, did it, Paulo?"

"Things are going to be handled different this time."

"No they aren't. You lied then, and you'll lie again this time."

The mood swing was startling. Vince had to bring back that guy with the sense of humor who answered the phone. "I won't lie to you."

"Like hell you won't. Liars always lie. And you are a total liar!"

"Falcon, come on, man."

"Just bring me my food and stop jerking me around."

"I'll call you just as soon as it gets here."

"No, don't you *ever* call me again. I don't want no cops calling me. The next voice I hear on this line better be Jack Swyteck telling me he's got my money."

"What about the food?"

"I just want my money."

"Calm down, okay?"

"Don't you be telling me to calm down! I'm in control here, not you."

"Let's work this out together."

"Together, my ass!"

"You've got two hostages. Why not let one go?"

"I ain't letting nobody go."

"Falcon, listen to me. Let one of the hostages go, and you can talk to Swyteck. You don't need two hostages. You only need one."

"That's exactly right. All I need is one. So get me Swyteck, and bring me my money, or someone's gonna die over here long before the battery on this phone ever does."

Falcon disconnected. Vince couldn't see the expressions on the faces around him, but he didn't need to.

"You okay?" said Chavez.

Vince felt his hand shaking just a bit as he put the phone down. "Yeah, I'm good."

"What now?"

Vince said, "I can't call him again without Swyteck standing by. As soon as his plane lands, let's get him here. ASAP."

25

"C an I *please* use the bathroom now?" she said.

The renewed plea from his fellow hostage made Theo cringe. Watching Falcon's meltdown in the middle of a phone conversation with the negotiator should have been more than enough to take her mind off of her bladder. Theo couldn't understand why she would say something to provoke him now. Either she was really stupid, or she really had to go. Or maybe, it suddenly occurred to him, she had a plan of her own.

She was sitting on the floor, her back against the wall, right beside Theo. He guessed she was nineteen, maybe twenty, but she was wearing way too much makeup, so it was difficult to tell. She was definitely Latin, with pretty features and a classic, heart-shaped face. Her getup, however, was strictly about sex appeal. Big gold-hoop earrings played against her olive skin and her long, chestnut hair. Her breasts were neither large nor small, but the contraption she was wearing beneath her low-cut blouse had pinched the B-cups together and nearly pushed them up to her chin. The deep red lipstick and heavy eye shadow were the perfect complement to her tight skirt, black heels, and fishnet stockings. Theo didn't like to judge people, but he knew he wasn't holed up with a nun.

"I need to go," she said. "I need to go *now*."

"Shut up!" said Falcon. "No one's going anywhere!"

"I meant to the bathroom."

Her response didn't seem to register with Falcon. He had a vacant look in his eyes, as if part of him had just checked out. "You can't drink now," he said.

"I don't want a drink. I need to use the bathroom."

"It's too soon."

"In thirty seconds, it will be too *late*."

"If you drink now, you'll die."

She and Theo exchanged uneasy glances. Falcon was speaking to the young woman, but it was as if he were having another conversation.

"What are you talking about?" she said in a tentative voice.

Falcon started to pace—not the slow, peripatetic movements of a man in contemplation, but a relentless and angry back-and-forth, from one side of the room to the other. "Just shut up, shut up!" he said, slapping his left ear with one hand, clutching the gun with the other. It was the most agitated Theo had seen him since the standoff's beginning. Neither he nor the young woman said a word.

"Quit your damn whining," said Falcon. "Ask the doctor. He'll tell you. If you drink water now, you'll die. Do you hear me? You'll just die on me! Is that what you want to happen?"

They weren't sure if Falcon wanted a response, so they were silent.

"Answer me! Is that what you want?"

She shrank against the wall, as if wishing that she could just disappear. It was a scary situation to begin with, and his harsh tone was clearly pushing her to the edge. Theo said, "Leave her alone."

"What did you say?" Falcon said sharply.

"I said leave her alone."

"*Qué es su número?*"

"Say what?"

"*Qué es su número?*"

"I don't speak Spanish, man."

The Latina whispered through her teeth to Theo, her lips barely moving. "He wants to know your number."

"What number? You mean my phone number?"

"No, no!" shouted Falcon. "*Su número!*"

"I got no idea what you're talking about, dude."

His eyes filled with rage. He pointed his gun at the woman. "You want me to shoot the bitch? Do you?"

"I don't want you to shoot nobody."

"Then why do you make me do these things? Why?"

"No one's making you do nothin'," said Theo. "Everybody's cool."

"I don't care if you're thirsty. Do you *want* to die? Is that it?"

"I said it's cool, dude," said Theo. "Ain't nobody here who wants to die."

"Because giving her water right now would be just like squeezing this trigger and putting a bullet between her eyes. Do you understand what I'm saying?"

He might as well have been speaking Spanish again. Or Chinese. "Makes perfect sense to me. No problem. Whatever you say, we're cool with it."

"Maybe you just wish you were dead. Is that it? Do you think you'd be better off dead?"

Theo said, "Hey, here's an idea. Just forget the water, the bathroom, and whatever else it is that's got you pissed. Forget everything she said. Okay, boss?"

Falcon kept pacing. A mixture of tension and confusion hung in the air. In the dimly lit room, and under these trying circumstances, it would have been difficult to read anyone's expression. Not even Sigmund Freud, however, could have made heads or tails of this character and this outburst. Did Falcon hear what they were saying and simply misinterpret their words? Or did the sound of their voices trigger entirely distinct and distant voices inside his head? Theo wasn't sure.

Falcon stepped away from them, shaking his head in disgust. "You know what? Go ahead and drink the damn water. See if I care." He began to pace again.

Theo made eye contact with the young woman beside him, and they came to a silent understanding. This was a bad situation, and it was only deteriorating. It was too dangerous to sit around and wait for rescuers. They had to help themselves.

They needed to enlist that man in the bathroom. Theo whispered, "What's your name?"

"Natalia."

"Okay, Natalia. Does your friend in the bathroom have a gun?"

Falcon wheeled and started toward them. She waited until he crossed the room, made the turn again, and resumed pacing in the other direction, his back toward the hostages. Then she leaned closer to Theo and whispered in a voice that quaked, "I sure hope so."

The door to the police command center opened. The footsteps were too heavy to be Alicia's. Paulo turned at the approaching sound. Blind for over six months, and sometimes he still wheeled to face whatever it was that startled him, as if he could see it. He wondered when that instinct would leave him, if it would ever leave him completely. "Chavez?" said Paulo.

"Yeah, it's me. Got Daden on the line from Nassau. He needs to talk to you." He put the cell phone in Paulo's hand.

Paulo felt a surge of adrenaline. He needed a fresh angle with Falcon, and he hoped that Daden and the Bahamian connection would supply it. "What do you have for me?" he said into the telephone.

Daden's voice was hurried, excited. "Fingerprint search on the handwritten note we found in the safe deposit box just came back. There was a match."

"Who is it?"

"Unfortunately, we don't have a name."

"You just said there was a match."

"There was."

"Then who is it?"

"Last week, when the lab pulled that extraneous print from Officer Mendoza's compact, they entered it into the FBI's data bank. Well, that's our match."

"Wait a second," said Paulo. "You're saying that the person who stole Alicia's purse from that bar in Coral Gables is the same person who took the money from Falcon's safe deposit box in the Bahamas?"

"That's not what I'm saying. That's what the fingerprint tells us."

Paulo thought for a moment, wondering if there could have been some kind of mistake. He knew better. "Fingerprints don't lie," he said.

"No, sir. They sure don't."

26

Jack kept his promise to Sergeant Paulo. He was back in Miami before sunrise—barely.

Seaplanes were meant to land at five a.m. Government Cut, the man-made channel that connected the Port of Miami to the Atlantic, was like a sheet of glass—no chop, no wakes, no beer-chugging morons showing off their brand-new boats and their total ignorance of the rules of right of way. Jack had managed to catch an hour of sleep on the flight from Nassau, not long enough to refresh him but he took what he could get. The landing was so smooth—or perhaps Jack was just so out of it—that he would have kept right on sleeping had Zack not shouted the operative word.

"Fire!"

Jack shot out of his chair like—well, like a man running out of a burning airplane. He caught his bearings, and when he finally managed to focus, he saw Zack smiling back at him. "Was that supposed to be funny?"

"Sorry, dude. I called your name fifteen times, and you just kept snoring."

Jack could have rattled off a dozen different ways to wake someone from a deep sleep, none of which induced cardiac arrest, but he let it go. Zack was obviously one of those delightful adults who still thought of wedgies and short-sheeting the bed as a barrel of laughs.

Man, do I miss Theo.

A City of Miami squad car was waiting at the dock. Jack got in the backseat, and they rode straight up Biscayne Boulevard, stopped at the traffic-control checkpoint, and then continued north.

A dawn of early-morning shadows crept across the evacuated city streets. The police presence had grown substantially since Jack's departure, much larger than Jack had expected. Every conceivable side street had been shut down. In addition to the MDPD and the City of Miami police, Florida state troopers had come onto the scene. Snipers were posted on rooftops. Squad cars and SWAT vans filled the parking lot outside the fast-food restaurant that was now the site of a mobile command center. Police air coverage had replaced the media choppers. As night turned into morning, members of the media and a few curious onlookers were beginning to gather at the police barricades on Biscayne Boulevard.

Seeing all this firepower in the morning hours, and seeing the crowd at the barricades, sent a strange image flashing through Jack's mind. He was reminded of a certain autumn night in northeastern

Florida, outside the Florida State Prison. A group of demonstrators—some supporting the death penalty, others against it—had gathered in an all-night vigil. They crowded as near to the prison gate as the state troopers would allow. A cold fog stirred in anticipation of the warm morning air, as if the sliver of sunshine on the horizon signaled much more than just the dawn of another day. Theo Knight was less than an hour away from his date with the electric chair. His head and ankles had already been shaved to ensure a clean contact for the electrodes that would pass twenty-five hundred volts through his body. Jack had said his good-byes. It was the closest he would ever come to losing Theo—much closer than any lawyer should ever come to burying a client who was innocent. Back then, it was the state doing everything within its power to put Theo Knight to death. Jack's own father, Governor Harry Swyteck, had even signed the death warrant. Now, years later, and just a few blocks away from the neighborhood in which a fifteen-year-old Theo had been arrested for murder, an army of police officers had been deployed to save Theo's life. The executioner this time was not Jack's father but one of Jack's clients. The guilty executing the innocent. The ironies were piling up too quickly for Jack to absorb. It was like his *abuela* used to say in yet another one of those Cuban expressions that her culturally challenged grandson could never seem to remember, but it boiled down to this: Life was full of sharp turns in the road.

Jack wondered if his client—his friend—would beat the odds again.

The squad car drove right past the mobile command center. Jack leaned forward and tapped on the steel grate that separated the front from the backseat. "We just passed it."

"We're not going there yet," the cop said.

"Where are we headed?"

He didn't answer right away. Jack said, "Paulo said he wanted me there ASAP. Where are you taking me?"

"The mayor needs to speak to you."

"What about?"

The cop didn't answer. They turned at the corner and pulled into a parking garage. The squad car stopped. The driver got out and opened Jack's door. Jack climbed out of the backseat. The cop nodded toward a dark blue sedan parked at the end of the row. The click of Jack's heels echoed off concrete walls as he approached the vehicle. Jack was two steps away when he heard the power locks release. The passenger door opened a little and then swung out all the way, as if pushed from the inside. Jack climbed into the passenger seat and closed the door.

Mayor Raul Mendoza was seated behind the wheel. "Hello, Jack."

"Mr. Mayor," he said flatly.

The mayor laid an unlit cigar on the dashboard. The tip had been chewed flat, as the mayor had been sucking tobacco to work off stress. "We didn't do so well in our phone conversation last week," said the mayor. "I was hoping that the personal touch might make a difference."

"That depends on what you want to talk about."

He paused, seeming to measure his words. "Look, you and I are on the same side here. I think we can agree on a few simple facts. One, this Falcon character is a nutcase who is fully capable of cold-blooded murder. Two, he has your friend. And three, he wants my daughter."

"Has he asked to speak to her?"

"Not yet. But he will. And when he does, I want your word that you will not let it happen."

"How is that my department?"

"I'm not saying that the City of Miami Police Department is a sieve, but I *am* the mayor. I'm told that Falcon wants to talk to you. And if he plays ball and gives up something in return, they'll agree to put you on the phone."

"They want me to negotiate with him?"

" 'Negotiate' might not be the right word. I'm sure that your dialogue will be scripted, or at least highly coached. But yes, they are going to let you talk to him."

"I'm okay with that, I guess."

The mayor flashed a sardonic smile. He took the cigar from the dashboard and tucked it into the corner of his mouth. "That's very nice," he said, the cigar wagging as he spoke. "But this isn't a pep talk, pal. It's about ground rules. My rules."

"Your rules?"

"Yeah." He removed the cigar and said, "When

you get on that phone, I'm sure that Falcon is going to demand to speak with Alicia. I don't care how much you want to appease this guy, or what Paulo tells you to say. I don't care if Falcon puts a gun to your friend's head or if he threatens to blow up the entire building. Do not hand that phone to my daughter. Period."

"Well, wait just a second. As I told you when we had our little telephone conversation about Falcon's bail, I'm sympathetic to a father's concerns for his daughter. But I intend to do what the negotiators tell me to do."

"Do you want to get your friend killed?"

"No, of course not."

"Then listen to me. Vince Paulo has this enormous set of balls that makes him believe that a face-to-face talk with a hostage-taker is a good idea. That's what happened last time, when everything literally blew up in his face. Now he's blind, and this time he'll need someone to take him by the arm and walk him into another death-trap. I'm not going to let that person be Alicia."

"Just because we put her on the telephone doesn't mean that she's headed for an up-close and personal talk with the gunman."

"It's the first step. Clearly, Falcon is obsessed with my daughter. For crying out loud, he stole her lipstick and sent her that sick 'It's only out of love that I seek you' e-mail."

"You need to check your department sources, mayor. They're not so sure it was Falcon who did either of those things."

"Are you denying that this guy has a thing for my daughter?"

Jack remembered his first meeting with Falcon, the look in Falcon's eye when they spoke about Alicia. "No. I don't deny it. But she's a cop, and if letting her talk to Falcon can get a hostage released, I'm all for it. I think we should trust the negotiators on this."

"I trust *nobody*, all right? Do you—" He started to say something, then stopped. At first, Jack thought he was trying to control his anger, but it seemed that some other emotion was at work. "Do you have any idea what it's like to lose—"

Jack waited for him to finish, but again the mayor stopped himself. The mayor was looking straight ahead, toward his own reflection in the windshield, making no eye contact with Jack as he continued in a solemn voice. "I don't talk about this very often, but Alicia's mother is my second wife. I was married once before. Had another daughter." He paused, then added, "She was eight years old when she died."

"I'm sorry."

"September sixteenth, nineteen seventy-four. Isabel and her mother were in a pastry shop in Buenos Aires. They had been out shopping, had their bags and packages with them. They decided to stop for something sweet before coming home. They were just sitting there at the counter, having a perfect little mother-daughter day."

Jack was watching him, but the mayor was still looking through the windshield, staring out at nothing.

"And out of the blue," the mayor said, his voice starting to quake. He swallowed hard to regain his composure. "Out of the blue, there was this huge explosion. A bomb. Some crazy terrorist son of a bitch had decided to blow up a bank branch right next to innocent shoppers. Can you imagine anyone doing such a thing?"

Jack could, but he wished he couldn't.

"About forty bombs were exploded around the country just on that day alone. My wife was dead at the scene. Our daughter died in the hospital, two days later."

"I had no idea. I truly am sorry."

The two men sat in silence. Jack wasn't sure what to say. Would it really have mattered if he had promised to do everything in his power to keep Alicia out of the hostage negotiations? Or was the mayor simply trying to close old wounds—trying to convince himself that, this time around, he was doing everything he possibly could to protect his daughter, even if his demands on Jack were not entirely reasonable, even if his fears for Alicia were not completely rational? Finally, the mayor leaned over the console, reached across Jack's torso, and grabbed the passenger-door handle. The invasion of personal space made Jack uneasy.

"Keep my daughter out of this," the mayor said as he pushed the door open for Jack. "Or we may both regret it."

It had almost sounded like a threat, but the situation was too delicate, too ambiguous, for Jack to challenge him on it. Jack offered a little nod, wanting to give the man something, if only out of pity for what had happened to the Mendoza family more than a quarter-century ago. Then he climbed out of the car and closed the door.

The engine started, and the mayor drove away.

27

It was still dark in Nassau when Riley returned home from the Greater Bahamian Bank & Trust Company. He was exhausted, annoyed, and determined to get another two hours of sleep before meeting with the bank's attorneys about the safe deposit box matter. He was forced to deal with lawyers far too often to suit his own preferences. Probably the only thing that wasn't secret about the offshore banking industry was that the secrecy regulations and the endless challenges to them had made plenty of lawyers rich.

Riley climbed the front steps to his townhouse slowly. The sprawling tropical canopy over his front yard blocked out the glow of the street lamp, and he'd neglected to turn on a porch light before rushing out the front door to meet Swyteck and the others at the bank. The door was unlocked, just as he'd left it. Crime wasn't exactly unheard of in the Bahamas, but something about island living seemed to encourage unlocked doors and open windows, as if to deny, or at least defy, the existence of evil in paradise. Riley entered the foyer and tried the wall switch. The room remained dark. No great surprise. Power outages were a way of life in his neighborhood. He closed the door and waited for his eyes to adjust before trying to cross the room. He was about to take his first step when, from the other side of the living room, he heard the distinctive cocking of a revolver.

"Stop right there, Riley."

He froze in his tracks. The voice was familiar, though he might not have recognized it so quickly if he hadn't just spent the night dealing with box 266. "News must travel pretty fast." He was trying to sound breezy, but he couldn't conceal his nervousness.

"It's a small world, Riley. Even a smaller island."

"That it is, mon." Riley's eyes were adjusting to the darkness, but the man was still just a shadow in a black corner of the room. Not that Riley would have recognized him. In their past dealings, he had only heard the man's voice, never seen his face. The fact that he'd cut off the electricity at the circuit breaker signaled his clear intention to keep it that way.

The gunman said, "I hear that someone finally cleaned out box two sixty-six."

"You hear correctly."

"Who was it?"

"I can't tell you that."

The man's chuckle was laden with insincerity. "Good answer."

"It's the only answer I can give you."

"I can live with that," the man said, and then his tone became sterner. "So long as it's also the only answer you can give to the police."

"That's up to the bank and its lawyers."

"Wrong answer."

Riley waited for him to say more, but there was only a long, uncomfortable silence. Several strands of speculation began to race through his mind, and none of them ended in a very happy place. Riley could not escape the conclusion that the man was simply debating whether to shoot him here, in Riley's own living room, or to take him somewhere else and do the job.

"Here's my problem," the man said finally.

Riley's throat was dry, and he had to force his response. "Yes?"

"Police are such nosy bastards. If you tell them who cleaned out the money, what do you think their next question is going to be?"

"I—I don't know, mon."

"Think about it."

"I'm having a little trouble concentrating right now. I'm sorry. I'm sure the bank's lawyers will have an answer."

"Screw the lawyers. You ask them for a straight answer, they'll give you six wishy-washy ones and bill you for twelve. Let's keep this simple. I'll answer it, and you tell me if you agree with me. All right?"

The gun made it difficult for Riley to disagree. "Sure, mon."

"When the police find out who took the money, they'll have just one question: How the hell did all that cash get there in the first place?"

Riley said nothing.

The gunman continued, "Don't you agree?"

"I suppose so," said Riley.

"Stop being coy with me. Do you agree or not?"

"Yes. I agree."

"Now, here's something else I'm sure we can both agree on. If the police unravel this money trail all the way to its source, things are going to get very ugly for you."

Riley said nothing.

"Can we agree on that, Riley?"

Riley swallowed hard. He wanted to speak, but his mouth wouldn't move. He was too afraid of saying the wrong thing.

The man said, "I need your agreement on that, friend. Because if I don't get it, I'm going to have to kill you right here and now."

Riley could hear himself breathing. He'd dealt with some unsavory characters in his time. Bank secrecy had its dark side. But no one had ever threatened his life, at least not in such a matter-of-fact tone. There was no doubt in Riley's mind that the man meant every word of it. "Okay," he said, his voice little more than a peep.

"Okay *what*?" the man said.

"No one will ever find out where that money came from."

"Good answer, Riley. That's a very good answer."

He rose from the chair, a silhouette in the darkness. The face was obscured in shadows, but Riley could detect the faintest outline of a gun.

"On the floor," the man said. "Face down."

Somewhere in the back of his mind, a voice cried out, begging Riley to resist. He tried to ignore it, but he continued to hear the warning over and over, as he lowered himself to the floor and laid his cheek against the rug. The man approached, and Riley could feel the vibration of each heavy footfall. The man stopped, towering over him, and Riley could see only the tops of his shoes.

He imagined that the gun was pointed directly at the back of his head, and tomorrow's headlines quickly flashed through his brain: "Banker Found Dead in Home, Shot Execution-Style."

"Count to a thousand, out loud," the man said. "Don't even think about getting up before you finish."

Riley started counting.

"Too fast. Slower."

Riley started over again. One, two, three. The man walked away. Nine, ten, eleven. The front door opened. Fifteen, sixteen, seventeen. Riley heard it close. He didn't move a muscle, but his voice was shaking.

He didn't stop counting until the first signs of daylight shone through the slatted wooden shutters.

28

Miami's cold wave was coming to an end. Theo could feel it. The motel room was getting hotter, stuffier by the minute. It was growing brighter, too. Flickers of sunlight filtered through the top of the old drapes and broke over the heaping barricade of overturned furniture and mattresses like dawn over a hilltop. If Theo could somehow crawl across the room and yank those drapes off the window, the snipers might be able to scope the interior, over the mound of furniture, and take a shot. He assumed there were snipers out there. Those guys lived for the chance to shoot something other than the ink out of a bull's-eye at two hundred yards. All they needed was an opening, one kill shot straight to the head. Game over. The cop-killer would be dead. Unless they were under the impression that it was Theo who had shot those police officers. Surely, Jack had explained to them that the black dude wasn't one of the bad guys. But would they believe it? Or would they see nothing more than a criminal defense lawyer covering for his old client? They must have pulled his record by now and seen that Jack had sprung him loose from death row. It wouldn't matter that DNA evidence had proved him innocent. Like everyone else who professed to "know" about Theo's past, they would assume that he'd gotten off on a technicality, that his clever lawyer had thrown some legal bullshit up against the wall and it stuck. They'd see a murderer in the crosshairs and a chance to serve the ends of justice—delayed but not denied. First shot, Falcon. Second shot, the black piece of shit who deserved to die. A tragic mistake. What a pity.

Calm down, Theo told himself. *Maybe the sniper's a brother.*

"Hey, mister," said Natalia. "Are you ever going to let us use the bathroom?"

Falcon looked in her direction. She'd apparently roused him from some very deep thoughts, as it took a moment for her request to register. "Use what?" he said.

"The bathroom," said Theo. "We been sitting here for six hours."

Falcon was standing at the front door. He pressed his eye to the peephole and stole one more quick peek of the parking lot, then turned and walked to Natalia. "She goes first."

"It's okay," she said. "Let him go."

"Shut up! If I say you're first, then you go first. Do you hear me?"

She glanced nervously at Theo. Their voices were loud enough to carry into the bathroom, and they both knew that all hell would break loose when Falcon opened the door. It would have been a stretch to call it a coordinated effort, but Theo was obviously the better point man on this side of the bathroom door.

"Okay," she said. "I'll go first."

Both Theo and Natalia had their hands tied behind their backs, and Falcon had bound their ankles tightly with electrical cords that he had yanked from the lamps. Falcon knelt down slowly, pointing his gun straight at her face. With the free hand, he loosened the cord around her ankles so that she could walk. Then he grabbed her by the hair and pulled her up so hard it cocked her head sideways, her cheek practically lying on her shoulder. She was sandwiched between Falcon and the wall as he jammed the gun under her chin and aimed straight at her brain. "Do not try anything," he said.

"Don't worry, I won't."

Her clothing was tight, and Falcon seemed to like the feel of his body against hers. "And the door stays open," he said.

"You mean you're going to watch me use the bathroom?"

A vacant smile creased his lips. "Aren't you used to it, *jinitera*?"

"Hey," said Theo. "There's no need to be calling her that."

"I thought you didn't speak Spanish."

"Do you seriously think there's a bartender in Miami who doesn't know how to say 'prostitute' *en español*?"

"Do you seriously think it's worth taking a bullet to defend this one's honor?"

Theo didn't answer. Falcon kept the gun trained on the back of Natalia's head as he nudged her forward and followed directly behind her. From the standpoint of a potential escape, it was unfortunate positioning. If Natalia's friend in the bathroom did have a gun, it would have been difficult to get off a clean shot at Falcon without wounding or killing her in the process.

Theo remained on the floor. It was just a few steps from his seat against the wall to the bathroom, and his angle offered a clear view of the door. He had been trying to loosen the bindings around his wrists for hours, with little progress. The cord around his ankles was equally secure. If something good was to come of this, it was up to Natalia and her friend.

Natalia was taking small, deliberate steps toward the bathroom door, as if plotting her next move. Theo wondered if the man inside was ready to rise to the occasion. Was he standing at the ready, hammer cocked and prepared to fire? Was he any kind of a shot at all, or would bullets fly wildly in every direction? Would he lose his nerve and freeze up? Did he even have a gun?

Falcon reached past Natalia and grasped the doorknob. Theo prepared to scoot forward and roll, if need be, to help overpower Falcon. Falcon turned the knob and pushed the door open.

Out of the darkness, a white blur shot, like a linebacker racing through the open doorway. With it came a scream so loud and shrill that it chilled

Theo and completely disoriented Falcon. The man emerged from hiding and slammed into Natalia, pushing her against Falcon. The momentum sent all three of them sailing across the dressing area and crashing against the wall. Falcon hit first, then Natalia, followed by her friend. The combined impact dislodged the gun and sent it flying through the air. Natalia was kicking furiously, and her friend was pummeling Falcon with both fists, as the gun hit the tile floor. Theo immediately rolled toward it, but it was sliding away from him. He was quickly entangled in the two-on-one dogfight against Falcon, but out of the corner of his eye, he noticed another woman hiding in the bathtub.

"Get the gun!" shouted Theo.

She didn't move. The bathroom had no windows, no source of light, making it difficult for Theo to see her. But he could see enough in the shadows.

"Damn it, get the—" he started to say, but Falcon's boot caught him squarely in the mouth. Falcon sprang to his feet, and he was regaining control. He shoved Natalia aside, grabbed her friend by the shirt, and slammed the man's head into the wall. The guy went down in a heap, dazed if not unconscious. Falcon rolled to his right and snatched up his gun.

"Nobody move!"

Theo froze. Natalia was on the floor, her shirt torn and blood coming from her nose. Her friend appeared to be breathing, but he was otherwise motionless, facedown.

Falcon was shaking, more angry than frightened.

"You planned this!" he said. "I told you not to try anything!"

Theo glanced toward the bathtub again. He could see her hand draped over the side of the tub, and the top of her head. *Come on, baby. It's now or never.*

"I should kill you for this!" said Falcon as he thrust the pistol in Natalia's direction.

"Don't shoot me, please!"

"Why shouldn't I?"

"I'm only eighteen. Please, don't do this to me."

Falcon was breathing heavy, staring at Natalia. Then he turned the gun toward Theo. "I guess that leaves you, big guy."

"I don't think you want to do that," said Theo.

"Oh, then you don't know me very well," said Falcon.

"You fire that gun, and the cops will be in here in two seconds flat."

"Who said anything about a gun?" Falcon reached inside his coat pocket and pulled out a steak knife. Homeless people were like walking kitchens. Theo wondered what else he had in there. Another ammunition clip, maybe? In the tussle, Theo had definitely felt something under that bulky coat. Falcon must have known that the police were searching for him after that body was found in the trunk of his car. Had he prepared himself for a standoff?

"The cops are probably on their way in here already," said Theo.

"Nice try," said Falcon.

There was a groan, then a gurgling sound, from inside the bathroom. Falcon and Theo both shot a look through the open doorway. The woman still hadn't moved from the bathtub, and she showed no reaction when Falcon pointed his gun at her.

"Don't move!" shouted Falcon, but she seemed to have no such intention. Falcon stepped into the doorway and flipped the light switch. Nothing happened. Apparently, he'd forgotten that they were without electricity. He dug into his coat pocket again, found a disposable lighter, and kicked up a flame that brightened the bathroom.

Only then did Theo notice the blood.

Falcon let out a scream that was beyond shock, beyond fear, beyond the most harrowing screech of a mortally wounded animal. It lasted a good ten seconds, and when he stopped to take a breath, he slammed the door and stepped away, trembling with each tentative step backward.

He was staring at the door, taking aim with his pistol, as if he expected it to open at any moment. Nothing happened. There was not another sound. Finally, he raised a fist and shouted toward the bathroom, shouted at the top of his voice, "No, no, damn it! Not *you* again!"

29

Vince Paulo was at the mobile command center when he caught a blip of radio squelch in his earpiece. The excited voice of one of the officers outside the motel room followed.

"I think we heard a scream from inside the room, Sergeant."

Vince keyed his microphone. "You sure?"

"Yeah. I heard it. Jonesy says he heard it too."

"Man or woman?"

"Man, I think."

Vince keyed his mike again and summoned up his audio specialist. "Bolton, what are you picking up in there?" She took a moment to respond, and Vince imagined that she was adjusting the controls, trying to get a clearer transmission. "It sounds like some kind of argument going on, sir."

"Do you have a video feed yet?"

"Negative. When Swyteck's car crashed into the building, it crushed the AC ducts leading to the room. There's no place to snake the transmission line. Our tech team planted these listening devices

as close as we could, but until we have a green light
to enter the next room and plant something right
on the adjoining wall, it's not going to give us what
we want."

"Can you isolate on anything?"

"I tried separating out some background noises,
but it's just a screech to me. If the officers on site say
it was a man's scream, I've got no reason to doubt it."

"Got it, thanks," said Vince.

Chavez said, "If he's savaging the hostages, we
need to breach."

Vince took a moment, thinking.

Chavez said, "What are you waiting for, gunshots?"

Vince picked up the phone and dialed. "If he
doesn't answer, we breach."

Falcon was staring at the cell phone on the floor as if
it were some kind of chirping alien. It rang a second
time, and then a third.

"You better answer it," said Theo.

"Quiet!" It rang two more times. Nobody moved.
Then, on the sixth ring, Falcon sprang like a cat,
grabbed it, and hit the talk button. "Swyteck?" he
said in a hoarse whisper.

"It's me, Vince Paulo."

"I told you I didn't want to hear from no more
cops," he said, the anger coming through, even in
a whisper.

"We heard a scream. Is everything okay in there?"

"Where's Swyteck?"

"Why are you whispering?"

He gnawed his lower lip, wincing like a man in pain. "Tell me where Swyteck is."

"He's on his way back from the bank. He'll be here in a little while. Now, like I said, we heard a scream in there, Falcon. It sounded like a man. I need to hear Theo Knight's voice, make sure he's okay."

"He's fine."

"I got guys chomping at the bit to beat that door down, Falcon. Help me out here. I need to hear his voice."

Falcon gritted his teeth, then walked over to Theo, who was still seated on the floor. Facing him, he put the gun to Theo's left ear, the phone to his right. "Say something."

"There's two more—"

Falcon slugged him with the butt of the gun and snatched the phone away before Theo could finish. "Not so damn loud," he said as he brought the phone back to his ear. He was furious but still whispering.

Paulo said, "Falcon, do you have two more hostages?"

"I want to talk to Swyteck."

"Why are you whispering?"

"Because she's here. In the bathroom."

"Who's in the bathroom?"

"It's her. I know it's her."

"Who is she?"

"I can't get rid of her!"

"Falcon, take a breath and tell me who else is there with you."

Falcon was pacing furiously, but he was careful with each footfall so as not to make too much noise. "She's always here. Everywhere I go, she just shows up."

"Who?"

"She comes to the river. She comes to my house. She sits on my milk crate. She won't go, she won't never go! I beat the living crap out of her with a pipe and stuff her in the trunk, and she's still here! Right here in the bathroom!"

"Falcon, tell me who you're talking about."

He cupped his hand around the receiver, containing his words so that no one would overhear. It made his whisper even raspier. "I have to tell Swyteck something."

"No problem. I can pass it on to him. What is it?"

"Tell him—first tell him I still want my money."

"Okay, he's working very hard on that. Anything else?"

"Yeah," he said as he shot a nervous glance toward the bathroom door. "Tell him I need, I really need, my fucking necklace." He closed the flip phone and disconnected.

30
.

Jack was in search of the Bushman.

Falcon's demand for his necklace had made absolutely no sense to Sergeant Paulo. Jack, however, knew exactly what his client was talking about. He wanted the necklace of metal beads that had held the key to Falcon's safe deposit box at the Greater Bahamian Bank & Trust Company. Problem was, Jack had last seen it around the neck of a homeless and extremely paranoid Jamaican called the Bushman.

"Would you know this Bushman if you saw him again?" asked Paulo.

"Sure. My guess is that he lives along the river, probably not far from Falcon's car. If someone can give me a ride, I'll find him."

"I'll go," said Alicia.

Jack had yet to tell anyone about his private talk with Alicia's father, but the upshot of that conversation made it seem like a good idea to take the mayor's daughter away from the command center and the lead negotiator. "Great. Let's go."

They took Alicia's personal car, so she had to flash her badge to get through the traffic-control perimeter. Miami Avenue took them south, toward the river. They parked at a metered spot near Tobacco Road, Miami's oldest bar, a place where Theo had on many occasions blown the saxophone until the wee hours of the morning. Jack wasn't searching for memories, but it was amazing how the prospect of losing a friend made you see him everywhere and in everything.

"What does this Bushman look like?" said Alicia as they walked along the north side of the river.

"The thing I remember most is that he had about three miles of dreadlocks tucked up under a bulging knit cap, and the whole blob on top of his head was wrapped in aluminum foil. It reminded me of Jiffy Pop."

"Of what?" said Alicia.

"Remember in the days before microwave popcorn how you would cook it on the stove in that little container that looked like a pie tin? As the corn popped, the foil on top would blow up like a big aluminum balloon? Well, that's the Bushman's head."

"There was popcorn before microwaves?" she said.

Jack was about to answer, but he noted the little smile, a signal that she was yanking his chain. *Nothing like being made to feel old by a young and beautiful cop.*

Jack walked around a heap of rusted metal that appeared to be part of an old barge. "Your father corralled me for a talk before I came back to the command center this morning."

She cast him a tentative look. "What about?"

"He's very concerned that you might play too active a role in this hostage negotiation. He made me promise that if I talk to Falcon, I won't even mention your name."

"My father means well. But you should do whatever Sergeant Paulo tells you to do."

They continued walking. The terrain was flat, but the piles of junk along the river were getting more formidable. With an active hostage-situation back at the hotel, Jack felt as though he should be running to find the Bushman, but he had to watch his step with all the twisted metal along the banks. "What can you tell me about Paulo?"

"He's excellent."

"How well do you know him?"

She hesitated just long enough for Jack to sense that it was a complicated question. "Very well," she said.

"I hope you don't mind my asking this, but is he *totally* blind?"

"Yes. Now, before you freak out, just remember that he's an experienced negotiator. Listening, talking, persuading—that's the essence of his job, and none of it is tied to his sight. It's not like he's a blind cosmetic surgeon about to feel his way through your nose job."

Jack did a little face-check. "What's wrong with my nose?"

"Nothing . . ."

"Good."

". . . that a little plastic surgery couldn't fix."

"Ah, cop humor. That's one thing we criminal defense lawyers just can't get enough of."

Alicia stopped and pointed. "Is that him?"

Just ahead, near the bridge, a man was asleep on the ground. His winter jacket was so dirty that his form nearly blended into the earth, but the morning sun reflected off his shiny headgear like a chrome globe. "Gotta be the Bushman," said Jack.

They approached with caution, the way anyone might approach a guy who slept alongside the river with his head wrapped in aluminum foil. He lay curled up on his right side. A charred, empty crack bowl was on the ground beside him. A stray cat was licking something off of his hand, but the Bushman wasn't moving. It was hard to tell if he was even breathing.

"Bushman?" said Jack. He still didn't move. Jack tried a little louder, "Hey, Bushman!"

The Bushman groaned and slowly propped himself up on one elbow. "What you want, mon?"

"Remember me? It's Jack Swyteck—your friend Falcon's lawyer."

The Bushman sat up, but he paid little attention to his visitors. He started smacking his lips, as if trying to decide whether he could live with the foul taste in his mouth.

Alicia said, "Falcon needs your help."

He stopped smacking. "Who are you?"

"She's with me," said Jack. He didn't want to sic the cop on him just yet. "Falcon wants his necklace back."

"You talked to him?" said the Bushman.

Jack didn't answer directly. "He's in a lot of trouble, and he just said he really, really needs his necklace."

A look of concern came over the Bushman. "She must be back."

"Who must be back?"

"That woman I was telling you about. I thought she was just another one of Miami's homeless. But Falcon explained to me, mon. She's not one of us. She's one of them."

"One of them?"

"Yeah, mon. They keep coming back, you know? You can't be nice to them. You can't take them at their word. They just never stop."

"Never stop what?"

"Stop looking. For the house."

"What house?"

He checked over his shoulder, as if to see if anyone was listening. Then he whispered, *"La casa de la bruja."*

"The witch's house?" said Alicia. Jack, too, had been able to translate it, but she was a tad quicker.

The Bushman winced. "Not so loud, lady. They'll hear us."

Jack said, "Who lives in the witch's house?"

"Nobody lives there. It's just where they go."

"Where who goes?"

"You know, who we talked about before. The Disappeared."

Time was precious, and Jack feared that the Bushman might be wasting too much of it. But with the mention of the Disappeared, Jack had to take a shot.

"Bushman, if I told you that Falcon sent me on an errand, and that when I got there I found a note that asks in Spanish, 'Where are the Disappeared?'—would you be able to answer that question?"

"Of course I would. *La casa de la bruja.* Don't you understand nothing I'm saying to you, mon?"

"No," Jack said, shaking his head slowly. "I wish I did, but I honestly don't have time to sort this crap out. We need the necklace."

"It's mine now."

"Falcon wants it back."

"Too bad. He gave it to me."

"What do you want for it?"

"It's not for sale."

"There must be something you want."

The Bushman considered it. Then he looked at Alicia and smiled. "I want to see her tits."

"No problem," said Alicia.

"Really?" said the Bushman.

"Yeah, really." She reached inside her jacket and pulled out her badge. "How's that for a rack?"

The Bushman swallowed the lump in his throat.

"Now give us the damn necklace," she said.

31

·

Theo watched with concern as Natalia tended to her girlfriend's wounded leg. She was still in the bathtub, and Natalia was kneeling beside her on the bloody tile floor. Theo and the other male hostage were seated in the dressing area just outside the bathroom, facing the open bathroom doorway, their backs against the wall and their hands and feet bound tightly. Falcon paced nervously from one end of the room to the other. He was sweating but refused to remove his coat. Theo was perspiring, too, as the room seemed to grow warmer with each passing minute. The lack of any ventilation gave the air a heavy, stale quality, as if they were drawing the same breath over and over again.

As best Theo could recall, this had all begun with a woman's scream. Theo had burst into the room, and Falcon had fired a single gunshot. The errant bullet had apparently passed right through the bathroom wall and hit Natalia's girlfriend in the thigh.

"How is she?" said Theo.

"Shut up!" said Falcon. He was still pacing, mumbling, as if struggling to formulate a coherent sentence. It seemed to frustrate him to no end that he was incapable of improving upon Theo's words. "How is she?" he said.

"The bullet tore through the skin and took a little piece of her thigh with it," said Natalia. "But the bleeding has stopped."

"Good," said Falcon. "No more bleeding. That's real good."

"It's good only if her heart's still beating," said Theo.

"Shut up, you!" shouted Falcon. Then he looked at Natalia and said, "It's still beating, right?"

"Yeah," she said. "She'll have a nasty scar when this thing heals, but it looks like she's going to be okay."

Theo winced at the response. Natalia was too far away to hear his whisper, so he waited until Falcon paced to the far end of the room, and then he spoke through his teeth. "Tell him that your friend needs a doctor."

Falcon wheeled and said, "I heard that! I won't have any phony emergencies around here. You hear me?"

"This isn't phony," said Theo. "Look at her. She's barely conscious."

"I decide who needs a doctor. That's my call. I'm in control here. Understand?"

Theo worried about pushing too hard, but he didn't want to let this drop. "Look, dude, you got three other hostages. Let this one go, okay? We're talking about a gunshot wound from a pretty mean pistol you're packing there. The bleeding may have stopped, but she's a bloody mess already. She could go into shock, and you don't need that kind of hassle."

Falcon's expression tightened. He seemed to be considering it.

Theo said, "You need to get her outta here."

"I know, I know! Everybody just shut up!"

Theo said, "Be smart, dude. Cut a deal. Give up the girl, but get somethin' in return. Maybe this is the bargaining chip you need to get that necklace you talked about."

Falcon clearly liked the idea of negotiating, but he seemed less than keen on giving up a hostage. He dug the cell phone out of his pocket and gripped it tightly.

"That's it," said Theo, egging him on. "Make 'em start talking."

"Swyteck," Falcon said, barking into Theo's cell phone. "Where's my damn money? And where's my necklace?" His face reddened with anger, as if he didn't like the response. "Don't give me any more excuses. I want my money and my necklace. You got five minutes. If my shit ain't here by then, I shoot the black guy. You hear me? I'm gonna take out my gun, and I'm shooting your smart-mouthed friend right in the head!"

He muttered something under his breath and shoved the phone back into his pocket. Theo shot him a knowing expression, fully conveying that Falcon hadn't fooled him.

Falcon said, "What are you looking at?"

"You didn't open the flip phone," said Theo. "You can't make a call if you don't open the flip."

Falcon smiled, as if suddenly this were all just a big joke. "Didn't open the flip phone. That's some really bad news for you, isn't it?"

"I'm not followin' you, dude."

Falcon stepped closer, speaking in a low, threatening voice. "Your friend Swyteck has a five-minute deadline," he said as he aimed his pistol at Theo's forehead. "And he doesn't even know it."

32

The command center was starting to smell like bad coffee. People came and went, but their coffee cups remained behind. Did anyone ever actually dispose of disposable coffee cups? Jack counted thirteen half-empty ones lying around. Theo would have counted thirteen half-*full* ones, even with a maniac holding a gun to his head and a sleep-deprived lawyer about to negotiate for his release. They were just wired differently, or at least they held fundamentally different perceptions of Jack's abilities. To Theo, Jack was a miracle worker, the tenacious young lawyer who had gotten him off death row. To Jack, Theo was the figurative sponge that had already soaked up Jack's lifetime allocation of luck—and then some.

"Try not to use the word 'no,'" Sergeant Paulo said to Jack. "No matter what Falcon says, no matter what he asks for, just don't slam any doors in his face."

The Bushman's request for a peep show suddenly

popped into Jack's mind. "What if he asks to talk to Alicia?" said Jack.

"That's a good example," said Paulo. "Tell him that you'll have to check on that. You'll look into it. Make no promises, but don't shut him down. You're in the perfect position, because there really isn't anything that you can give him without getting approval from the police, the mayor, Alicia, or whoever."

"Do I raise this issue of the Disappeared?"

"Don't force it," said Paulo. "If it comes up, go with it. But remember, he has yet to use that term with us. I'm afraid to raise it with him until we understand the concept better. If we just spring it on him, we may unleash some personal demons that could cause him to freak out and hurt one of the hostages."

"His arrest record said he came here from Cuba," said Jack. "Maybe we should check and see if *los desaparecidos* is a way of referring to the homeless in Cuba."

"That's a good thought," said Paulo.

Jack looked at Alicia and said, "What do you think?"

The question seemed to jar her from deeper thoughts. "Me?"

"Yeah. Your Spanish is excellent—a heck of a lot better than mine, anyway. What do you think about the notion of the homeless being the Disappeared?"

"Hard to say. I suppose it's worth looking into."

"Do you have a different theory?"

She paused before saying, "No. Not really."

Jack sensed that something was being left unsaid, though as a criminal defense lawyer he often got that feeling when talking with cops. He glanced at Paulo but couldn't read his expression. Jack let it go.

"You ready to make the call?" asked Paulo.

"Yeah," said Jack. "Let's do it."

Alicia slid the phone to the center of the table and dialed the number. Jack drew a deep breath and let it out with the first ring. It rang twice more before he inhaled again. On the fourth ring, Falcon answered.

"Joe's Deli," he said.

The stupid joke threw off Jack's rhythm momentarily. "Falcon, it's me. Swyteck."

"You got my necklace?"

"Yes, as a matter of fact I do."

"What about the money?"

Jack searched for the mantra that Paulo had planted in his head. "We're working on the money."

"What's the problem?"

"No problem. Just typical offshore banking hassle. Be cool."

"I want my money."

"I understand. But right now we've got the food Paulo promised you—some burgers, fries, and nice cold drinks. And we have your necklace. That's a pretty darn good start, don't you think?"

"Minimal," he said.

"But you know the drill. Even little things count for a lot, especially when you're dealing with cops. If it were up to me, I'd just give all this stuff to you. But these guys always want something in return.

So, I hate to do this to you, pal. But what are you gonna give me?"

"Let me think about that."

"How about—"

"I said let me think!"

"Okay, take your time."

In the ensuing silence, Paulo made a slow, palms-down gesture, as if telling Jack to be patient.

"I got it," said Falcon. "I'll give you shit in return. How's that sound?"

Jack considered it, wondering how to handle such an offer within the parameters of Paulo's never-say-no rule. "What kind of shit?" said Jack.

"Horseshit. Bullshit. Whatever kind of shit you want. We got it all, and every time you bastards call me, the inventory just keeps piling up. Now, for the last time," he said, his voice rising, "where's my damn money?"

Jack measured his words. He could hear the strain in Falcon's voice. "I'm not going to lie to you, all right? But we need to have an understanding here. If I tell you the truth, you have to be able to deal with it. Can you do that?"

"Just tell me where my money is."

Paulo made another hand gesture, this time a sharp, cutting signal, which Jack read as "Stay away from the truth." Jack said, "Let me check on your money, okay? I'll work on it, I promise. But you have to give me something."

"You don't deserve anything."

"Do you want your necklace or not?"

"Don't hang that over my head."

"I talked to your friend, the Bushman. I know how badly you need it."

There was silence, and Jack's instincts were telling him that he'd played exactly the right card. Paulo, however, was making that slashing signal again, silently but emphatically telling Jack not to go down the road of the Disappeared.

"Here's the deal," said Falcon. "I'll give everyone here a turn on the telephone. Ten seconds, no more. They can tell you who they are, and they can give you the name of a friend or relative to call. You cool with that?"

"What do you mean by 'everyone'? Exactly how many people do you have in there?"

"Do you want my deal or not?"

Jack glanced at Paulo, who gave a quick nod of approval. "Okay. Agreed."

"But first I get my necklace," said Falcon. "Send it in with the food."

Paulo shook his head firmly. Jack spoke into the phone, "First you let the hostages make their phone calls. Sorry, Falcon, but that's just the way it has to be."

Jack heard him muttering under his breath, and, in his mind's eye, he saw Falcon swinging his fist at no one, on the verge of an explosion. Falcon said, "Am I going to have to shoot one of these people?"

"Don't do that," said Jack.

"Is that the only way I can get your attention?" Falcon said, his voice suddenly racing.

"Please, don't even think about it."

"Because I can play the game that way, if you want me to."

"That's not what anyone wants."

"I can hurt people."

"I'm sure you can."

"If I put my mind to it, I can *really* hurt people."

Jack heard a sudden scream in the background—a man, though it didn't really sound like Theo. "Falcon, if you do that one more time, you'll have SWAT all over you. Just get it under control."

There was a brief silence, and then Falcon spoke in a halting voice. "It's under control, Jack. It's totally under control."

"Did you hurt someone?"

"No. *You* did. Now bring me my damn necklace."

The line disconnected.

"It's all right," said Paulo. "That was Falcon screaming, not your friend Theo."

"You sure?"

"I'm blind, not deaf," he said. "Trust me. You got us off to a good start."

Jack wanted to believe him, but his hand was shaking as he handed Paulo the telephone. "What's he going to do when I tell him that his money's gone?"

"Hopefully, this standoff will be over before we get to that point."

"What if it's not?"

Paulo was looking straight at him, and it was obvious that he could hear the concern in Jack's voice. "Like I say," said Paulo. "Hopefully, it will be over before then."

33

Theo listened carefully to Falcon's every word. The phone call seemed real this time, and it struck Theo as a positive step that Falcon was speaking directly to Jack and not the police. Theo didn't want anyone putting his own interest higher than that of the other hostages, but at least he felt confident that Jack wouldn't hold his any lower.

"Impressive," said Falcon as he tucked away the cell phone. "Your buddy made his five-minute deadline with twenty seconds to spare."

"I wasn't worried. Jack is psychic, you know."

Theo gave no outward indication that he was joking, which clearly made Falcon uncomfortable. "You messing with me?" said Falcon.

"That's for you to figure out," said Theo.

His eye twitched nervously, and then Falcon turned away. Theo noticed that his face was taking on a constant red and puffy quality, but it wasn't anger. It was the winter coat. Miami's cold snap was over, clearly, and the closed-in room was heating up in a hurry. Falcon had to be roasting. Still, he wouldn't remove that bulky coat.

"Listen up," said Falcon. "I'm gonna let you make some phone calls. Keep it short. Just give your name and the phone number of a friend or relative who the cops can call and say you're doing just fine. That's it. Anybody breaks the rules, I break your head. Got it?"

No one answered.

"Good. We'll start with the girls." He poked his head into the bathroom. "Natasha, how's your friend?"

"My name's Natalia. And my friend is in no shape to speak on the telephone, if that's what you're asking. She's still fading in and out."

"Then wake her up."

"I think we should let her rest."

"I think she could use a little cold water in that tub."

Theo said, "Are you crazy? You'll send her into shock, for sure."

"The doctor says it's okay."

"What doctor?"

"We don't do the water treatment unless the doctor says it's okay."

"What doctor?" said Theo.

Falcon didn't answer. He went to the tub and turned on the cold water. It spit out a few drops before going dry. "Bastards! They cut off the water."

"Must be what the doctor ordered," said Theo.

"Okay, smart mouth. We'll start with you, and then the pretty boy next to you. But first, I gotta take a dump. You can watch or look the other way. Don't make no difference to me."

With the bathroom door open, Theo had a clear view of the toilet, so he looked the other way as Falcon lowered his pants. The coat stayed on.

The man next to Theo leaned closer and whispered, "I can't get on that phone."

"Why not?"

"Because—Can't you see what was going on here, man? These girls aren't exactly what you'd call my friends."

"So that must make you their priest who came here trying to save the hos."

"Nice try. I've already worked that one through my mind, and it won't fly. But I have to say something when the crazy man hands me the phone."

"Just tell them that your name is John and that you're here on business."

"Make fun all you want. But how would you feel if the world was about to know that you were in a two-bit hotel room with a pair of eighteen-year-old prostitutes."

"Eighteen?" Theo said with a light chuckle. "You can only hope, buddy."

"Will you stop being such an ass, please? This could be the death of my career."

"What do you do for a living?"

The guy didn't answer, but Theo did a double take. "Hey, now I know. Ain't you the weather guy on Action News?"

"Weather guy?" the man said, straining to show confusion. "You must be thinking of someone else."

"No, dude. I watch you every night at eleven. Walt the Weather Wizard."

"That's not me."

"Like hell. Dress you up with some hair gel and one-a those snappy Armani jackets, and you're definitely Walt the Weatherman. But I thought you was gay."

"No, I'm married."

"You mean, *was* married."

The weatherman closed his eyes and then opened them, as if in mortal pain. "Dear God, I'm screwed."

"Oh, yeah," said Theo. "You are *so* screwed."

"I can't believe this is happening. All over a stupid shopping bag."

"What?" Theo had heard it all as a bartender, but this was one story that not even a psychologist/mixologist could have been expected to endure without being tied down—literally. It seemed that the weatherman's teenage daughter needed to return a pair of jeans that she'd borrowed from a friend at school. Stupid husband put the jeans in a regular old grocery bag. Angry wife nearly had a stroke. "You can't use a bag from Winn-Dixie!" she shrieked as she ran off to the closet. Moments later, she returned, the jeans wrapped in packing tissue and tucked neatly into a signature powder blue shopping bag from Tiffany.

"She was ready to kill me over a shopping bag," he told Theo, "all because she doesn't want some rich girl's mother to find out that we shop at Winn-Dixie. So I look at her and say, 'When did the funny and sexy woman I married turn into such a pretentious bitch?'"

"Ouch."

"Was I wrong?"

"You're always wrong," said Theo. "It's in the contract. Read the fine print."

"You think I should have apologized?"

"Hmmm. Apologize or run out the door and hire yourself a couple of teenage hookers? Let's call Dr. Phil about that one."

The weatherman breathed a hopeless sigh, as if hearing it from Theo made things even worse. "What should I do now?"

"You do whatever it takes to get out of here alive."

"Then what?"

"You do the honorable thing."

"Which is what?"

"Shoot yourself."

"Shoot myself?"

"Yes. But not on her duvet cover. She'll hate you for that. You don't mess with a woman's duvet cover."

The guy nodded, as if it all made sense. "Thanks."

"No problem."

The toilet flushed, and out with Falcon's waste went the last liter of water left in the hotel room. "All right, smart guy," Falcon said to Theo. "You're first."

The weatherman whispered, "Please, I can't get on that phone."

"Don't worry," said Theo, "he ain't gonna get to you."

Falcon dialed the number, waited for an answer, and dispensed with all pleasantries. Theo couldn't even tell if he was speaking to Jack or the cops. "Here's your roll call," said Falcon, speaking into the phone. He held the gun in his right hand, the phone in his left. "Ten seconds," he told Theo. "Your name and a contact."

As soon as the phone was in place, Theo blurted out Falcon's secret in rapid-fire fashion. "He's wired with explosives under his coat and—"

"Asshole!" Falcon yanked away the phone and kicked Theo in the belly with the force of an angry mule.

Theo slid to the floor, unable to breathe. He hadn't been one-hundred-percent certain about the explosives, but he'd felt *something* earlier when they wrestled on the floor, and Falcon's refusal to remove his winter coat despite the rising heat only fueled Theo's suspicions.

Falcon kicked him again, and with all the cursing, Theo knew he was right. The guy was definitely wired.

"I make this promise," Falcon said, seething as he put the gun to Theo's head. "No matter what happens, *you* are not walking out of here."

34

Explosives changed everything—especially for Vince Paulo.

Since losing his sight, Vince had heard all the amazing stories. The guy who blew his nose so violently that his eye popped out. The firefighter whose eye was left hanging by the optic nerve after a blast from a fire hose. The child who ruptured her eye on a bedpost while bouncing on the mattress. Metalworkers with steel shards embedded near the optic disc or with splashes of molten lead on the eyeball. A soldier shot at arm's length, the projectile entering the inner canthus of the right eye and lodging under the skin of the opposite side. What made these cases remarkable was that in each instance, the ultimate visual impairment was nonexistent or negligible, or so the tales of medical miracles went. On the other side of the spectrum were patients who seemed to suffer only minor ocular trauma, the globe still intact, but whose vision was lost forever. They were the unlucky ones, the Vince Paulos of the world.

"Bomb squad is standing by, Sergeant."

Vince heard the message over his earpiece, but he didn't answer right away. Theo Knight's mere mention of explosives had Vince seeing that pockmarked door again, the opening at the end of the hallway to his personal and permanent tunnel of darkness.

"Vince?" said Alicia. She was standing at his side.

"Yeah, I heard. I was just thinking for a minute." It was a lie, of course—at least the part about "a minute." Vince had been thinking and rethinking for months, imagining how different things might have been if he just hadn't pushed open that door. He keyed his mike and told the bomb-squad leader to stand down until he made one more attempt to reestablish contact with Falcon.

Alicia said, "Just because this Theo says there's a bomb doesn't mean Falcon has one."

"We have to assume the worst."

"Do you really think he has the know-how to make one?"

"He had two hundred thousand dollars in a Bahamian safe deposit box. He's packing a nine-millimeter pistol with plenty of ammunition. He shot two officers in a gunfight in the dark, and now he's more than holding his own in a hostage standoff against the entire City of Miami. I think it's time we all erase from our minds the image of a hapless homeless guy atop a bridge and focus more on the sick bastard who for no apparent reason beat a defenseless woman to death with a lead pipe."

"I was just asking, Vince."

He could hear the change in Alicia's tone, and he

realized that his own intensity was getting the best of him. It was time to get control over those feelings that lingered just below the surface and never really went away, time to quell the useless anger over a risk he should never have taken. "Sorry," he said. "Guess I should just catch my breath and chill a little, huh?"

He felt the gentle touch of her hand on his forearm. She said, "This is a different ballgame than the one Chief Renfro and I invited you to. Are you okay with it?"

"Why wouldn't I be?"

"I don't know. Too much like the last one, maybe."

"No, you're wrong. It's nothing like the last one. This time I have a warning. I can see what's coming." The unintentional pun drew a mirthless chuckle from somewhere inside him, like a reflex.

The phone rang, but it wasn't on the dedicated line to the hotel room. It was Vince's cell. The call was from Detective Barber, the lead homicide investigator. "Got an update for you on the body in Falcon's car," he said.

"Good. Alicia Mendoza is right here with me. Let me put my cell on speaker."

"I'd rather you didn't do that," said Barber.

Vince wasn't sure how to interpret the detective's concern, but he obliged. "Okay, no speaker."

Barber said, "In fact, I'd prefer that this information and everything you say in response to it be just between us. It might be important to your negotiations."

"All right." He covered the phone and said, "Alicia, could you excuse me for a minute?"

He sensed some confusion on her part—just a vibe that he picked up from her hesitation—but it was only for a moment.

"No problem," she said. "I'll get some coffee."

Vince waited for the door to open, then close. "I'm back," he said into the phone.

"I have an eyewitness who claims to have seen a well-dressed, twentysomething-year-old man, either light-skinned black or dark-skinned Hispanic, speaking to Falcon two nights ago by the river."

"What time?"

"Just after dark. If I tie that in with the medical examiner's report, it's not long before our Jane Doe ended up dead and stuffed inside the trunk of Falcon's car—Er, home."

"Any idea who it might be? Your physical description could fit half the young men in Miami."

"True. But fortunately our witness got a license plate number."

"How did it come back?"

"This is where it gets interesting. It's a guy named Felipe Broma. He works security for Mayor Mendoza."

Vince suddenly understood why the detective wanted Alicia out of earshot. "You talked to Broma yet?"

"No."

"How about the mayor?"

"Not yet."

"What are you waiting for?"

There was silence on the line, then Barber said,

"I've been a detective a long time. I listen to my instincts."

"What are your instincts telling you?"

"There's only one way to find out what's really going on here. And talking to the mayor or his bodyguard is not the answer."

"What are you suggesting?"

"I need to talk to Falcon," said Barber. "Through you."

Vince considered it. "Let me see if I can get him talking again. We'll take it from there."

"One other thing," said Barber. "Not a word of this to the mayor's daughter. Agreed?"

Vince wasn't entirely sure what the detective had on his agenda, but he wasn't hot on the idea of keeping secrets from Alicia—at least not without a more compelling explanation from Barber. "Like I say: I'll see if I can get Falcon talking, and we'll go from there."

35
.

Things were finally coming clearer to Falcon. Even without electricity, enough sunlight seeped into the room to show the faces of all his prisoners. The girl in the bathtub was not the woman he'd originally thought she was, not the past he feared. She was just a girl without a name, like many others he'd known years earlier.

"I think she's getting a fever," said Natalia.

"Quiet!" shouted Falcon.

"You should really get her to a doctor," said Theo.

Falcon glared and said, "I told you before, the doctor has already given his blessing."

"What the hell doctor are you talking about? Are you a doctor?"

"Do I look like a doctor?"

"From my HMO? Absolutely."

Falcon shot him an angry look. "I've met clowns like you before, always getting in their little jokes. The minute I let my guard down, you sneaky bastards go right for the gun."

He glanced at the girl in the tub, then turned and

started pacing across the room again. No food, no money, no necklace. Swyteck had told him that they had the necklace, but now it would be more difficult than ever to work out a delivery. The big-mouthed black guy had screwed up everything by telling the cops about the magic coat. Who in their right mind would come near the hotel room?

The girl in the tub groaned. Natalia said, "She's definitely getting a fever."

"She needs a doctor," said Theo.

"Shut up!" he shouted, thrusting the gun toward Theo. "I've had it with you. Enough already!"

Falcon could feel the heat rising. It was as if someone had switched on the furnace, which he knew wasn't possible. Or was it? The cops could have been pumping hot air through the AC ducts. They'd already turned off the water and the electricity, so why not turn the place into an oven? He crossed the room and pressed his hand to the vent. He felt nothing, save for the sweat that continued to run down his face. How people in Miami survived in these concrete boxes before air-conditioning was beyond him. There was something to be said for living in a car with the windows busted out. If you got cold, you put on a coat. When it turned hot, you took the coat off. Not this time, however. Not this coat.

The coat stayed on.

There was a whimper from the bathroom, then a sustained groan. Falcon knew the sound of pain, but he was impervious to it. That was not exactly true. Once upon a time, he had thought himself to be impervious to it. He'd failed to realize that every grunt, every groan, every shrill scream in the night had seeped right through the psychological walls that he'd built around his conscience. For years, he'd kept them locked in the basement, but they kept creeping up the stairs and knocking on the cellar door until the locks finally broke. The memories came flooding back to him. They were no longer his past. They had become his every waking hour—his past, present, and future.

"She needs a doctor," he heard someone say, but it only confused him further. The present was mirroring the past. Or the past was coloring the present. His mind could no longer distinguish between the two, and he was suddenly returning to the basement, trapped with his memories.

"Are you looking for the Virgin?" asked El Oso.

The question had the intended effect. Prisoner 309, the young woman with child, was well acquainted with the horrors that had unfolded at the feet of the Virgin Mary. A gang rape before the statue of the Blessed Virgin was a particularly effective way of telling a subversive young woman just how far she had strayed from acceptable behavior.

El Oso acknowledged her fear by telling her not to worry. "The Virgin is not here," he said, his voice laden with a perverse satisfaction. "There are no virgins left at *la casa de la bruja*."

He pushed her forward, and they continued to the end of a long, dark hallway. Her belly was way out in front of her; she had to be due any day. El Oso stopped and unlocked the metal door. The moment it opened, a sharp scream pierced the darkness. It sounded like a woman, but El Oso knew it was a man. It was something the guards liked to tell jokes about, the way men could be made to scream like girls.

"Would you like to watch?" he said. They were standing outside the room, as yet unable to see inside. Party music was blaring from a radio, a tune strangely at odds with what was obviously going on in there.

The young woman shook her head.

"Are you sure you don't want to see?" he said. "It could be someone you know."

It was a possibility that she seemed unwilling to consider, but he could see her defenses breaking down. They always did. Instinct may have cautioned that it was better not to know, but in the end, the prisoners craved answers.

"Come, let's have a look." He was speaking softly but not out of concern. The insincerity was palpable, and it pleased him to see the heightened anxiety in her eyes. He nudged her forward, and there was another scream from inside the room. This one was so loud and lasted so long that even El Oso stopped to listen. It ceased only when the prisoner had no more voice, no more ability to express his suffering.

Had to be the testicles, thought El Oso.

The party music continued to play.

"I don't want to go in there," said the woman.

"That's not important."

"No, please. Don't make me go."

"It's your only chance. In a minute, he'll be crying

for his mama. They always cry for their mamas."

The tears started to come. Her body trembled. "I don't want to see."

"That doesn't matter."

"Who's in there?"

"The enemy."

"What's his name?"

"He has no name."

He pulled her forward, but she resisted. "I can't go in there!"

A slap across the face silenced her. Then he jerked her by the arm with so much force that she slammed into the wall. In her advanced state of pregnancy, her balance was not what it might have been. With another quick shove from behind, she stumbled through the open doorway. She collided with the counter, which rattled the guards' empty beer bottles, and then she fell to the floor.

"Look, woman!" one of the guards shouted. "See who's on the grill now."

The grill was a metal table in the center of the room. A male prisoner was strapped to it, completely naked and flat on his back. The soles of his feet were purple and swollen. A guard stood at the foot of the table with a length of hardwood, ready to swing it at the prisoner's arches like a baseball bat. Another guard tended to the electric transmitter and several strands of wire that ran directly to the prisoner's torso and genitals. His chest and stomach were dotted with black burn marks. His testicles were grotesquely discolored and three times their normal size.

"Fernando!" the pregnant woman screamed, but the prisoner did not respond to her. He managed only to groan and whisper, "Water . . . please."

"No, you can't drink now!" said El Oso.

"I'm so thirsty," the prisoner said, his voice fading.

"He can't drink now or he'll die!"

"He's going to die anyway," said another guard. He laughed as he forced metal beads down the prisoner's throat—electrodes that would make the voltage cut like lightning through his insides.

"Swallow!" the guard with the beads ordered.

At the turn of the dial, the current flowed. The prisoner's entire body tensed and then quivered. There was suddenly a bizarre symphony of party music on the radio, howling from the guards, and the blood-curdling screams of a dying man.

"You animals!" the woman shouted through tears, but she was no longer watching the torture of her husband. She remained on the floor, grimacing. El Oso assumed that she simply couldn't bear to look, but the pained expression told more than that.

"My water just broke," she said as she slumped onto her side, sobbing.

The guards stopped laughing. The prisoner lay utterly motionless. The pregnant woman was wailing. Party music continued to play in macabre fashion.

"Shit, now what?" said the man with the metal beads.

"Quick, help me carry her," said El Oso. "Let's find the doctor."

36

The moment Jack came through the door, the silence in the mobile command center didn't seem natural to him. He understood that negotiations were in many ways a strategic game of chess, but some of the best chess players he'd ever seen— the old Cuban men in Little Havana—could talk *beisbol*, order espresso, and argue politics, all while contemplating their next move. Some could even engage in a simultaneous game of dominoes. To be sure, a hostage situation was no game. Still, Jack was beginning to fear that Sergeant Paulo might be overanalyzing things.

He also sensed more than a little tension between Paulo and Alicia. "Did I interrupt something?" said Jack.

"No, not at all," said Alicia.

"Come right in," said Paulo.

Each of them had spoken in a tone that was a bit too upbeat, voices that tried too hard to convince Jack that nothing was wrong. Jack said, "I can come back in a minute."

"No," said Paulo. "We need to do this now. Ready?"

Jack nodded, then realized that it was a dumb-ass thing to do when speaking to a blind man. "Ready," he said.

Jack was definitely picking up some added stress in Paulo's voice. Perhaps it was Theo's outburst about explosives that had changed the lead negotiator, or at least affected his demeanor. Jack was about to say something about it, but Alicia was already dialing up Theo's cell. Whatever it was, it seemed that Alicia was even less inclined to discuss it than Paulo.

The hollow sound of unanswered rings echoed in Jack's ear—five times, then a sixth. Another ring and the call would go to voice mail, but finally Falcon picked up.

"Boom," he said.

Jack gathered himself and said, "That's not funny, Falcon."

"Swyteck, is that you? Can't say I was expecting that. What happened? Is my friend Paulo afraid to talk to the mad bomber?"

Jack glanced at Alicia, then at Paulo. He should have simply said "no," but Jack couldn't help himself, at least not when part of him was wondering the same thing. "Our only fear over here is that you might do something really stupid. You should be afraid of that, too."

"You got my necklace?"

"First, we need to talk about your coat. More specifically, about what's under your coat."

"What do you want to know?"

"Are you wired with explosives?"

"Come on. That's ridiculous. Where would I get a bomb?"

"My friend Theo says you have one."

"Your friend Theo's an asshole."

"Maybe. But he's not a liar."

"He doesn't know what he's talking about."

"Most of the time that's true. But every now and then he nails it. Here's how we can settle this real quick. Theo's cell phone has a camera function."

"A what?"

Jack realized that a guy who'd been living in a car for over a decade might not know anything about camera phones. "Trust me, the phone takes pictures. Theo can explain how to use it. Take off your coat, snap a picture of your torso, and send it to us."

There was silence, and Jack took some comfort in the fact that Falcon didn't immediately tell him to take a flying leap.

"Anything else?" said Falcon.

"Yeah. We want the coat." Jack didn't want to explain why, but Falcon could probably guess that they wanted to examine it for traces of explosives.

Falcon said, "So, let me get this straight. First you tell me that if I let everyone talk on the phone, you'll give me food and my necklace. I try to keep up my end of the deal, and your friend screws everything up. Now, to get the same food and necklace that you promised me before, you want me to start snapping photographs of myself and give you, literally, the coat off my back. Is that what you're saying?"

"I'm just trying to do what's fair for everyone."

"Like hell. You keep changing the deal, and I'm tired of all this stalling."

"The coat changes things."

"Not for me it doesn't. If you get more, I get more."

"What do you want?"

"I want my damn necklace. *And* I want Alicia Mendoza to bring it to me."

Jack glanced at Paulo, not sure how to answer that question. Paulo picked up Jack's hesitation, scratched out a message on a scrap of paper, and slipped it toward him. It read: *NO WAY . . . But never say never.*

"That's a tall order," said Jack. "I won't lie to you. It's going to be very, very tough to pull that off."

"Tough my ass."

"Seriously. For starters, I'll have to track down Alicia."

"If you're telling me she's not there with you, I know you're lying."

Jack didn't respond, but it was obvious that his bluffing needed some improvement. "If Alicia is going to get involved, I'm sure I'll need to get clearance from Mayor Mendoza himself."

"That's easy. Your dad's the governor of Florida, right?"

"Used to be the governor."

"He's still a politician, just like Alicia's father. Those guys are always sucking each other off. You get your old man to call her old man, and you make it happen, you hear me?"

"I can try, I guess. But I can't make any promises."

"This is going to be easier than you think, Swyteck."

"What makes you say that?"

"Here's a little incentive for her. Tell Alicia that if she blows me off again this time, then we're going to have to call the doctor."

It took Jack a moment, but then he deciphered what Falcon was saying. "Threatening the hostages is a very bad tactic, Falcon. SWAT is just looking for a reason to bust down those doors."

"I'm not threatening anyone, you idiot. Just be sure to tell her exactly what I said. She'll know what I mean."

Jack looked at Alicia, who gave him nothing in return. It wasn't clear that she understood what Falcon was saying. But it wasn't clear that she didn't, either.

"All right, Falcon. I'll be sure to pass along your exact words to Alicia. But I can tell you right now, I'll need some serious time to work on this."

"How much time?"

Jack looked at Paulo, whose instincts again told him that Jack needed guidance. He held up six fingers. Said Jack, "Six hours."

"You got one," said Falcon, and the call was over.

37

Jack walked across the parking lot from the mobile command center to the fast-food restaurant. He was in search of caffeine. He found mostly testosterone.

Law enforcement had taken over the entire restaurant and surrounding property, and the SWAT members were in the dining area, waiting for the green light. Jack had bumped up against plenty of machismo before, as few Miami courtrooms were large enough to hold the average trial lawyer's ego. But there was simply nothing quite like the collective bravado of a tactical team in full gear. It was a bizarre thought—and one that seemed unnerving to no one in the room but Jack—but in a matter of minutes, one of these guys might be pumping hollow-point ammunition into a man's skull. The outcome depended entirely on the words Jack chose, the nuances of his tone of voice, the way he steered his next telephone conversation with Falcon. His job suddenly seemed even more overwhelming.

Jack passed by the coffee machine and went straight

to the restroom. He stood at the sink, splashed cold water onto his face, and then took a good look at the man staring back at him from the mirror. He needed a shave, for sure. He removed the bandage, and there was some purple swelling around the cut at his right temple, where Falcon had said hello with the butt of his pistol. There wasn't much other color to his skin. The worry lines appeared to be carved in wax, the stress written all over his face. It reminded him of the time his father had signed Theo's death warrant and Jack went running into the bathroom to throw up. "Damn, you look worse than I do," Theo had told him when he arrived at the penitentiary. It was no joke. When it came to matters of life and death, Theo seemed to have a leg up on everybody. Jack hoped that was still the case.

"Hang in there, buddy." Jack was speaking aloud, but in his mind, he heard Theo talking.

Jack dried his hands and started toward the door. It opened before he got there, and a plainclothes officer entered. Jack recognized him as Detective Barber from the night they'd found a woman's body in the trunk of Falcon's car. Jack said a quick hello, then excused himself and tried to pass. Barber closed the door and leaned back against it, blocking Jack's way.

"You used to work with Gerry Chafetz, didn't you?" said Barber.

It seemed like an odd time for small talk, but Jack went along. "He was my supervisor at the U.S. Attorney's Office, back when I was a prosecutor."

"Chafetz and I rode together when he was on the

force. I called him after you and I talked the other night. He speaks highly of you."

"That's nice to hear."

They stood in silence, each sizing up the other. Jack knew that this had to be about more than his old boss. "Is there something you and I need to talk about, detective?"

"Chafetz tells me that you can be trusted."

"I like to think that's true."

Barber narrowed his eyes, as if to press his point. "I had a private conversation with Paulo this morning. Did he mention it to you?"

"No."

"I need some information from Falcon, but Paulo tells me that you're the one doing most of the talking."

"It's not my choice, but that seems to be the way Falcon wants it."

Barber nodded slowly, as if Jack's version were consistent with what Paulo had told him.

Jack said, "What are you trying to find out?"

Barber hesitated, seeming to weigh in his mind whether it was enough that Jack's former boss had vouched for his integrity. Either it was, or Barber had run out of options. "I need to know why the mayor's bodyguard was snooping around Falcon's car on Thursday night."

"You mean the night the woman was murdered?"

"That's exactly what I mean."

"What does the mayor have to say about that?"

"Haven't discussed it with him yet."

"Why not?"

"Couple reasons. Can't really share them with you. Except for one, which you may have already figured out."

"What's that?"

"Oh, I'm sure you've heard by now how upset the mayor is that Vincent Paulo is heading up this hostage negotiation. How afraid he is that Paulo is going to get his daughter involved."

"Oh, yeah," said Jack. "This morning I got a police escort straight to the mayor's car. He made it absolutely clear that Paulo is not his first choice."

"See, that's so very interesting to me."

"How do you mean?"

"Because I know for a fact that it was a phone call from Mayor Mendoza to Chief Renfro that got Vince Paulo assigned to this case in the first place."

Jack needed a few seconds to process that one. "How do you know that?"

"I'm a detective, okay?" That seemed to be all the explanation that Barber cared to offer.

Jack said, "Why would the mayor pretend that he doesn't want Paulo in charge if he was the driving force behind the assignment?"

Barber gave a slow, exaggerated shrug, as if to say "Good question." "Figure out a way to make your client tell us what the mayor's bodyguard was doing down by the river the other night. Maybe we'll get the answer."

Jack considered it, then checked his tired expression in the mirror one last time. "Yeah," he said quietly, "maybe."

38

On his way out of the restaurant, Jack stopped at the doughnut bar. He was hungry, and there was plenty to choose from. In Miami, doughnuts were to doughnut bars what sea turtles were to turtle soup. There were *pastelitos*, warm and flaky Cuban pastries with guava and other fillings that Sara Lee never dreamed of. Some had ham or ground beef inside, and the sweet crust with salty meat produced a surprisingly tasty combination. There were *capuchinos*, which were not misspelled cups of coffee but delicate sponge-cake cones drenched in sweet syrup. The empanadas and *croquetas* smelled pretty amazing, too, though not nearly as good as the ones Jack's *abuela* made. The bottom line was, not a plain old doughnut to be had. Perhaps it was a trend. Jack had read in the *New York Times* or somewhere that cupcakes were now all the rage in New York precincts. Those guys still had a long way to come.

Jack grabbed a coconut *pastelito* and stepped outside to make a call. Talking things out always helped him think. His *abuela* told him that he got that from his mother. Even though Jack had never known his mother—she'd died in childbirth—he was quite confident that Ana Maria Fuentes Swyteck's favorite sounding board had been nothing like Theo Knight. With Theo held hostage, however, Jack turned to his father to help him brainstorm. Jack wasn't sure if the former governor could help, but Falcon had told Jack to call him. If nothing else, it might help Jack lie more convincingly if he could at least say, truthfully, that he had indeed spoken to Harry Swyteck.

"You know me," said Jack. "I've never been a good liar."

"Then you should give up defense work and go back to being a prosecutor."

What else could he expect from a former police officer? "That's a real belly-buster, Dad."

"Sorry. I can hear the tightness in your voice. My bad attempt to loosen you up a little for your own good."

"I appreciate that."

"Have you spoken to your grandmother?" asked Harry.

"No."

"You should try to take a minute and do that. Your name is all over the television. She's going to be worried sick about you."

"I'll try. Can you call her for me, tell her I'm doing all right?"

"Are you?"

"What?"

"Doing all right?" said Harry.

Jack didn't answer right away. "I'm doing better than Theo. Right now, that's the test."

"Well, it must seem absurd to hear me say this, but your friend Theo is definitely a survivor."

He was right. It seemed beyond absurd, coming from the man who'd signed Theo's death warrant. But Jack didn't want to rehash that history. "I need your help."

"Sure. What can I do?"

"I'm trying to figure out what the hell is going on inside the City of Miami Police Department."

"How do you mean?"

Through the plate-glass window, Jack caught a glimpse of the television that was playing inside the restaurant. The SWAT members were gathered around it. "Dad, turn on channel seven. I'll call you right back."

"What's going on?"

"Mayor Mendoza is speaking live on television. I need to hear this. I want *you* to hear it, too." Jack switched off his phone and ran inside. He found a spot in back, behind the crowd of SWAT members in tactical fatigues, where he had a clear line of sight to the television. The volume was set at the max, making the tinny speaker rattle with each voice inflection.

On screen, Mayor Mendoza was standing in front of Miami's city hall, having completed his prepared statement, poised to take questions from the media. He was dressed in the same dark suit that he'd worn for his conversation with Jack in the backseat of his limo, but he had changed neckties. It was how publicists earned their keep, Jack presumed, assuring the Mayor Mendozas of the world that a pink tie was all wrong and that the red one conveyed the necessary firmness and resolve.

"Has the gunman demanded to speak to your daughter again?" a reporter asked.

"Not to my knowledge," said the mayor.

"Will she speak to him if he does make that demand?"

"Absolutely not," he said.

"Has your daughter told you that directly?"

"Both Sergeant Paulo and Chief Renfro have given me that assurance."

Another reporter jumped in, an old muckraker who used to pester Jack all the time, back when Harry Swyteck was governor and Jack was the young and rebellious thorn in his father's side. His name was Eddy Malone. "Mr. Mayor, can you assure the families of these hostages that you're doing all you can to secure the release of their loved ones?"

"That is our unfailing commitment."

"But how can you give that assurance if you won't even entertain the possibility of letting your daughter—who is a trained police officer—speak to this Falcon character?"

"The best way to answer your question is to point out that I'm not the one drawing the line here," said the mayor. "Sergeant Paulo has handled many of these crisis situations, and it's his very firm view that you don't feed a stalker's sickness by giving in and letting him talk to the very woman he is obsessed with. I'm following his advice on this point."

Jack's mouth dropped open, ready to release an involuntary "What?"

The mayor kept talking. "I simply want to add that I have the utmost confidence in Vince Paulo."

Malone said, "So, you're not at all concerned that Sergeant Paulo might not be ready for this crisis, given his recent leave of absence?"

"If by 'leave of absence' you mean his blindness, the answer to your question is an unqualified 'no.' He wouldn't be in this position if he weren't the best man for the job. Period. That's all the time I have now for questions. It's time to let the police do their work. Thank you all." He gave a simple wave, turned, and went back inside City Hall.

Jack didn't stick around to listen to the newscaster's recap. He grabbed his phone, ready to dial his father back, then thought better of it. He knew the cops were tweaking his cell calls to keep the press and other eavesdroppers from picking up his conversations with Falcon. At the moment, there were probably enough technological gadgets crammed into the surrounding city block to turn his cell phone into a virtual party line. He hurried outside and dialed from the pay phone on the wall.

"Did you see that?" said Jack.

Harry seemed puzzled by the urgency in Jack's voice. "Yeah, but I can't say that I heard anything that surprised me. The mayor obviously doesn't want his daughter talking to that lunatic any more than I want you talking to him."

"Believe me, the mayor's feelings are much

stronger than yours. Too strong for his own good, perhaps."

"What do you mean?"

Jack told him about the conversation in the back of the mayor's limo and the surprise visit from Detective Barber in the bathroom. Then he said, "The medical examiner says that the woman I found in the trunk of Falcon's car was beaten to death on Thursday night."

"Okay. What of it?"

Jack checked over his shoulder, making sure no one was around. He waited for two patrol officers to disappear inside the restaurant before continuing. "What would you say if I told you that the mayor's bodyguard was seen down by the river, near Falcon's car, right about that same time?"

"I'd probably want to ask the guy what he was doing down there."

"Let's assume he's not talking. And neither is the mayor. Then who do you ask?"

"Crazy as he might be, I suppose you would ask Falcon."

"Yeah," said Jack. "Unless . . ."

"Unless what?"

"Unless they take Falcon out of that hotel room feet first."

Harry paused, seeming to process what his son was implying. "That's a very serious accusation, if you're making it."

"Yeah," said Jack. "It is."

"So . . . are you making it?"

"Do you think it sounds crazy?"

Again, there was silence. Jack thought he was about to get the patented Harry Swyteck lecture again—how the whole world thought there was a "conspiracy" out there. Finally, Harry said, "Let me do some checking. Call me in a couple hours."

"No, don't do that."

"I want to help you."

"You already have. Just the fact that you're willing to check into it tells me that I'm onto something. It's best if I follow up from the inside. Maybe through Paulo. Or maybe even Barber."

"I think you should pick one or the other."

"I agree."

"So which one is it going to be?" asked Harry.

"I don't know yet. I'll see how it plays out over the next couple of hours and just go with my instincts."

"Okay. But son?"

"Yeah?"

"Be very careful with this."

"I will," he said, then hung up the pay phone.

39

Vince could smell the rain approaching.

He was standing outside the mobile command center, getting some fresh air. A northwesterly breeze caressed his face and ran through his hair. Rain was on the way, no doubt about it. His nose picked it up with ease, and it had nothing to do with any souped-up olfactory senses that came with blindness. The smells that warned of rain in Miami were as portentous as the sight of thunderclouds over the Everglades. With eyes closed, even those with perfect vision could sense a coming storm.

Rain was Vince's new best friend. The bond had formed on his first rainy day without sight, just moments after he'd stepped out the front door and onto his porch. His mind was gearing up for the usual mental exercise, the memorized flower-beds, shrubbery, and footpaths that defined his morning walk. But the rain changed all that. More precisely, it was the sound of falling rain that brought the outdoors and all of its shapes, textures, and contours back into his world. Where there was once only blackness, suddenly there was water sloshing down a drainpipe. The patter of raindrops on the broad, thick leaves of the almond tree. The hiss of automobiles on wet streets. Even the grass emitted its own peculiar expression of gratitude as it drank up the morning shower. A sighted person would have heard nothing more than rainfall in its most generic sense, a white noise of sorts. To Vince, it was a symphony, and he reveled in his newly discovered power to appreciate the beautiful nuances of each and every instrument. Nature and his old neighborhood were working together, calling out to him, telling him that everything was still there for his enjoyment. He heard the drumlike beating on his mailbox, the gentle splashing on concrete sidewalks, and even the ping of dripping water on an iron fence that separated his yard from his neighbor's. Rain, wonderful rain. It made him smile to find this new friend.

Rain, however, was no *amigo* to a negotiator. It made everything that much more complicated, especially with a hostage-taker wrapped in explosives. If things went south and they were forced to neutralize him, it would have to be a head shot. Snipers worked in a world of zero margin for error. A precision shot from atop a building, a hundred yards away, through a hotel window, was tricky but doable. Even to the skilled marksman, ambient conditions mattered. Nobody liked rain—except Vince, who knew better than any sighted person that sometimes the only opportunity to see things clearly was in the midst of the storm, that you might never find answers if you hide away in a shelter until after the rain.

Vince heard footsteps, then Alicia's voice. "I need to speak to you," she said. "Inside."

They retreated into the mobile command center, and before Vince could ask what this was about, Alicia said, "Did you see the TV broadcast?"

A month earlier, he would have corrected her and said, no, he'd only listened to it. He was maturing as a blind person, he supposed. "Yeah," he said.

"Then you caught what my father said. About the assurances he received from you that I would not under any circumstances talk to Falcon."

"I was hanging on his every syllable."

"Did you tell him that?"

"Nope. Never told Chief Renfro that, either."

He heard her sigh and take a seat. "Now if I have to talk to him, everyone on the force is going to assume that you broke your word to Chief Renfro and the mayor. Why is he tying your hands like that?"

Vince could tell that she was upset, and he was absolutely certain that his answer to her question would only upset her more. It might even insult her. He tried a less direct approach. "Did I tell you about the dream I had after you called to invite me to the jazz festival?"

She hesitated long enough for Vince to know that she was shooting him an incredulous look. "Vince, can we focus on what I'm talking about?"

"No, this is important. I need to tell you this."

She breathed out a little noise that Vince took for reluctant acquiescence. "Okay," she said. "Tell me about your dream."

"I've actually had it a couple of times, twice in the same night. It's kind of weird because it's one of the few dreams I've had where I'm blind. I'm married to you."

He stopped right there. He hadn't intended to create such a dramatic pause, but he suddenly wasn't sure if sharing this dream was such a great idea, after all.

"We're married?" she said.

"Yeah. And we take our daughter to the park. She's maybe four years old. Kids are playing all around us. I can hear them all happy and squealing with delight on the monkey bars. Little pockets of conversation surrounding me. Music is playing from the band shell in the distance. I'm tired and have to sit down on a bench. Then all of a sudden, a child comes and sits in my lap. I'm pretty sure it's a girl, because of the length of her hair, but she doesn't say a word. She just slides into my lap and nuzzles up against me. I wait for her to say something, but she's completely silent. I don't know what to do. I think it's our daughter, but without the sound of her voice, I can't be sure. Of course, I'm afraid to come right out and ask if it's her. What would that make her think, if her own father can't even recognize her when she's sitting right in his lap? And so we just sit there, this child in my lap, and me in the dark, not knowing who she is or what to do."

Silence. Insufferable silence. He'd thought that

telling her about it would loosen the emotional knot in his stomach, but it was only worse to have it out there with no reaction at all. Now, more than ever, it was driving Vince crazy that he couldn't see Alicia's face.

Finally, she said, "That child will speak to you, but only if you let her."

"In my dream I want her to speak."

"No. She's just going to sit there and be quiet, until you're ready. Until *you* decide what you want to do. About us."

More silence, and then he heard the approaching footfalls. He could almost feel her standing right before him, looking into his face. He wanted to reach out to her, but he wasn't sure what she wanted, and something inside him wouldn't let him take the risk. Then her arms went around his shoulders, and instinctively his hands found their way around the curve of her back, locking the two of them in a tight embrace. It wasn't the reaction he'd expected, and it was beyond even what he had hoped for. It felt so good.

"Vince, I'm glad you're sharing this with me." She was trying to control it, but there was real emotion in her whisper as she released him and took a step back.

He smiled a little, trying to put her at ease. "Hey, I didn't bring this up so that we get all sloppy on each other."

"Your timing *is* kind of weird," she said.

"I actually have a point."

"What is it?"

"I guess what I'm trying to say is that my feelings for you haven't changed, but—pardon the pun—that doesn't make me blind."

"I don't follow you."

All traces of a smile ran away from his face, and he summoned up his most serious expression. "Don't be offended by what I'm about to tell you. And please don't say that I'm losing my mind."

"Tell me," she said, concerned.

"I think I'm only beginning to understand why I've been put in charge in here."

40

•

Theo was counting bullets. Again.

He'd been trying to keep track of spent ammunition since Falcon's first shot had shattered Jack's sunroof. At some point Falcon would need to reload his pistol. That was any gunman's most vulnerable moment. Theo still had to figure out a way to loosen the cord around his hands and ankles. Assuming he could get that done, he would ideally make his move when Falcon was out of bullets and searching frantically for another magazine. Thirteen rounds would be standard. Some guys loaded only twelve to prevent misfeeds. Counting the number of rounds already fired, however, was not as easy as it might seem. Falcon's second shot had hit the girl in the bathroom. One to each of the downed officers made four. Another had taken out the police searchlight. Or was that two shots? Theo couldn't remember, couldn't distinguish Falcon's shots from the return fire by police.

"Where'd you learn to shoot?" said Theo.

Falcon stepped away from the draperies. "None of your damn business."

"What is that you got, anyway? A Browning?" A Browning Hi-Power, was Theo's guess—a long-standing favorite with military forces around the world.

Falcon didn't answer.

"Pretty efficient use of ammunition so far," said Theo. "The girl, two cops, a searchlight. What'd it take you—five bullets, four bullets?"

Falcon only smiled, as if amused by Theo's transparency. "Don't worry. Pretty sure I got one in here with your name on it. But let's go ahead and remove all doubt."

For a split second, Theo thought he was about to be shot. Instead, Falcon hit the pistol's slide-release button with his right thumb, dropping the magazine to the floor, while pulling a new magazine from his coat pocket with his left hand. He inserted the new magazine and finished with a quick slap to its bottom, ensuring that thirteen new rounds were locked in place. A complete tactical reload in about two seconds.

The guy was definitely no stranger to a sidearm.

"You can start counting all over again," said Falcon as he picked up the old magazine.

A loud thud at the door startled everyone in the room.

"What was that?" said the weatherman.

"Quiet!" said Falcon. He pulled the weatherman up off the floor and held him as a human shield. If SWAT came flying through the door, guns firing, the weatherman would be the first to get it.

"Don't use me, use the big guy," the weatherman said in a quaking voice. "You can hide behind him better."

Theo made a mental note to nominate this jackass for *Profiles in Courage*, loser's edition.

Falcon said, "Be still, *everybody*." No one moved, except for Falcon himself, who couldn't seem to make up his mind whether to aim the pistol at the door or the weatherman's brain. They listened for another thud, any sound at all that might explain the intrusion.

A moment of loud electronic feedback resonated from somewhere in the parking lot, and the public address system clicked on. Paulo's voice followed. "Falcon, there's a knot of rope outside your door. Pull it, and it will draw a wagon toward you. There's food in the wagon."

Theo watched as Falcon calculated his next move. Not a thought passed through the guy's head without an exaggerated blink of the eye or twitch of the mouth, as if some kind of facial contortion were part of his normal brain function.

The PA system keyed again. Paulo said, "Your necklace is in there, too."

That clinched it.

"You," Falcon said to the weatherman. He pressed the gun against the man's right temple. "I want you to open the door."

"Okay, sure. I'll do whatever you say."

"You're going to open the door and pull the rope. Take what's in the wagon and grab the rope, too.

Leave the wagon outside. If you try to run, I'll shoot smart-ass here in the head and you in the back."

"You won't have to shoot anyone. Just save your bullets, okay?"

"I got plenty of bullets. Now don't move until I tell you to." He went quickly to the bathroom door and said, "I don't want to hear a peep from you girls."

"You don't have to worry about her," said Natalia, speaking of her injured friend.

"Good." Falcon closed the door, then turned his gun toward Theo. "You. Face down on the floor, over against that wall, away from the door."

His ankles and wrists still bound, Theo rose up on his knees and crawled to the other side of the room. He lay on his belly, but he cocked his head to the left, so that he could still see what was going on.

Falcon cleared away the furniture that was piled up against the door. He untied the electrical cord that bound the weatherman's wrists, and then he stepped back against the far wall, having searched out a spot that would be outside the line of SWAT sniper fire once the door opened. His gun moved back and forth from Theo's head to the weatherman's back. "Now open the door," he told the weatherman, "and do exactly what I told you to do."

The weatherman didn't immediately comply. It seemed less an act of disobedience and more the paralysis of fear.

"Do it!" said Falcon.

The weatherman drew a breath, then let it out, clearly unaware of just how loud his breathing was. The bindings around his ankles forced him to shuffle rather than walk to the door. He turned the deadbolt, reached for the doorknob, and then stopped. "Let me go, please."

Falcon didn't answer.

"I have a wife. Kids, too." The words caught in his throat, perhaps out of fear, perhaps because he was in a hotel room with two young prostitutes.

"I don't give a shit," said Falcon.

"Please. I want to see my family."

"Then do as I say. If you run, hop, or try to roll yourself to safety, you and your big-mouth buddy die. Now open the damn door."

Theo could see the man's hand shaking as he turned the knob and pulled the door open. The room brightened, but not as much as Theo had expected. He'd either miscalculated the time of day, or it was completely overcast.

"Pull the rope," said Falcon.

The weatherman bent over, grabbed the knot of rope at the doorstep, and started pulling.

"Faster!" said Falcon.

Hand over fist, he pulled, and Theo could hear the wagon wheels rolling on the pavement. The whirring grew louder until the wagon was at the door, and the weatherman stopped pulling.

"Quick, empty it!" said Falcon.

Everything was in one bag. The weatherman grabbed it and set it behind him on the floor.

"The rope!" said Falcon. "I want the rope!"

The weatherman untied it from the wagon and dropped it on the floor beside the bag.

"Shut the door!"

The instant it closed, Falcon hurried across the room and pushed the weatherman to the floor. He took the knife from his coat pocket, cut a two-foot length of the rope, and tied the weatherman's hands behind his back. Then he locked the door and piled up the furniture to barricade the entrance. He was about to open the bag when Theo's cell phone rang. Falcon dug it from his pocket and answered on the third ring. Theo was close enough to hear Jack on the other end of the line. He always kept the volume on his cell phone at the maximum setting, since he worked in a noisy bar, and Jack had one of those voices that carried like a loudspeaker. Falcon was holding Theo's phone a good two inches away from his ear to save his eardrum.

"We made good on our end of the deal," said Jack. "Now we need that camera-phone picture we talked about."

"I told you, I'm not wired with explosives."

"Good. Then just take off your coat, take off your shirt, and take a picture. Then put your coat in the wagon and send it back to us. When we see there's no bomb, then we'll all be happy."

"Screw you."

"Falcon, I won't be able to talk the cops into meeting any more of your demands if you don't keep up your end of the deal."

"I said screw you!" He ended the call and stuffed the phone back into his pocket. The expression on his face went completely blank. Finally, he glared at Theo and said, "What are you looking at?"

"You should listen to Jack. He's a straight shooter."

"He's a liar. They're all liars."

"Right now, I'd say you're the one who looks like the liar."

"Who asked you?" He went to the bag, opened it, and looked inside.

Theo could smell the food from across the room. He hadn't realized how hungry he actually was. "We gonna eat or just talk?" said Theo.

"I'm not eating this crap," said Falcon. "The bastards probably put sleeping powder in it."

The guy sounded paranoid, but Theo wasn't so sure that he was wrong. Falcon grabbed a burger from inside the bag and unwrapped it. The aroma was irresistible, and Theo's stomach growled. Falcon went to him and put the burger to his lips. "Lucky you. You're my food tester."

Never in his life had Theo refused food, especially if it was free. Even when he was on death row, he was the one-man exception to a prisonwide hunger strike. But the prospect of some sort of drug in the food didn't seem so far-fetched. "I'm not hungry."

Falcon pressed the barrel of the gun to Theo's forehead. "I'm not asking. Eat it."

Theo took a huge bite.

"That's it," said Falcon. "Let the big dog eat."

Theo took another bite. It tasted amazing, even at gunpoint.

Theo chewed, swallowed. "What are you hiding under the coat?"

"Nothing."

"Then take a picture and show Jack that it's nothing."

"Nah. I kind of like letting those jerk-offs think I have a bomb."

"If it's not a bomb, then what are you hiding under there?"

"What makes you think I'm hiding anything?"

"I felt it when we were wrestling on the ground. There's something under there. Something with wires."

Their eyes locked, and Falcon's expression changed dramatically. He seemed less nervous, less intense, and he was suddenly more distant and vacant. It was an expression unlike any that Theo had ever seen in his life, and Theo had stared down some pretty scary characters in his checkered past. He felt a strange sensation that he had probed into another part of Falcon's world and that Falcon was not sure how to deal with the intruder. The room seemed hotter. Falcon was sweating as he unzipped his coat, though Theo was dead certain that it had nothing to do with the room temperature. Theo braced himself—for what, he wasn't quite sure.

"You mean *these* wires?" said Falcon. He held them in his fist, pulling them out from inside his coat just far enough for Theo to see.

"Oh, shit!" said the weatherman.

"Take it easy," said Theo. "If there's a bomb in there, this is no time to be yanking on any wires."

Falcon clutched the wires tighter with his free hand. Carefully, he continued to unzip the jacket with his gun hand, his index finger still on the trigger, his middle finger pressing the metal zipper tag to the gun butt. He didn't stop until the jacket was completely unzipped. Slowly, he swung open the right half of the heavy coat, like a model showing off the lining to a tailored suit.

Theo could see the bulge in the inside pocket—and the wires leading to it.

"Curious?" said Falcon.

The weatherman's eyes were like saucers. "You don't have to prove anything. Just leave it alone, all right?"

Falcon was perfectly still for perhaps a minute, though it seemed much longer to Theo. Then his hand started upward. The wires went taut, and the bulge in his pocket began to climb.

Theo said, "The weatherman is right. Just leave it alone."

Falcon ignored him. He was like a magician pulling a rabbit out of his hat in slow motion. The weatherman cowered in the corner. "Stop, just stop already!"

Falcon's expression changed once again, the vacant look giving way to something that Theo could only assume was pure amusement. He jerked the wires upward. The weatherman screamed, and Theo rolled toward the wall, as if that would save him from the blast.

Nothing happened.

Theo looked back and saw a small black metal box dangling from the end of the wires. "What is that?"

Falcon flashed a sardonic smile. "It's just an old generator," he said.

Theo's heart was in his throat. It did appear to be some kind of battery-powered generator, which was better than a bomb, but it was still confusing. Falcon was apparently one of those homeless people who kept his treasured possessions with him at all times, no matter how bizarre or useless. Theo said, "I guess you never know when you're going to need your own electricity."

Falcon went to the bag, reached inside, and ran the strand of metal beads through his fingers as if it were a fine pearl necklace. "You'll know," he said in a voice that seemed to come from another place, the remote part of Falcon's world that Theo had intruded upon. "Trust me, smart mouth. You *will* know."

41

The relief was written all over Sergeant Paulo's face.

Jack felt exactly the same way, and to that extent, looking at Paulo was like looking in the mirror. It had been Paulo's idea to plant the tiny electronic listening device in the bottom of the double paper bag, buried between the seams. No one, however, had expected such a big payoff so soon: *no bomb*. On some level, it seemed bizarre to rejoice in the fact that they were dealing only with a paranoid killer who had plenty of ammunition and was a crack shot with his pistol. Small victories, however, were a relative concept, especially in hostage negotiations.

"So, who's the weatherman?" said Jack.

"We think it must be Walt the Weather Wizard from channel seven," said Paulo. "He left the station at eleven-thirty last night and never came home. His wife reported him missing this morning."

"His wife?" said Alicia. "I thought he was gay."

"Everybody does," said Paulo. "Maybe that's how he ended up in a hotel room with two prostitutes. A metrosexual with something to prove."

"More to the point," said Jack, "we now know that there are two male hostages and two females. That's an awful lot for Theo to deal with."

Alicia said, "You mean it's a lot for Falcon to deal with."

"No, I meant Theo," said Jack. "I know how my friend thinks. He won't come out of that hotel room unless they all come out together. Now it turns out that he's stuck in there with two teenage girls and Walt the Weather Wizard. It's all on Theo's shoulders."

No one disagreed.

"At least there's no bomb," said Alicia.

Paulo said, "It's interesting, though, the way he talks about his generator. You can hear it in his voice. It's as if he thinks a generator is more scary than explosives."

"I heard it, too," said Jack. "But it's hard to imagine how that could be."

"Depends on your imagination, I suppose," said Alicia.

"What do you mean?" said Jack.

She hesitated and looked away. "Just, you know, this Falcon has already shown himself to be highly delusional. There's no telling what he thinks his little generator can do. Maybe he's convinced himself that it has the power to change the magnetic charge of the earth's poles or the gravitational pull of the moon."

"You sure that's what you meant?"

"Yeah. What else would I mean?"

Several possible answers to that question tumbled through Jack's mind. The same intuition that had raised his antennae a few hours earlier was gnawing at him again. He could have sworn she was back-pedaling. "Tell me something, Alicia. What scares you the most about Falcon?"

She gave him a curious expression. "That he'll kill the hostages, of course."

"Let me ask a different question. What does your father fear most about him?"

"The same thing, I'm sure."

"How do you know that?"

"Because I know my father."

"Do you?"

"Yes," she said, somewhat annoyed.

"Do you know what your father's bodyguard was doing along the river, down by Falcon's car, the other night?"

"I don't know anything about that."

"How about you, sergeant?"

Jack had hoped to catch Paulo off guard and get some kind of reading from his expression. Paulo was too savvy for that. "Funny thing about people with something on their chest. If they're afraid to get it off, they usually end up with a chip on their shoulder."

"Meaning what?"

"Spare us the cross-examination mode, counselor. If you've got something to say, just say it."

"All right," said Jack. "I'm all for the direct approach, so long as it's a two-way street. Does somebody want to tell me what the mayor's bodyguard was doing down there, or are you going to keep pretending that you didn't know anything about it?"

"I'm sure he had a good reason," said Alicia.

"I'd sure like to hear it. Because a woman was killed that night."

"She was beaten to death with a lead pipe that has Falcon's fingerprints all over it," she said.

"Alicia," said Paulo. It was clearly an admonishment, as she was sharing confidential details about the investigation with a guy who was (or at least had been) Falcon's lawyer.

"I don't care," she said. "I see where you're headed with this, Swyteck, and it's nothing but a distraction. You think something smells fishy. Maybe you even think my father sent his bodyguard down to the river to make sure Falcon doesn't come after me again."

"Maybe I do," said Jack.

"*Alicia*," said Paulo.

"No, I want to clear this up right now. It's ridiculous. Even if my father were the type of man to do such a thing—which he's not—your insinuation just doesn't make any sense. If Falcon himself had ended up dead, maybe you would at least have some semblance of logic on your side. But why in the world would my father's bodyguard kill a defenseless woman who has been homeless for so long that not even the medical examiner can identify her body?"

She had a point, but at this stage of the discussion, Jack wasn't ready to concede anything. "I'm working on that."

"Your work would be better focused on helping Vince solve this crisis."

"*That* I agree with," said Paulo. A moment later, his phone rang. It was the outside line, not their negotiation line. Paulo answered, then covered the mouthpiece and spoke to Jack. "It's Darden, the Miami officer who went with you to the Greater Bahamian Bank and Trust Company. Can you excuse me for a minute please?"

Jack didn't move. "Two-way street, remember?"

Paulo was about to object, then seemed to think better of it. Perhaps he saw an opportunity to regain Jack's trust by not making him leave, but he didn't go so far as to put Darden on speaker. It turned out to be a short conversation, with Paulo doing a lot of listening and very little talking. He hung up after just a couple of minutes.

"Did something turn up at the Bahamian bank?" said Jack.

"Quite the opposite, actually. Darden just gave me a little update on Mr. Riley, the manager who let you into the bank this morning."

"What about him?"

"He's gone missing."

It took Jack a moment to process that one. "'Missing' as in he ran away? Or 'missing' as in foul play?"

"Don't know yet. But according to the Bahamian police, every computer record relating to Falcon's safe deposit box has been destroyed. Every hand-written record, including the access log book, is gone also."

"Sounds like you need to find Mr. Riley."

"Yeah," said Paulo. "I'd say that sounds about right."

·

42

·

Theo kept waiting for the buzz.

Had the food from the wagon been laced with any kind of sleeping agent, some noticeable effect should have kicked in by now. Theo felt nothing. It was like the time Jack had decided to walk on the wild side and bake pot brownies, only to discover that he'd paid his Colombian yardman a hundred bucks for a bag of oregano. Actually, it was Theo who had made the discovery. Jack thought he was stoned. Poor Jack.

How will that guy ever survive without me?

"I want out of here," said the weatherman. He spoke softly, to no one in particular. It wasn't even clear that he'd intended to utter his thoughts aloud.

"What did you say?" said Falcon, challenging him.

"I didn't say anything. It was him," the weatherman said, pointing with a nod toward Theo.

In another setting, with hands untied, Theo

would have snapped the little twerp in half. For his own sake and that of the girls, he kept his cool. "I want a beer," said Theo. "That's all I said."

"Ain't got no beer."

"Try room service."

"Try shutting your damn mouth."

"Can you at least give the men a turn in the bathroom?" said the weatherman.

Falcon nodded. "Go ahead."

"Aren't you going to untie us?" said Theo.

"No. Hop on over there and let Natalia the *jinitera* hold it for you."

They did exactly that, and when they finished, a tense silence gripped the room, like the calm before the storm. Falcon had finally removed his coat, but he showed no sign of complying with Jack's demand that he turn it over to the police for examination. It was bundled up in the corner next to the little generator. Theo had been eyeing the contraption for several minutes. The thing looked to be about a hundred years old, except that portable generators probably didn't exist that long ago. Maybe twenty-five or thirty was more like it. The black metal box was scratched and dirty, with a nasty dent in one corner, as if it had been dropped off a building. One of the knobs or dials was missing, and all that remained was a screw protruding from a round hole in the box. There were two meters—amps and volts, Theo presumed—and the glass casing over one of them was shattered into a spiderweb of cracks. At one time, this might have been a working generator, and perhaps it had even been overworked. Theo had to wonder if it was still operational.

He wondered, too, about the metal beads in the bag.

Twelve hours. That was Theo's best guess as to the duration of this standoff so far. He wondered how long the cops would let it go before sending in SWAT and breaking down the door. A day? Two? He seemed to recall that the FBI's infamous siege of the Branch Davidian compound in Waco had dragged on for nearly two months. Things were always more complicated when dealing with a crazy man. Falcon was beginning to make David Koresh seem sane.

"I want out of here," said the weatherman. It was a whimper, just above a whisper. His face was pinched, and his eyes were closed tightly, as if he were trying to wish away the misery. The guy was on the verge of losing it.

"Quiet!" said Falcon. "Or you're next on the grill."

The grill? Theo wondered. What did he think they were now, hot dogs and hamburgers?

"It's too hot in here!" shouted Natalia. She and her injured friend were still inside the bathroom with the door closed. "Please, open the door."

Falcon didn't move.

Theo felt for the girls. It was boiling hot in the main room. Opening the front door had brought a three-minute blast of fresh air, but that was gone already, and they were again breathing the same air over and over. A triangle of sweat pasted Theo's shirt to his back, and after his quick bathroom break, he could only imagine what it must be like for those two girls trapped inside the tiny bathroom with a toilet that didn't flush. Theo said, "You need to open the bathroom door."

Falcon was staring at the paper bag, silent.

"Hey, genius. They could suffocate in there."

Falcon's gaze remained locked on the paper bag, as if he were in a trance.

Natalia shouted, "She's getting worse. Open the door!"

Falcon didn't flinch. Theo was about to shout and tell him to snap out of it when, finally, Falcon rose and started toward the bag.

Falcon said, "You just won't listen, will you?"

Theo wondered if Falcon was talking to him, but he didn't think so. Falcon seemed to be drifting into another one of those delusional episodes of his.

"You hear me, Swyteck?" said Falcon. "I told you to ask Paulo what I want. Why don't you listen to me?"

He waited a few moments, and finally he answered his own question, speaking as if he were Jack. "I'm listening, Falcon. I just don't want to play any more guessing games."

Another sudden change of expression, and Falcon was himself again. "You'll play whatever game I want you to play. Tell me, Swyteck. It's not a secret. What do I want? What do I *really* want?"

He mulled it over, now playing Jack. "To speak to Alicia Mendoza?"

"Nah, that's old news. This bullshit has gone on way too long. You can't solve things that easy. Not this late in the game."

Another role change. "Then just tell me what you want."

He was suddenly Falcon again, leaning closer to the bag, as if to stress the importance of his point. "Okay, here's what I want: I want to hear Alicia *beg* to talk to me."

Falcon chuckled in reply, the way Jack might. "That's not going to happen, pal."

"Oh, yes, it will, Swyteck. Before long, she'll want to talk to me so bad it hurts. She'll want it so bad that she won't ever forget who Falcon is. And when we're done, she'll thank me. She really will. She'll thank me."

It was strange to watch a man carry on a conversation so convincingly, as if Jack were in the room, but it suddenly occurred to Theo that Falcon wasn't delusional. This time, he was crazy like a fox. Falcon had figured it out before Theo. There was a microphone in the bag, and from the look in Falcon's eye, Theo could tell that he was about to tear the bag apart and destroy it. Before that happened, Theo wanted to convey one last bit of information to Jack. "Hey, Falcon."

He looked in Theo's general direction, but he was still too busy keeping up both ends of his conversation with Jack to focus on Theo.

Theo said, "The girl in the bathtub really needs a doctor."

Falcon didn't answer.

"Did you hear me?" said Theo, speaking in a voice that was loud enough to be picked up by the listening device. "I said, the girl in the bathroom is hurt and really needs a doctor."

Falcon picked up the paper bag and dumped the food, drinks, and metal beads onto the floor. He took the beads and laid them in the corner beside his generator. Then, slowly, he tore the grocery bag at the corners and laid the brown paper flat on the floor like a doormat. He began walking on it, ever so carefully, like a man fearful of stepping on a landmine.

"A doctor, huh?" he said with his second step. "You say the girl needs a doctor?" Another step. "That's really too bad. Because the doctor is nowhere to be found."

He took two more steps, inching closer to the crisscrossing seams of the bag's double bottom. "But if you find him," he said, raising his foot, as if poised to kill a cockroach, "if you do manage to talk to that chickenshit doctor, you be sure to ask about *la bruja*."

He brought his foot down with full force, and the smashing of the tiny microphone between the seams made a small pop that could be heard across the room. "The witch," he added, but only for Theo's benefit.

43
·

In a reflective moment outside his mobile command center, Vince allowed himself to wonder what he was missing.

Vince didn't think of himself as an existentialist, but, ironically, his blindness almost forced him to step outside his own body and see himself. Sometimes he saw a happy Vince adapting to a world that didn't depend on sight. He knew the smell of Alicia's perfume and how it faded as the day wore on. He could hear footsteps around him and even differentiate between the heavy plod of SWAT members and the lighter step of Alicia as she walked away, toward the restaurant, leaving him alone with his thoughts. He could feel the breeze on his face and smell the Laundromat down the street. He heard helicopters overhead, the buzz of traffic a block away as it was being rerouted around the barricades on Biscayne Boulevard. With a little extra concentration, he could suddenly distinguish buses from trucks, trucks from cars, little cars from gas-guzzlers. Nearby, a pigeon cooed, then another, and it sounded as though they were scrapping over a piece of bread or perhaps a bagel that someone had dropped in the parking lot. A car door slammed. Men were talking in the distance. No, not just men—there was a woman, too, though Vince couldn't make out the words. In some ways, he was more aware of his surroundings, or at least of certain details of his surroundings, than many sighted persons.

Other times, however, he looked at himself and saw a foolish Vince who blithely skated by in a world that acted upon him and described itself to him through sound, smell, taste, and touch. The foolish Vince failed to realize that he lived his life largely in a reactive posture, failed to appreciate that things still existed even if they concealed themselves and did not call out to him for recognition.

He wondered where the patches of silence lay in this assignment, and he wondered what secrets they held.

"Paulo," said Sergeant Chavez.

Vince turned at the voice and faced the SWAT leader. "Yeah?"

"Chief Renfro's on the line. Wants us to conference. Come on, in the SWAT van." He took Vince by the arm and tried to steer him toward the van. Vince resisted, not because he didn't want to go but because Chavez was apparently of the mind that blind folks should wear a brass ring in the nose so they could be led around like stray calves. "My hand at your elbow will work just fine," said Vince.

They entered the van through the side door. Chavez directed Vince to one of the captain's chairs, took the other one for himself, and slid the door shut. "We're all here, Chief," Chavez said into the speakerphone.

"Good," said Renfro, her voice resonating over the speaker.

"You want another update already?" said Vince.

"Not unless something's changed in the last five minutes."

"No change."

"Good," said the chief. "Chavez and I were just talking, and we have both reached the very same and firm conclusion. I know you won't like this, but it's time to start angling for a kill shot."

"What?"

"We're going to take him out," said Chavez, as if translating.

"But he just admitted that he has no bomb," said Vince.

The chief said, "We don't give that any credence. Falcon clearly knew there was a listening device hidden in the bag when he said there was no bomb."

"I don't think he was trying to trick us."

"Doesn't matter," said Chavez. "The message from Theo Knight was loud and clear. There's someone inside the bathroom who's hurt and needs a doctor."

"I agree," said Vince. "I was just working out my next phone call in my head. Let me see if I can talk Falcon into letting her go to the hospital."

"That's ridiculous," said Chavez.

"Let him talk," the chief said. "Paulo, how do you propose to get the injured hostage out of there?"

"We can roll a gurney up to the door, just like we did with the food in the wagon."

Chavez scoffed. "Falcon won't trust that. We planted an eavesdropping device in the food bag. He'll probably think a gurney rolling into the hotel room is a Trojan horse loaded with specially trained, three-foot-tall SWAT members."

Vince said, "Maybe he'll let a doctor come in and see her."

"Maybe he'll hold the doctor hostage, too. Chief, you and I have been over this already, and time is a-wasting. That girl could be dying in there for all we know."

There was silence, then the chief said, "That's where I keep coming out on this, Paulo. I can't let you keep talking indefinitely, knowing that there's a hostage in need of medical attention."

"So we're going in, right?" said Chavez. "That's the plan."

"That's not a plan," said Vince. "Not unless you want dead hostages on your hands."

"Paulo's right," said the chief. "I want to try a sniper shot before we break any doors down. Maybe we can get him to open the door or come to the window. Paulo, I need you to help us set it up."

Suddenly, it was as if all the questions were answered, as if the real reason for his involvement were being trumpeted from the hilltops. Vincent Paulo wasn't there to negotiate for the release of hostages. His highly conceived role was to facilitate and assist in Falcon's execution. And he had the sinking feeling that this had been the foolish blind man's role from the beginning.

"All right, Chief. Let me see what I can come up with."

44

Jack was standing by the Dumpster behind the restaurant, ready to make a follow-up phone call to his father. He'd punched out six numbers when a uniformed officer interrupted.

"There's someone at the barricade who insists on seeing you," she said.

It was one of those eerie *doo-doo, doo-doo* moments, as Jack got the impression that his father had shown up just as he was about to place the call. "Who is it?"

"Says she's your *abuela*. I told her you were kind of busy. But she's, to put it mildly, persistent. Kind of a crazy old lady. No offense. My *abuela*'s crazy too."

Not like mine, thought Jack. He put his phone away. First things first, and *Abuela* never came second. "All right. Lead on."

Abuela, of course, was Jack's maternal grandmother, his chief source of information about the mother he had never known. Jack's mother died while he was still in the hospital nursery. His father remarried before Jack was out of diapers. Jack's stepmother was a good woman with a weakness for gin martinis and an irrational hatred for Harry's first love and, by extension, all things Cuban. As a result, Jack was a half-Cuban boy raised in a completely Anglo home with virtually no link to Cuban culture—a handicap that his *abuela* was determined to rectify. The results were mixed, at best.

"Jack Swyteck, *ven aca*." Come here.

She was standing behind the striped barricade with arms folded across her bosom, a disapproving scowl on her face. Jack remained on the other side of the barricade. This was not going to be pretty, and some official separation from her wrath couldn't hurt.

He leaned closer, kissed her forehead, and said, "What did I do now?"

Her love for talk radio had improved her ear for English (Dr. Laura was her favorite), but when speaking, she often stuck to the present tense. "Your father calls to tell me what you are doing."

"I asked him to," said Jack.

"Then I turn on television news and hear your name. Is this how I should find out what you are doing?"

"I'm sorry. I've been very busy."

"Too busy to pick up the phone and tell me you are okay?"

"*Abuela*, I'm negotiating for the release of hostages."

"On an empty stomach, I am sure."

"I really haven't been that hungry."

"So you eat nothing?"

Jack suddenly felt like a five-year-old. "I had half of a coconut *pastelito*."

"Hmm. *Por lo menos, lo que comiste fue algo Cubano*." At least what you ate was something Cuban.

There was a picnic basket at her feet, and Jack could suddenly smell the food. She picked it up and said, "I bring you this."

Jack took it, and all he could do was smile. "*Gracias*."

"Share with your friends."

"I will."

A look of genuine concern came over her. "How is Theo?"

Jack tried to be positive. "You know Theo. He'll be all right."

She nodded, then returned the conversation to a lighter subject, as if sensing that Jack needed the diversion. She pulled back the red-and-white checkered cloth covering the basket. "There are four Cuban sandwiches, still hot from the press, the way you like. The *papas fritas* are *deliciosa* with the green-olive-and-garlic *mojo*. For dessert, there is *tres leches*, which you know is my own invention."

Jack smiled. It had been a while since *Abuela* had made herself the laughingstock of Spanish-language talk radio by phoning in and claiming to have invented *tres leches*, the Nicaraguan specialty. But who was Jack to take sides? "It's your legacy," he said.

She leaned forward and kissed him on the cheek.

"No, you are." Then she looked at him sternly and said, "Do *not* be stupid."

"I won't."

"Good. Try this," she said, handing him something sweet.

Jack took a bite, and it was delicious. "I love Torinos."

"*Aye, mi vida*," she said with a roll of her eyes. "*Turones*."

"Sorry." You could say that Jack had a mental block about that word. Then again, you could say the same thing about Jack and roughly two-thirds of the entire Spanish language. But his idiomatic bumbling did bring a pertinent thought to mind.

"*Abuela*, tell me something. Did anyone back in Cuba ever refer to homeless people as *los Desaparecidos?* The Disappeared?"

"Why do you ask that?"

"Because Falcon is homeless, and he has used the term several times in our discussions. We're trying to figure out what it means. I thought it might be some kind of Cuban slang for homeless people."

"Not that I've ever heard of. But you know that man is not Cuban, no?"

"Actually, he is. I saw his file when I was his lawyer. He came here from Cuba in the early eighties."

"He may come here from Cuba, but he is not Cuban."

"How do you know?"

"I watch the television this morning. They show film from the last time, when the police take him down from the bridge over to Key Biscayne. He is yelling in Spanish, cursing at the police when they arrest him and say he can't speak to Mayor Mendoza's daughter. That is not Cuban Spanish. I have an ear for these things. Trust me. *Ese hombre no es Cubano.*"

That man is not Cuban.

Abuela was not always right on the money, but Jack knew one thing. When it came to all things Hispanic, her word was gold. Falcon was not Cuban. Jack could take that one to the bank. "Thank you," he said.

"Of course. Is nothing."

She obviously thought he was talking about the food, which he wasn't.

"No," he said as his gaze drifted up the barricaded boulevard in the general direction of the mobile command center. "I have a feeling that this is definitely something."

45

Alicia rushed home, not to her Coconut Grove townhouse, but to the walled and gated Mediterranean-style villa in which she'd grown up. The Mendozas had lived in the same house since Alicia was seven years old. It wasn't a palace by any stretch, especially compared to the new ten-thousand-square-foot McMansions that seemed to blanket South Florida like the dreaded red tide, but it was a great old house. Twin pillars covered in purple bougainvillea stood like sentries at the driveway entrance. Beyond the wrought-iron gate was the circular driveway where Alicia had learned the hard way that it was a very bad idea to roller-skate on Chicago brick.

She parked beneath the largest of several sprawling oak trees that shaded the property, then made her usual entrance: one ring of the doorbell to warn anyone inside who might be walking around in their underwear, and then she let herself in with her key. She was passing through the kitchen when her mother greeted her.

"Alicia, I wasn't expecting to see you today," she said with a warm smile. Graciela Mendoza was actually a striking Latin beauty who took excellent care of herself, but today she was sporting the Marjorie Stoneham Douglas look, dressed in a floppy straw sunhat and blue jeans stained at both knees with rich black potting soil. Gardening was her passion.

Alicia said, "This is sort of unexpected from my end, too."

"Did they resolve that hostage situation?"

"Not yet. I have to get back, but I need to check on something quickly."

"Here?"

"Yes." She knew that she couldn't possibly explain, so she didn't even try. "Is all my old stuff still in the bedroom closet?"

"Yes, of course."

"This probably sounds weird, but there's something I need to find."

"What is it? Maybe I can help."

"No, that's okay. It's sort of official police business." *Sounding weirder by the minute*, Alicia realized.

"Okay," her mother said. "Holler if you need anything."

"Thanks, Mom." She turned and went straight to her old bedroom, which no longer resembled the shrine to Alicia that had existed for years after she'd left home. Her parents had finally turned it into a home office, though it was still decorated with a few of her adolescent touches, including a message board filled with names and phone numbers that were so vitally important to a teenager and not even remotely a part of her present life. There was no time to reminisce. She went to the closet, which was like a time capsule filled with awards, toys, school yearbooks, and other mementos. Her search was very narrow: she was looking for Manuel Garcia Ferre.

Ferre created some of the cartoon favorites from her childhood. Not many Americans knew of his talents, except for a few foreign-film buffs who might recall that his animated film *La Manuelita* was Argentina's official entry to the 1999 Academy Awards. Truth be told, surprisingly few Argentines even knew that bit of movie trivia. Alicia was no expert on her ancestry, but it had long been her passing observation that Argentina showed too little enthusiasm for its own contributions to culture. Argentines didn't even embrace the tango (born in bordellos) until it caught on in Paris, and the country continued to revile its greatest tango composer, Astor Piazolla, even as Europeans hailed him as a genius. Argentina had a history of being equally standoffish about local films, many of which were of first quality but lagged far behind Hollywood blockbusters and European films at the Argentine box offices. But Alicia's father, thousands of miles away from his native country, made sure that his daughter knew Ferre's work, which for decades has delighted Spanish-speaking children. He'd supplied her with comic books and videotapes of cartoons that had once aired on Canal 13–Buenos Aires and other Argentine television stations. It was his way of connecting her at a young age to her homeland and to her parents' native tongue.

Alicia went from top shelf to bottom in search of the right box. Naturally, it was in the last place she checked. She pulled it off the shelf and laid it on the floor, then unfolded the flaps and peered inside. Another era was staring back at her. The comic books were on top. Her favorite was *Las Aventuras de Hijitus*, the adventures of an orphan kid who fought the forces of evil. Simply by saying magical words, Hijitus could transform himself into Súper Hijitus, a boy in a blue suit who is propelled through the air by a little propeller atop his head.

Alicia gave a little nostalgic smile and laid the comic books aside. Wouldn't it have been nice if Vince had simply called Hijitus?

Beneath the comic books, she found the videotapes, packed across the bottom of the box like spine-out books on a shelf. Alicia couldn't recall ever having made a conscious decision to save them all these years, but she suspected that somewhere in her heart lay a plan to share them with her own children. She allowed herself to wonder for a moment if Vince would be the father, and it saddened her to think that he would never see any of this. She cleared her mind of such thoughts, however, as it had nothing to do with her mission. The important thing was that her old favorites were still there. She ran her finger lightly across the titles, searching for one of particular interest. She didn't find it. She checked again, knowing that it had to be there.

It was gone.

She felt a slight chill, but her suspicions were not yet confirmed. Maybe she'd loaned it to a childhood friend and forgot about it. Maybe for some reason she'd decided not to save this one. Neither of those possibilities seemed likely, however. She guarded her collection like gold.

Her gaze swept the room and settled upon the PC that her parents had set up in the corner of the room. It was running, and the screen saver of bright blue sky and puffy white clouds beckoned. She went to it, clicked on the Internet browser, and typed a few pertinent words into the search engine. It came back with exactly what she needed. She opened the link and went straight to the Web site.

On screen, a pitch-black background transformed itself into impenetrable night sky with flashes of lightning and a blanket of twinkling stars. To one side, a dead, leafless tree shivered. The vacant eyes of two orange pumpkins flashed back and forth from white to black. A creepy old Victorian-style house soon took center stage, the doors and windows of irregular shapes, as if the whole structure were in danger of collapsing at any moment. A black bat fluttered in the wind, between the house and the old tree. And in bright orange letters, the title appeared against the black sky.

La Covacha de la Bruja Cachavacha.

Finally, in a high-pitched, scary voice that still gave Alicia the shivers, the witch—*la bruja*—said, "*Bienvenidos a mi casa.*"

Welcome to my house.

This witch was no Elizabeth Montgomery or

Nicole Kidman. Her orange hair and pointy hat made her scary enough, and she was plenty ugly, with a big, long nose and missing teeth. For a cartoon character, particularly one created for children, she was unusually macabre. The thing that Alicia remembered most about her, and the very thing that had lured her back to her old bedroom, was the strange magic this witch possessed.

She had the power to make people disappear.

Alicia was still looking at the computer screen, this modern-day window to her childhood, but she was no longer really focused. She was thinking more about Falcon's words—be sure to ask about the witch—and about his apparent obsession with "the disappeared." She had yet to sort it out and think it through completely, but there was enough to make Alicia wonder.

How does that creep know anything about my childhood?

46

Jack needed some straight talk from Sergeant Paulo.

On paper, the line between good and evil seemed easy to draw in a hostage situation: hostage-taker, bad; hostage-negotiator, good. In Jack's mind, however, the line was starting to blur. It wasn't Paulo who was causing the confusion as much as the people around him, both on and off the scene. The mayor was sending mixed messages about his support for Paulo as lead negotiator. His bodyguard's appearance at the river on the night of the murder remained unexplained. By nature, SWAT leaders were bursting with confidence, but Sergeant Chavez was becoming so arrogant that he seemed to have his own agenda. At times, even Alicia sent out confusing signals. For Jack, the interpersonal dynamic was starting to resemble a complicated trial in which he represented one of several co-defendants, where everyone professed to stand together at the outset, but where ultimate survival depended on covering your back in dagger-proof armor. Things were nowhere near that extreme—not yet, anyway—but Jack still found himself trying to figure out who could be trusted to act in the best interest of Theo and the other hostages.

He chose Sergeant Paulo.

Alicia was away when Jack returned to the mobile command center. Paulo was giving himself a quick shave with an electric razor. Another member of the crisis team was seated beside him, but he was more than willing to take a short break when Jack asked for a few minutes alone with Paulo. The door closed as the officer left the command center. Paulo switched off his razor, and the ball was in Jack's court.

"I need to know the plan," said Jack. "The whole plan."

To Jack's mild surprise, Paulo skipped the police doubletalk. "Falcon is going down," he said.

"I'm sure that if it comes to that, no one will blame you."

"It's no longer just an option. You wanted to know the plan; that is the plan. They've made their decision."

It was interesting that Paulo put it in terms of a decision *they've* made. "SWAT is going in?" said Jack.

"They want to try a sniper shot first."

"How do they plan to set it up?"

"That's my job—our job, actually, to the extent that you'll be doing at least part of the talking."

"What am I supposed to tell him? 'Hey, Falcon,

would you mind stepping closer to the window please? Good. Head up a little. That's it. Now hold it.'"

"Ideally we'll come up with a ruse to make him open the door and provide a clean shot. Drawing him to the window and somehow getting him to reveal himself is a possibility, but it's not the preferred method. Even a trained marksman loses some degree of accuracy when shooting through a pane of glass."

"What's the difference? It's clear glass, not a Coke bottle."

"It can still affect the bullet's trajectory, depending on distance and angles. And it's been looking like rain all day. If it comes, that's another issue. Even in clear weather, the safest assumption when shooting through a window is that the first shot will miss. But now that they have a green light, our snipers don't need more than a split second to get off a second shot."

Jack considered his response. He wanted this standoff to end as quickly as possible, but up until now he'd at least held out some hope that Falcon would put down his gun and surrender. Negotiating with the sole objective of putting a bullet in a man's head changed the tenor of things. "When was this decision made?"

"I was just told about it five minutes ago."

Something in Paulo's voice conveyed that the question wasn't being answered directly. "But when was it made?" said Jack.

"Sometime after we found out about the injured hostage, is what they tell me."

Jack still sensed some equivocation. This was no time to let anything slide, even at the risk of offending. "Do you believe what they're telling you?"

There was silence, and if Vince had been a sighted person, Jack sensed that they would have exchanged one of those long, ambiguous stares in which two equally cautious men size each other up and decide how much honesty their evolving relationship can handle. Strange, but Jack had the feeling that Paulo was doing exactly that, albeit on some level that didn't depend on sight.

Paulo said, "I'm a suspicious man. It's my nature."

"So you have some questions in your mind."

"Sure I do."

"Do you ever wonder about the real objective here?" said Jack.

"I have only one objective, and that's to get these folks out alive."

"Does it matter to you if Falcon lives or dies?"

"Of course it matters. But the safety of the hostages is paramount."

Honesty. That was all Jack wanted. "Can we cut the bullshit?"

Paulo's expression changed, as if he'd suddenly realized he was talking in platitudes. "Yeah, sure."

Jack had a theory, but he wasn't quite sure how to present it. He took an indirect route. "You know the history between me and Theo, right?"

"In a general sense. You were his lawyer. Got him off death row."

"Theo was my one innocent client in four years with the Freedom Institute."

Paulo shook his head slightly. "Don't know how you lawyers do that. Defending the guilty, I mean."

"Maybe we can have that talk over beers when this is over. The funny thing is, the client on my mind right now isn't Theo."

"It's Falcon?"

"No. It's a guy named Dusty Boggs. Dusty was at a bar and got into an argument over whose quarter was next in line on the edge of the pool table. Dusty said it was his game; the other guy said it was his. So Dusty went out to his car, got his gun, walked back inside the bar, and shot the guy in the head."

"You represented Dusty?"

"Yeah. He was my very first client. I was just a few weeks out of law school, still studying for the bar exam. My boss and I went down to the prison to interview him. For whatever reason, Dusty showed more confidence in me than in my boss, even though Neil Goderich was a seasoned trial lawyer with more death cases under his belt than any lawyer I've ever known. Anyway, at the end of the interview, Neil told Dusty that he would be defending him at trial. Dusty got this angry look on his face. Then he banged his fists on the table, looked at me, and said, 'I want Swyteck!'"

"Before you'd even passed the bar?"

"Yup. So Neil agreed to supervise me, and I was Dusty's lawyer. I essentially did the whole trial myself. Thought I did a pretty good job, too."

"You got him off?"

"Are you kidding? He was convicted of murder in the first degree and sentenced to death. But here's the point of the story. Dusty appealed his conviction, and guess what his lead argument was."

"I don't know. The butler did it?"

"Ineffective assistance of counsel. He claimed that a recent law-school graduate who hadn't even passed the bar exam wasn't qualified to handle a death penalty case. The court of appeals agreed and ordered a new trial. But as time dragged on, witnesses started to disappear and some of them even changed their stories. We ended up plea bargaining, and Dusty got life instead of the electric chair."

"Sounds like old Dusty was crazy like a fox."

"That's exactly right. He knew he had zero chance of an acquittal, no matter who his lawyer was."

"So he set you up."

"He set me up," said Jack, repeating Paulo's words slowly enough to underscore his point. He waited another moment, giving the sergeant sufficient time to catch his drift. It was a delicate subject, but Jack felt as though it needed to be broached. "You ever feel like you've been set up, Vince?"

Paulo didn't flinch. He simply seemed to be processing Jack's intimation. Jack said, "I have this theory."

"Talk to me."

"I think someone has wanted Falcon dead all along."

The suggestion didn't seem to shock him. Paulo said, "I don't know if I'd go that far. But they don't seem to want him alive."

"Who are 'they'?"

Paulo didn't answer. Jack didn't let it drop. He

said, "I think they want him dead almost as much as they want the hostages freed."

"I would never want to believe that."

"Believe it."

"What makes you say that?"

"As soon as I returned from the Bahamas this morning, I was taken straight to the mayor for a private talk. He laid it on heavy, how he wanted my solemn word that I would do nothing to jeopardize Alicia's safety in these negotiations, even if that meant disobeying certain instructions from you."

"That's no surprise. At least among insiders, it's no secret that I'm not his first choice to head up these negotiations. I'm smart enough to realize that his show of support for me in the press conference this morning was just talk. Law enforcement always wants to present a united front."

"Forget what the public has been told. I'm talking about what's going on within the department. Internally, as far as all the players in the negotiation are concerned, Mayor Mendoza has led everyone to believe that Vincent Paulo is the last person on earth that he'd like to see in charge of this negotiation. But according to my sources, you were put in charge because the mayor called Chief Renfro and told her to do it."

"Your sources?"

Jack did not want to implicate Detective Barber at this point. "You have to remember who my old man is."

"Your daddy has an ear to the wall on this?"

"Only because I asked him to. And the walls can

be pretty thin for a former governor who was once a City of Miami cop."

Paulo started working a pencil through his fingers like a miniature baton, and it was as if Jack could see the wheels turning inside his head. Finally, Paulo said, "Let me see if I follow your logic. Someone has wanted Falcon dead all along. The mayor tells the chief to put me in charge of the negotiations. As soon as the opportunity arises, the chief tells me to step aside and let the snipers take Falcon out. I'm in charge, but I'm not in charge."

Jack was silent. It sounded harsh coming from Paulo's own lips.

Paulo continued, "Falcon is my Dusty Boggs. I've been set up to fail."

"It's just a theory," said Jack.

"It's an execution they want, not a negotiation," said Paulo. "If it takes one bullet to drop Falcon, mission accomplished. If something goes wrong and a hostage goes down in the crossfire, it's my fault. The blind guy takes the fall."

"I'm not saying it's true," said Jack. "It's just something to consider."

"I have considered it," said Paulo, his voice turning very serious. "You and I are on the same page."

It was more honesty than Jack had expected, and he wasn't going to squander the opportunity. "Why do you think they want Falcon dead?"

"Mendoza can be a vindictive man, I'm told. Maybe the message is simply 'Don't mess with the mayor's daughter.'"

"Or maybe it's something else," said Jack.

"You got a theory on that, too?"

"I'm working on it," said Jack.

"Work faster," said Paulo. "We're running out of time."

"Theo's running out of time," said Jack.

"Maybe we can buy a little more." A hint of a smile creased Paulo's lips. "They've got the guns, but you and I are still the only two people who Falcon will talk to. All I need to know is that you're willing to work with me on this."

"That's exactly what I was hoping to hear," said Jack.

47

Jack placed the call from his own cell phone. Sergeant Paulo wanted it that way. Paulo refused to be anyone's puppet, and Jack was more than willing to help cut the strings. If that meant calling from the mobile command center on a wireless phone that wasn't encrypted, Jack was on board, even if he did not yet fully understand Paulo's strategy. There was no time to debate every decision, and Jack figured that his show of trust in the sergeant's instincts would only serve to solidify their alliance.

The phone rang several times, but Jack was certain that Falcon would answer soon enough. Falcon was using Theo's cell phone, and Jack's number was programmed into it. The display would identify Jack as the caller.

"Changing phones on me, Swyteck?" said Falcon.

"Yeah. I figured it was time to shake things up a little."

"I thought that was my job."

"We've got the same job. Let's end this thing and keep everyone safe."

"Did you get my money from the Bahamas yet?"

Jack had been hoping to avoid that matter, and the abrupt change of subject caught him somewhat off guard. "Soon," he said, but the bluff rang hollow even in his own ears.

"You're stalling," said Falcon.

"No, I'm working on it."

"You're lying."

"It's more complicated than you think."

"You stole it, didn't you?"

"No. I didn't steal it."

"You stole my money, and now you think you can just keep on talking in circles."

"That's not true at all."

"You stole my money, and I want it back *now*!"

"I just need a little more time."

"Time? How much time do you think I've got here? Time is up, Swyteck. Tell me where my money is, or I swear, I'm going to—"

"It's gone," said Jack. He cut off Falcon before he could say the words "shoot a hostage," which would have unleashed an immediate breach by SWAT.

"What did you just say?" said Falcon.

Jack collected himself. Paulo offered a nod of encouragement, as if to say that the truth was out, there was no taking it back, and perhaps it was even better this way. Jack said, "We went to your safe deposit box, just like you told me to. A manager named Riley met us there. When we opened the box, the money was gone."

"All of it?"

"Yes. Even Riley was shocked. The only thing

inside was a note. It was handwritten in Spanish."

"Really?" said Falcon. The shrill edge was gone from his voice. He sounded genuinely intrigued. "What did it say?"

"It read: '*Donde están los Desaparecidos?*' Where are the Disappeared?"

The words were met by stone-cold silence. Jack waited for a reply, and, after several moments of dead air, he wondered if Falcon was still on the line. "Falcon?" he said.

Falcon replied in a soft, calm voice, a tone that Jack had not heard in any of their previous conversations. It was a combination of pleasure and relief, punctuated with a hint of sheer joy. "She came," he said. "I can't believe it. She finally came."

"Who came?" said Jack.

There was no reply.

"Falcon?" said Jack. "Who came? Who are you talking about?"

The silence on the other end of the line was suddenly more profound, and Jack realized that no response was coming. The call was over. Falcon was gone. Jack closed his flip phone and laid it on the table in front of him. He stared at it for a moment, trying to comprehend the exchange that had just ended.

Paulo said, "Not exactly according to plan, was it?"

"No," said Jack, looking off to the middle distance. "At least not *our* plan."

48

Falcon shoved the cell phone in his pocket and resumed pacing. In his years of homelessness, he often went for long walks along the river, up Miami Avenue, and down Biscayne Boulevard. Confinement to a tiny, closed-in motel room made him feel like a caged animal. Walking helped him to clear his head, settle the confusion, and silence the voices. Swyteck had laid a huge mind-blower on him. On the streets, he could have walked all the way to Fort Lauderdale and back just processing this one.

The money was gone. It disappeared.

The money. The Disappeared. The play on words brought a bemused expression to his face.

"You want to share the good news with the rest of us?" said Theo.

Falcon turned and saw his reflection in the full-length mirror on the closet door. He did look like someone who had just received good news. But it was no one else's business. "Speak when you're spoken to," he said.

"That girl still needs a doctor," said Theo.

"Shut up! Don't you think I know that? Of course she needs a doctor."

"So what are you going to do about it?"

"What do you want me to do? The doctor isn't here."

"Then let her go to one."

"We can't."

"Sure you can," said Theo. "Just open the door. I'll carry her out into the parking lot only as far as you say, and then I'll come back inside."

"Sure you will."

"You have my permission to shoot me in the back if I try anything funny."

Falcon was pacing again, furiously this time. The last telephone conversation with Swyteck had brought a long-awaited clarity to his thoughts, and then Mr. Big Mouth had to mention the girl again and scramble everything. It wasn't his fault that she needed a doctor. It wasn't his fault that the doctor wasn't around. There was only so much he could do, only so much abuse he could stand, only so much self-loathing he could inflict.

"What do you want from me?" he shouted, but he didn't wait for Theo or anyone else to reply. Demons that he'd kept locked deep inside were taking control and forcing their way to the surface like a volcanic eruption. He went to the wall and started kicking it with the force of a soccer star. "Why . . . the hell . . . did you . . . have . . . to be . . . *pregnant*?" he said, a swift kick to the wall marking each break in his sentence. He didn't even notice the horror on the hostages' faces, didn't hear the girl shouting that he had it all wrong, that neither she nor her injured friend was pregnant. It was as if the hostages were no longer in the motel room, as if Falcon himself were in another place, another time. In his mind's eye, he was seeing other faces, ones that had haunted him for over a quarter-century.

"Faster!" shouted El Oso. He was in the backseat of the car with the expectant mother, prisoner 309. She was flat on her back, belly protruding, knees bent, her feet squirming in El Oso's lap. She was wearing a loose-fitting cotton dress, but it was hiked up to her hips, all sense of modesty abandoned.

"You must drive faster!" she cried.

"Two more minutes," said the driver.

She let out a shriek that belonged in the torture chamber. That kind of noise coming from a man on the grill was something that El Oso heard every day, all just a part of the job. The same sound coming from a woman in labor affected him in ways that he had never anticipated.

"I have to push," she said.

"No, you can't!"

She started breathing loudly through her mouth, in and out, trying to build a rhythm and control the pain. Her face was flushed red and glistening with sweat. Her legs quivered, and her eyes bulged as if ready to pop from her head. Every pothole in the bumpy road elicited another grimace of pain. "I *really* have to push."

"Not yet!" said El Oso.

She rolled from her back onto her left side and drew her knees up, assuming more of a fetal position. It seemed to help slightly.

"This is the turn," said the driver.

"Just hold on a few more minutes," El Oso told the woman.

The car squealed around the corner. Gravel flew as they turned off a paved highway and continued down a long, narrow alley. It was almost midnight, and with no streetlights in the alley, they sped like a freight train through a long, dark tunnel. The car suddenly screeched to a halt. The driver jumped out and opened the rear door. He grabbed the woman by the armpits, and El Oso took her by the legs. Together, they carried her to a metal fire escape at the rear of a rundown apartment building. In their haste, they knocked over a trash can, which sent a pack of rats scurrying toward the gutters. Up the rickety metal stairs they climbed, all the way to the third floor.

"Where are you taking me?" the woman said in a voice tight with pain.

Neither man replied as they reached the top of the fire escape. They were standing at the rear entrance to an apartment. A light shone through the kitchen window, but the door was closed and made of solid wood. El Oso was still holding the woman's legs with both hands, so he knocked on the door by kicking it so hard and with such urgency that the steel toe of his military boot splintered the lower panel. "We're here, let us in!" he shouted.

The deadbolt turned, and the door opened a few

inches. El Oso immediately pushed against it, practically pulling the pregnant woman and the driver across the threshold. The old woman who had unlocked the door was suddenly pinned behind it, her back to the wall. Before she could speak, El Oso shouted, "Look the other way, woman!"

She complied without protest, averting her eyes from the pregnant woman as the men carried her inside. "Take her to the back bedroom," she told the men.

El Oso and the other man carried her through the kitchen and down the dimly lit hall to the bedroom. She seemed to be getting heavier with each step, and the men were so exhausted that they dropped her onto the mattress.

"Please, get this baby out of me!" she cried.

The older woman was still waiting in the kitchen. "Are you ready for me?" she asked.

"Wait!" said El Oso. He took a black cloth from his pocket and put it over the prisoner's head. She resisted and tried to pull it off, but El Oso grabbed her by the wrists. "The hood stays on, or you and your baby die."

"Okay, whatever you say," she said, her voice trembling. "Please, let's just do this!"

El Oso called into the next room. "We're ready!"

The midwife rushed through the open doorway and went straight to the prisoner. Everything she needed for the delivery was arranged neatly on a table beside the bed. "Let's get those underpants off," she said.

The men lifted her hips, and the midwife slid

the underpants down the woman's legs. They were soaking wet with fluid from her broken membrane. "She's ready to push," said the midwife.

"No kidding!" the woman cried, her voice only slightly muffled beneath the black hood.

"How far apart are your contractions?"

"I don't know. Not very long. Hurry, please. I can hardly breathe with this stupid hood over my head!"

The midwife asked each of the men to take one of the woman's feet and raise her legs into the air. Then she probed with her whole hand into the vagina, stopping just before she was in up to her wrist. "The head is right there. Clearly you've been pushing already."

"I tried not to."

"One more good one and I'll be able to grab a shoulder."

The woman's body tightened. Another contraction was coming. "It hurts so much!"

"Push through it," said the midwife. "Just ignore what your brain is telling you and push right through it!"

El Oso could not see the woman's face, but he knew that beneath that black hood was the contorted face of a woman in utter agony. She screamed again, and the midwife assured her that she was doing great. El Oso was starting to feel dizzy.

"Keep pushing!" said the midwife.

The woman rose up on her elbows so that her shoulders were elevated above the mattress. She was half sitting and half lying on the bed, trying to find the best angle to push out the baby and end this ordeal. The next scream was loud enough to be heard throughout the neighborhood. The crown of a newborn's head emerged between her legs.

The next few moments were a blur to El Oso. He heard the woman screaming, fighting to rid herself of something far too large to possibly come out of another human being. He heard the midwife praising her, yelling at her, encouraging her, ordering her to keep pushing. It took El Oso completely by surprise—after all the torture he had witnessed, all the pain he had inflicted—but he felt his own knees weakening, and he had to look away to get through the final stage of delivery.

Then the baby let out its first cry, and El Oso turned to see the midwife cutting the umbilical cord. The mother collapsed on the mattress, her torso swelling with each breath. The midwife washed the baby in a basin of warm water, which did nothing to stop the crying. She cleared the baby's eyes and nostrils, wiped the baby's entire body clean. When she was through, she wrapped the healthy newborn in a soft blanket and started toward the mother, who was still wearing her black hood.

"I'll take that," said El Oso.

The midwife halted. "Surely you are going to let her hold her own baby."

"I said, I'll take it," El Oso repeated sternly.

The prisoner sat bolt upright and screamed again, which caused her to push out the placenta. The midwife hurried into position to collect the blood and tissue, but the mother couldn't have cared less about her own body. "What are you doing with my baby?" she cried.

The other guard grabbed her by the wrists and tied her hands behind her back so that she could not remove the hood.

"I want my baby!"

"We do not punish the innocent," said El Oso. "Your baby will be well cared for."

"No. Don't take my baby!"

El Oso turned to the midwife and said, "Your job is done here."

"No, it's not. She's torn. I have to sew her up. And she needs to be cleaned up to prevent infection."

"That won't be necessary," said El Oso.

"It will only take a few minutes."

"None of that matters. I need you to come with me."

The mother tried to rise up from the bed, but the other guard held her down. "Where are you taking my baby?" she shouted.

El Oso did not respond. He simply looked at the other guard and told him to wait at the prisoner's side until he returned. Then he took the midwife by the arm and said, "Come."

"No!" screamed the prisoner.

"Gag her," El Oso told the guard. The prisoner was beyond exhaustion, but she resisted with all her remaining strength. El Oso handed the baby back to the midwife and directed her toward the door. The prisoner continued to scream and resist as the guard tried to place a gag on her mouth. El Oso and the midwife left the bedroom and walked down the hallway together, the crying baby in the midwife's arms. She unlocked the back door to the fire escape, and they were almost clear of the apartment when they heard one last cry from the back bedroom, a desperate plea that was audible even though the woman was wearing a hood over her head, even though the guard was struggling to gag her. It was a voice that El Oso would never forget.

"My name is Marianna Cruz Pedrosa!" shouted prisoner 309.

El Oso hesitated for a split second, exchanged glances with the midwife, and then closed the door.

The baby cried all the way to the car. El Oso climbed behind the wheel, and the shiny new Ford Falcon disappeared into the night.

49

The midafternoon rain began to fall.

It fell gently at first. Then, in typical Florida fashion, it suddenly came down in sheets, beating like a drum on the aluminum top of the mobile command center. This was one of those aberrant moments where Vince didn't welcome the sound of falling rain to help him visualize his surroundings. Today, the rain was not his friend. Neither, it seemed, was Chief of Police Megan Renfro. By telephone, she was in the process of dressing down Vince for having allowed Jack to call Falcon on his own cell phone, a nonencrypted line.

"I know that was no mere slipup on your part," she said. "You did that by design."

"It was imperative that the call go through. I thought Falcon would be more likely to answer if he saw Swyteck's name come up on the caller ID."

"I want to believe you," she said, "but I don't. You used Swyteck's cell because you wanted someone other than law enforcement to be able to hear the conversation. Like the media."

"Why on earth would I want the media to over-hear our negotiations?"

"Because you don't agree with the decision to take Falcon out. You think you can still talk Falcon into releasing that injured girl. And if you are somehow able to convince the media that negotiation remains a viable alternative, this department will have hell to pay if we go in with guns blazing."

Vince didn't deny the accusation, at least not directly. "Negotiation is still workable."

"Not in my judgment. So stop trying to back us into a corner with leaks to the press. Your job is to position Falcon for a kill shot."

"Do you really want to take that shot in the pouring rain?"

"We need to work for the right opportunity. Obviously a window shot is not our first choice. You need to get him in the open doorway. If you can't pull that off, SWAT will breach."

Paulo's other telephone rang. The caller ID told him that it was from Falcon. "It's him," Paulo told the chief.

"Answer it. And remember, get him in the open doorway." Chief Renfro hung up, and Vince answered the other call. "Talk to me, Falcon."

"Just had a nice talk with Jack Swtyeck."

"So I hear."

"I'm cool with the missing money," he said.

"That's good news."

"I like Swyteck's honesty."

"I wouldn't put him on the phone to lie to you," said Vince.

Falcon chuckled lightly. "I don't know about that. But he does seem to be the straightest shooter in the bunch."

Falcon had no idea how "straight" the police snipers could shoot, but Vince let the unintended pun slide. "We need to deal with the injured hostage," he said. "It sounds like she needs to see a doctor."

"Maybe so."

"If she needs medical attention, we need to work something out."

"All right. Swyteck bought you that much. A little honesty deserves some reward."

"That's what I like to hear, Falcon. Let's just agree here and now that this is the way we're going to deal with each other. Nothing but honesty."

There was silence on the line, and then a slight change of tone. "Don't make agreements you can't keep. Just tell me what you want to do about the girl."

"What kind of shape is she in?"

"I don't know. I'm not a doctor. That's the problem, remember?"

"Is she conscious?"

"Yes. Most of the time."

"Is she bleeding?"

"Not anymore."

"But she has lost some blood?"

"Yeah."

"A lot or a little?"

"Some."

"Is it a gunshot wound?"

"Hardly. A bullet grazed her thigh. It's not like

she's going to die or anything. She's just in pain."

"I'd feel a whole lot better if I heard those words from a doctor."

"Well, that's a real bummer, because last time I checked, nobody here went to med school."

"What if I could get a doctor to come into the motel room and examine her?"

"No way."

"It can work, Falcon. I've done it in these situations before."

"Sure you have. You send in a SWAT guy dressed up like Marcus Welby. He takes one look at me and prescribes two bullets and a burial in the morning."

"I don't play those games."

"That's what you told me on the Powell Bridge, when you said I could talk to Alicia Mendoza if I came down from the lamppost."

"What happened the last time wasn't my fault."

"Well, it sure as hell wasn't *my* fault."

"It was a different situation."

"Not to me it wasn't. Just forget it. I'm not letting any doctor come inside here."

Vince tightened his fist, then released, relieving a little stress as he searched for the right words. "Okay, I'm not going to force the issue. But we can still work this out. Tell me something. Can the girl walk on her own power?"

"I don't think so. She's pretty weak."

That was exactly the answer Vince was hoping to hear. "Do you think you could get her to the door?"

"Yeah, no sweat. She's a toothpick."

"Okay, listen to me. Here's how this can work.

We agree that Swyteck's honesty bought some goodwill, right?"

"Yeah, some."

"Good. Then here's what we can do. If it's just a leg wound, you can pick the girl up and take her to the door. Open the door, and lay her right outside on the stoop. Then just close the door, and leave her there."

"Then what?"

"Then we'll send someone to pick her up."

"No cops."

"No. It will be paramedics with a stretcher."

"No, it will be SWAT guys dressed up like paramedics. Forget it."

"I give you my word."

"Your word isn't worth dirt. Not after the Powell Bridge."

"Trust me on this."

"Never. If you want to send someone to pick the girl up, send someone I can recognize—someone who I know is not a cop."

Vince paused. The silence lingered a good bit longer than he would have liked, but it was still nowhere near as long as it felt. That recurring and unnerving image suddenly flashed in his mind—the pockmarked door at the end of the hallway, the unexpected percussion of flash grenades, the burst of light, and then the darkness. Unceasing darkness. Vince couldn't believe the words were coming from his mouth, but it was like a reflex. "What if I come to pick her up?"

The suggestion seemed to have caught Falcon by

surprise. "Now there's a twist. A blind cop turned escort."

"It's perfect," said Vince. "You don't have to worry about me busting down the door and shooting the place up."

"You got a point there."

"So it's agreed? You bring the girl to the door, I'll come and pick her up."

"Let me think about it."

Vince tried not to push too hard, but Falcon didn't seem to appreciate how urgent the situation was. "There's no time to think about it. We need to cut a deal on this girl, or things are going to get ugly in a hurry."

"Is that some kind of a threat?"

"I'm just being honest with you, like we agreed."

"I'll call you back."

"Please. I'm not messing with you, my friend. This is something that we need to work out right now."

"Stop rushing me."

"It's the best deal I can offer." Vince braced himself for a hang-up, but he could tell that Falcon was still on the line. He gave him a little time to think it over, but too much time would cost him his momentum. Vince said, "So, is it a deal?"

Falcon let out something between a sigh and a groan. "All right. You can come."

"Good."

"But bring Swyteck with you."

"Why?"

"It's like I told you. I don't trust cops. Not even blind ones."

"I'm not going to lead the cavalry through your door."

"Probably not. *Definitely* not, as long as there's a civilian in the line of fire."

"The wounded girl is a civilian."

"The girl is a prostitute from Colombia," Falcon said, scoffing. "Call me crazy. I get more comfort with the son of a former governor at risk."

"I can't guarantee that Swyteck will be willing to do it."

"He'll do it, if he wants to talk to his buddy Theo again."

Vince was about to say something, but he heard the line disconnect. The call was over.

50

A licia should have been driving faster.

More than an hour had passed since she'd left the mobile command center and headed home. Vince hadn't called for her, but she still felt like she was letting him down, as if it was important for her to be with him. She was the one who had talked him into taking this assignment in the first place and, after all, he . . . She halted that train of thought, which of course would have ended with "was blind." She knew that Vince wanted no part of that pity party, and thinking along those lines was the quickest way for her to earn a permanent ticket home.

The police barricade on Biscayne Boulevard was just ahead. The rainstorm had driven most of the onlookers off the street and sidewalks, though many still watched from higher and drier ground, through the windows of apartments and office buildings. The only folks braving the weather were law enforcement and, in even greater numbers, adventurous members of the media, who seemed to relish strong winds, driving rain, tsunamis, or anything else that made it even more challenging to bring a story into the comfortable living rooms of couch potatoes. Alicia stopped at the police roadblock and rolled down her window. The cool rain was falling so hard that, just in the short time it took a patrol officer to check her badge and grant her clearance, her sleeve was completely soaked. She raised the window and adjusted the windshield wipers as she continued up Biscayne Boulevard. Squad cars, vans, and a variety of police vehicles still filled the parking lot that served as the staging area. Alicia found a spot as close to the mobile command center as possible and killed the engine.

She reached for the door handle and then stopped. Why hadn't Vince called her? She was running almost twenty-five minutes late. Vince was dealing with a hostage-taker who had a history of making public demands to speak to the mayor's daughter. Surely, in the past seventy minutes some question of strategy had arisen that involved or at least related to Alicia. Yet her cell phone and BlackBerry had remained silent. Maybe Vince was trying to prove something—that he didn't need her. Maybe he didn't see her as helpful any longer, or worse, saw her more as a hindrance.

Or perhaps Vince was starting to wrestle with the same questions and suspicions that she was finally facing.

Alicia's BlackBerry chirped and vibrated in her purse, which wrested her from her thoughts. Without even checking, she was certain that it was from Vince, and that this phone call would settle once and for all that he respected her judgment and that, despite all the personal history and the intervening tragedy, they could work together as a team. She smiled a little as she grabbed the phone and prepared to deliver some pithy greeting. But it wasn't Vince. It wasn't even a phone call. It was an e-mail. It came from a server she didn't recognize, and the screen name wasn't even a name, just an apparently random combination of letters and numbers. The subject line took her breath away. It read simply, "It was only out of love that I sought you," harking back to the e-mail she'd received that same night her purse had been stolen. Alicia scrolled down to the body of the message, her hand shaking.

And now I'm sure that I have found you,

the message read.

Meet me in the lobby of the Hotel Intercontinental. Today at 4:00. Please come alone. Please, please come.

Alicia read it again, which only delivered a double dose of chills. She checked her watch: 3:40 p.m. She could make it to the Hotel Intercontinental by four o'clock, but only if she left at that very moment. She thought about it, then decided to trust her instincts. She restarted her car and tucked the BlackBerry into her purse, right beside her Sig Sauer pistol.

* * *

The phone call in Jack's ear sounded like a buzz saw. He held his flip phone about six inches away from his head, and only then did he realize that it was Theo's friend Zack shouting over the roar of a seaplane engine.

"I can't hear a word you're saying," said Jack. He was shouting in reply, even though he was standing in the relative quiet of the parking lot outside the mobile command center. Two Miami cops happened by and wondered if Jack was speaking to them.

"Just a sec," shouted Zack. The engine noise in the background suddenly cut off, then Zack was back on the phone. "Is that better?"

"Much."

"Guess who I have sitting here next to me," said Zack, though he didn't wait for a response. "It's our pal Riley."

"You mean Riley the Bahamian bank manager?"

"The one and only."

"I thought he was missing."

"'Hiding' is a better word for it."

"How did you track him down?"

"Made it my mission to do so. I've been flying back and forth from the Bahamas for ten years. I got my share of contacts. Let's just say that my resourcefulness would have made even our buddy Theo Knight proud."

Jack knew exactly what Zack was saying: Don't ask. He had visions of Riley bound, gagged, and hanging upside down by a thread over a vat of bubbling acid to prevent his escape, à la Adam West and the old *Batman* TV show. Jack said, "Does Riley know what happened to the money in Falcon's safe deposit box?"

"My friend, there is no end to the secrets this man knows."

"Does that mean yes?"

"It means that the answer is so long and complicated that you'd better ask him yourself."

"That's fine. Bring him here to the mobile command center. Sergeant Paulo and I will question him."

Zack hedged. "Uh, there's a reason this guy went into hiding. Taking him to the police is probably not such a hot idea."

"Is he running from the law?"

"No. He just doesn't have any faith that the cops can protect him."

"Then who is he running from?"

Again, Zack's pause conveyed that same "Don't ask." Jack said, "Have you processed him through immigration?"

"That depends on what you mean by 'processed.'"

"Zack, I hope you haven't—"

"Stop right there. This is Theo Knight we're talking about here, remember? If that was you or me stuck in that motel room with some pistol-waving lunatic, Theo would have sprung us free two hours ago. We'd be back at his bar shooting pool, drinking beers, and laughing about the whole thing by now. Theo would do whatever it takes. You understand what I'm saying?"

Jack considered it. In every way that mattered—

friendship, loyalty, and the kind of brotherhood that transcended the luck of the genetic draw—Zack was making perfect sense. Jack said, "Okay, so tell me, exactly what is it going to take?"

"About five minutes of your time. There's things you know that I don't, and vice versa. If you and me put our heads together, Riley could be the key that unravels this thing. It's like that guy Deep Throat telling the *Washington Post* reporter how to figure out what was really going on with President Nixon and the Watergate scandal."

"Follow the money?"

"Yeah. Follow the money."

"And you're telling me that Mr. Riley is our roadmap?" said Jack.

"Well said. Now, get your butt over here."

"I really can't get away from this place. At least not for long."

"I'm not bringing Riley to the mobile command center. Dropping him in a sea of cops is the quickest way to make him clam up for good."

"Can you meet me somewhere halfway? How about the people-mover station over by the college? I forget the name."

"The one next to that huge construction site?"

"That's it."

"I can be there in ten minutes."

Jack checked his watch. "Be there in five," he said, then switched off his phone.

Surrounded by polished walls and towering columns of green Brazilian marble, an old woman waited in the three-story, open lobby of the Hotel Intercontinental. On a typical South Florida day, streams of sunlight would be shining through the skylights and bathing the lobby in a warm, natural glow. The afternoon rain and dark clouds, however, gave the marble interior a cold, dreary feeling. A huge modern sculpture dominated the center of the lobby, and in its shadow, the old woman found a comfortable leather armchair. From there, she had a perfect view of the hotel's grand entrance. She eyeballed each person who entered through the revolving glass doors. If it was a man, she let him pass without much notice. Only the younger women warranted her scrutiny, attractive Latinas in their midtwenties. Miami seemed to be full of them, and this particular hotel lobby was no exception. One of the major cruise lines was in the process of booking hundreds of guests for an overnight stay, and the old woman was beginning to worry that she might miss her expected rendezvous in the long lines of confusion.

A waiter cleared away the empty cocktail glasses that previous patrons had left behind on the table beside her. "*Algo de tomar?*" he asked. Something to drink? Miami waiters didn't always assume that their guests spoke Spanish as a first language, and she wondered why he had made that assumption correctly in her case.

"No, *gracias*," she said.

As the waiter turned and tended to the next table, it suddenly occurred to her why he had spoken to her in Spanish. She was clutching her purse tightly, and protruding from it was a thick file. It was plainly marked: LA CACHA, CASO NUMERO 309. La Cacha, Case Number 309.

The waiter must have noticed the Spanish wording on the file. Or maybe not. Paranoia was getting the best of her. She didn't exactly look Swedish, for heaven's sake. Even so, she turned the folder around so that the label was concealed against her bosom. She continued to clutch it tightly, hopefully. Almost as an afterthought, as if for support, she reached into her purse and clutched an old white nappy. It was just a piece of cloth, but it was rich with personal history and years of struggle.

Finally, she spotted a beautiful young woman at the revolving doors. Her pulse quickened. She rose and peered through the crowd for a better look. The young woman climbed the marble stairs, and the prospects looked even more promising.

The old woman started toward her, weaving through a human obstacle course. A group of pilots and flight attendants wheeled their baggage toward the reservation desk. She bumped into one of them and was nearly knocked to the floor. The man stopped to help her, but she was in too much of a hurry to wait for his assistance. She quickly collected herself, forced her way across the lobby, and then froze in her tracks.

She made direct eye contact with the young woman, who also came to a sudden halt.

The old woman had never been more certain of anything in all her years. It was definitely her.

There was a moment of confusion, a flurry of activity as another tour bus unloaded in front of the hotel. Yet another group of tourists trooped across the lobby. The never-ending flow of guests raced toward the long and disorganized line at the reservation desk. She pushed forward, trying to keep an eye on the young woman, of whom she suddenly lost sight.

"Alicia!" she shouted.

Still no sight of her.

"Alicia Mendoza!"

The old woman hurried through the crowd, but she saw only strange faces. People were starting to stare, as if something was wrong with her. Breathless, she could go no farther. From the top of the stairs, she spotted Alicia racing toward the revolving door. Her instincts told her to give chase, but it was pointless. In utter desperation, she reached inside her handbag, grabbed a tube of lipstick, and hurled it down from the top of the steps. It flew across the lobby, and, like a dart finding the bull's-eye, hit Alicia squarely in the back.

Alicia stopped.

The women exchanged glances from afar. Then Alicia saw the tube on the floor and picked it up.

She seemed to recognize it as her own.

The old woman was about to climb down the stairs, hopeful that Alicia would speak to her. Before she could move, however, Alicia hurried through the revolving door. The old woman could only stand and watch helplessly through the plate-glass window as Alicia ran across the parking lot, jumped in her car, and even burned a little rubber in her haste to get away.

51

In downtown Miami, construction sites were out-numbered only by traffic jams. Jack passed seven or eight of the former before he was ensnarled in the latter. He left his car in a loading zone near Flagler Street and hoofed it down the sidewalk. After a couple of wrong turns, he came to the construction site that marked the way to the people-mover station where he and Zack were supposed to meet.

No city on earth had more skyscrapers in the works than Miami—not New York, not Tokyo, not even Hong Kong. Many would eventually be built; just as many, if not more, would develop no further than the weedy construction site that served as the landmark for Jack's destination. The downtown people-mover was an elevated tram that ran on rubber tires and a concrete track. As Jack climbed the stairs to the station's platform, he had an unobstructed view of a vacant lot surrounded by a chain-link fence. Most of the fencing was covered with a green nylon mesh, but the long stretch facing the street had been transformed into an architectural gallery of sorts, with impressive drawings of a future seventy-story multi-use facility. The sign at the gate boasted that sixty percent of the condominium units had already been sold. The big question was, "To whom?" Miami was to condo speculation what Las Vegas was to roulette wheels, and Jack figured that many of those units had been bought in bulk by the type of investor who would stash away his money at an institution shrouded in secrecy, like the Greater Bahamian Bank & Trust Company, all with the help of a man like Riley.

When Jack arrived, however, there was no sign of Riley. Zack was leaning against the lighted billboard by his lonesome—all seven feet of him.

"Where's Riley?" said Jack.

"Sorry," said Zack as he stepped toward him. "You may be Theo's best friend, but any lawyer makes me nervous. After the way you were talking on the phone, I half-expected you to show up with the cops in tow. I left Riley behind."

Images of that vat of boiling oil suddenly resurfaced in Jack's brain. "Where?"

"Back at the hangar. He's cool, okay? Frankly, he's glad to be out of the Bahamas. So long as the guys who are out to get him don't know he's out of the Bahamas."

"Who's out to get him?"

"I'm not sure. Somebody showed up at his house yesterday morning, pulled a gun, and told him to keep his trap shut about Falcon's box. I pressed Riley pretty hard on it, but honestly, I'm not sure that he even knows who it was."

"Not everyone in the islands follows the Swiss model of 'know your customer.' I'm not so sure the Swiss even follow it. Bank secrecy has more exceptions than rules."

"I wouldn't know about that. But if you grew up where Theo and me did, you know this much: nobody sings like a scared canary."

Somewhere in Zack's sentence was a more familiar cliché, but Jack got the drift. "What did you get out of Riley so far?"

"First off, your boy Falcon set up the safe deposit box and did all the paperwork himself."

"We knew that. His signature specimens were on file with the bank."

"Yeah, but here's something you didn't know. He did all this years ago, probably before he started living on the street. And here's something else. Falcon never even opened the box."

"You mean after he put the two hundred grand in it."

"No. I mean *never.*"

"How can that be?"

"That's what I asked Riley. But he says Falcon just rented the box sight unseen. Never put a thing in it."

"Then how did the money get there?"

"According to Riley, some other guy shows up about two months later. He's got a key and a power of attorney signed by Falcon to let him open the box. Now, we don't know what he did when he opened the box, but Riley says the guy came with a briefcase."

"Big enough to hold two hundred thousand in cash?"

"Yup. He used the name Bernard Sikes. Totally bogus identity, of course."

"So this guy Sikes, or whatever his real name is, puts two hundred thousand dollars cash in an empty safe deposit box rented by Falcon. That's what you're telling me?"

"You got it."

"Why?"

Zack shrugged. "Hell if I know. Why don't you ask Falcon?"

"I just might do that. But obviously there has to be more to the story. There was two hundred thousand in the box when Theo and I went there. I took ten thousand for Falcon's bail. So who came after me and took what was left? Riley?"

"No," said Zack. "He swears he didn't."

"Sikes?"

"Uh-uh. Riley says it was a woman. An old woman at that. The way Falcon set things up with the bank, three people were authorized to access the box. Falcon, Sikes, and the woman."

"She got a name?"

"Marianna Cruz Pedrosa."

Jack searched his mind for some recognition, but there was none. "Have the Bahamians tracked her down?"

"This is where it gets interesting. I didn't hear

this from Riley, but I was talking to a buddy on the Bahamian police about this."

"And?"

"As you can imagine, there are more than a few women by this name in the world. But the local cops have checked all kinds of databanks and computer lists, and one woman has really caught their interest."

"Why?"

"A woman named Marianna Cruz Pedrosa went missing over twenty-five years ago. She was a university professor in La Plata, Argentina, back in the mid-seventies. She and her husband were taken from their home in the middle of the night. No one ever heard from them again. It's like they just vanished."

Jack fell silent for a moment. "No," he said finally, "I'll bet they disappeared."

"Vanished. Disappeared. Same thing."

"Not exactly," Jack said, as the pieces to Falcon's puzzle finally started to fall into place.

52

Vince was not getting the response he wanted from headquarters. He was listening to Chief Renfro on speakerphone, and she didn't like the idea of Vince—with or without Swyteck—approaching the motel in any kind of swap for the injured hostage. Vince was prepared to make a host of arguments to the contrary, but he was a lone voice. The mobile command vehicle was starting to feel less like the nerve center of negotiations and more like a SWAT staging area. Sergeant Chavez, two members of his tactical team, and his best sniper were standing near the door, as if waiting for the chief to say "Go." The Miami Dade Police Department had its negotiator in the room, but if body language meant anything, she was actually standing behind the MDPD's SWAT leader. The MDPD director himself—the local equivalent of the county sheriff—was participating by conference call, and he was siding completely with Chief Renfro.

"Look," said the director, "the guy has already

shot two officers, killed one. It appears that he's wounded one hostage. It makes no sense to send in a negotiator with a civilian in the hope that a known killer has suddenly lost his itchy trigger finger."

"We're not sending anybody *in*," said Vince. "The deal is that he puts the injured girl outside the door. Then Swyteck and I go and get her. We never set foot inside the motel room."

Chavez said, "I like the first part of that plan. When he opens the door and lays the girl on the stoop, that's our chance to take him out."

Renfro said, "What's the likelihood of success on that shot?"

Chavez deferred to his lead sniper, who answered in a thoughtful monotone and without any sense of arrogance. It was simply the best judgment from a highly trained professional who fully understood the gravity of his work. "Subject in the open doorway. Girl on the ground. He'll probably be moving quickly, perhaps even erratically, since we are dealing with an agitated and clinically paranoid subject. Definitely won't be standing still. Second story of the apartment building directly across the street offers the clearest line of sight. Distance is just about one hundred yards. Slight angle should have only minimal adverse impact on bullet trajectory. We do have rain and wind to contend with. Unless this rainstorm turns into a hurricane, I'd say we're close to a sure thing here."

Renfro said, "I don't want to wing him now. Last thing we need is for him to go back inside and tear into those hostages like a wounded animal."

"Understood," said the sniper. "I'm talking about a kill shot to the head."

Vince said, "Nothing's a sure thing. Any attempted takeout brings a chance of dead hostages."

"We breach at the crack of the sniper fire," said the director. "If the shot doesn't take him out, we will."

"No offense," said Vince, "but that won't do much good, unless your team can fly faster than one of Falcon's speeding bullets."

The SWAT leader spoke up. "You'd be surprised how quickly we can move. We've been studying the blueprints. There's a maid-service hallway that runs directly behind the rooms on this eastern wing of the motel. We can cut through the back wall. It's just sheet rock on studs. Conservatively speaking, we should be able to position a team as close as two rooms away without Falcon ever knowing we're there."

"If he hears you cutting through walls, it's disaster," said Vince.

"He won't hear us."

"And what if he comes to the door with a hostage in tow?"

"Then we'll respond accordingly," said Chavez.

"What does that mean?"

"It means we've done this before. We adapt."

Vince could have debated that point, but he knew when he was outnumbered. In truth, he didn't totally disagree with the strategy. He hoped it was because they were right. He feared that it was because of the way things had gone so horribly wrong the last time, his disastrous face-to-face confrontation with that monster who had stolen a five-year-old girl, and then stolen Vince's eyesight.

"You on board, Paulo?" asked the chief.

Vince didn't answer right away.

"Paulo, you with us?"

"Yeah," he said without much enthusiasm. "I'm all in."

"Good," said Renfro. "Then proceed as planned. Tell Falcon to bring the girl to the door, and give him every assurance that you and Swyteck will come and pick her up. Any questions?" The mobile command center was silent. "Excellent," said Renfro. "Good luck, team."

Vince ended the call. The SWAT members headed toward the door. Chavez was the last to leave. He stopped on his way out, laid a hand on Vince's shoulder. "Look at the bright side, Paulo. Falcon won't live long enough to know you lied to him."

Vince couldn't tell if it was a bad joke or if Chavez was just being a total jerk. He gave him the benefit of the doubt by simply not responding. He turned, walked the familiar path back to his chair, and was about to take a seat when he heard radio squelch in his headset. He adjusted the earpiece, and the voice came clear.

"Sergeant Paulo, you there?"

Vince didn't recognize the speaker. "Paulo here. Who's this?"

"Officer Garcia, perimeter control."

"Go ahead."

"Got a little situation here at Biscayne and Seventeenth."

Rookies, thought Vince. He couldn't imagine why it took the lead negotiator to handle perimeter control, but he wasn't too harsh in his response. "I'm sure it's nothing you can't handle, Garcia."

"Actually, sir, it's a little complicated. There's someone here who insists on seeing you."

"Who is it?"

"Wouldn't give me a name, says it wouldn't mean anything to you anyway. But she says she can definitely be of help to you."

Vince was tired, stress was high, and this interruption seemed so inane that he was on the verge of losing his temper. "Tell her we don't need any help, thank you."

"She says she knows who Falcon is."

"She does, does she?"

"Yeah. I hear your skepticism. I didn't put much credence in it either, and I wasn't even going to bother you with it. Except that she has something that she wants to give you."

"What is it?"

The cop paused, as if taking care not to be overheard by any bystanders. "Looks to be about two hundred thousand dollars. Cash."

The rookie suddenly had Vince's undivided attention. "Bring her in right away," said Vince. "Tell her that I'd be delighted to speak with her."

53

Alicia made it from downtown Miami to Coconut Grove in record time. The last time she'd been in such a hurry to reach 311 Royal Poinciana Court, she was seventeen years old, it was three a.m., and her fake ID had worked like a charm on South Beach. This afternoon, the circumstances could not have been more different. The charming Mediterranean-style villa was no longer where she lived, of course, though she'd probably heard it from her parents a thousand different times, a hundred different ways, that it felt so much more like home whenever she came to visit. She understood that sentiment perfectly. This old house was where she'd grown up. It was filled with memories of birthday parties, sleepovers, after-school snacks, skinned knees, girl talk, and boy troubles. It was like a giant box filled with all the hopes and dreams that marked her journey from daddy's girl to womanhood. She'd scored a thousand soccer goals in the yard with her father as goalie. She'd practically killed her mother in the living room for trying to "fix" her hair five minutes before her prom date arrived. It was a cliché to say that not every house was a home, but this one brimmed with the kind of endless love and inevitable parental overkill that an only child could either understand or endure. For a moment, Alicia felt like she was a kid again as she sat directly across the kitchen table from her mother.

Another part of her, however, felt more like a cop.

"Why the oh-so-serious expression?" her mother said.

Alicia was a tangle of emotional knots, and the words seemed trapped inside her. She laid her handbag atop the table, the lipstick tube concealed from her mother. She reached inside, removed her wallet, and opened it. The billfold was empty.

Her mother could not contain her disapproval. "Alicia, how many times have I told you never to go around without a dollar to your name?"

"Mom, please."

"You should always have a little cash. What if you had a flat tire or an emergency?"

"If there's an emergency, I have a fully loaded nine-millimeter pistol. Mom, can you please just listen?" It was a tone she rarely used with her parents, and her mother was clearly taken aback.

"Okay," her mother said quietly. "I'm listening."

Alicia reached into the photo section of her wallet and removed a colorful piece of paper currency that was pressed behind plastic. She laid the bill on the table between them, facedown. "Do you know what this is?"

It required only a cursory glance for the recognition to kick in. "It's an Argentine banknote. Twenty pesos. But why is it torn in half?"

Alicia took the bill, and with her elbows on the table, she held it at eye level. The smooth natural edge was between her right thumb and index finger. The rough edge, where the note had been torn down the middle, was in her left. "Six years ago, just a few days after my twenty-first birthday, a woman gave this to me."

"Who was she?"

"I'd never met her before. She found me on campus after one of my classes and asked if she could speak to me. I had nothing else to do, and she seemed nice enough. So we sat down at one of the picnic tables on the lawn and talked."

"What about?"

"At first, it seemed that we weren't really talking about anything. She told me that she had a friend whose daughter was thinking about enrolling in the spring, and she wanted to know how I liked the university, what campus life was like, that kind of thing. It was all about me. Too much about me, actually, and after a while I started to feel a little uncomfortable with the personal nature of the questions. I came up with an excuse to leave, and that was when she admitted that she wasn't just scouting out the campus for the daughter of a friend. She said she'd come all the way from Argentina just to talk to me."

Her mother suddenly showed more concern than curiosity. "Why on earth would she come that far just to talk to you?"

"That's what I wanted to know. She said she knew my family back in Argentina."

"Really? Your father's side or mine?"

It was a simple enough question, but suddenly Alicia was having second thoughts about this entire conversation. She'd avoided it for years, out of respect, love, and probably a host of other emotions that she might never fully sort out. Fear had certainly been part of it—fear of the truth. But it was too late to turn back now. She searched within and found the strength to say it. "Neither."

Her mother let out a little nervous chuckle. "What do you mean, 'neither'?"

"She told me that she didn't want to ruin my life, that she was not trying to upset me, that she would not make me into another victim by turning my world upside down."

"Victim of what?" Graciela said, seemingly annoyed. "This woman sounds like she was crazy."

"I had the same reaction. I didn't want to hear any more, but the interesting thing is that she never really came right out and said anything directly. Even so, I somehow sensed what she was implying. In hindsight, I think she wanted me to figure things out for myself, rather than dump a lot of painful information in my lap."

"Figure *what* out for yourself?"

Alicia laid the torn Argentine peso on the table, facedown. "Before she left, she took this bill from her purse and tore it in half. She kept part of it for herself, and she made a point of giving me this half, the one with the handwriting on it."

Alicia turned the bill faceup. Directly on the bill, in blue ink, a message was handwritten in Spanish. The translation read: "The military is taking our children. Where are the Disappeared?"

Alicia's mother showed no reaction.

"I kept the bill, and over the next few months I did some research on this."

"What kind of research?"

"Being raised in Miami, I realized that I didn't know much about the country of my birth. It turns out that I was born during Argentina's Dirty War, which I had heard of but never really studied."

"Plenty has been written about it."

"I know. But it wasn't until I met this woman and had this torn banknote in my purse that I started to learn about *los Desaparecidos*—the Disappeared. It was so amazing to me, how everyone was afraid to talk about what the military was secretly doing to people who opposed the regime. Some of the Disappeared were left-wing extremists."

"Terrorists. Like the ones who set off the bomb that killed your father's first wife and daughter."

"Yes, I know about that. But others were just ordinary people who spoke out against the government: trade unionists, social reformers, human-rights activists, nuns, priests, journalists, lawyers, teachers, students, actors, workers, housewives, and on and on. Some were guilty of nothing. They were simply accused or suspected of being a subversive or conspiring to undermine the 'Western Christian way of life.' It was like Nazi Germany, except that in the case of Argentina, the rest of the world stood by until the very end and let it happen. Even within the country, practically no one had the courage to say or do anything, except for the mothers of the disappeared children. They met secretly in churches, they organized, they marched in the town plazas with little white nappies on their heads and carried photographs of their missing children. They put themselves at risk to make the public aware of the fact that people were disappearing and that the military dictatorship was behind it."

Alicia paused to catch her breath, then gestured toward the torn Argentine peso on the table. "And one of the ways they got their message across was by writing notes like this on money. It was a way to make sure that the word would spread from one person to the next, all across the country."

"That was all a very long time ago," her mother said in a quaking voice. "And it has nothing to do with our family."

"It was probably the implication otherwise that got me so angry and made me tell this woman never to contact me again. And you know what? She promised to respect my wishes. She said I would never hear from her again. Unless . . ."

"Unless what?"

Alicia took the tube of lipstick from her purse. She opened it, but the lipstick was gone. Inside was another torn Argentine banknote. Alicia unrolled it and laid it flat on the table beside the other half. The ripped, jagged edges fit perfectly, like the pieces of a puzzle. Said Alicia, "She promised never to contact me again, unless she could prove all of the things that she wanted to tell me."

"What kind of proof is this?" her mother said, scoffing.

"This was the tube of lipstick that was stolen from my purse. I got it back today."

"From who?"

"The same woman who came to see me before."

"She stole your lipstick?"

Alicia's expression turned very serious. "Notice how the lipstick has been removed. Only the tube is left."

"Yes, I see that. Who would do something like that? She must be absolutely crazy."

"No. She actually did something smart."

"I don't see how stealing lipstick can be smart."

"It was ingenious, actually—if the purpose was to collect my saliva."

Her mother halted, as if the big picture were suddenly coming clearer.

Alicia said, "What kind of proof do you think there might be in my saliva?"

The color seemed to drain from her mother's face. Matters of biology had always been irrelevant in the Mendoza family, and it pained Alicia to watch her mother start to unravel emotionally. For an instant, it seemed as though the air had been sucked from the room.

"People are sick. The things they say and do just to hurt others."

"No, Mom. That's not what this is about."

Her mother swallowed hard, seeming barely able to speak. "This . . . I just don't understand how this could be happening. I love you, Alicia. I love you with all my heart."

"I know that."

"Then what do you want from me, my darling?"

"I want to know just one thing," said Alicia.

Her mother's eyes welled, and she seemed on the verge of tears. "Tell me, please."

"Do you want to talk to me, Mom? Or do you want me to talk to *her*?"

54

There were many things that Jack had yet to figure out about Sergeant Paulo. Jack was normally a quick study, but Paulo was a complicated guy by anyone's measure, and Jack had known him only a matter of hours. A crisis, however, had a way of breeding a certain amount of instant familiarity, as it was difficult to conceal "the real you" when both the stakes and the level of tension were sky-high. At the very least, Jack understood him well enough to appreciate just how serious Paulo was when he told Jack to come inside the command center, meet the old woman who had Falcon's cash, and hear firsthand what she had to say.

Paulo was alone with her when Jack entered the room. She sat in a stiff, upright position, the fingers of each hand interlaced to form a tight ball in her lap. She was clutching a handkerchief, perhaps Paulo's. Jack's first impression was that she was younger than his *abuela*, but he could have easily envisioned her at his grandmother's card table with a half dozen elderly Latinas just like *Abuela*, talking and drinking coffee for hours at a time, perhaps even pulling Jack aside and telling him about a beautiful niece that he should meet. Her hair was short, stylish, and mostly gray. Behind the wire-rimmed eyeglasses were big, dark eyes that were equally sad and sincere. Although her face was wrinkled, her healthy olive complexion had retained some of its youthful quality, as if the creases in her skin were more the product of worry than age.

"So, you are the lawyer who represented this monster?" she said as Jack took a seat at the table.

"I'm Jack Swyteck," he said. "I was Falcon's lawyer for a short time, but I'm not here on his behalf. I'm here because he's holding my best friend hostage, and I'm doing everything I can to help Sergeant Paulo get him and the other hostages out safely."

Vince said, "She understands all that. We had a lengthy talk before I called you."

Jack said, "Do you actually know Falcon?"

"Yes," she said. "That's why I contacted Sergeant Paulo."

"I don't mean to sound like a doubting Thomas, but why did it take you so long?"

"I tracked down Sergeant Paulo as soon as I saw Falcon's face on television."

"The local news stations have been airing this hostage standoff all day long, and Falcon's mug has been all over the media for at least two days, ever since that woman's body was found in the trunk of his car."

"I just arrived in Miami a few hours ago."

"This has been on CNN and some of the other national newscasts as well."

"I was in Argentina. This wasn't news there."

"No, I guess it wouldn't be," said Jack.

"I was in my hotel room when I first saw a news-flash update of a hostage situation involving a man named Falcon. The name, of course, piqued my interest. When I saw his picture, I grabbed my bag and came straight here."

"You mean the bag with Falcon's money in it?" said Jack.

"Yes."

"How did you end up in Miami with all that cash?"

Paulo interjected, "That's getting a little ahead of things. Jack, I think you might want to start by asking how she came to know Falcon in the first place."

Jack was starting to sense that there were only certain things that Paulo wanted him to know. But as a member of law enforcement, Paulo didn't have to share any of this information with an outsider, so Jack wasn't going to pitch a fit about it. "Okay, tell me, ma'am. How do you know Falcon?"

"He first contacted me several years ago. It was by letter. He identified himself only as Falcon. He said that I should get in touch with a twenty-one-year-old woman in Miami, named Alicia Mendoza. She could help me with my search."

"Your search for what?"

"That is between Alicia and me." Both her tone and tight expression conveyed that it was an intensely personal matter. Jack decided to move on rather than press the point, perhaps come back to it later.

"Did you contact Alicia?"

"Yes. I came to Miami and talked to her in person."

"Why?"

"Like I said, that is between Alicia and me." She glanced at Paulo and said, "Right, Sergeant?"

It was apparent that she and Paulo had reached an understanding about the things that she would and would not share with Jack. Paulo said, "Jack, why don't you ask about the next time she saw Falcon?"

She was quick to correct him. "I didn't see him on either occasion."

"Okay," said Jack. "Tell me about the next contact."

"I didn't hear from him again until just recently. A little more than a week ago, I received a package by international courier. Inside was a key and enough money for a plane ticket to Nassau. He told me to go to the Greater Bahamian Bank and Trust Company and open safe deposit box number two sixty-six. He said that I should take everything that was inside the box, and that I should be sure to use the name Marianna Cruz Pedrosa."

"And you just dropped everything and went?"

"When he mentioned Marianna's name, of course I went."

"So, you are not Marianna Cruz Pedrosa?"

"No."

"Do you know her?"

"*Sí.*"

"Do you know where she is?"

Her voice was so laden with sadness that even one-word responses took considerable effort. "No."

Jack treaded lightly, sensitive to her heavy heart. "What can you tell me about her?"

She drew a breath, then let it out as if it were her last. "*Era mi vida.*"

She was my life.

The words chilled Jack. His own *abuela* often used the same term of endearment to convey how much he meant to her, so he had some appreciation of the depth of this woman's feelings. Still, Jack realized that he was barely scratching the surface of this mysterious triangle—the woman, Marianna, and Falcon. It was obviously a triangle filled with pain and born in Argentina, though it somehow intersected with Alicia Mendoza's life in Miami. The trial lawyer inside him wanted to ask a thousand follow-up questions and sort everything out immediately. Who was Marianna? What happened to her? Why did Falcon give this old woman so much money in her name? Why did the woman bring it to Miami? But with each passing moment, the old woman was showing signs of increasing distress, and Jack could only begin to sense the breadth of her personal loss and suffering. It seemed only humane to shift gears for a moment, albeit slightly, and let her collect her wits.

Jack said, "Can we take a step back and clear up something you mentioned just a minute or two ago?"

"Sure," she said as she used the handkerchief to dab away a tear from the corner of her eye.

"You made a point of telling Sergeant Paulo that you never actually saw Falcon in either of the two communications you had with him."

"That's right."

"Then how did you recognize Falcon's picture on the television this afternoon?"

The sorrow drained from her face, replaced by a surge of strength and stoicism that could only spell anger. "At first I didn't recognize him, because he has aged so much. But it was in the eyes. I looked into those eyes on the TV screen and realized that I'd seen that monster before, in his younger days. I had just always known him by another name."

"What name is that?"

"I knew him as El Oso."

"The Bear?" said Jack. "What kind of a name is that?"

"A nickname," she said. "None of those men in his position used their real names."

"So, who is El Oso?"

Her eyelids flittered as she struggled to keep her whole body from trembling. "That's the reason I've come to you," she said in a voice that faded. "You are dealing with such a *very* dangerous man."

55

Theo could feel it in his bones that something big was about to break loose.

He'd overheard Falcon's end of the last telephone conversation with the negotiator. As best he could tell, they'd cut a deal that somehow involved Jack coming to retrieve the injured girl. Theo was all for getting the girl out safely from that hot, stuffy motel room. He just hoped that Jack wasn't stupid enough to try and be a part of any rescue effort.

Falcon, for his own part, was proving to be anything but stupid.

"You two slobs," he said, pointing at Theo and the weatherman. They were seated next to each other on the floor, their backs to the wall, bound at the wrists and ankles.

"Are you talking to us?" said Theo.

"Yeah, the both of you." This time he pointed with his gun, which drew a whimper from the weatherman. It was everyone's biggest fear that Falcon would shoot a hostage, but no one wore it more plainly on his face than the weatherman.

Theo said, "What do you want?"

"You're going to carry the wounded girl outside and lay her on the stoop."

"Is that the deal you cut?"

"It's none of your business what deal I cut."

"I just didn't hear you mention anything over the phone about me and lover boy stepping outside the motel room."

"All I can tell you is that it ain't gonna be me who opens that door. You think I don't know there's snipers out there?"

"Snipers?" the weatherman said nervously. He leaned closer to Theo and whispered, "What if they shoot us by mistake?"

"Then you don't have to tell your wife what you and those girls were doing in here last night," said Theo.

The response almost seemed to satisfy him. Almost.

"No talking between prisoners!" shouted Falcon.

Prisoners? *Here we go again*, thought Theo. *Next he'll be telling us we can't drink any water.* "You're going to have to untie us if you want us to carry the girl anywhere."

The look on Falcon's face suggested that he hadn't considered that part of the plan. His eyes darted across the room, as if he had no idea where the solution lay. "Okay, forget what I said about it being both of you. One of you is going to carry her." Again, he pointed with his gun, this time only at the weatherman, which made him gasp. "You carry her," said Falcon.

"I can't carry her by myself," the weatherman said.

"I can," said Theo.

"Who asked you?" Falcon said sharply.

Theo said, "The girl may be alive, but she's dead-weight. If you want it done right, not to mention quickly, then let me do it."

The part about "quickly" seemed to register with Falcon. "All right, big mouth. You got the job. But if you try to run for it . . ."

"I know, I know. It's a bullet in the back."

"That's just for starters," said Falcon. He pulled his strand of beads from his pocket, rolled the little balls of metal around in his hand, then added, "You can't even imagine what will happen to the ones you leave behind."

Jack hesitated before hitting speed dial on his cell phone. It suddenly occurred to him that, depending on how Paulo's latest plan played out, this might be the last time he would ever dial Theo's cell.

Theo was *numero uno* on Jack's speed-dial list, which Jack liked to think said less about his love life and more about the kind of friend he had in Theo. Having a bad day in court and needing a guy who really knows how to pour a drink? Dial 1 for Theo. Your classic Mustang's been torched and you want to find the punk who did it? Just punch 1 for Theo. Is your client a hit man who needs to show his attorney a little more respect? Theo again. There was no limit to what Theo would do for Jack, which only exacerbated Jack's feeling that he wasn't doing nearly enough for Theo in his hour of need. For most people, it probably would have made perfect sense to follow orders and stand aside so that the police could do their job. That wasn't Jack's style, however. Couple that with the guilt Jack felt about having gotten Theo into this mess in the first place, and Jack was glad to take on a more active role in the rescue operation.

He hit speed dial, and Falcon's voice was on the line. "Are you coming to get the girl, Swyteck?"

"Is that what you want?"

"I couldn't have made it any clearer. You and Paulo. The dumb leading the blind." He laughed way too hard at his own joke.

"That's a real knee-slapper, Falcon."

"Lawyers," he said, his laughter ending with a scoff. "No sense of humor."

"It's hard to laugh when you know the truth."

"What's that supposed to mean?"

"I know who you are."

"Well, that makes one of us."

"I know all about Marianna Cruz Pedrosa."

"What's there to know? It's just a phony name on the access list to my safe deposit box."

"No. I know much more than that."

"You're so full of crap."

"I know about El Oso."

Jack wished that he could have seen Falcon's reaction, but it was almost unnecessary. The silence on the line was profound.

Finally, Falcon said, "Exactly how much do you know?"

"Enough."

"How much is enough?"

"Enough to keep my friend Theo alive. Unless you'd like me to share what I know with the media."

"What makes you think I care?"

"The fact that you changed your name, lied about being from Cuba, went and lived in a burned-out car. The fact that you climbed up on a bridge and got arrested for trying to talk to the mayor's daughter, and then holed yourself up in a motel room with hostages, and yet for some reason, you've never mentioned your dark side to anyone. Or should I say *darkest* side."

Falcon's voice took on an edge, rising with agitation. "I'll mention it when I'm good and ready."

"Or I'll steal your thunder and do it for you."

"You keep your mouth shut!"

"No problem. Just keep Theo and the other hostages alive."

He didn't respond right away, but Jack could hear him breathing out his anger. "Don't push me, Swyteck. I don't like it."

"Nobody's pushing you. All I'm saying is that if you harm any of the hostages, you lose your stage, your soapbox, your platform—whatever the hell it is you're angling for."

"How do you know I want a stage?"

"Because none of your other demands makes sense. And I don't think you're anywhere near as crazy as you lead people to believe."

Falcon's tone changed again, less argumentative, more respectful of Jack's insight. "I like you, Swyteck. Deep down, I really like you."

"I'm truly honored."

"That's why I want you and Paulo to come get the girl."

"Fine. But then what?"

"Then . . ." Falcon's voice trailed off, and for a moment Jack thought he'd lost him.

"Falcon? Then what?"

"Then, it's curtain time," Falcon said, and the call ended.

56

The drive back to the mobile command center was practically unbearable for Alicia. At least a half-dozen times, she had to fight off the impulse to jump onto I-95 and just keep going. She had no particular destination in mind. It was simply about getting away. Running, however, was rarely the answer. With the lives of at least four hostages still hanging in the balance, it wasn't even a remote option.

She switched on the car radio and caught the tail end of a news update at the top of the hour, delivered in rapid-fire cadence.

"The hostage standoff between police and the homeless man accused of stalking Mayor Mendoza's daughter now enters its eighteenth hour," the announcer reported, "with no outward signs of progress. At least four hostages remain holed up in a motel room with the gunman, one of whom is now believed to be Walter Finkelstein, better known as Walt the Weather Wizard, the colorful meteorologist with Action News in Miami. More news at the bottom of the hour."

Alicia switched off the radio. To her knowledge, the identity of the hostages had yet to be released. The leaks were starting. With more than a little concern, she wondered what other secrets might find their way into the media.

She returned to the staging area just before dark and found a parking space a few car-lengths down from the mobile command center. The rain continued to fall, though no longer in the blinding sheets that had made her drive to Coconut Grove so treacherous. Still, completely overcast skies and plenty of threatening dark clouds made for a premature dusk. Darkness came early in December, and on a miserable day like today it would come even sooner than usual, which gave her an uneasy feeling. She was no expert in hostage negotiations, but Vince was. He was living and walking proof that nightfall often triggered action in a hostage situation—for better or for worse.

Alicia dodged raindrops as she darted toward the mobile unit and pushed the door open, entering with more of a flurry than she'd intended. "It's me," she said upon seeing the startled expression on Vince's face.

"You're back," he said. "I was beginning to think you'd left us for good."

"No, there was just something . . . something that came up. Can I speak to you alone for a minute, Vince?" Alicia glanced at the second negotiator from MDPD, who was gracious enough to volunteer that he needed another jolt of espresso. He pulled on a windbreaker that was already rain-soaked, stepped out into the drizzle, and left Alicia and Vince alone in the command center.

"What's up?" said Vince.

Alicia pulled up a chair that faced him and sat close enough for him to feel her presence. She felt an urge to reach out and take his hands in hers, but she resisted, in this setting. "Vince, what do you know about Argentina's Dirty War?"

The question didn't seem to surprise him the way she had thought it would. "Up until this afternoon, I'd say I knew virtually nothing."

"That probably puts you in the same boat as most Americans, except for the fact that your answer implies that you now know something about it."

"I have learned a few things."

"Did something happen while I was gone?"

"Someone came forward with some information. A source."

"Who?"

"An old woman who cleaned out the cash from Falcon's safe deposit box in the Bahamas."

"She stole it?"

"No. It appears that he authorized access. He gave it to her."

"Why?"

"She claims she knew Falcon. Told us all about him."

Alicia knew exactly whom he was talking about, and she was glad that Vince couldn't see her reaction. "What did she tell you?"

"Lots of things. Turns out that he spent most of the Dirty War torturing prisoners at one of over three hundred secret detention centers that the military dictatorship set up around the country to deal with dissidents. He was known as El Oso."

"How did she know him?"

"Her daughter was detained there."

"I see."

"Do you?" said Vince.

She wasn't quite sure how to read his tone, but he didn't wait for her response.

"Interesting thing is that the detention center was called La Cacha. The guards gave it that name. It was short for La Cachavacha. Apparently there was a popular cartoon in Argentina called *La bruja de la cachavacha*, about a witch who could make people disappear."

"I know the cartoon," she said.

"El Oso and his buddies must have been a real bunch of comedians. I guess that's what Falcon was hinting at when he kept talking about the witch and the Disappeared."

"What do you expect? You've seen him, talked to him. He's crazy."

"No, he's not crazy. He's more of a sociopath."

"Is that what your source told you?"

"She didn't use that word, but she told us the stories. If it quacks like a duck and walks like a duck . . ."

"What kind of stories did she tell you?"

"Some pretty horrible things," said Vince.

"*What?*" she said, conveying more urgency than she would have liked.

"Basically, her daughter was seven months pregnant when she was taken into La Cacha. Believe it or not, she was one of nineteen pregnant women detained and tortured there. Nobody ever saw her again, but there were rumors that she lived long enough to give birth."

"Does anyone know what happened to the baby?"

"I couldn't tell you."

"You didn't ask her?"

"She wouldn't discuss it."

"You didn't push it?"

"It didn't seem pertinent to the hostage negotiation. And when I say she wouldn't discuss it, I mean she would *not* discuss it."

"You were okay with that?"

"Actually, that was part of our deal. She was willing to tell us everything she knew about Falcon, but the more personal details about her daughter were her business."

"Was she hiding something?"

"Could be. Or maybe it's still too painful for her to discuss it. Either way, I always honor my deals with sources. She gave us plenty of helpful information about Falcon, and she asked for just one thing in return."

"What?"

"She asked that I give something to you."

"To me?" she said, trying to act more surprised than she was. "What is it, the money?"

Vince shook his head. He laid two files on the table. Alicia could see the entire label of the top file, which was written in Spanish. In translation, it read: SECRETARY FOR PUBLIC HEALTH. BUENOS AIRES. DURAND HOSPITAL. ATTENTION: DR. DI LINARDO. Only a portion of the label was visible on the second folder beneath it. This one, however, was written in English: AMERICAN ASSOCIATION FOR THE ADVANCEMENT OF SCIENCE. WASHINGTON, DC. An abbreviation of some sort followed: CONADEP.

Alicia had never seen the files before, never had any dealings with a Dr. Di Linardo or any of the listed entities. "What is this?" she asked.

"I don't know. It's not for lack of interest, but obviously I didn't read it."

"Your source didn't tell you?"

"No. That was our deal. She tells me all about Falcon, and I give you the files. But she insisted that what's in there is between you and her."

Alicia was looking straight at the files, but she didn't answer.

"What's wrong?" said Vince.

"Nothing."

"Come on. The old lady said it was personal, but she also promised that you wouldn't hate me for giving it to you."

"I don't kill messengers, Vince."

"Then what is it?"

Alicia couldn't tear her gaze away from the files, but she was hearing that voice inside her head again—the one that had told her to get on the interstate and just keep driving. "I think it's more than I want to know," she said quietly.

57

Sergeant Chavez was in a SWAT power struggle, and he was determined to win it.

As lead representative of the City of Miami's tactical team, Chavez was inside the SWAT van with the head of Miami-Dade SWAT. Joining the debate by telephone were Chief Renfro from the city and the MDPD director. Paulo was not invited.

"I thought this was settled hours ago," said the director. "If a breach was necessary, Miami-Dade SWAT would lead it."

Chavez said, "It's a different ballgame now. We're not staging a straight breach. The breach occurs only if the city's sniper misses the target."

The director asked, "How does that change things?"

Chavez said, "The timing of the breach is tied directly to the sniper's shot. My sniper is taking the shot. I'm in direct communication with him. We're talking about split-second coordination here. It makes no sense to link the breachers from one law enforcement agency to the sniper of another and expect everything to come off with precision. Pile on top of that the fact that if we need a negotiator to intervene for any reason, Paulo's also from the city."

Chief Renfro chimed in. "I think the sergeant has a point, Director."

Chavez was ready to press his argument further, but to his surprise, it wasn't necessary.

"All right," said the director. "We'll serve as backup. The city takes the lead."

Chavez wrapped up the phone call quickly, before the director had a chance to change his mind. As they headed for the door, he extended his hand to the MDPD's SWAT coordinator, but the return handshake was lukewarm. Chavez didn't care. Already, it was as good as "mission accomplished," and not a single shot had been fired. He stepped down from the SWAT van and started toward the restaurant. Before sharing the news with his team, however, he picked up the telephone and dialed. Right at "Hello," he went straight to the bottom line.

"It's done," he said. "I'll lead my team in first. MDPD's SWAT will serve as backup."

"Very good," was the reply. "I can't tell you how much I appreciate this."

"It's nothing."

"No, it's *everything*. This Falcon is a stalker and a murderer. If your sniper misses and SWAT breaches, I don't want a bunch of guys going in who are so afraid of losing a hostage that they can't pull the trigger."

"The safety of the hostages is always paramount."

"Absolutely. That said, I want to be damn sure that if that door gets busted down, there's at least one man on the team who is sharp enough, brave enough, and talented enough to take this guy out even if the place goes wild with screaming hostages. You understand?"

Chavez could have launched into a lecture on the critical importance of knowing when not to shoot, but he decided just to shut up and take the compliment. "Yes, sir," he said. "I read you loud and clear."

The injured girl was deadweight in Theo's arms. She was only semiconscious.

It was getting darker by the minute inside the motel room. Theo had lost track of time, but it was obviously near nightfall. Daylight was no longer seeping into the room around the edge of the draperies, and they would have been in total darkness but for the very white, artificial glow that had replaced the natural light of day. Theo surmised that the police were aiming high-powered search lamps at the door and window.

The two other hostages, Natalia and the weatherman, were seated on the floor, back to back. Their ankles and wrists were bound tightly, and with hands behind their hips, they were tied together at the elbows. Theo was standing before the door, which remained closed, though the pile of furniture had been pushed aside for a clean exit. His ankles were tethered together by a two-foot length of lamp cord, a makeshift version of the shackles he'd worn in another life on death row. He stood a full head taller than his captor. Falcon came up from behind and pushed the barrel of his pistol against the base of Theo's skull.

"I have no problem shooting you," Falcon said in a calm voice.

The feeling was entirely mutual, but Theo didn't say it.

"So don't even think about running," Falcon added.

"Don't worry," said Theo.

"No ducking, no sudden jerks from side to side. I'm standing right behind you. You're my human shield, big guy."

The girl shifted in Theo's arms, and Theo rocked forward onto the balls of his feet to keep his balance.

"Don't move till I tell you to!" Falcon said, pushing Theo's head forward with his gun to emphasize the point.

Theo froze, which forced him to hold the girl in a somewhat awkward position. "I'm not going anywhere. Just staying loose."

The gun remained in place, aimed at the back of Theo's brain, as Theo listened. There was very little sound, like the eerie calm before the storm. He heard the discomfort in the injured girl's breathing. He heard the distant hum of helicopters hovering somewhere above the motel. He could hear Falcon rummaging through his pocket for the cell phone and then punching out the number.

"We're coming out now," Falcon said into the telephone. "If I open that door and see anything I don't like, if I even *sense* something I don't like, your friend Theo is dead."

Theo heard the close of the flip phone, Falcon's call to Jack having ended. Two things were now certain.

Falcon was ready to make his move.

And so was Theo.

58

•

Theo let the plan run through his mind one last time.

The moment of opportunity would arise when he bent down to lay the injured girl on the stoop. Crouched like a football lineman, he could let his right leg fly back with the force of a mule kick. Falcon would never know what hit him. Theo would sweep up the girl and roll away from the open doorway, out of the line of fire. The cops would see Falcon go down and immediately send in the SWAT to save the other two hostages. That was the plan, but Theo was nothing if not a realist.

Things never went according to plan.

"Open the door," said Falcon.

"How? I'm holding the girl."

"Hold her tight with your right arm, drape her knees over your left forearm. That will give you a free hand."

Theo complied, and Falcon was right. The girl weighed maybe a hundred pounds, and he could easily free up a hand and still manage to carry her. He turned the deadbolt, and the door unlocked with the portentous sound of a shotgun shucking.

"Nice and slow now," said Falcon.

Theo reached for the doorknob, grasped it tightly, and turned it to the right.

"Even slower," said Falcon. "Now open it."

Theo pushed the knob away from him, and the hinges creaked as the door swung outward. Building codes required external doors to swing out in south Florida, to prevent hurricanes from coming inside. This time it seemed that the hurricane might be going the other way. Theo, however, suddenly felt very small standing in the open doorway. Night had indeed fallen, and searchlights cut through the darkness like giant lasers. One was aimed directly at Theo, and it was momentarily blinding. Had he not been holding the girl, he would have shielded his eyes. He couldn't see very far—that was probably one of the intended effects of the searchlights—but he sensed or at least hoped that somewhere out there was a huge police presence.

"Take the shot," Chavez said into his bone microphone. He spoke in a hushed voice, albeit with urgency.

The sniper came back in his earpiece, "It's a black male, one of the hostages. I don't have a shot."

Chavez was with his tactical team in room 105, just two doors down from Falcon and the hostages. It was as close as they felt they could get to Falcon without tipping their hand that SWAT was on the way. The entire team was dressed in black SWAT regalia with Kevlar helmets, flak jackets, thigh guards, and night-vision goggles. Each was armed with an M-16 rifle and .45-caliber pistol. The front door was open for a quick exit. The men stood in the ready position in anticipation of the crack of a sniper shot that would be their starter pistol.

"Can you see Falcon?" said Chavez.

"Negative. The black male is holding the injured female in his arms, but there is no sign of— Check that. There's Falcon. He's standing directly behind the male hostage."

"Then take the shot."

"There is no shot."

"If you can see Falcon, there's a shot."

"It's too risky. He's using the hostage as a shield."

"What about the north-south snipers? Any angle for a shot to the side of the head?"

"Negative. The hostage is standing at the threshold. Falcon is still inside."

"Then back off. It's time to breach."

"If you breach now, Theo Knight is dead."

"Then take the shot, damn it!"

Take the shot.

For a brief instant, Falcon thought he was hearing voices in his head all over again, but it sounded unlike any voice he'd heard before, and it was coming from a place that seemed all too real—specifically, one of the nearby rooms.

"Back inside!" shouted Falcon as he grabbed Theo by the collar and pulled him out of the doorway.

59

Vince listened intently as Jack described what was unfolding on the command center's closed-circuit television—Falcon retreating into the hotel room with both Theo and the injured girl still held hostage. Vince's telephone rang almost immediately. He answered just as quickly, only to get an earful of Falcon's most hysterical screams yet.

"You tried to screw me, Paulo!"

"No one's screwing with you."

"I heard your SWAT guy or sniper or whoever talking to someone in the next room. He said to take the shot! Now call them off, or *I'll* take the shot. This is no joke. Somebody's gonna die here!"

"Just calm down, all right?"

"Calm down? You send in a shooter, and now you're telling me to *calm down*?"

"Hear me out, Falcon. If SWAT or anyone else is anywhere near you, it's not my doing. Let me check into it, and I'll get them to back off."

"I don't buy that for one second. It's just like you

did to me on the bridge. You're lying through your teeth all over again."

"Look, for what it's worth, I didn't lie to you on the bridge. When I said you could speak to Alicia if you came down from the lamppost, that was a firm deal in my mind. Someone else—someone higher up—pulled the plug on us."

"It's never your fault, is it, Paulo?"

"I know I must sound like I'm full of excuses, but I swear I'm not lying to you."

"And I swear right back that I don't believe you."

Vince could see that this conversation was going nowhere, along the lines of the timeless are-too-am-not playground debate. He needed another tack. "Falcon, let me make good on this, all right?"

"How?"

"First, let's agree upfront that you are not going to hurt the hostages. If you can make that promise to me, then we can talk about what it is that you really want."

"You know what I want."

"Not until you tell me, I don't."

"You've known all along."

"Spell it out, Falcon. Tell me what you want, and I'll see if I can get it done."

"Anything I want?"

"Within reason. Just don't hurt the hostages."

He paused, as if he enjoyed keeping Vince in suspense. Finally, he said, "I want to speak to Alicia."

"Okay. I think we can do that."

"In person."

Vince didn't want to use the word "no," even if the

answer was "no freakin' way." "How about we start with a phone conversation?"

"No, I want to—" Falcon said, then stopped. "You know what, Paulo? I'm calling your bluff. Put her on."

"Unfortunately, she's not here right now."

"Damn you and your lies! Don't you ever keep a promise? Don't you *ever* stop stalling?"

Vince wasn't sure how to convince him that he was being truthful, but based on what he was hearing in Falcon's voice, it appeared that he didn't have nearly enough time to redeem his own credibility. "If you don't believe me, talk to Swyteck. Here, he'll tell you."

He handed the phone to Jack, who had been listening to the conversation on speaker. Paulo would have liked to coach him on what to say, but there was no time for that, either.

Jack spoke into the telephone. "He's not messing with you, Falcon. Alicia is not here, and we're doing our best to find her."

"It's time she talked to me. It's beyond time."

"What do you want to say to her?"

"Just bring her here. *Now!*"

Jack hit the mute button and spoke to Vince. "Where the hell is Alicia?"

"She rushed out of the command center after I gave her some files from my source. I sensed something was wrong, but she wouldn't say what. I honestly don't know where she went."

"Find someone who does."

"We're working on it."

"Work harder!" said Jack. He disengaged the mute function and spoke into the telephone. "She's on her way, Falcon. Just give us a couple minutes."

Falcon didn't answer.

Vince slipped Jack a note that read, keep him talking.

"Falcon?" said Jack. "Are you there? Come on buddy, talk to me. Tell me more about that stage you wanted. You know, 'curtain time.'"

Falcon paced across the room, the cell phone
pressed to his ear. Swyteck was clearly stalling, but his exact words were lost on Falcon. The
lawyer's voice was just noise on the phone line.
Falcon couldn't focus on conversation. His mind
was roaming elsewhere, and the noise was growing
louder. At first, it was a hum, then a buzz, and finally
the roar of engines. Airplane engines.

"I want to speak to Alicia, damn it!" Not even his
own voice, however, could drown out the rumble of
airplane engines inside his head.

It had been a moonless night, and the sky was
a vast, impenetrable blackness in his darkest
memories. He was flying in a retrofitted Skyvan, a
propeller-powered aircraft so squat in its design that
it was nicknamed the Flying Shoebox. This craft was
owned by the Argentine Coast Guard. Nearly all of
the passenger seats had been removed to expand the
plane's cargo capacity, and El Oso was buckled into
one of the few that remained. The plane's normal

flight crew was in the cockpit. El Oso was part of a working crew that included a noncommissioned officer and a petty officer. The military rotated different working crewmembers onto each flight—involving as many operatives as possible—so that no one who worked at the detention center could point fingers without implicating himself or a friend. El Oso had, of course, heard rumors about the flights, and he had begun to speculate about the nature of his assignment from the moment he received orders to report to the landing field at ESMA, one of the largest and most notorious of all the secret military detention centers. For El Oso, however, the exact purpose of this particular flight was not confirmed in his own mind until he saw about twenty naked, unconscious prisoners laid side-by-side on the floor of the aircraft.

"Falcon, are you there?" It was Swyteck's voice on the telephone, somehow cutting through the deafening airplane engines.

"Just shut up and get Alicia on the line!"

Swyteck kept talking, more stalling, but Falcon wasn't even listening. He was barely aware of the fact that he was still inside a motel room, let alone that he was on the telephone. There was so much noise inside his head, those damn engines roaring from the past. *But why so loud?*

They had left the hatch open. The Skyvan had a rear hatch that slid down to open, and there was no intermediate position. It either had to be closed or fully open. On the Wednesday-night flights, the hatch definitely remained open. El Oso was staring directly into the night, a black hole in the aft of a noisy aircraft. Between him and the gaping hatch lay the rows of naked bodies on the floor. He wished that each and every one of them were dead, but he knew better. Only the living would require the injection of a sedative from a medical doctor. *The doctor.* He was making his rounds, so to speak, moving from one prisoner to the next, administering a second injection that would keep them unconscious. El Oso hadn't noticed at first, but as the doctor worked his way up the row of naked bodies, emptying his syringe, his face came clear. Finally, El Oso made the connection. This man was no stranger. This was the very same navy doctor to whom he had taken prisoner 309's newborn baby just two months earlier.

"A couple more minutes, Falcon," said Swyteck. "Alicia's on her way."

Falcon grunted a reply of some kind, but it wasn't even in English. His memories had him thinking in Spanish, his native tongue.

Mandar para arriba. Send them up. El Oso had been waiting for the order, and it came in those exact words from the commissioned officer. It came just as soon as the doctor had administered the last of the injections and disappeared into the cockpit, literally turning his back on the prisoners—his patients. The physician's own "disappearance" was an ironic charade, a way to serve the regime and maintain merely technical compliance with his Hippocratic oath. When the doctor was gone, El Oso's work began. He unbuckled his seat belt, rose, and started toward the row of naked, sleeping prisoners. Among them were the young and not so young, men and women alike. Some bore the burn marks of the grill. Others were bruised from relentless beatings. A skilled torturer could implement the tactics of "special interrogation" without leaving such marks, but finesse of that sort was completely unnecessary in the case of prisoners who were being "sent up." El Oso worked in a two-man team. They started with the prisoner nearest the hatch, a man who was perhaps in his early twenties, perhaps even younger. El Oso took his arms. His teammate took the prisoner's ankles. They lifted him up from the floor. In the prisoner's unconscious state, his body sagged between them and hung before the open hatchway like a broad, sadistic smile.

"Are you still there, Falcon?"

"I've had it with this! Stop stalling. Where's Alicia?" It was a coherent response, and it took every ounce of psychological fortitude for Falcon to string the words together. Even so, he wasn't strong enough to pull himself up from the past. The lucid moment, however, had managed to shift his focus slightly. It was suddenly as if El Oso were another man entirely, someone whom Falcon didn't even want to know. This stranger called El Oso was working furiously but in sync with his teammate, swaying the bodies back and forth as if rocking a hammock. They would release on the count of *tres*, "sending up" the prisoners only in the most figurative sense, as the bodies would soon plunge into the cold, black ocean below, into the depths of the disappeared. The young man went first, then a woman, followed by two men who looked like brothers, an older woman, and so on. Grab the ankles, swing the body, and release. El Oso was on autopilot, discharging his duty with "subordination and courage, to serve the Fatherland," in accordance with the detention center's ritual salute. He'd lost count of the prisoners that had, by his own hands, passed through the hatchway. His movements became almost robotic as he disposed of one subversive after another. Their faces were without expression, their transformation into zombies having begun hours earlier, back at the detention center, with the first injection of penthonaval. They went out without a sound, without any knowledge of their fate, without any final scorn for their murderers—until it was the turn of a certain young woman, who suddenly slipped free from El Oso's grasp and grabbed him by the wrist.

Perhaps she hadn't been dosed properly. Or maybe it was her extraordinary will to survive that had fought off the sedative and roused her to a state of semiconsciousness. Whatever the explanation, she had found the strength to reach for El Oso and grab him tightly enough to draw him halfway into the open hatchway. At the last second, he managed to brace himself against the frame with his right foot, and his teammate snagged him by the arm. He was staring into empty space, inches away from his own death at the hands of this young woman whose face was no longer without expression. She was no longer just another subversive. She fought with the determination of the young mother she was, and before she disappeared into the darkness, El Oso was struck by a bolt of recognition: he knew that it was La Cacha prisoner 309.

"Damn it, Swyteck! Put Alicia Mendoza on the phone right now!"

"I just need another minute. I swear, she's almost here."

Falcon pushed his memories aside, shoved them right through that yawning black hole in the back of the Skyvan, but the young mother's face was forever lighted in his mind.

He went to Theo and put a gun to the prisoner's head. "You've got one minute, Swyteck. *Your buddy's* got one more minute."

61

I'm here!"

Jack heard Alicia announce her arrival just a split second before the door flew open and she hurried into the mobile command unit.

"Where the heck have you been?" said Jack.

"My parents' house."

"Sergeant Paulo has been psycho calling you for almost fifteen minutes. Why didn't you answer?"

"It's complicated."

Jack couldn't contain his reaction. "What do you mean it's—"

"It doesn't matter," said Vince, interrupting. "She's here, and there isn't time for this. Alicia, I need you on the phone right now."

"Okay." She moved closer to the desk and took the empty seat by the phone. "What should I say?"

"Just say 'Hello, this is Alicia Mendoza.' Then hand the phone back to me."

Jack said, "That's not going to satisfy him. In fact, teasing him like that might only infuriate him and make him take it out on Theo."

"This is negotiation, not capitulation. We let him know that Alicia's ready to talk to him. Then I get back on the line and make him give up a hostage to get past 'hello.'"

Jack felt a moment of anxiety, but he knew that if it were anyone but his best friend in that motel room with a gun to his head, he would have agreed wholeheartedly with Paulo's negotiation strategy. Jack had to remain objective. "All right. But Falcon's very close to the edge."

"We all are," said Paulo. He handed the phone to Alicia. She breathed in and out to compose herself, then spoke in a voice that was almost too pleasant for the circumstances. "Falcon, this is Alicia Mendoza."

There was silence. Vince took the phone back, but he didn't speak.

"Alicia? Is that you?" said Falcon.

"It was," said Paulo. "She's ready and willing to talk to you, Falcon. All you have to do is let one hostage go."

"Put Alicia back on."

"I will. But I need something in return. It's not too much to ask. Just let one of the hostages go."

"I need to speak to Alicia."

"I understand that."

"I just want to say two words to her."

"I'll give you two minutes with her if you let one of the hostages go."

"I don't need two minutes! Now put her on the phone, damn it!"

"I can't do that, Falcon."

"Don't lie to me! You can do whatever you want."

"I'm glad to hear you say that, because all I really want is to get the hostages and you out of this mess safely. So let's help each other here, Falcon. Let's help each other get what we want."

"Okay, how's this for help? I got a gun to the black guy's head. Just let me talk to Alicia, and you can have him alive. Just two words."

Paulo paused, considering it. "Two words, and you give me Theo Knight."

"That's all I want."

"All right," said Paulo. "I'll put her on."

He hit the mute button and handed her the phone. "When I cut off the mute button, tell him you're back on the line. But don't tell him anything more. I'm cutting him off after two words."

Jack said, "I don't think he literally meant two words."

"I don't care," said Paulo. "The deal was that he gets to say two words to Alicia and then he releases Theo Knight."

"Yeah, but he also said that he has a gun to Theo's head. If by 'two words' he meant a sentence or two, you could piss him off bad enough to make him pull the trigger."

Paulo showed no reaction. He laid his index finger atop the mute button. "Two words," he said, as if to close all debate. He counted aloud—one, two, three—and then pressed the button.

On cue, Alicia spoke into the phone. "Falcon, it's me again."

There was silence on the line.

Alicia waited, and then, on Paulo's hand signal,

she tried again. "Falcon, is there something you wanted to say to me?"

A muffled noise carried over the line. It was unmistakably human, so it was clear that Falcon had not hung up, but no words were discernible. It sounded like crying, perhaps from one of the hostages.

"Alicia?" said Falcon.

Paulo raised one finger, indicating that Falcon had just spent one of his two words.

"Yes?" she said.

The sound of her voice triggered a sob over the line, and the source of the crying was no longer in question. "I'm sorry," said Falcon.

Paulo seemed confused by the words as much as the tone. He was slow to reach for the telephone, apparently not quite so intent on limiting Falcon to his two-word deal.

"Sorry for what?" said Alicia, but as the question left her lips, the crack of a single pistol shot exploded over the line.

"Theo!" shouted Jack, fearing the worst for his friend.

62

·

Jack practically flew out of the mobile command center and ran toward the Biscayne Motor Lodge at full speed. Alicia was right behind him, but with his adrenaline pumping, Jack was gaining separation with each stride.

Jack couldn't count the number of times Falcon had threatened to shoot Theo, from the carjacking, which had started this whole crisis, to the final telephone conversation, which had ended with a gun blast. By closed-circuit TV transmission, he had watched Theo step into the open doorway with the injured girl in his arms. He'd caught glimpses of Falcon shielding himself behind Theo, pressing a gun to the back of his head. In any hostage crisis, the safest strategy for someone in Theo's position was to keep quiet and melt into the background, but lying low and playing the wallflower was definitely not Theo's style. It would have been impossible, Jack knew, for Theo to stand by and watch the abuse of other hostages, especially the girls. After four years on death row for a crime he hadn't committed, Theo would never bet his life on law enforcement swooping in to save him. Theo was the kind of hostage who made negotiators nervous—strong, fearless, and determined to save himself and to save the others, even at the risk of pushing a crazed gunman over the edge.

Jack had no doubt that if Falcon's bullet had found a hostage, it was Theo.

"Hold it right there!" a police officer shouted as he nearly tackled Jack. It took the strong arms of two motorcycle cops to keep Jack from breaking through the yellow crime-scene tape. He was at the street entrance to the motel's parking lot, about thirty yards away from the open doorway to room 102.

"Did SWAT go in?" said Jack.

"They got it under control."

"Then I need to get by you!"

"You need to wait here," the cop said with attitude.

Alicia caught up. "He's with me," she said, breathless from the run.

"Sorry," said the cop. "You can't go either. No one goes past this line until I get the all-clear from SWAT."

A member of the tactical team suddenly appeared in the open doorway. Jack believed it was Chavez, but he wasn't sure. He lowered his M-16 rifle and gave a hand signal, which needed no interpretation, but Alicia offered one anyway.

"There's your all-clear," she said. "Come on, Jack."

They ducked beneath the yellow tape and sprinted toward room 102. Two teams of emergency medical technicians had also been waiting for the signal, and even with their gear, they kept pace with Jack. As Jack neared the open door, he could hear other SWAT members inside as they tried to calm the hostages. He heard cathartic crying from the girls and hysterics from a man who sounded nothing like Theo.

Chavez allowed the EMTs to enter, but he stepped up to prevent Jack from entering the room. "Crime scene," he said. "That's as far as you go, Swyteck."

Jack looked past him and saw the SWAT members and EMTs tending to the three other hostages. Then he saw Theo. He was lying on the floor, his face, neck, and shoulders covered with blood.

"Theo!"

Theo sat up, obviously disgusted. "Can somebody clean this shit off me?" he said. On the floor beside him was Falcon, his body in a heap. Beside him was the pistol that he had used to turn the right side of his head into red-and-gray splatter.

"He shot himself," said Jack.

"Really?" said Theo. "Are you sure your name isn't Jack *Sherlock*?"

"Are you hurt?" a paramedic asked Theo.

"No."

Another team of EMTs hurried past Jack, and Chavez stepped aside to let them enter. They put the injured girl on a gurney and rushed her to the ambulance. The other team stayed behind and checked on the remaining hostages.

Jack turned as Sergeant Paulo came up behind him. Alicia said, "It looks like they're all going to be okay, Vince."

"All but Falcon," said Chavez.

"Go figure," said Jack. "A guy threatens to jump off a bridge, gets himself arrested, even kills a police officer and takes hostages. He finally gets what he wants and has the mayor's daughter on the telephone, and what does he do? He falls apart, says he's sorry, and can't tell her any of the things he's been dying to tell her."

Vince said, "I think he said everything he wanted to say."

"What do you mean?" said Alicia.

"If I'm to believe that old woman who passed along those files to you, Falcon gave you something that thousands of other Argentine families have never gotten."

"What?"

"An apology."

Alicia tried, but she couldn't dodge the impact of Paulo's words. Jack took notice.

"Hey," said Theo. "You guys heard tonight's forecast yet?"

"The forecast?" said Jack.

"Tell 'em, Wally," said Theo.

One of the SWAT guys said, "Hey, ain't you Walt the Weather Wizard? My wife watches you every night."

The weatherman groaned, as if resigning to the fact that it was time to face the music. "Yes, yes. Walt the Weather Wizard was shacked up in a flea-bitten motel room with a couple of teenaged hookers. I'm guilty as charged, all right? You happy now?"

The SWAT guy checked out the Latina, then, as if the weatherman weren't even there, he gave his teammate a little shrug and said, "Who knew? I thought he was gay."

63

Theo wanted nothing to do with the media.

For two full days, one reporter after another tried to land an exclusive interview and brand him a hero. Theo turned them all away. In his mind, true heroes were never motivated by self-preservation. They ditched their own safety and thrust themselves into danger to save others. The actual words he used to convey those thoughts, however, were slightly less than quotable: "Ain't nothing heroic about lifting your own black ass out of a crack."

In some ways, it took more courage for him to pick up the telephone and call Officer Mendoza.

The Mendoza family had also been hounded by the media, and Theo could only assume that Alicia had managed to avoid the frenzy by crawling into a bunker. Her father, of course, was all over the television and newspapers, praising "a job well done" by the City of Miami Police Department. Chief of Police Renfro was almost as much of a media hound. She and the mayor spoke most highly about Sergeant Chavez and "the brave men of SWAT." They made little mention of Jack and the active role he had played in the negotiations. Even Sergeant Paulo was relegated to the I-also-wish-to-thank category. Jack and Paulo seemed okay with that. After the hour-by-hour intensity of a hostage crisis, a chance to relax and sleep was more than welcome, and a little time to step back and plan the next move was a good thing. At some point, however, it was time to stop planning. Theo was ready for action.

Alicia sounded somewhat surprised to hear from him, but she took his phone call nonetheless. She was pleasant enough in thanking Theo for doing all that he could to keep Falcon from harming the other hostages. Theo was never one for small talk, however, so he cut to the chase.

"I'm calling because there are things Falcon told me while I was stuck in that motel room with him. Things that I think you should know."

She hesitated, as if not sure how to respond.

"Did you hear me?" said Theo.

"Yes, sorry. What kind of things are you talking about?"

"Personal stuff. Family matters."

"Do you mean my family?"

"I don't mean the Sopranos."

"There's no need to be sarcastic about it."

"Sorry, but being a smart-ass is kind of like therapy. It's about the only thing that separates me from the guys who tell the mayor's daughter that they're sorry and then blow their brains out."

"I have no idea what you mean by that."

"That makes two of us. But look, what I called to tell you is that Falcon talked plenty before he killed hisself. I haven't gotten into the details with anyone yet. Not the police, not the newspapers, not even Jack."

"Do you plan to share with them?"

"Right now, I ain't got a plan. I think you and me need to talk about it first."

"What could we possibly have to talk about?"

"For starters, a guy named Sikes."

"Are you talking about the guy who deposited two hundred thousand dollars into Falcon's safe deposit box in the Bahamas? Do you mean that Sikes?"

"Sort of. Dude used a phony name, you understand? So maybe you'd like to know who this Sikes really was."

Again, she paused. "Falcon told you who Sikes was?"

"Yup."

"Who was it?"

Theo laughed. "Not so fast. I had to work real hard to get that information out of Falcon. Real hard."

"I don't understand."

"I don't work for nothing."

"Are you asking me for money?" she said, suddenly indignant.

"Money? Nah. That wouldn't be right."

"Then what do you want?"

"Well, I hope I don't sound too much like Falcon the crazy man," he said with a light chuckle, "but I just want to meet with you."

"Why?"

"Because this is too important to discuss over the telephone."

"And if I refuse, then what?"

"Then you'll never know who Sikes is."

"You do want money, don't you?"

"Like I was saying, this is way too important for you and me to handle over the telephone."

There was silence, as if she were mulling things over. "All right. I think I'd like to talk with you, Theo."

"Good. Let's say eleven o'clock tonight at my bar. I own Sparky's Tavern down on—"

"I know Sparky's," she said.

"Cool," said Theo. "And if you decide to come, you'll know Sikes." He said a quick good-bye and ended the call with a touch of the speakerphone button. His use of the handheld receiver had made it impossible for Alicia to know that she was on speaker.

"Did I do good, boss?" asked Theo.

Jack was sitting across the table from him. "You were perfect," he said. "Just perfect."

64

Jack reached Sparky's Tavern around ten forty-five p.m. Tuesday was not Jack's regular night, as it was common knowledge that a visit to Sparky's was best followed by at least a full weekend of detoxification. Tonight, however, he made an exception.

Theo was blowing on his old Buescher 400 saxophone and just finishing up a set when Jack entered the tavern. A few appreciative regulars stood to applaud Theo's efforts, but most of the patrons kept right on drinking, talking, and laughing, as if Theo were little more than elevator Muzak. Sparky's was not a true jazz club by any stretch, and on most nights, it was whatever the paying clientele wanted it to be. If the Latino band of bikers craved a little meringue with their *cerveza*, so be it. If the pretty redneck girls raced to the jukebox for yet another round of the electric slide, it wasn't Theo's place to stop them. Any bartender worthy of his honorary degree in pop psychology could see that Sparky's struggled with a multiple-personality disorder

Sunday through Thursday just so that Theo could pay the rent and do Charlie Parker proud on the weekends.

Theo stepped down from the stage to meet Jack at the bar. Jack had a beer, and Theo drank bourbon, which told Jack that he was done playing for the night. Theo never drank alcohol when he was performing, but he sure made up for it when he wasn't. Time passed quickly, as it always did for Jack at Sparky's. By eleven-fifteen p.m., it was pretty clear that Alicia would be a no-show.

By eleven-thirty p.m., it was equally clear that Jack's plan was working perfectly.

"Well, look who's here," said Theo, pointing with a nod toward the door.

Jack swiveled his barstool to see a handsome Latino coming toward him. He was built like a football player, had the haircut of a marine, and bore the chilling expression of a racist cop who'd just spotted a busload of rap musicians doing eighty in a thirty-five-mile-per-hour zone. He walked up to the bar, ignored Jack, and spoke directly to Theo. "You Theo Knight?"

"Who wants to know?"

"My name's Felipe." He didn't offer a handshake. "I work for Mayor Mendoza."

Jack said, "Did the mayor send you?"

Felipe didn't even acknowledge the question. "I need to talk to Theo."

"He's cool," said Theo, speaking about Jack. "These days, I don't talk to anyone without my lawyer at my side."

Felipe wouldn't even look at Jack, seemingly determined to keep the lawyer out of the picture. "The mayor just wants to talk to Theo."

"What about?" said Jack.

Felipe's gaze finally shifted toward Jack, but the look in his eyes made it clear that only big hunks of humanity named Theo were welcome. "The mayor said that Theo would know what it's about."

"Fine," said Theo. "Let's talk. Where is he?"

"On his boat."

"That's rough. Dixie Highway's a bitch by boat."

"He wants you to come to him, asshole."

Theo glanced at Jack. "He must have been talking to you, counselor. Because the last guy who talked to me like that ended up swallowing his teeth."

Jack raised his hands like a boxing referee. "Time out, guys. Can we take the testosterone level down just a wee bit here?"

Theo locked eyes with Felipe. Jack didn't like the way the conversation was going, but he respected Theo's street smarts. If the big guy took an immediate dislike to someone, it was usually for good reason. Jack said, "How do we get to the mayor's boat?"

"There's no we," said Felipe. "It's just Theo."

"If he doesn't go, I don't go," said Theo.

Had it been up to Felipe, Jack would have expected to hear something along the more profane lines of "Go take a flying leap." But Felipe obviously had his orders, and returning without Theo was not an option. "Fine," said Felipe. "The both of you can come."

"I need five minutes," said Theo. "Let me close out the cash register."

"I'll meet you in the parking lot," said Felipe. He turned and headed toward the door.

Theo removed the cash drawer from the register and went to the back room. Jack followed him. An elderly woman was seated at Theo's desk. She looked up hopefully, then reacted quickly to the expression on Jack's face. It was as if she'd seen that same look of disappointment too many times before.

"I told you she wouldn't come," she said.

"It has nothing to do with you," said Jack. "She just doesn't want to get involved in the whole Bahamian bank-account mess. Alicia didn't even know you were going to be here waiting for her."

"So, if I invite her myself, do you think she will agree to see me?"

Jack and Theo exchanged glances, neither of them sure how to answer that question. "I think we'll know more after we talk to the mayor," said Jack.

65

It was after midnight before Jack and Theo reached the Coconut Grove Marina. A gentle breeze blew in from the bay, and Jack's ears tingled from the steady ping of halyards slapping against the tall, barren masts of countless sailboats. Motorboats and yachts of every size and description slept silently in their slips, though a few figurative snorers gurgled from their bilge pumps. Somewhere in the distance, a diesel engine rumbled toward home, and the lonely sound in the darkness only added to the moonlit marina's eerie aura. Felipe spoke not a word as he escorted Jack and Theo to the end of the long, floating pier, where they boarded a forty-six-foot Hatteras Convertible.

For a career politician, Mayor Mendoza did not lack for the finer things in life. His house, though not a mansion, was loaded with Old Spanish character; his yacht, though more than two decades old, was still a floating lap of luxury. It was technically a fishing boat, but the mayor had rigged the salon for entertainment, complete with club chairs, a wet bar, handcrafted teak cabinetry, and even a flat-screen television. The mayor invited his guests to take a seat at the old wooden wheel of a ship that had been turned into a round, glass-top table—floating proof that money doesn't buy taste. Felipe stepped aside, removing himself from the main circle of conversation, but he remained in the salon.

"Something to drink, gentlemen?" said the mayor, standing at the bar. He made the offer with a smile, but it seemed strained to Jack. The bags under his eyes had almost doubled in size since Jack had first spoken to him in the privacy of his limo. His skin had taken on an unhealthy, ashen hue. Had Jack been forced to guess, he would have said that the mayor hadn't slept in at least three days.

"Nothing for me, thanks," said Jack.

"You got any smoothies?" said Theo.

Jack tried not to roll his eyes.

"Uh, no," said the mayor.

Theo looked around and said, "I ever trade in my little open fisherman for one of these babies, it's gonna have smoothies. Strawberry. Banana. Mamey."

Jack resisted the urge to strangle him.

"Papaya, carambola, kumquat—"

"Theo, we get it, all right?" said Jack. "The man doesn't have any smoothies."

"Funny," said Theo. "Falcon didn't have any either. It's weird, the things you crave when you're being held hostage. I couldn't stop thinking about smoothies. But Falcon didn't want to hear anything about it. Said I was just making him hungry, all this talk about food. So you know what we did?"

The mayor filled his glass with ice and scotch. "I can't even imagine."

"We talked about money."

Jack detected a rise of concern in the mayor's eyes. "Is that so?" said the mayor.

"Yeah," said Theo. "But I guess you already knew that. Alicia must have told you about our phone conversation."

The mayor used his finger to stir the ice around in his scotch.

Jack said, "Alicia didn't tell her father anything."

"She had to tell him," said Theo. "Why else would Felipe show up at my bar in her place?"

Jack glanced at Felipe and said, "Because somebody tapped her phone."

"That's a lie," said Felipe.

Jack was bluffing, but Felipe's quick denial was as good as an admission. Over the past five days, he'd heard and seen enough to formulate his own theories. The old Argentine woman with her DNA files—the work of modern-day scientists trying to solve the crimes of the Dirty War—had confirmed his darkest suspicions. "Alicia doesn't want to know the truth. That's why she didn't show up tonight. That's why she didn't dare tell her father anything about her conversation with Theo. She simply doesn't want to know that her dad is Sikes."

Felipe stepped closer, his tone threatening. "You don't know what you're talking about."

"It's okay," the mayor told his bodyguard, "I want

to hear what he has to say. Go ahead, Mr. Swyteck. I'm finding this very interesting."

"Interesting," said Theo, scoffing. "One of those great fudge words. Sex is *interesting*. The Holocaust is *interesting*."

"So is blackmail," said Jack.

"Meaning?" said the mayor.

"That's what it was, right? Two hundred thousand dollars cash deposited in a Bahamian safe deposit box. You make the drop under a fictitious name. Falcon agrees never to tell anyone that you took a baby from one of his disappeared prisoners. It's blackmail, with a little twist at the end. Falcon doesn't keep the money for himself. He apologizes to the daughter of the woman he murdered, and he gives the money to the grandmother, who has spent over a quarter-century searching for her."

"Justice from the Dirty War," said Theo.

"Dirty Justice," said Jack.

"Is this the best you morons can come up with?" said Felipe, his anger rising. "You come up with this totally bogus story to get a little blackmail of your own going?"

"We're not here for money," said Jack.

"That's a shame," said the mayor. He laid a briefcase on the table and popped it open. "Because that's all I can offer you."

Jack did a double take. Stacks of crisp hundred-dollar bills were laid out before him.

"How much is that?" said Theo.

"A hundred thousand dollars," said the mayor. "That'll buy a lot of smoothies."

"We don't want your money."

Theo said, "The boat, maybe, but not your—"

Jack kicked him under the table.

"Look here," said the mayor. "If it's simply a matter of negotiation, we can work something out."

"It's not negotiable. We came here for the truth, and you gave it to us the minute you opened that briefcase."

"So what do you want to do now, ruin me?"

"I think that's up to Alicia and her grandmother. Her biological grandmother."

"You don't know what you're doing. Nothing positive can come of this. You're just destroying a happy, loving family. Until Falcon called and asked me for two hundred thousand dollars in hush money, I didn't have the slightest clue that Alicia had been stolen from her birth mother."

"That's another lie," said Jack.

"How would you know?"

"Because you adopted a two-week-old baby with a birth certificate that said she was two years old. And you did that for one reason only: to make it harder for her blood relatives to find her."

The mayor fell silent, but his expression spoke volumes. Suddenly, his complicity in the most horrible crime imaginable was as plain to see as the briefcase full of money on the table.

Felipe said, "Mayor, you don't have to listen to these insults."

The mayor had gone pale. "You really should take the money, Mr. Swyteck."

"We don't want your money."

"Please," said the mayor. "Take the money."

"We're leaving," said Jack, rising.

"No you're not," said Felipe. He was pointing a pistol at Jack. "Now sit back down."

"Felipe," the mayor said in a shaky voice, "this is not the answer."

"It worked fine when you sent me down the river to get Falcon to back away from Alicia. It worked just as well when you sent me over to Nassau to talk some sense into Riley about where all that money came from."

"I never told you to threaten anyone's life. Put the gun away."

"I'm just protecting both of us, Mayor. It's best if you went back to shore now."

"Listen to your boss," said Jack. "Put the gun away."

"Shut up! You're nothing but trouble, Swyteck, starting with the way you tried to make me into a bad guy for going down the river and telling your client to stay away from the mayor's daughter. You had the cops thinking it was me who killed that homeless woman in the trunk of the car."

"That went nowhere," said Jack. "We know it was Falcon who killed her. So just put away the gun before you end up facing a real murder charge."

"Just shut your trap! If you didn't go sticking your nose where it didn't belong, we wouldn't be in this mess."

Theo was suddenly a blur diving across the cabin. His shoulders hit Felipe in the midsection, and the two men tumbled to the deck. Felipe somehow managed to land on top. They were locked in a struggle when the gun went off and shattered a window.

"Theo!" Jack shouted as he dived behind a club chair. Theo finally broke free and grabbed Felipe's gun hand, but in the fight, another shot cut through the cabin.

The mayor went down.

Theo had Felipe in a hold that nearly broke the man's arm, and the gun dropped to the floor. Jack hurried to the mayor's side.

"Hold on, Mayor," said Jack. "We'll get you to a doctor."

The mayor coughed up blood, and a mirthless chuckle followed. "I am the doctor," he said in a fading voice.

Jack felt chills as he watched the mayor—the doctor—draw his last breath.

66

Jack was having a hard time understanding Alicia's grandmother, and the language barrier had nothing to do with it.

The rumors surrounding Mayor Mendoza's death were scandalous even by Miami standards. The high-octane ingredients were all in place: a cash-stuffed briefcase and a scuffle on the mayor's yacht, a dead politician and his pistol-packing bodyguard, a death-row survivor and the son of a former governor—all on the heels of a dramatic hostage stand-off. Walt the Weather Wizard was the happiest man alive. Just when it seemed that the media couldn't get enough of his sex-for-hire disaster, he was suddenly yesterday's news.

Officially, the cause of the mayor's death was under investigation. The police department was in its tightest "no comment" mode, and details about what was said that night on the yacht were not generally known. The mayor still had many friends and supporters, however, both inside and outside the police department. They were actively spinning the cause of death as an "accidental shooting." They dismissed all leaks about the mayor's alleged link to Falcon and the Disappeared as the senseless ranting of a delusional homeless maniac. Jack did nothing to educate the press or the public, though standing mute was not a decision he had come to on his own. Nor was he minding the homicide detectives' concerns that he not comment on an ongoing investigation.

Jack was simply honoring the wishes of Alicia's grandmother.

To be sure, Alicia's family history was complex. Jack didn't even pretend to understand the depths of the tragedy, though his own experiences surely framed his perspective. Jack's grandmother had spirited her teenage daughter away to Miami when Castro came to power in Cuba. Sadly, *Abuela* wasn't able to escape Cuba for another forty years, long after Jack's mother died in childbirth. In a manner of speaking, Jack and his mother had been stolen from *Abuela*, and when his grandmother landed in Miami nearly four decades later, she latched onto Jack with the heartfelt intention of never letting go, even if he was a grown man in his thirties. Jack would have expected the same sense of urgency from Alicia's biological *abuela*, now that she had the DNA and other proof she'd longed for. He was wrong.

"Yours is a completely different situation," the old woman told Jack.

"I realize that. My mother wasn't murdered."

"And even though she was driven out of her native

country and died so young, you always knew who your real mother was."

"But you have all the proof you've ever needed. You have every right to push forward on this."

"It's not a question of my rights," she said. "For any parent or grandparent, it's always a question of what's best for the child. Even if that child is grown."

Jack wished for a better answer, but anyone who knew the biblical story of King Solomon could understand the old woman's reasoning. The real mother would never cut the baby in half—physically or emotionally—to serve her own maternal needs and desires. Neither would the real grandmother. After years of searching, she finally heard from Falcon, who told her exactly where to find her granddaughter. Right then, she could have ambushed Alicia with accusations if not evidence against Mr. Mendoza. She could have gone to the newspapers. She could even have gone to court, though at the time the Argentine judiciary did not have a history of siding with mothers of the Disappeared who reached out to lost grandchildren, no matter how much the child looked, walked, or talked like his or her dead mother. The point was that forcing the issue would have earned her nothing but Alicia's contempt. Instead, she gave Alicia the soft sell, starting with that first face-to-face visit when Alicia was in college. As difficult as it was to exercise emotional restraint, she simply planted seeds and, on occasion, dug them up to see how they were growing, knowing that she and her granddaughter could never have a future together unless Alicia followed her own heart.

Jack, however, was of the view that even the hungriest of hearts needed a nudge now and then. And when Alicia's phone number showed up on his caller ID, he was certain that his slightly more aggressive strategy was about to pay off.

"Thanks for returning my call," said Jack. He was on his cell phone, standing somewhere in the middle of a very ill formed line at the walk-up counter of a sidewalk espresso bar called La Cabana Havana. Little hole-in-the-wall joints like this one were a Miami staple, part of a ritual that brought together everyone from lawyers to street cleaners for an afternoon jolt of caffeine Cuban-style.

"You mean *calls*, don't you?" she said coolly. "Five times in three days is borderline stalking."

"My apologies. It's just very important that we talk. First of all, I wanted to say how sorry I am about your father."

"Thank you. But any discussion that begins with 'first of all' also includes a 'second of all,' and invariably the 'second of all' is the real point of the conversation."

"Fair enough," said Jack.

"I know what this is about," she said. "I'm sorry. I don't want to see her."

Jack stepped away from the busy espresso counter and found a little privacy beneath a shady oak with gnarled roots that had long ago outgrown the allocated square of dirt in the sidewalk. He was struggling to strike the right tone in his response, trying not to sound argumentative. "I wish you would reconsider."

"I can understand how you might feel that way. But you have to see this from my side, too."

"I'm trying hard to do that, and pardon me for saying this, but it just seems harsh."

"There's no easy answer."

"To me there is. So maybe it would help to hear it in your own words—your own take on what's driving this decision."

"You want the honest truth?"

"When all else fails, it usually comes down to that."

Jack could hear a sigh on the other end of the line. "The truth is," she said, then stopped, seeming to collect herself before continuing. "There are things I don't want to know about my family."

"Alicia, I don't mean to sound insensitive, but some bad things are going to come out anyway. It's inevitable. Mayor Mendoza was a public figure. His secrets won't die with him, no matter what decision you make."

"I'm not talking about that family," she said. "I'm talking about my biological family."

"I don't understand."

"My mother and father disappeared in a secret detention center for subversives."

"Yes, I'm aware of that," said Jack.

"What if it turns out that they were leftist extremists—terrorists who killed or maimed innocent people? What good would it do for me to know that?"

Jack was suddenly reminded of something Alicia's grandmother had told him about the blind eye of a nation—friends and neighbors who watched teachers, journalists, and housewives taken by force from their homes and did nothing about it, except to nod in agreement when someone at a cocktail party shrugged and with a dismissive wave of the hand remarked, "They don't take people away for no reason." Jack said, "Somewhere between eighteen and thirty thousand people disappeared in the Dirty War. Many of them were completely innocent."

"Exactly. And right now, I can count myself among the lucky ones who have that consolation. My biological parents are dead. They were the innocent victims of a terrible dictatorship. My adoptive father may or may not have been part of that hellish regime, but I still have the only mother I've ever known. She loves me unconditionally, and she has no one's blood on her hands. For me, that's the only happy ending to this story."

A city bus rumbled past him, and Jack stepped away from the gritty black cloud of diesel fumes at the curb. "What about your grandmother? How does this end for her?"

"I'm not numb to her suffering. I realize that she has to find some kind of closure."

"You're the only one who can give it to her."

"Don't you think I know that?"

"Then please, do something about it."

She paused, seeming to consider it.

Jack said, "People have gone to a lot of trouble to bring you two together. Innocent people have died."

"You can't mean Falcon."

"No. He was the one who tipped off your grandmother as to your whereabouts, but I didn't mean him. I mean people like the midwife who delivered you."

"What are you talking about?"

"Your mother was a numbered political prisoner with a hood over her head when you were born. But she shouted out her real name during the delivery. The midwife had a conscience. She tracked down your grandmother and told her about you."

"Is that true?"

"Yeah. And then the midwife went missing. She's among the Disappeared."

"How do you know that?"

"Listen to what your grandmother has to say. She knows."

There was another long pause, and Jack sensed that he was getting through to her.

"All right," said Alicia.

"Do you mean it? You'll see her?"

"Yes," she said, clearly struggling. "I mean—no. I can't. I can't do it."

"But you agree that she needs closure, don't you?"

"I'm so confused. Can't you see what a mess my life is? The Mendozas are either a bad joke or a terrible tragedy, depending on who you talk to. My mother needs me now more than ever."

"Isn't there something you'd like to say to your real grandmother?"

"Of course. But I want you to do it for me. Please. Just tell her . . . tell her that I love my mothers. Both of them."

"After all she's been through, do you really think that's enough?"

There was silence on the line, and after several long, contemplative moments, her reply came in a barely audible voice. "It's the best that I can do. I'm sorry."

Jack heard the click as she hung up, which triggered a flash of emotion. It was as if he were watching his own grandmother's heart breaking in the exact same place and for the very same reasons that it had broken so many times before. The pain, however, was quickly followed by a deep sense of dread. Jack wasn't at all sure that he could do it, but he had no choice.

He tucked away his cell phone and prepared to deliver Alicia's final message to her grandmother.

67

Alicia drove Vince and her mother home from the cemetery. It was a sunny Saturday afternoon, and even the first day of winter was way too hot for their black attire. Alicia cranked up the air-conditioning, but her mother switched it off. An earlier attempt at conversation had drawn a similar reaction. Her mother seemed averse to consolation of any kind, as if an overall state of misery were a prerequisite to a widow's proper grieving.

The graveside service had been private—just Alicia, her mother, Vince, six of the mayor's closest friends who served as pallbearers, and a presiding Catholic priest. The funeral mass, on the other hand, had been public in the extreme. The Church of the Epiphany was South Florida's version of the Crystal Cathedral, an award-winning architectural gem with soaring ceilings, towering windows, and so much natural light that you couldn't help but feel God's presence. Though outside the Miami city limits, it was the only church large enough to accommodate the crowd, and it was packed to capacity. Alicia sat between Vince and her mother in the front row. Behind them was a virtual who's who in Miami politics, friends and foes seated shoulder-to-shoulder. Their ranks stretched all the way to the vestibule, like so many waves of power. Among them were a former governor and U.S. senator, the lieutenant governor, a congresswoman, state representatives, mayors from around the state, and judges, not to mention the entire city council, the county commission, and the lobbyists who controlled them. The business community was equally well represented, as there was nothing like the death of a Latin leader to bring out living proof that Miami—land of *opportunidad*—had more self-made Hispanic millionaires than any city on earth. As yet, neither the mayor's secret past nor his final words to Jack Swyteck—"I am the doctor"— had leaked to the public, so Alicia alone noted the irony that was buried in the third verse of one of the church's oldest funeral hymns:

Often were they wounded in the deadly strife.
Heal them, Good Physician,
*   with the balm of life.*

The eulogies were delivered in both English and Spanish, heartfelt and even a few humorous stories about a compassionate man, a doting husband, a loving father. For the moment, Mayor Mendoza had officially joined the ranks of those beleaguered

souls who had escaped the wrath and judgment of
mere mortals through the expedience of untimely
death.

Invited guests gathered for food and refreshment
at the Mendoza house after the service. Parked cars
lined both sides of the street for several blocks. The
press was not allowed on the property, but they
blanketed the neighborhood. It was as if the local
media had decided to hold the tough questions until
the mayor was buried, and now they were ready for
the real dirt. Editorials called for a complete investigation. Talk radio was buzzing with all kinds
of theories, some of them crackpot, some not. A
local television station did a segment on the Disappeared and the Argentine Dirty War. The *Tribune*
dispatched its Pulitzer Prize–winning investigative
reporter to Buenos Aires. It would only be a matter
of time before the mayor's dark past came to light.

Police officers stood outside the front gate at the
end of the driveway, directing traffic. There were
more guests than expected, and many of them
flocked to the mayor's widow and daughter the
moment they entered the house. Alicia accepted the
sincere condolences of several well-wishers and then
quickly excused herself.

"Are you okay?" Vince asked. They were standing outside the carved double doors to her father's
library.

"Yes, I'm all right. Really." She could tell that
he wanted to speak with her alone, away from her
mother. Vince had been supportive all week, but

something was clearly weighing on his mind. Whatever it was, Alicia wasn't ready to deal with it. "I just need some time to myself."

"You go ahead," he said. "I'll get something to eat."

She thanked him with a little kiss, then retreated into the library and closed the door behind her.

As long as Alicia could remember, it had been an unwritten house rule that the library belonged to Mr. Mendoza. Rules, however, were made to be broken, and Alicia was the biggest offender. There was something uniquely comforting about a room filled with books, and Alicia had always felt drawn to this place. Celebrated Argentine author Jorge Luis Borges once said that he could not sleep unless surrounded by books, a sentiment that sang to Alicia from the country of her birth. Just a quick glance at the titles was like a trip down memory lane, a reminder of the various stages of her life—*Alice in Wonderland*, *Don Quixote*, *The Great Gatsby*. Her prized collection of the Argentine comic strip *Mafalda*, however, had disappeared years ago. Apparently, Mr. Mendoza didn't like the political leanings of the artist who created the smart little girl that couldn't help speaking her mind. Still, so many times over the years, the library had been Alicia's escape, and she could still feel some of the magic within these four walls. No other place on earth had the power to suppress the negativity of the past week. Had she succumbed to that power or magic or whatever it was that energized this roomful of memories, she might have found a better place—an emotional equilibrium where, despite everything that she'd learned recently about her father, it would have saddened her to see the empty chair behind his desk. She would have remembered climbing up into his lap as a little girl and promising to go to bed if he would read her just one more story. She might have even smiled at the sight of the humidor on the credenza, recalling the only time in her life that he'd offered her a cigar. It was on the night she'd graduated from the academy, and she would never forget the look on his face when she took it. They laughed and drank twenty-year-old scotch until the Monte Cristos were reduced to a pair of smoldering nubs.

Strange, but those memories didn't even seem to belong to her anymore. They felt more like somebody else's musings about a man very different from the one her father had turned out to be.

The door opened, stirring Alicia from her thoughts. It was her mother, still wearing her black hat and veil.

"There are people here you should see," she said.

"Can we talk for a minute?"

Her mother balked. All week long, she had been dodging a one-on-one conversation, which Alicia figured was the reason she'd given the okay to invite Vince along for the family-only events. "But we have guests."

"They can wait a few minutes," said Alicia.

The older woman paused to consider it. A houseful of guests offered her the perfect excuse to cut things short, but she seemed to recognize that she'd put off Alicia long enough. "What is it that you want to talk about?"

At Alicia's lead, they sat in the matching leather armchairs in the center of the room, separated by an antique marble pedestal that had been in the family for generations and that now served as a cocktail table. As a young girl, Alicia got into serious trouble for wrapping herself in a bedsheet, covering her body with talcum powder, and then climbing up on the pedestal with arms pinned behind her back à la Venus de Milo. This room was so full of conflicting emotions.

She looked at her mother directly and said, "Do you think I should forgive *Papi*?"

"For what?"

"Surely you don't need me to answer that."

"Your father loved you more than most men love their own natural offspring."

"His whole life was a lie, and he made me the center of it."

"His love for you was not a lie."

"That's not the point," said Alicia.

"What else matters?"

"Truth," said Alicia. "The truth matters."

"The truth is that your father was destroyed by some crazy terrorists who exploded a bomb near a crowded café and murdered his wife and daughter. It took him a long time to find a reason to go on living, and he found it in you and me."

More of those conflicting emotions. Alicia backed off just a bit, her tone softening. "Why did you adopt?"

"We desperately wanted a child. We tried on our own, but I couldn't get pregnant."

"Did you know about my parents?"

"Of course not. I thought you came through normal adoption channels."

"But *Papi* knew everything."

She struggled, as if the answer were better left unstated. "Like I said, those people destroyed his life. He must have justified it that way."

"Wait a second. Are you saying that my biological parents planted that bomb that killed his family?"

"No, no. I don't know anything about them or what they did. But they were part of the insurgency."

"Guilty by association, is that it?"

Her mother didn't answer, but Alicia waited, refusing to let it drop. Finally, her mother said, "You have to understand the times. I'm sure your father's only thought was that he was providing a loving home and a bright future for the innocent child of not-so-innocent parents."

Alicia nodded, not because she agreed with what her mother was saying but because she understood her position. "For the moment, let's put aside the question of whether that rationalization holds water or not. I still have a real problem with what you're telling me."

There was a sudden uptick in the noise level outside the closed doors. More guests were arriving, and apparently, no one was leaving. "We really should get back," her mother said.

"I'm almost finished."

"We can talk more about this later," Graciela said, rising.

"No, I want to talk about it *now*."

The stern voice made her mother do a double take, and it surprised even Alicia. Until this day, she'd told herself and others that there were certain things she just didn't want to know. But now she was in a different place. Her real grandmother was no longer an abstraction. She'd also been affected deeply by Jack's mention of the innocent woman who had sacrificed herself to expose the truth. Alicia couldn't stop thinking about the midwife who'd heard a numbered prisoner shout out her real name, who'd followed her conscience and sought out the baby's grandmother, only to pay the price with her own life. Alicia was tired of hiding behind lies.

Her mother lowered herself back into the armchair.

Alicia asked, "Do you remember the videotapes of those Argentine cartoons Papi and I used to watch together? The ones about the witch?"

"*La Bruja de la Cachavacha.* Of course I remember."

"My biological parents were held in a detention center called La Cacha. It was named after that cartoon, because of the witch who could make people disappear."

Her mother looked down. "That's a very macabre coincidence."

"Unless it's not a coincidence."

"Oh, come on now, Alicia. There is no way that your father could have known the name of the detention center."

"Why not?"

"How could he—how could *anyone* sit down with a little girl and watch those cartoons knowing that her parents had disappeared from La Cacha? That just wouldn't be human."

"I agree."

"Your father would have to have been some kind of sociopath."

"Yes," she said in a matter-of-fact tone. "He would."

Her mother took her meaning and nearly erupted from her chair. "This conversation has gone on long enough. After all that's been said this past week, and after all that you've been through, I can understand that you would have some questions. But I won't have you dishonoring your father like this on the day he was laid to rest."

"I also have some questions about the woman he married."

"You're going to insult me now, too?"

"The birth certificate. It said I was two years old when I was really just two weeks old."

The older woman covered her ears. "I don't have to listen to this."

"That means *Papi* knew it was false."

"I'm leaving now," Graciela said as she started toward the door.

"And so did you."

Alicia's final accusation stopped Mrs. Mendoza cold in her tracks. She stood there for almost a full minute, saying not a word, her back to Alicia.

Alicia said, "I went all the way through school wondering why I was the oldest kid in my class, thinking I'd been held back. I was actually the youngest."

Her mother refused to turn around.

Alicia said, "You don't have an answer for any of this, do you?"

Graciela started to turn around, then stopped. It was as if she couldn't face Alicia. Or perhaps she simply didn't want Alicia to see her tears of shame.

"I didn't think so," said Alicia. She rose and walked right past her mother on her way to the double doors.

"Alicia!" her mother pleaded, but Alicia opened the door and kept right on walking.

The house was filled with guests, scores of people grouped into smaller clusters of conversations. They held drinks or plates of food with one hand, and, in the time-honored Latin tradition, spoke with the other hand. Several guests tried to catch Alicia's eye and engage her as she cut through the crowd. Alicia made a beeline past everyone, exited through the French doors that led to the patio, and found a little privacy in the backyard near the tall ficus hedge.

She dialed Jack Swyteck on her cell phone.

"Hey, it's me, Alicia Mendoza," she said.

"Well, isn't this a surprise."

"I wanted to ask you a favor."

"Sure. What is it?"

Alicia glanced back toward the house. Through the French doors, she could see her mother inside the family room, working the crowd with the skill of a seasoned politician. She had managed to compose herself completely, as if nothing had happened— just like the last twenty-seven years.

Perhaps she and the mayor had been alike in more ways than Alicia could imagine.

"Tell my grandmother—" she started to say, but a wave of confusion and conflicting emotions washed out her voice.

"Tell her what?" said Jack.

She drew a breath and said, "Tell her that her granddaughter would like to meet her."

68

Jack never really expected Sergeant Paulo to show up.

At the height of the hostage standoff, Paulo had asked Jack how he could defend the guilty and still live with himself. Jack had suggested that they have that discussion over beers someday. That was not an offer he extended casually. Life was too short, and Jack would sooner call his college roommate in Chicago and do shots by long distance than waste time drinking with people he didn't like. Paulo was definitely one of the good guys, and when they finally parted ways, Jack mentioned that he could be found at Sparky's Tavern on just about any Friday night, if ever Vince wanted to have that beer.

It took a few weeks, but Paulo actually showed up. The even bigger surprise was that he'd brought Alicia with him. Apparently, she'd finally reached the turning point and could go out in public without the media hounding her about her father. That was the great thing about Miami. There was always a bigger scandal to come along and take you out of the limelight.

Theo showed them to "the best table in the house," which for anyone who knew Theo meant the one that happened to be available at that particular moment. They talked over drinks. Fortunately, Theo exercised relatively good judgment by waiting for Alicia to break for the restroom before offering a couple of toasts. The first went to Sergeant Chavez, who, according to the newspapers, was demoted from head of SWAT pending the outcome of an internal investigation into whether his determination to take out Falcon was purely a favor to the mayor. The second was to Felipe, who (through Jack and Theo's cooperation with the grand jury) would soon be indicted for taking his job as the mayor's bodyguard way too far.

When Alicia returned to the table, Theo got up and played "a special set for some special guests," which, of course, meant the one that he had been planning to play all along. Vince and Alicia sat extremely close to each other as Theo played out his set, and seeing Alicia in this setting gave Jack a fuller appreciation of what a captivating woman she was. He was trying not to eavesdrop, but he was only human, and it was a scientifically proven fact that fifth wheels were cursed with excellent hearing.

"Do you remember that dream I told you about?" Paulo said to her. He was speaking loudly enough to be heard over the music, but Jack had to presume that it was intended for Alicia's ears only.

"Which one?" she said.

"The one about the little girl who sits in my lap."

Okay, it's the kinky cops, thought Jack, but he soon realized that he had it wrong.

"Yeah, I remember," she said. "You and I were married, and this little girl comes up to you in the park and sits in your lap. But she doesn't say anything, so you can't tell if she's our daughter or somebody else's child."

"Right. And I'm afraid to ask her who she is, because I don't want our own daughter to know I don't recognize her. So I just sit there, waiting for her to say something, so I can hear her voice. Do you remember what you told me about that dream?"

"Yes. That the little girl would never speak to you until you decided what you wanted to do about us."

"Well," said Vince. "Guess what. The little girl spoke to me last night."

Jack couldn't hear the rest. All he knew was that they were up and saying good night to him before Theo even finished his set. Paulo reached for his wallet, but Jack told him to put it away. "On me," said Jack. "Just promise to come back sometime."

"We will," said Alicia. "Maybe when I get back from Argentina."

Jack had been dying to know how Alicia's conversation had gone with her grandmother. Now he didn't have to ask. It made him smile, but not too much. He knew it would be an emotional journey for her. "Have a safe trip."

"Thanks," she said.

"See you around, Jack," said Paulo, and they headed for the door.

Jack was alone at the table when Theo returned. He saw the empty chairs and shot Jack a look of disbelief. "I leave you alone for one lousy set and you scare away the new customers?"

"They had to go somewhere."

"Where?"

Jack didn't answer. He hadn't even heard the question, really. "Theo?" he said in a philosophical voice. "Do you think it's a sin to be jealous of a blind guy?"

"Jealousy is always a sin. In fact, it's one of the seven deadly ones. Even worse, it's a terrible waste of time and energy."

"Yeah, I know. But look at me. I've fallen for two women since my divorce. One of them dyed her hair, changed her name, and fled the country. The other one would rather live in a hut in West Africa than with me, except for the few times a year she plants herself in my bed and tries to cram six months' worth of sex into a weekend."

"Okay, now you got me jealous. You happy?"

"No, I'm not happy. That's my point. When it comes to women, I'm starting to feel like the guy who didn't get the memo."

"Dude, please don't tell me this is going to turn into one of those nights when I have to tackle your ass to keep you from running up on stage and doing your pathetic rendition of Rod Stewart's 'Some Guys Have All the Luck.'"

"I have *never* done that."

Theo smiled like the devil. "You just don't remember," he said as he pulled a shot glass from each pocket. Then he slammed them down on the table.

"No way," said Jack. "No tequila. Not tonight."

Theo pushed the shot glasses aside. "How about martinis?"

"Since when do you drink martinis?"

"In case you haven't noticed, business isn't exactly booming. I been wracking my brain trying to figure out how to give it a jump start."

Jack's selection finally rolled over on the juke-box—Don Henley's "Boys of Summer." It was one of his all-time favorites, but it triggered a thought. "A few selections from artists who've actually peaked in the last ten years might do some good."

"The music ain't the problem. It's the image."

Jack looked around. The building was actually a converted old gas station, the term "conversion" used loosely, the way a high school gymnasium might be converted into Margaritaville for a 1970s retro ball. The grease pit was gone, and only recently had Theo gotten around to blocking up the openings for the old garage doors. There was a long, wooden bar, a TV permanently tuned to ESPN, and a never-ending stack of quarters on the pool table. "Granted, the image could probably use a little polish," said Jack.

"Polish my ass," said Theo. "What Sparky's needs is a signature drink. That's what got me thinking about martinis."

"All right, I'm with you. But aren't martini bars kind of passé?"

"I'm talking about a Sparky's original. The smoothie martini."

"Will you quit with the smoothies already? That practically got us killed on the mayor's boat."

"It's not just a smoothie. It's a smoothie martini. Smartini."

"Smartini? Sounds like brain food for drunks."

"What?"

"Never mind. It will never catch on."

"How can you say that?"

"Because . . . who in his right mind would put vermouth in a smoothie?"

"Somebody who drinks vermouthies?"

"You need a new concept, buddy."

"All right, fine." Theo signaled the bartender and shouted, "Two belt-and-suspenders martinis, Leon."

"Two what?" said Jack.

Theo grinned. "Belt-and-suspenders martinis. Shaken *and* stirred. Now there's a signature drink fer ya, eh, dude?"

Jack shook his head. "You know what? Let's just do the shots."

"Now you're talking." He handed Jack a glass. The bartender brought over a bottle and didn't stop pouring until a little drop of tequila spilled over the rim.

Jack raised his glass, careful not to spill any more, then stopped. "Did I really stand up and sing 'Some Guys Have All the Luck'?"

"Yup."

"When?"

"About two hours from now."

Jack downed the shot in one quick hit, then wiped the tequila expression from his face. "Sure hope I didn't embarrass myself."

Acknowledgments

Making up stories is a great way to earn a living, and it's especially wonderful when you're supported by incredibly talented people. Carolyn Marino has been my editor since the mid-nineties, and this novel feels like the product of a ten-year degree in creative writing. Her assistant, Jennifer Civiletto, is also top-flight. I'm equally grateful to Richard Pine, my agent from day one in my literary career. There is no one better in the business.

Thanks also to my usual cast of early readers, Eleanor Rayner and Dr. Gloria Grippando. Gordon Van Alstyne again lent his expertise on firearms. Of course, any screwups are all mine.

The American Federation for the Blind was of more help than they realize in my effort to understand the world of the visually impaired, but no one was more helpful than my own father, James V. Grippando. He lives by his motto: "It's about attitude, dummy." We should all be so courageous and upbeat.

My knowledge of Argentina was limited before I began researching this book. Thankfully, South

Florida has a proud and vibrant Argentine community, and I want to thank the many families who shared their stories. All were fascinating, and I'm especially grateful to those who tapped into some painful memories.

This novel also marks the close of a chapter in my life. My "office mate" for the last nine years was my golden retriever, Sam. We did eleven novels together, and this one was our last. I miss him terribly, so don't be surprised if at some point in the future Jack Swyteck gets himself a sidekick even more loyal than Theo Knight. (If you're a pet lover, please check out my story about Sam at www.jamesgrippando.com.)

As always, none of this would be possible without the love and support from my wife, Tiffany. People often ask where my ideas come from, and I don't have a clue. But I do know where my inspiration comes from.

Finally, I often struggle over character names, so I want to thank David Boies for making my job a little easier. In recognition of his generous contribution at a fund-raising auction in support of the Boys & Girls Club Marti Huizenga Unit (the largest Boys & Girls Club in the country), the "Richard Boies" referred to as "Uncle Ricky" in chapter 4 is named in honor of Richard James Boies, David's younger brother. He was "Rick" to his friends and "Ricky" to his family, and with his warm heart and mischievous spirit, he was loved by all who knew him. A nice tribute to a good man in support of a good cause.